SUBSTRATUM

A Jasper O'Malley Novel

SUBSTRATUM

A Jasper O'Malley Novel

Jonah Buck

A
Grinning Skull Press
Publication

Substratum
Copyright © 2016 Jonah Buck

All rights reserved. No part of this book may be used or reproduced in any manner whatsoever without written permission except in the case of brief quotations embodied in critical articles or reviews.

This book is a work of fiction. All characters depicted in this book are fictitious, and any resemblance to real persons—living or dead—is purely coincidental.

The Skull logo with stylized lettering was created for Grinning Skull Press by Dan Moran, http://dan-moran-art.com/.
Cover designed by Jeffrey Kosh, http://jeffreykosh.wix.com/jeffreykoshgraphics.
Published by Grinning Skull Press, PO Box 67, Bridgewater, MA 02324

ISBN: 0-9984055-3-1 (paperback)
ISBN-13: 978-0-9984055-3-7 (paperback)
ISBN: 978-0-9984055-4-4 (ebook)

DEDICATION

For Mom and Dad

CONTENTS

Chapter 1 Hell Hole	3
Chapter 2 Fitzhugh Gets Served	15
Chapter 3 Oh Snap	27
Chapter 4 Welcome to Detroit	39
Chapter 5 With a Grain of Salt	50
Chapter 6 Blood Diamonds	58
Chapter 7 I Bet Your Say That to All the Girls	66
Chapter 8 Queen of Diamonds	76
Chapter 9 Come into My Parlor	81
Chapter 10 Making Enemies	92
Chapter 11 Trouble Brewing	94
Chapter 12 Double Trouble	96
Chapter 13 Three of a Kind	98
Chapter 14 Bad Medicine	99
Chapter 15 Going Clubbing	110
Chapter 16 The Dark at the End of the Tunnel	112
Chapter 17 In the Flesh	122
Chapter 18 Tanks a Lot	133

Chapter 19 Bottoms Up	135
Chapter 20 Things Get Worse	151
Chapter 21 Countdown to Midnight	159
Chapter 22 Look on My Works, Ye Mighty, and Despair	169
Chapter 23 Smorgasmorgue	172
Chapter 24 Hell to Pay	177
Chapter 25 Salting the Land	184
Chapter 26 Razing Hell	192
Chapter 27 U-235 Complete Me	196
Chapter 28 Salt in the Wound	209
Chapter 29 Pillar of Salt	220
Chapter 30 Fire in the Hole	230
Chapter 31 Salt of the Earth	241
Chapter 32 The Hungry Earth	245
ABOUT THE AUTHOR	247

GEOLOGY, n. The science of the earth's crust — to which, doubtless, will be added that of its interior whenever a man shall come up garrulous out of a well. The geological formations of the globe already noted are catalogued thus: The Primary, or lower one, consists of rocks, bones or mired mules, gas-pipes, miners' tools, antique statues minus the nose, Spanish doubloons and ancestors. The Secondary is largely made up of red worms and moles. The Tertiary comprises railway tracks, patent pavements, grass, snakes, mouldy boots, beer bottles, tomato cans, intoxicated citizens, garbage, anarchists, snap-dogs and fools.

– Ambrose Bierce, *The Devil's Dictionary*

Thus He overthrew those cities and the entire plain, destroying all those living in the cities — and also the vegetation in the land. But Lot's wife looked back, and she became a pillar of salt.

– Genesis 19:25–26

Chapter 1
Hell Hole

June 26, 1925

Hugh Corbett ran for his life. Probably his soul, too. He'd been running for a long time, trapped down here, and he was breathing hard. A stitch pulsed in his side, but he continued onward. It had been a long time since he ran the police department fitness test, and he felt it. His flashlight beam sent crazy shadows jittering in every direction as he ran. His lungs burned, and he slowed down. It was like being trapped in a giant funhouse, facing identical tunnel after identical tunnel. The mine's gritty, white walls bore no distinguishing characteristics. For all Corbett knew, he'd been running in circles the entire time.

He was lost in the Detroit Salt Combine's mining tunnels. Each of the salt mine's shafts looked exactly the same, and he had no idea how he was going to get out of this pit. The mine was laid out as a series of long, straight tunnels radiating out from a center chamber. Cross shafts connected all the main tunnels at regular intervals, creating a nice, circular grid pattern like a spider web. Hell's suburbs. The tunnels were a marvel of the industrial age, a modern day labyrinth even larger than the city they were buried under. Stretching beneath Lake Erie in some places, the massive network of tunnels ran for miles. A man could get lost down here and starve to death before finding a way out. Hugh Corbett was very lost.

That wasn't the bad part, though. Not even half of it. There were things in the darkness. Corbett had seen them, and now he wished to God he hadn't. He wanted to run until he reached daylight, chew his way straight through the rock to the surface if he had to. He didn't want to be trapped down here with those things, but he had to stop and rest. His legs were screaming at him, and his spit tasted sour in his mouth. He was pretty sure he'd lost his pursuers somewhere deeper in the mine anyway.

Each of the tunnels was peppered with alcoves so workers could get out of the way of mechanical borers or other heavy equipment. Corbett slipped into one of the dark corners and stopped. His legs trembled, and he forced back the sudden urge to puke. He leaned over, hands on his thighs, regaining his composure.

Gradually, his ragged breathing leveled off, and he listened. He looked around and tried to shake off the vice grip of panic that had sent him running for miles through this maze. In the subterranean gloom, his flashlight was the only source of light. It allowed him to see, but it also highlighted his location to anyone else in the tunnels. Any*thing* else in the tunnels. He flicked it off, and the darkness descended on him. Corbett strained his ears, ignoring the sound of his own heartbeat hammering like a timpani drum.

The arc lights that normally illuminated this stretch of tunnel were all dead. His fellow police officers cut the power themselves, thinking it would befuddle their quarry and give them the advantage. Now Corbett was the one being hunted.

Corbett knew how to move in darkness. Slipping through Detroit's back alleys at night and staking out speakeasies had taught him how to move confidently in minimal light. He befriended the night years ago, learning to cloak himself in shadow when needed. This was different, though. This wasn't some shadowy alley. This darkness was complete, absolute. It engulfed Corbett, swallowing him whole. He was but a tapeworm in the earth's guts.

At 791 feet high, the Woolworth Building in New York City was the tallest building in the world. Corbett was more than 1,100 feet below the earth's surface. That far underground, there was no light. None at all. Right now, Corbett's eyes could only pick up visual static. Black noise. He was literally in the underworld, gobbled up by the earth. He struggled to remain calm. He was all but suffocating on the blackness. It seemed like it was pouring into him the way water swept into a drowning man's lungs as he went under for the final time.

A monsoon of sweat had sprung up on Corbett's face as he ran, but he still felt a chill that penetrated down to his soul as he thought about what he'd seen deeper inside the mine. Wiping his brow, he tried to concentrate.

Nothing could have followed him, not in this plutonian blackness, but he didn't completely believe that. A particular part of Corbett's brain had risen to the forefront and seized the reigns from his rational mind. It was the part that prehistoric shrews used to avoid being eaten by dinosaurs. It was the part honed in primitive man as he explored caves that might be infested with saber-toothed cats. It was pure survival instinct.

When he was a boy, Corbett had a stuffed rabbit he kept with him under his covers when the darkness in the closet was too terrible to contemplate any longer. Now that he was an adult, he wished he had his service pistol — it offered the same form of comfort — but he'd lost it back in the tunnels when those things killed his partners. Five cops had gone into the tunnels with Corbett, and now he was the only one left.

Somewhere, maybe miles away, machines boomed and squealed. Men shouted to each other and threw salt rock into carts. The collective bustle echoed and re-echoed down the tunnels, creating an eerie blanket of meaningless sound. Clanks and whistles sounded at random intervals, and he jumped each time. Sometimes the mine itself popped or groaned as millions of tons of rock settled. Even under the best of circumstances, Corbett didn't know how the miners kept their sanity. If the mine caved in, they'd be buried alive almost a quarter of a mile underground or, more likely, crushed like screaming wine grapes. Of course, harrowing as they were, those were the best of circumstances. There were much worse dangers in these tunnels now.

He needed to find the central shaft and make his way back to the surface. It was imperative that he get back to the upper world, not just for his own survival, but to warn everyone. He was the only one left who could tell them what he'd seen. They'd have to quarantine the mine tunnels and send in the military. Hell, never mind the military. They should just blast all the mine's support columns and let the tunnels crumble in on themselves, crushing everything down here. The things Corbett had seen could never be allowed to —

What was that?

Corbett stopped breathing. He'd heard something. It was a quiet, stealthy shuffle, almost hidden by the whispers and groans of background mine noise. Something new had just entered the mine's echosystem.

It was a faint *tap*, almost like someone with a hammer was knocking on one of the walls deeper in the tunnels. The sound emanated from the direction he'd just fled from. Anything moving in that section of the tunnels was not going to be friendly.

Even though he couldn't see anything, he automatically reached for his gun. It wasn't there. Of course, it wasn't there. He'd lost it in the hungry darkness. But his sleeve brushed against the rough wall as he reached. The fabric whispered against the rough surface.

Corbett grimaced. In the darkness, the sound of his sleeve rasping against the salt rock sounded as loud as a scream. He remained perfectly still, listening. His teeth bit into his lower lip as he held his breath.

Seconds ticked by. In the cloying gloom, they could have been eons. Corbett thwarted the urge to turn his flashlight back on. No matter what meager comfort it might provide, switching it on would give away his position as surely as if he'd been illuminated with a spotlight. The seconds stretched into minutes. Maybe the minutes stretched into hours. Trapped in the darkness, his senses deprived of input, it was impossible to tell. Nothing else sounded from the tunnels behind him.

Whatever he heard must have been a trick of the mine's acoustics.

His heart spelunked its way back down his throat as he decided the danger had passed. Corbett slumped as he suddenly became aware of how tense his muscles were. God, he was exhausted. The adrenaline keying through his system began to fade, leaving his nerves stripped raw.

He and his fellow police officers had been patrolling the tunnels in one of the Detroit Salt Combine's survey trucks. Half of Detroit's police force was down here doing the exact same thing, running a dragnet. Miners had been disappearing from the tunnels, and the city had dispatched every beat cop it could spare to comb the shafts. At the time, he'd thought it was a fool's errand. The entire state of Michigan didn't have enough cops to thoroughly search the tunnels in a systematic manner. Hundreds of miles of tunnels stretched below Detroit in a subterranean mirror of the road network above. It was like a giant ant nest. They couldn't patrol every single tunnel any more than a doctor could check every single capillary in a sick patient. If they ran into whoever was responsible, it would be purely a matter of luck. Bad luck, as it turned out.

Corbett's squad had been puttering down one of the abandoned sections of the mine, shining a truck-mounted searchlight into every nook and cranny they could find. All six of them were tired after hours of poking their noses into dark corners. The other patrols had fanned out and gone into different parts of the mine, hopelessly separating everyone. The rock walls meant radios were worthless, and nobody could see anyone else. There was simply no way to keep what was supposed to be a cohesive search force organized. It was like sending a gaggle of blind kids out trick or treating without supervision.

Corbett had been an infantryman in the Great War, and he remembered columns of men scrambling out of their trenches for assaults. The formations quickly hit barbed wire, craters, and machinegun fire, and the highly organized mobile armies turned into individual squads of frantic soldiers within thirty yards. All the brilliant planning in the world couldn't fix some boondoggles, and this expedition had not been brilliantly planned.

They'd been maybe four miles out from the mine entrance when they got hit. Murphy had been complaining about how the mine's stale air messed with his sinuses and how the salt grit got into everything. Corbett had been standing in the bed of the truck, swiveling the light into tunnel after tunnel, wishing Murphy would shut up already. The man never seemed to stop complaining.

Suddenly, something had darted past the headlights. Corbett had only caught the briefest glimpse of it, but it had looked like a hunched figure scampering into a side tunnel. Scraps of cloth clung to its frame as if shuffled into the shadows. Nelson, the driver, had slammed on the brakes, nearly throwing Corbett onto the hood of the truck in the process. The searchlight had careened around at a cockeyed angle as Corbett grabbed onto it. Regaining his footing, he had drawn his service revolver. "Freeze!"

Hot metal clicked and pinged as everyone struggled to scramble out of the truck at once. "The hell was that?" Murphy had asked, pulling at his door handle.

As Corbett tried to track the figure they'd seen with the searchlight, he had become aware that they weren't alone in the tunnels. Murphy had finally managed to unfasten his door when a set of claws clamped down on the frame and tore it off the vehicle's chassis. Another set of misshapen talons had reached inside and ripped Murphy himself out of the truck.

Corbett had only seen the thing that did the ripping for a split second, but he knew it was a vision that would live in his nightmares for the rest of his life.

Once upon a time, the creature had clearly been human. Now it was a mass of twisted, organic chaos. It looked like a graveyard had had an abortion. More shapes were moving through the shadows just outside the searchlight's beam. They had come from everywhere. Dozens of them. Each one had looked like something that would send the Frankenstein monster screaming into the night. They seemed to be coming straight out of the damned walls, slithering bonelessly out of every available crevice. The shadows had suddenly become alive with writhing, shambling movement.

The monsters hadn't encircled the back of the truck yet, and Corbett hadn't waited. He'd jumped to the ground and ran for his life as the truck's other doors were being torn open. Something had climbed over Murphy's empty seat and fastened its teeth to the driver's face.

Corbett had fired his revolver a couple of times as he ran. He didn't know if he'd hit anything. The gun had been knocked out of his hand as something tried to grab his arm. Dodging away, he'd sped down the tunnel as fast as he could, the screams of his friends following him as he ran.

Now, all Corbett had was his flashlight and his wits. He needed to get out of the mine. He had no way of contacting any of the other patrols, and he couldn't guarantee his fellow officers would find him before those things did.

There was another *tap* from somewhere else in the mine. Thinking about what he'd seen, Corbett shuddered. He wasn't sure what that noise was, but it was time to get moving.

Some of the mine intersections were fitted with signs to direct the workers. He hadn't stopped to read them while he was running, but they might save his life now. They labeled every cross shaft. Some of them must point to the mine elevators.

His thumb rested on the flashlight's switch. He was going to need to use it if he wanted out of here. Hopefully, its batteries had enough juice to get him to a part of the mine where somebody could help him.

Tap. Tap. Tap.

Corbett's blood turned to ice. There was that noise again, and it was definitely closer. Maybe it was just a natural sound of the rock shifting, but if it wasn't...

Some primal sense told Corbett that things weren't right. The air had changed in the tunnel. It wasn't something he could articulate, but all the hair on his arms suddenly stood at attention. He couldn't see anything, couldn't hear anything, couldn't even smell anything, but alarm bells were ringing in his head. Long-buried instincts were sending up smoke signals to his higher brain. He needed to move.

Taking a deep breath, he flicked on the light. And screamed.

A face stared back at him from only a few feet away. At least, it used to be a face. Now, it was little more than a crater of bone and teeth and split, flaking skin.

The monstrosity had once been a man, but something had gone very wrong with nature's plans. In places, the flesh was pierced with what looked like layers of fingernails growing like scales. The jaws jutted forward where the bone itself had twisted and changed. Hyper-elongated teeth pierced through the cheeks at obscene angles. Dozens of new fangs grew in a jagged row behind the first set. Corbett could see the thing's fleshy tongue through the holes in its cheeks. It was raw and mottled, as if the uppermost layer had sloughed off. Blood blisters pebbled the tongue like a layer of scavenger beetles. However, the worst part of the ruined face was the eyes. The right eye was glossed by some sort of nictitating membrane, a semi-transparent second eyelid streaked through with a riot of veins. Corbett could see the monster's pupil jittering about, constantly moving. The other eye ... Well, there was no other eye. It was just a hole, but it wasn't empty. More teeth — little, stumpy canines — rimmed the socket and continued deeper into the skull in neat, concentric orbits. Most of the flesh had peeled away from the socket like yellowing wallpaper, and the underlying bone was split open towards the temple. The flaps of bone opened and closed, snapping mindlessly, creating a secondary mouth on the side of the man's head.

Corbett knew that he'd never forget that little mouth trying to grow out of the side of the man's head. It would be with him when he ate, and when he read the paper, and when he sat on the can. It would be rattling around in his brain, pinballing through his thoughts like a loose ball bearing, for the rest of his life. A little part of his sanity choked on its own vomit and died just then.

The thing that had once been a human being was dressed in the remains of a Detroit Salt Combine miner's uniform. More of the creatures stood in the shadows just outside the reach of Corbett's beam. They'd followed him, tracking him perfectly through the stygian gloom of the mine tunnels. They too were dressed in the shredded remains of mining coveralls.

The miner directly in front of him reached out a scaly claw. Corbett ducked, swinging the flashlight. The metal tube crashed into the creature's ribs with a sickening crunch. Corbett felt something inside the monster's chest snap like old, rotting wood.

Darkness consumed the tunnel again as the flashlight fizzled out, but Corbett was already running. Inhuman hands grasped for him, clawing at his arms and face. He slammed straight into one of the creatures, auguring his shoulder into the monstrosity's center of mass like a football player steamrolling a smaller opponent out of the way. The creature's innards felt spongy, like a sack of rotten cheese.

Corbett heard a strange sound echoing down the tunnel, and he realized he was still screaming. He propelled himself down the passageway at full speed. Completely blind in the blackness, he ran in the first direction his legs took him.

Sometimes divers became disoriented in sea caves and lost track of which direction was up. They might travel in the wrong direction for minutes, thinking they were heading toward the surface. Sometimes they became so confused they ran out of oxygen and died down there before they could find their way out. But Corbett didn't have minutes. He might have a few seconds at most to choose the right direction. He lunged in the general direction the tunnel led, flailing in the darkness.

Tap. Tap. Tap.

That knocking sound came again from somewhere behind Corbett, even louder than before. Whatever was making that noise, it was following him.

Without any warning, Corbett slammed into one of the mine's walls, nearly knocking himself unconscious. His nose snapped like a twig as he met the rocks face first. His teeth rattled in his skull as the air blasted out of his lungs. He bounced off the wall and landed on his butt, cracking his flashlight against the ground as he fell.

Weak, wavering light spat out through the broken lens, blasting Corbett in the face and sending purplish rings across his vision. Blood ran down his face in a warm torrent from his shattered nose, but he put all that out of his mind. He could hear shuffling footsteps behind him.

Struggling to regain his feet, Corbett flipped himself up onto his knees before collapsing again. Running into the wall had knocked him nearly senseless and turned his thoughts fuzzy. He managed to get to his knees again, steadying himself against the wall. He grabbed the flashlight and wrenched himself back onto his feet, nearly falling down again in the process. His mind was sluggish, his limbs uncooperative. It would be so much easier to rest ... just for a minute. He could close his eyes and let the mushiness drain from his mind.

No! He had to get out of this hell hole; he had to escape. A single thought sliced through the stunned cobwebs clinging to his brain: *"RUN!"*

With a supreme effort of will, Corbett stumbled forward, half bent at the waist like a drunk trying to escape a speakeasy raid. He went to his knees again and began to pull himself up when something splattered against the ground next to him.

He glanced down. It was some sort of clear, viscous liquid. Another rope of the syrupy goop dribbled down from the ceiling, landing on his shoulder. More globules began to rain down all around him. The stuff was unpleasantly warm and ... and ...

Corbett suddenly realized what the stuff on his shoulder was: saliva.

Tap.

The knocking sound came again, directly overhead this time. Slowly, almost unwillingly, Corbett raised the flashlight and looked up.

"Oh God," he said, and then he started running as fast as he could. He knew he couldn't outrun the thing on the ceiling, knew it with a cold, bone-hard certainty. He wished he still had his gun. Not that the weapon would offer him the least bit of protection. No, he wanted the gun so he could at least kill himself quickly and cleanly. There was no doubt he was about to die. The only question was how horribly.

His eyes burned when he'd looked at the thing, but that was nothing compared to the inferno raging in his head. It felt like just the mental image of the thing was chewing through his head like acid, soaking into his mind. Hot chills and frozen fire crept up his spine. His brain chafed as strange ideas and images squirmed through his head, clamoring over each other as they overran the ramparts of his sanity. He realized the monster was in his head. He could feel it rummaging through his thoughts, sniffing his memories. Impossible, inhuman thoughts crawled across his cerebellum like electric spiders.

Something huge and powerful slammed into Corbett's back, knocking him to the ground. He landed on his stomach and instantly tried to scramble to his feet. He rose to all fours before an immense weight landed on his back.

The pressure was horrendous, crushing. Corbett wriggled and squirmed, tried to struggle out from under the massive weight of one of the creature's legs. He was pinned by one of the monster's talons, like a prized butterfly on an entomologist's display board. It hurt like hell. He could feel the innards in his midsection compressing, squeezing together as he was pressed into the rocky earth. His spine strained, the vertebrae creaking and grating together. Corbett flailed his arms, desperately seeking purchase to help him crawl out from under his attacker.

Suddenly, the thing pinning him jerked backward, dragging him across the floor feet first. Something new clamped down on each side of Corbett's midsection, just below the ribs, and Corbett screamed again. An entire galaxy of white hot agony blinked into existence behind his eyes. He nearly passed out then and there.

There was a horrible squeezing sensation and a thick ripping noise, and then Corbett was free. The pressure relented. His shirt must have ripped, freeing him from the horrible thing's grasp.

Corbett crawled forward on his elbows commando-style, pulling away from the thing. It must have ripped more than his shirt. His entire torso felt like it was on fire, and hot, wet stickiness coated his sides.

He pushed himself up on his arms to get to his feet again, but he just flopped down on his face. Corbett suddenly realized that he couldn't feel his legs at all. He was paralyzed. Oh shit. Shitshitshit. The creature must have broken his back.

Writhing like a worm on a hook, Corbett tried to push himself onto his feet again. He willed feeling into his legs. The thing on the ceiling hadn't grabbed him again yet. If he was going to escape, this was probably his only chance. Hot tears of frustration and pain rolled down his cheeks as he fell onto his chest again. Flipping himself onto his back, Corbett shined the flashlight back toward his attacker.

As it turned out, he wasn't paralyzed. His legs were just gone. Corbett had been scissored in half just above the navel. The flashlight beam revealed a river of blood where Corbett had crawled away. He was trailing lengths of his own intestines, and his organs were starting to spill out of his ruptured body like groceries out of a ripped sack. Most of the pieces were already partially encrusted with a layer of salt crystals from the mine floor.

Corbett moaned and grabbed some of the warm, sticky viscera, trying to stuff it back inside his body, but it was no use. Touching the ragged flesh around the stump of his torso only caused more of himself to spill onto the ground.

Casting the flashlight madly about, Corbett caught one last sight of his limp legs. A set of gigantic mandibles stuffed the appendages into an equally gigantic mouth. Corbett watched his legs disappear into the huge maw, slurped down like jointed spaghetti.

He was beginning to feel light headed, distant. Even the pain was beginning to recede into a dull throb. More blood jetted out of his wounds onto the floor with each heartbeat, but the pulses were growing further and further apart. Or maybe it just seemed that way. Corbett couldn't tell anymore. Dark fog was beginning to creep into the corners of his vision, and he felt so tired. So very tired. Everything was slowly disappearing into the blackness that was engulfing him.

The thing approached him, little more than a shadowy outline against the midnight devouring Corbett's sight.

Tap.

Corbett's breathing grew increasingly unsteady. Red foam bubbled up his throat from his lungs, and he tried to cough, but only a little dribble of red came out. He stared at the monster hovering over him. Suddenly, it ducked its head, and Corbett felt himself being lifted off the ground in the thing's mouth. He tried to scream one last time.

The mandibles snapped down on Corbett's body, piercing his chest and mashing his lungs to pulp. Without waiting for the man to stop twitching, the mandibles pushed what was left of his body further down its gullet.

The flashlight slipped out of Corbett's limp hand and plummeted through the air. The bulb smashed, and the mine returned to perfect darkness.

Chapter 2
Fitzhugh Gets Served

One week later

Jasper O'Malley stood across the street from the laundromat. As always, bedlam reigned on the streets of Chicago. Traffic cops blew their whistles to little effect as vehicles whizzed past. Street vendors hawked everything from fruit to cigarettes to pulp magazines. The city smelled of factory fumes and hot asphalt. Pedestrians flowed around him like water pushing past an obstinate river rock. A few of them gave him odd looks as he stood perfectly still, waiting, watching. He ignored them. There was business to attend to.

Jasper owned seven suits. He was wearing suit number six. Not that it mattered; all of his suits were an identical slate gray and expertly tailored to his tall, wiry frame. Under the jacket, he wore a plain white shirt and a blue silk tie. A matching gray hat sat perched on his head at a rakish angle. He kept the hat tipped at an angle to conceal the fact that his left ear was missing. His face might have been handsome if he were smiling, but he rarely smiled. A large, aquiline nose, the kind that would have looked good on a Roman emperor, sat in the middle of his face. Two dark green eyes rested above the nose. They moved back and forth like big jungle cats restlessly pacing their circus cages, never stopping to focus on any one thing for too long before sliding on to the next point of interest. They were the sort of eyes that quickly made people uncomfortable. Boyish freckles dappled his face. Despite the warm summer day, Jasper remained buttoned up in his suit.

He watched the crowds milling past the laundromat on the opposite side of the street. His eyes flicked from person to person, assessing each before moving to the next. Jasper saw a few potential targets, but none of them went into the laundromat.

He waited.

Ten minutes passed. Then twenty. Jasper continued to stand and watch the laundromat like a big gray shark watching the beach, waiting for swimmers to splash into the water.

Finally, Jasper spotted someone who matched the description he'd been given. The man was big and broad shouldered, built like a boxcar. He was wearing an expensive-looking coat, but it fit poorly around his massive arms and stumpy neck. He had strong, classical features. His square jaw was currently thrown open in a laugh as he put his arm around the shoulders of a short-haired blonde woman.

She was dressed in a green flapper dress and a floppy hat. The big man's arm practically engulfed her. Jasper noticed she wasn't laughing. Her feet wobbled on a pair of glittery heels.

As he watched, the man opened the laundromat's front door and stepped inside, not bothering to hold it open for the woman. She had to grab the handle to keep the door from slamming shut on her face.

Jasper waited. A minute ticked by.

At last he decided he'd given them enough time, and he began walking toward the laundromat. His polished shoes padded off the sidewalk and onto the street. A horn honked at him, but he ignored it.

A length of bells hung on the inside of the laundromat's door, but they barely made a sound as Jasper opened the door and stepped inside in one fluid motion. He glanced around the dark room.

Neatly pressed clothes hung from dozens of racks situated all around the room. Little numbered placards were attached to each hangar. A counter stood directly in front of him, but there was no one there to help him. Steam wafted gently through the air like a sauna. Jasper spied several large cauldrons bubbling like witches' brews and a set of wringers, but there was no sign of the man and woman he had tracked in here.

He walked up to the counter, curled his hand into a fist, and knocked on the wooden surface.

Tap. Tap. Tap.

A door at the back of the room popped open and an elderly Asian woman appeared. Her hair was streaked gray, and her face was a roadmap of wrinkles. She smiled when she saw him. "Hello. You pick up or drop off?" Her English was heavily accented, but passable.

"Actually, I'm looking for someone," Jasper said.

The elderly woman's face instantly hardened into a mask of suspicion. "Pick up or drop off?" She put her palms on the counter and squared her shoulders, looking unhappy.

"He was a big fellow," Jasper continued, unfazed. "A woman was accompanying him."

"No one like that here," she insisted, her voice cold.

"I saw them walk in here."

"You see wrong."

"My apologies for bothering you then, Ma'am. I guess I'll just pick up my clothes." Jasper's hand crept inside his jacket and grabbed something.

"You have number?" she asked, suspicion in her voice.

"Of course." His hand emerged from his jacket with a ten dollar bill poking out from between his long fingers. "I seem to have lost my stub, but I believe I was number ten."

"I don't think that was your number."

A five appeared beside the ten as if by magic. "You're right. How silly of me. I was number fifteen."

She stared at the two bills for a moment, obviously trying to decide if she should push for more. Then she looked up and saw Jasper's eyes and decided to settle for what she could get. This one could be trouble if he wanted to be.

"Ah, yes. I believe I have your items back here. Follow me and I'll get them for you." She dropped her falsely halting speech and slipped into perfect, Chicago-clipped English. The elderly woman turned around and began walking toward the back of the laundry without waiting to see if he followed.

She approached the litter of hangers lining the back wall. Coats and dresses of every color hung from the racks. Sticking her hands between two suits, the woman spread the clothes like Moses parting the Red Sea.

With the space now cleared, Jasper could see a door behind the clothes. "There's only one rule back there — don't cause trouble. I don't know what your business is, but if it interferes with *my* business, you'll regret it."

"I shall endeavor to keep that in mind." Jasper tipped his hat and opened the door.

"You do that. Welcome to Madame Mai's," she said as Jasper stepped into the secret room behind the laundromat, and the door shut behind him.

The place was a "blind tiger," a type of speakeasy. Prohibition made the manufacture, transportation, and sale of alcohol punishable by law, but it was still perfectly legal to drink the stuff. Or give it away, for that matter. Thus, enterprising criminal minds had come up with a solution of sorts. If patrons bought a ticket to see a performance or an exotic animal, they could be served a "complimentary" beverage. Patrons could buy as many tickets as they liked, receiving a drink each time. Often the "tigers" they were paying to see were mangy alley cats, but no one seemed to mind. A halfway-decent prosecutor could still nail the proprietors for transporting the alcohol and probably any number of other charges, so the illicit bars continued to exist only in the shadows.

The deception, for the most part, was for the customers. They could come in and enjoy themselves without the feeling that they were participating in anything illegal. It was a quaint, little illusion to set people at ease, transforming the illicit business into a secret club. It calmed customers' nerves, and they probably bought more product as a result.

The building's construction was spartan, with large, wooden beams holding up the roof. A banner hung between two of the rough-hewn pillars. "WELCOME TO MADAME MAI'S," it said. "COME SEE AGATHA, THE WONDER CHICKEN. 50¢."

From the outside, the building probably looked like just another rusting warehouse or anonymous storage depot. The interior, though, resembled a posh restaurant. Dozens of small tables lined the high-ceilinged structure like a Parisian café. A phonograph in the corner warbled a jazz set. Reproductions of famous oil paintings lined the walls. A sixty-foot long bar took pride of place along the back wall. Hundreds of bottles lined the shelves behind the bar, some of them of pre-Prohibition vintage. The fifty cent price tag to see Agatha, the Wonder Chicken, might buy a man two of the cheaper, newer drinks, but some of the aged, amber-colored whiskeys would likely require several tickets.

His work took Jasper into speakeasies more often than he liked. From his experience, most of them were dark, unpleasant holes that stank of desperation and stale vomit. Usually, they were located in abandoned garages or hidden sub-basements, and they were only open at odd hours. After a few years of operation, every available surface, from the stools to the walls, became sticky with cigarette tar. Because the main concern for such structures was usually muffling sound, ventilation was poor. The bottled-up funk of tens of thousands of chain-smoked cigarettes built up until it clung to the structure's very studs. Often, the speakeasies were too primitive for plumbing, so there was sometimes just a trough in a dark corner of the room. Sometimes the trough was directly in front of the bar stools so that the men at the bar didn't have to risk losing their spots by getting up. Most of the drinks themselves were strongly flavored to hide the raw, volatile taste of pure alcohol. Sometimes the drinks were tainted, either with chemicals or some outside effluvia, and the customers would become violently ill.

Of course, there were always exceptions, and Madame Mai's obviously catered to a different type of clientele. All of the customers were well-dressed, dapper-looking chaps and well-groomed dames. Jasper spotted the deputy mayor sitting at one table, slowly working his way to the bottom of a tumbler. Other patrons appeared to be lawyers, bankers, and other professionals from the nearby districts, chatting with their colleagues.

Usually, a successful place like this would be guarded. If the owners weren't already associated with organized crime, mobsters would almost certainly come a-calling to offer protection. Less-prosperous booze barons might employ a few local street toughs to keep tabs paid, fights broken up, and undesirables out. Jasper had once seen someone crush a man's larynx because he owed three dollars. The body had been dragged into a back room, and there was a minute-long pause before everyone went back to the business of drinking. For a ritzy joint like this, the hired muscle would probably quietly lead you to the back alley, club you over the head, and load you into a truck to be anonymously buried in a field outside of town rather than just killing you on the spot. Pure class, that.

Jasper spotted Madame Mai's goons almost as soon as he stepped through the door. They stood out like a couple of turds in a punch bowl. Their matching suits were both cut from the same cheap, black cloth with the same overdone shoulder pads to make them look bigger and more intimidating. One was a squat man built like a fire plug. He was leaning against the nearest pillar, watching the door. The second thug was a big bruiser with a shaved head. He continually swept the room with a sour gaze. Whereas most of the customers were wearing pointed wingtips, the guards wore heavy, blunt ankle boots. Boots like that had many utilitarian functions, chief among them, kicking the crap out of people.

Jasper continued looking. He was searching for the big man he'd seen enter Madame Mai's laundromat. Sawing his eyes back and forth over the tables, Jasper began to stalk through the room. There was no one matching the big man's size. The bouncers were the only ones who even came close.

One of the patrons locked eyes with Jasper and raised a friendly glass. Jasper nodded to Tycho Vedel, but didn't bother to stop or further acknowledge his presence. There was business to be done.

The big man was not at any of the tables, nor was he at the bar. Jasper eyed a doorway at the back of the speakeasy. A sign hung over the door: "AGATHA, THE WONDER CHICKEN. 50¢."

A pretty girl stood next to the door selling cigarettes from a tray. She smiled as he approached. "How many tickets to the show, sweetheart?"

"Just one." Jasper did not return the smile. He reached into his pocket and removed five dimes, dropping them into the girl's hand one at a time. Once they were all in her outstretched palm, she counted them again.

"Thanks for visiting, hon. Once you're done, you can redeem your ticket for something special over there." She pointed in the direction of the bar, but Jasper was already through the door, hunting.

The small room was dimly lit. More for form's sake than anything else, hard, uncomfortable-looking benches lined three sides of the room, providing ample viewing space for the star attraction. A small cage stood atop a simple podium, but Jasper's focus was on the two people standing to either side of the pedestal. The big man and the woman were peering into the cage.

Blonde locks bouncing around her face, the woman tittered as she watched the big man. He had stuck his fingers through the bars of the cage and was pinching Agatha, the Wonder Chicken's tail feathers. Agatha was struggling to get away, but her feet just scrabbled uselessly against the floor of her cage. She made undignified noises as she ran in place.

"But Edwin, they're *so damn adorable*. Are you sure I can't have one?" The blonde's voice was high pitched and grating. She took a drag on a long, thin cigarette and exhaled a stream of fragrant smoke into the cage.

"Beulah, you wouldn't know how to take care of a chicken if they came with instruction manuals."

Agatha finally managed to break free of Edwin's grasp, losing a couple of tail feathers in the process. The blonde pouted.

"C'mon, I didn't bring us here to play with chickens. Let's go get those drinks," Edwin said.

The blonde immediately brightened. "Okie-dokie," Beulah said, and giggled again. Jasper noticed that her eyes weren't quite focused, and the pupils were dilated. She was unsteady on her feet, at risk of toppling right out of her sparkly heels. She was more than just drunk. On laudanum, maybe.

She seemed unsure what to do with her exhausted cigarette, so she stuffed it through the wires of Agatha's cage. Edwin grabbed her hand and started to lead her out of the room.

"'Scuse me, Bub." The big man attempted to shove his way through the door.

Jasper moved out of the way and let them pass, then walked over to the cage and examined a small plaque glued to the side of the podium.

> *Behold the rare Mongolian Steppe Chicken. These chickens were carried by Genghis Khan as his endless hordes of barbarian horsemen swept across Asia. Easily transported over a long distance, the chickens were valued for their meat, eggs, and plumage. Often, the chickens roamed free after a battle and were known to peck flesh off the bodies the Mongols left in their wake. Agatha is the only example of Mongolian Steppe Chicken in the Western Hemisphere, a true marvel of the mysterious Orient.*

It was a good story, but Jasper recognized the small chicken as a

Bearded d'Uccle, a Belgian breed. She had creamy tan feathers accented with points of blue-grey. A big muff of feathers under her beak gave her an exotic appearance. She sat in the middle of the cage, unhappily preening her tail. A clutch of tiny, peeping heads poked out from under her wings, chattering incessantly. One of the fluffy chicks, resembling a small, yellow cotton ball, escaped out from under Agatha and ran over to investigate the cigarette smoldering in the bottom of the cage. Curious, it poked at the embers.

A small padlock latched the cage's door. Jasper dipped his fingers into the cuff of his jacket and pulled out a lock pick. Within a few seconds, the padlock snicked open, and Jasper reached into the cage.

Peeping frantically, the chick scampered back under the warm, safe confines of its mother's feathers. Jasper snagged the smoldering butt. A hint of bright red lipstick lined the cigarette's base.

He flicked the cigarette onto the ground and relocked the cage. They were beautiful chickens, and the cage was much too small for them.

Jasper turned around and walked out of the room. Back to business.

The job sounded simple. All he had to do was serve Edwin Bartholomew Fitzhugh III with divorce papers. But no one came to the Attican Detective Agency with simple problems.

Normally, it would be a task for a certified court courier. Someone would deliver the papers, hand them to Fitzhugh, and leave. That was all the law required. Simple. Easy-peasy. Applesauce. But that was before three couriers in a row "lost" their deliveries in transit. Fitzhugh came from old money. His grandfather expanded into Chicago's slaughterhouse business early in the city's growth and made great heaps of money in the process. Granddaddy Fitzhugh's stockyards provided countless rations of tinned meat to Union soldiers during the Civil War.

As the scion of a meat-packing family, Fitzhugh had cash to spare and friends in every corner of Chicago. Jasper had done research on the man, trailing him for the better part of a week to learn his habits. Madame Mai's was his favorite hangout, and he visited nearly every day, a different girl slung across his hairy arms each time. All Jasper needed to do to find his quarry was stakeout the speakeasy's laundromat front.

Fitzhugh was built like a tyrannosaurus with a growth condition, and he had the personality to match. He was a hedonistic, boorish playboy prone to fits of extreme anger. As near as Jasper could tell, the man's favorite, and possibly only, hobby consisted of betting on dog fights.

The Fitzhughs virtually shanghaied Edwin into a marriage with Georgina Whittacker, the daughter of a prominent railroad family. Maybe the family thought marriage would settle Edwin down. Maybe it was just a cynical attempt to forge a permanent alliance in an industry that could transport meat products to all corners of the nation. Jasper didn't know, and it wasn't his job to care.

Georgina Fitzhugh contacted the Attican Detective Agency ten days ago, asking if one of their operatives could serve her husband with divorce papers. After two years, she'd had enough of Fitzhugh's abuse and philandering. She wanted out, and she needed someone who wouldn't be intimidated or bribed into ditching the papers.

Fitzhugh didn't give an eighth of a damn about the marriage. He probably didn't even care about the potential business aspects. The slaughterhouses could churn out meat products under the command of a board of directors indefinitely. No, Fitzhugh refused to grant the divorce because it would be a black stain on his social standing. He was a vain creature, and he knew higher circles would talk about it behind his back if he allowed the marriage to dissolve.

Georgina feared that if she couldn't get rid of Fitzhugh legally, he might use his connections to get rid of her. Legally or not. It was much easier to walk among Chicago's elite as a widower than a divorcee. And if Fitzhugh wasn't served the divorce papers, the process couldn't begin.

Jasper turned around and walked back out the door. He spotted Fitzhugh immediately, perched on one of the barstools with Beulah by his side. One of the barkeeps was pouring something expensive-looking for the pair. The stool looked like it was about to snap in half under Fitzhugh's girth.

At six feet, Jasper was taller than most of the men in the speakeasy, but he was primarily composed of ropy sinew and tough gristle, like a jackal. Fitzhugh, on the other hand, was built like a gorilla. He had at least four inches of height on Jasper and a chest like a steam boiler. His shirt was of an expensive cut, but tight, clearly chosen to show off his muscular physique rather than for any fashion qualities. The man looked like he could probably snap a yak in half if he wanted to.

Treading across the floor on silent feet, Jasper watched Fitzhugh slug back an entire glass of fiery liquid. Fitzhugh raised a finger, and the barkeep began to prepare another drink. Fitzhugh slid a ticket across the counter in payment. Jasper tapped him on the shoulder.

"Edwin Bartholomew Fitzhugh III?"

Edwin Bartholomew Fitzhugh III spun around on his stool. "Yeah? What's it to you?"

"Necessary for identification. I'm glad I found the correct man. Allow me to introduce myself; I'm Jasper O'Malley, with the Attican Detective Agency." A badge appeared in Jasper's hand, was flashed at Fitzhugh, and then disappeared just as quickly.

The barkeep finished Fitzhugh's drink and left it on the counter. Beulah twisted around to look at Jasper. She would have been pretty if she hadn't been plastered out of her mind. Her eyes were round and glassy. One of the straps of her dress had slipped, and the already low neckline sagged considerably.

"Can I help you, Detective, or are you just here to waste my time? If you know my name, you must recognize that I'm a very busy man." Fitzhugh flashed a big, carnivorous smile.

"Of course. This won't take but a moment." Jasper reached out and fixed the strap of Beulah's dress, slipping it back over her shoulder. The barkeep, who had been enjoying the view, moved on to serve a new customer. Jasper then reached into his jacket and removed a large, manila envelope. "I have some documents from your wife. I am hereby serving you with —"

"Oh, Christ. Not this again," Fitzhugh reached into his back pocket and removed a thick leather wallet. Without looking, he reached into the billfold and peeled off a wad of bills. "Listen, Sport, my wife isn't well. She's in the hospital; it's her nerves, you see? Just take this and scram. For the inconvenience she's put you through and all. Once she's better, I'm sure she'll agree that she's being silly."

Eighty dollars dangled in front of Jasper's nose. He brushed Fitzhugh's hand out of his face using the back of his fingers. "I am aware that Georgina is in the hospital. I visited her. Her nerves seemed just fine. Her primary ailment appeared to be that her legs were broken, an injury not inconsistent with being picked up and tossed out a third-story window. If the hospital told you the problem was her nerves, perhaps you should take that money and hire some competent doctors."

"Hey, pipsqueak, this doesn't concern you, okay? It's a purely private matter. I don't care who you are. I'm not accepting those papers."

"Drat. It would seem that we're at an impasse. I was hired to ensure that you accept these papers." Jasper held the envelope out again.

Fitzhugh irked him. Time to try a different tact. "Out of curiosity, does Fitzhugh Meat Packing have a specialty item? I'm guessing you deliver quite a bit of horse's ass. You seem to have a lot of it on hand."

"Here," Fitzhugh snatched the papers out of Jasper's hand. Jasper didn't try to grab them back. Fitzhugh ripped open the top of the envelope and pulled the papers out. He crumpled them in one massive fist without looking at them. His face was beginning to turn an unhealthy shade of red.

Technically, Fitzhugh had just accepted the papers. In the eyes of the law, he was officially on notice. Mission accomplished. Nevertheless, the man had put Jasper's hackles up.

Fitzhugh took the wad of papers and tossed them at Jasper. They bounced off the lapel of his suit and fell to the ground. "Stick it where the sun don't shine, pal." Fitzhugh turned back to the counter, ready to quaff down his drink.

"That can be arranged," Jasper said, picking up the wad of papers. He tapped Fitzhugh on the shoulder.

The big man swiveled around on his stool again. That was a mistake. He should have stood up immediately, using his height and weight to their maximum advantage. Sitting down, he was shorter than Jasper, and precariously balanced on the too-small stool.

"Get out of my face, or *GLUARG!*" Jasper jammed the wad of court papers in Fitzhugh's mouth. Fitzhugh's eyes went wide in disbelief. He grabbed for Jasper, but missed as the wiry detective stepped backward.

Beulah snorted high-pitched laughter. Fitzhugh swung his arm around the full length of his body and delivered a vicious backhand to Beulah's face. The blow knocked her clean off her stool, and she fell backward with a squawk.

Fitzhugh spat the papers out onto the floor. He didn't look at Beulah, who was on the floor squalling.

"You," he snarled. "You're a dead man."

Chapter 3
Oh Snap

The two bouncers instantly sprang into action. Jasper watched the big goon with the shaved head pause for a second, trying to figure out how to best enter the fray. Rather than take on the enraged Fitzhugh, the bouncer chose to grab at Jasper.

It was a solid theory. Jasper was smaller and lighter. That strategy was probably part of Thuggery 101: always go for the weakest-looking of the herd. However, like many theories, application quickly proved it wrong.

Jasper grabbed the bouncer's outstretched hand and pulled him forward, using his momentum against him as he rushed into the fracas. The bouncer stumbled, and Jasper brought his other arm around in a full uppercut. His fist connected with the man's jaw and the bouncer reeled backward into Fitzhugh, but Jasper may have bitten off more than he could chew with this one. He had hoped that the stunned bouncer would slow Fitzhugh down. Instead, Fitzhugh grabbed the goon by the pants and ridiculously overstuffed shoulder pads and lifted him over his head like a man tossing a medicine ball. The bouncer flailed, trying to escape Fitzhugh's grasp.

With a heave, the big man threw the bouncer at Jasper, who dropped into a crouch. The screaming guard sailed over his head and landed in a heap on top of a row of tables, flipping them over amid a crescendo of shattering glasses.

Madame Mai's patrons bolted, streaming out of the speakeasy in droves. A bottleneck formed around the door leading to the laundry as people scampered away from the burly brawl. Madame Mai herself, looking mad as hell, was struggling to come through the door from the opposite direction, but it was no use against the crush of people. She wasn't Jasper's main concern right now anyway; Fitzhugh charged him, swinging his fists in wide, sloppy haymakers. Size and endurance had probably tipped the scales in Fitzhugh's favor in every fight of his life. He had no reason to learn technique. He came at Jasper like a tsunami of fists. Jasper took two steps forward, moving directly into Fitzhugh's warpath. The angry giant didn't slow his charge.

A huge, ham-sized fist rocketed toward Jasper's face. The massive blow probably would have snapped Jasper's neck if it connected, but the private eye was already gone. He dropped low, hunkering into a stoop below the arc of Fitzhugh's swing. The attempted blow already had Fitzhugh off balance. Jasper grabbed the enraged man midstride just above the ankles. He launched himself into Fitzhugh's shins. Fitzhugh flipped like a massive tiddlywink and crashed face first into the floor behind Jasper.

Roaring incoherent anger, Fitzhugh tried to right himself. Jasper lunged backward to avoid the second speakeasy guard, Fire Plug, who now wielded a baseball bat. Hoisting the bat, Fire Plug wound up for a horizontal swing, as if he were preparing to hit a home run. Jasper stepped forward during the backswing, inside the length of the bat. It took precious time to swing a baseball bat. The bat's power depended on its handler's ability to bring the heavy, blunt weapon all the way around in a crushing blow. He grabbed the handle of the bat below Fire Plug's hands and yanked as hard as he could. The bat slid out of the man's grip.

The bouncer's eyes boggled at his empty palms.

Without hesitation, Jasper thrust the handle into the man's face like he was hitting a cue ball. The bat hit with a loud, unpleasant crack, knocking two of the guard's teeth out in a spurt of blood and spittle. Fire Plug clutched at his face as he reeled away from Jasper and floundered away. His fight was done. There was no need for Jasper to pursue him. He had more pressing matters to attend to.

Chuck-chck.

Like the barkeep who had just produced a shotgun from below the counter.

The bartender raised the big, double-barreled shotgun in Jasper's direction. More than twenty feet separated Jasper from the bar. There was no way for him to reach the counter without having a hole blown through his midsection, so he raised the baseball bat and hurled it like a javelin. It wasn't a particularly accurate throw. The bat missed the shotgun-toting worker by over a foot, smashing into the bar display behind him. Bottles plunged off their shelves, exploding like whiskey mortars on the floor.

Jasper followed close behind the bat. Even if his throw hadn't hit the barkeep, he'd accomplished his goal. The barman instinctively dodged to the side, twisting away from the projectile. For a few precious seconds, he couldn't train his weapon on Jasper, and that was all the time Jasper needed. He sprinted up to the bar and vaulted onto the counter like a gray-clad gazelle, planting a perfectly polished wingtip in the barkeep's face. The man's head snapped back and, with a streamer of drool escaping his mouth, stumbled backward into the shelves. More liquor bottles crashed to the floor.

Unfortunately, the barkeep didn't drop the shotgun. He clamped one hand to his forehead. Blood oozed out from behind his fingers from a cut near his hairline and flooded his eyes.

Half-blinded by the flow of blood, the barkeep raised the shotgun again and tried to focus his aim on his assailant. Jasper swatted the barrels away with one hand and grabbed a half-full bottle of Finley's Finest Whiskey off a shelf with his other hand. His arm became a gray blur as he brought the bottle around and smashed it against the side of the barkeep's head. The bottle shattered, spraying whiskey in every direction. The barkeep went down, unconscious and drenched in alcohol. His shotgun lay on the floor next to his limp body. Jasper grabbed the weapon.

A bottle of red wine rested on the shelf next to Jasper's head. The wine bottle exploded into a million pieces as a bullet struck it. Shards of glass sprayed Jasper's face, and droplets of wine spattered his suit. Jasper scanned the room to see who was shooting at him.

All Madame Mai's customers had fled, but the woman herself was marching through the door like a small, wrinkly tank. And, boy, did she look *pissed*. She was holding a heavy duty, pearl-inlaid M1911 semi-automatic pistol. The gun was enormous in her tiny hand.

Jasper darted below the counter as Madame Mai marched forward. The pistol *pop-pop-popped*, peppering the bar with bullets. The thick wood stopped the .45 caliber missiles from puncturing Jasper. Several more bottles exploded over Jasper's head. He dabbed at the wine spattering his suit. That was going to leave a stain.

More lead slammed into the bar, and then there was a sudden silence. Jasper popped up from the bar and unloaded both the shotgun's barrels in twin blasts. He instantly ducked back below the bar, but a loud, shrill screech told him he'd hit his mark.

He vaulted back over the bar. Madame Mai was trapped under the large, heavy banner welcoming patrons to her establishment. Jasper had peppered the two lengths of rope holding the welcome banner with .20 gauge shotgun pellets, and it collapsed on top of Madame Mai like a net.

Something slashed at Jasper, and he scuttled away before he could even see what it was.

Fitzhugh had recovered and pulled a switchblade from his pocket. The small blade looked ridiculous in his massive hands. The man was big. Huge. Gigantic. Hercules's pig-headed brother. But that made him slow. His tight shirt, meant to show off his muscles, also restricted his movement. His wide-arcing swings had all the finesse of a windmill.

Jasper launched himself backward. Fitzhugh lumbered after him. The detective managed to remain just out of range. He would pause for a split second, creating the illusion of an opening to induce Fitzhugh to strike, then retreat again.

This fight had probably already lasted longer than any in Fitzhugh's life. Sweat dripped from the big man's forehead as he leveled blow after blow at Jasper, thrashing at him like an angry tide. The punches came slower and slower as Fitzhugh tired. Jasper continued to bait him, springing away at the final second each time. The big man had used a stupendous amount of energy in his initial flurry of blows, intending to end Jasper in the first few seconds of the fight. He didn't have the stamina for a prolonged battle of attrition.

Pressing the advantage, Jasper surged forward, going for Fitzhugh's knife, which was still clutched in the man's massive fist. There was no easy way to get to the knife free from those thick, powerful fingers. It was like trying to pry the blade out from a tangle of oak roots.

There was a weak point, though.

Jasper grabbed Fitzhugh's thumb and wrenched it violently backward. A loud, hideous cracking noise sounded through the entire speakeasy.

A full-throated scream followed half a second after the sound of crunching bone. The switchblade clattered to the floor as Fitzhugh cradled his mangled hand. Jasper scooped up the knife. Leaping forward, Jasper swung the knife as hard as he could.

The cold steel sank home as Jasper buried it in the wood of the nearest pillar. He twisted the knife, and the tiny screw that held the blade in place snapped in half. Jasper yanked on the knife. The deadly blade remained stuck in the hard wood, but the handle came away in Jasper's hand.

He tossed the useless handle away, sending it skittering across the floor.

"You son of a bitch," Fitzhugh frothed. "You broke my thumb." He looked as if he didn't quite believe it himself.

"So I did," Jasper agreed.

Fitzhugh launched himself forward, hurling obscenities. He kept his right hand, the thumb kinked at an unnatural angle, cradled against his chest. His other hand came around for another pass at Jasper. The man did not know how to admit defeat.

Jasper was forced to retreat. It was like fighting a cargo freighter. There was only so much he could do to harm Fitzhugh.

Fitzhugh was panting. The veins on his forehead stood out like angry worms. A low, feral sound was coming from somewhere deep in Fitzhugh's throat as his lips peeled away from his teeth. Jasper shuffled backward as quickly as he could, but with every swing, Fitzhugh's strikes came a little closer.

Finally, one came too close.

Jasper threw an arm up, deflecting the weight of the blow away from his face. The punch struck his shoulder instead, spinning him around and drilling him backward.

Fitzhugh was right on top of him, boozy breath blowing in Jasper's face in great, ripping gusts. Jasper peddled backward. If he didn't open up some space, Fitzhugh would pull him apart in a matter of seconds.

Then, Jasper's back hit one of the structural wooden beams. There was nowhere for him to go. Fitzhugh smiled like a wolf about to tear out an elk's throat. The prey had given him a good chase, but it was all over now.

Fitzhugh's hand curled into a brutal-looking meat brick. His elbow cocked back as far as it would go, lifting up like a mechanical rock crusher. Then, the huge, terrible fist rocketed forward.

Jasper watched the blow arcing toward his face in a sort of creeping slow motion. He gazed at it the way the dinosaurs must have watched the meteor that ended their reign hurtling through the atmosphere in a cascade of fire.

Fitzhugh hadn't counted on one thing, though.

At the last second, Jasper simply disappeared. He moved with the spooky, liquid speed of a veteran gunslinger drawing a familiar weapon from its holster. In the blink of the eye, he was there and then not, having ducked straight down as if a hole had opened in the earth's crust and swallowed him.

He'd needed Fitzhugh to get closer. It would be impossible to end the fight simply by staying out of Fitzhugh's reach and delivering mosquito bite volleys. Jasper needed to get in close and use the man's sheer power against him. Taking the hit on the shoulder, fooling Fitzhugh into thinking he had a chance, that he was on the cusp of victory even, had been worth it.

Now, where Jasper's face had been, there was only a sturdy wooden beam that was thicker than a telephone pole and placed for structural stability. Fitzhugh had fully committed to the swing; there was no stopping it.

Fitzhugh's hand was made of a bit of skin, some tendons, and lots of small, fragile bones. His fist plowed into the wood like the Titanic at an iceberg derby. A series of pops, so close together that they sounded like a single noise, rattled through the speakeasy. Jasper recognized it as the sound of all of Fitzhugh's knuckles breaking at once. Fitzhugh's hand folded in on itself like a wilted petunia, snapping in half midway down his palm, creating a jagged, unnatural joint between his wrist and knuckles.

Fitzhugh drew his arm back, and Jasper saw a faint outline of a tiny crater where the man's fist had compressed the wood. Fitzhugh's hand dangled like a broken child's toy, smashed into something that no longer exactly resembled a hand. The man made a noise somewhere between a howl and a bleat. His hand flopped like a dead octopus.

Jasper didn't give him time to recover. So long as Fitzhugh was mobile, he was dangerous. One of Jasper's polished shoes shot out, the tip of which connected directly with the side of Fitzhugh's knee. There was a *crack* even louder than the sound of Fitzhugh's hand destroying itself against the post. At the end of his shoe, Jasper felt something shift and then give altogether.

Folding up like a cheap accordion, Fitzhugh's knee bent sideways at a horrific angle. For a second, Fitzhugh continued to stand as if nothing had happened, but then gravity took over. His leg collapsed under him, ligaments ripping like wet tissue paper under his weight.

In less than five seconds, Fitzhugh had gone from certain victory to a tangle of oddly cocked limbs on the floor. Jasper took two slow steps closer, the tips of his shoes coming to rest a few inches away from Fitzhugh's nose.

"No need to fret," Jasper said. "I know some doctors who can tell you it's probably just your nerves. Now, about those divorce papers."

Fitzhugh tried to reach out and claw at Jasper's leg using the hand where only his thumb was broken. A valiant effort, but ultimately futile.

Jasper casually lifted his foot up and brought back down on Fitzhugh's hand. Fitzhugh shrieked like a girl watching her kitten being eaten by wolverines.

"As I was saying, about those papers." Jasper reached into his jacket and withdrew a second manila envelope. "I took the liberty of creating duplicate documents in the event that anything should happen to the first set. People seem to keep losing these, and it never hurts to be prepared." He dropped the envelope next to Fitzhugh.

Fitzhugh gurgled some profanity at Jasper.

"Look at it this way, Mister Fitzhugh. Now you have something to read in the hospital. There is the slight matter of my suit, however. I'm afraid it's gotten some wine on it. Not very good wine at that. I'll be needing a new jacket."

Jasper reached down and plucked Fitzhugh's wallet out of his back pocket. More unhappy noises came from the floor.

"Georgina has graciously offered to pay for my expenses while I am in her employ. Technically, you two are still temporarily married, so I'm sure she won't mind if I take my fees from your joint resources."

Fishing his fingers into the wallet, Jasper removed four twenty dollar bills, the same eighty dollars Fitzhugh had tried to bribe him with earlier. The bills disappeared from between Jasper's fingers.

"Additionally, I paid fifteen dollars for access to this place, a rather steep sum given the abominable service." He reached into the wallet and removed a ten and a five. The new bills pulled the same vanishing act as their brothers. Jasper tossed the thick leather wallet off to the side.

"Oh, and I also paid fifty cents to see a chicken." Jasper brushed his hands over Fitzhugh's pockets and removed two quarters. He slipped the coins into his own pocket. "Fantastic. I believe that leaves us even."

Fitzhugh mewled, maybe in disagreement or maybe just in pain.

"There is one final matter I'd like to discuss with you, Mister Fitzhugh. I understand this must be a stressful time in your life, what with the divorce and all, but I'd like to leave you with one last thought."

"Piss up a rope, you son of a —" Fitzhugh screamed as Jasper's foot came to rest atop his shattered hand again. Jasper didn't apply any pressure. He didn't need to.

"The Attican Detective Agency values its clients. Their problems are our problems," Jasper said.

Sirens were approaching from the distance, but they were still a few minutes off. The gunfire and stream of fleeing customers must have caught someone's interest.

Madame Mai finally worked her way out from under the banner's heavy fabric. She glared poison-laced daggers at Jasper for a second before running out the door herself. She would have some explaining to do once the police stormed into her laundromat and discovered this backroom speakeasy.

Jasper bent down so he could whisper to Fitzhugh. "My Agency takes care of its clients, and Georgina is a perfectly nice woman. I like her. If anything should happen to her after this, I will blame you. If she should pass away in a suspicious accident, I will blame *you*. If she's attacked on the street by muggers, I will blame *you*. If a freak lightning bolt strikes her, *I will blame you*. Do you understand what I'm telling you, Mister Fitzhugh?"

Grimacing, Fitzhugh nodded, but pure, unadulterated hate glimmered in his eyes.

"Splendid. I'm glad we had this conversation. Now, if you'll excuse me, I have other matters to attend to." Jasper raised himself back to his full height.

He walked back to the rear of the speakeasy and entered the door to Agatha, the Wonder Chicken's chambers. No one asked him to buy a ticket this time. He walked in and examined the cage. It was secured to the podium by two heavy-duty padlocks of a much higher quality than those keeping the cage shut.

Jasper produced his lock pick again. Both padlocks were of the highest quality, and they used fairly sophisticated tumblers. It took Jasper almost a quarter of a minute to unlock both of them.

Agatha, the Wonder Chicken, squawked in alarm as Jasper picked the cage up and tucked it under his arm. He turned around and marched back out of the room.

Tycho Vedel, the man who had nodded at Jasper when he entered, was waiting for him at the bar. Jasper hadn't seen him escape the speakeasy with everyone else. He must have retreated to some hidden corner until everything blew over. An array of bottles was lined up in front of him, and a bottle of brandy rested in his hand.

"Was that really necessary?" Tycho gestured with the brandy bottle in Fitzhugh's direction. Though it had branch offices in numerous cities, the Attican Detective Agency was headquartered in Chicago. Vedel handled the Agency's dispatches in the city because he had the almost supernatural ability to know exactly where all the detectives would be at any given time, sometimes seemingly before they knew themselves. No one had a clue how he did it.

"Yes," Jasper responded. He set the small chicken hutch down on the counter of the bar. Vedel held the brandy bottle out to him, but Jasper held up a hand, declining. The police sirens were growing closer.

"Good choice," Vedel said. A thin seal of wax was wrapped around the bottle's stopper. Tycho twisted the bottle around and pointed to a tiny hole in the wax. He quickly stripped the seal and revealed that the hole extended into the rim of the bottle as well. "It's fake. The bottle's original, but they just refill it with swill through this little gap here."

Tycho pulled the stopper out with his teeth and took a swig straight from the bottle. He pursed his lips and spat a stream of liquor onto the floor. With a flick of his wrist, he tossed the bottle behind the counter, where it shattered on the floor. "Tastes like it came out of the wrong end of a camel," he said.

"I wasn't aware that there was a right end of a camel to drink out of," Jasper commented. "Much as I enjoy your company, Tycho, I assume you're here on Agency business."

"You sure I can't offer you something, Jasper? This over here is the real deal," Tycho hefted a bottle of whiskey. "Also, what's with the chickens?"

"Respectively, I'm fine, and I like these chickens. Now, what have you got for me?"

Vedel tucked the whiskey bottle under his arm and stood up to walk around to the other side of the bar. In doing so, he revealed the reason he only worked the Agency's dispatches and not as a field detective. He walked with a curious rolling gait, almost like a sailor who hadn't gotten used to dry land again. Thousands of men across the nation walked exactly the same way. Anyone who had lost a leg below the knee walked that way. Vedel had lost his leg during the Great War when a mortar exploded in his trench, and the shrapnel took most of the meat off everything between his knee and boot. He couldn't walk much faster than a swift limp.

The Attican courier began sorting through the liquor shelves. He picked up a bottle and examined it. After a moment, he tossed it over his shoulder onto the floor.

Agatha began clucking concernedly.

"You're agitating my chickens, Tycho. I know you have something for me."

"Oh, you *'know'* I have something for you? And here I was beginning to think you were a real detective. Don't you realize that the only true wisdom comes from knowing you know nothing?" Vedel enjoyed being a gadfly and quoted Socrates liberally to prove it.

"You wouldn't be here if you didn't have another job for me."

"Don't you have any hobbies, Jasper? You should take some time off between jobs. You take more jobs than anyone else in the office. The old philosophers told us to beware the bareness of a busy life. Sage advice then. Sage advice now."

"I seem to recall something about Socrates being executed after annoying the wrong people with incessant chattering."

"Touché, Mister O'Malley. You're a philistine, but touché."

"I'm mostly Irish, actually. Now, out with it."

The police chose that moment to storm into the speakeasy. A dozen uniformed officers poured through the door in tight precision, guns drawn and at the ready. They fanned out in a trample of boots, sweeping the room. Several of them split off to examine Fitzhugh, the unconscious bouncer, and the barkeep.

"You two, freeze," one of the officers commanded.

Jasper kept his hands dutifully planted in plain sight on the bar. Tycho raised his arms, a bottle of booze in each hand.

"Stand down. It's O'Malley and Vedel," Lieutenant Sam Black said, entering the speakeasy behind his men. Guns were holstered.

"Drink, Lieutenant?" Tycho tipped one of the bottles in Black's direction. The lieutenant waved away the offer. Vedel shrugged and took a slug from one of the bottles, smacking his lips in enjoyment. "A chicken, maybe?"

Black ignored the comment and pointed at Jasper. "You do this?" He swung his arm wide, gesturing to the speakeasy in general.

"Officer," Tycho jumped into the conversation. "Did you see the size of that man back there? And what's been done to him? Do you really think a spindly, waifish thing like Mister O'Malley could do that? I'd start looking for a real brute if I were you. Maybe put out an APB for any escaped medical experiments."

"I wasn't talking to you, Vedel." Black pulled out a small notepad from his breast pocket while his men began examining the speakeasy. One of them gave an all clear, and a pair of medics carried a stretcher into the speakeasy.

"I did that," Jasper pointed behind the counter to the still unconscious barkeep. He twisted around on the stool to point to Fitzhugh. "And that."

Jotting something in his notepad, Black glanced over at Fitzhugh. The medics were arguing with each other about what to do. Apparently, Fitzhugh was too big to fit properly on the stretcher.

"That's ... genuinely impressive. Care to explain what happened?"

"I was here to serve Mister Fitzhugh over there with some court papers, and our discussion became somewhat heated. We've settled the matter now, though."

"Sounds like a classic case of self-defense to me," Black said, snapping his notepad shut. Fitzhugh's head snapped up from the floor in the background, and it took both medics to restrain him. They finally succeeded in strapping him down to the stretcher, pulling the adjustable leather straps to their maximum length in the process.

"I'm not sure Mister Fitzhugh agrees with you, Lieutenant," Jasper commented.

"Mister Fitzhugh was just captured in a raid on an illegal liquor-distribution facility. He doesn't have much say in the matter."

The Chicago police force — and Lieutenant Sam Black, in particular — owed Jasper a bucket of favors. Both parties found it mutually beneficial to simply ignore each other. The police got to claim all the credit, and Jasper got to operate without any rules but his own. Everyone was satisfied.

"Now if you'll excuse me," Black said, "I have to go coordinate this with the Prohibition Office. They'll be interested to hear about this."

"Good day, Lieutenant. Let us know if we can render any assistance." Jasper touched a finger to the brim of his hat.

Vedel was watching the exchange in apparent disgust. "It must be nice having the city's finest eating out of your hand like that. Do you think you could get me my own pet cop now that you've got some chickens to take care of?"

"It must be my enormous personal charm," Jasper said. "Now, what do you have for me?"

Sighing, Tycho pulled out his own manila envelope, virtually identical to the one Jasper had dropped in front of Fitzhugh. He handed it over, and the clasp popped open in Jasper's fingers. A single page of instructions and contact information slid out.

"You're being dispatched to Detroit. They've got problems. Big ones."

Chapter 4
Welcome to Detroit

Jasper sat behind the wheel of a sleek, cream-colored Peerless as it prowled down the streets of Detroit. The large, predatory-looking car belonged to the Attican Detective Agency.

Its original owner had been a two-bit gangster who tried to muscle in on the wrong neighborhood and got pumped full of bullets for his trouble. The car was impounded by the police and eventually auctioned off.

A second owner bought the high-powered vehicle as a getaway car. His plan worked perfectly, leaving the police in the dust after a successful bank robbery, but his compatriots slit his throat and took his share of the earnings once they'd arrived back at their hideout. Again, the car was impounded by the police.

The Peerless had one final owner before it came into the Attican Detective Agency's possession. Impounded by the police yet again, buyers became less anxious to get their hands on the pale-colored luxury vehicle. A young prosecutor eventually bought the car, hoping to rehabilitate the automobile from its criminal past. Maybe he even succeeded. No one would ever know; the man disappeared without a trace a few months later. He simply drove home from the office one day, and then he was never seen again. The prosecutor had a reputation as a crusader against organized crime. Speculation thundered through the press that the mob was responsible, but nothing ever came of it, and the case eventually faded from the headlines.

When the car came up for auction next, the Attican Detective Agency was the only bidder, snatching the car up for less than a quarter of its value. From its black leather interior to its smooth V-12 engine, it was an automotive masterpiece.

And now the Peerless stalked through Detroit's traffic like a pale tiger and nosed its way down the city's roads with a hungry purr.

Traffic moved with its own ebb and flow, like individual blood cells pumping through the veins of a great mechanical god. Detroit was rapidly becoming the new industrial center of the United States. Workers flocked to its factories from every corner of the nation, looking for jobs amid its endless assembly lines. The city was growing into a nascent metropolis that seemed ready to rival New York and Chicago in a few short decades.

Resting on the Detroit River, a thin strip of water separating Lake St. Clair from Lake Erie, the city lay just south of the "thumb" on Michigan's left-handed mitten outline. Immediate access to the Great Lakes provided Detroit a major transportation conduit. Raw materials and finished products alike could be shipped in or out on barges. Just across the river, a mere bridge away, stood Windsor, Canada, allowing the city to easily send goods northward. Railheads connected Detroit with the rest of the country, hooking the city into a global distribution network.

Manufacturers of every stripe called the city home, but Henry Ford had truly transformed the city into a mechanical Mecca. Half of all the automobiles in the country were Model T's, and other companies trying to emulate Ford's success had set up shop in the city. Soot belched from hundreds of smokestacks as mass industry roared on. Every breath Jasper took was tinged with the faint chemical vapors that came with smelting, processing, and rendering.

Of course, Detroit had its share of problems as well. Prohibition was in full force in the United States. In the province of Ontario, just next door to Detroit, there was no ban on alcohol. This had led to a particularly virulent brand of organized crime surfacing in Detroit. Every night a cat-and-mouse game played out between police and rum runners trying to smuggle hooch across the border. Many were caught, but the police might as well have been King Canute trying to order back a tide of booze. Clashes between rival importers were frequent and violent.

There was also the matter that had brought Jasper to Detroit in the first place. The city's industry was not entirely in manufacturing, nor was it entirely above ground.

Engineers and miners had spent the last two decades hollowing out the earth deep below the city, harvesting the colossal salt deposits for the Detroit Salt Combine. Thousands of miners worked in the hidden depths, blasting and gathering rock salt, making Detroit one of the major suppliers of salt to the world. Even though only the Great Lakes remained, the area was once covered in a vast inland sea. When it retreated, it left behind huge salt deposits. Mining was the city's original industry before it became a manufacturing hub.

But the miners were being picked off. According to the sheet Vedel had given Jasper, more than one hundred men had disappeared down in the tunnels. Even after the Detroit Salt Combine shut down most of the operations, the disappearances continued.

Nor was it lone miners being picked off one at a time. Groups of up to five had wandered into the darkness and never come back. This had been going on for nearly two months, meaning at least one person, and usually more, disappeared every single day. The remaining miners were leaving in droves, refusing to work. Many of them had friends who had gone missing and never returned. Apparently, the police had no meaningful leads, so the miners had joined their resources to hire a detective of their own.

Jasper was driving to the Hotel Montclair, where he was supposed to meet Victor Pecos. Pecos was the self-appointed head of the group of miners who had contacted the Attican Detective Agency. Eventually, Jasper would need to contact the Detroit Police Department, too; then he could start working leads and checking angles.

So far, all he had was one simple, inescapable conclusion about the case: *he was being followed.*

Checking his mirror again, Jasper watched the beat-up Model T trail his Peerless like a shark shadowing a lifeboat. The Ford always stayed exactly three cars behind him.

He was in Detroit. There were thousands, maybe tens of thousands, of cars nearly identical to the one stalking him. Jasper might not have noticed his tail at all if not for the fact that it had one distinguishing characteristic. All of its windows were tinted, and the only part of the driver Jasper could see was a pair of oddly dainty, white driving gloves hooked around the Ford's steering wheel. Everything else was a vague shadow behind the dark glass.

Purring like a steel tiger, the Peerless sat at a street light, waiting for the signal to turn. Jasper tightened his grip on the wheel. With the exception of a few select individuals, no one was supposed to know he was in Detroit. If the tail were working for either the Agency or Pecos, it would have pulled up beside him and identified itself. Instead, it retained its three-car distance, which meant it belonged to some third party, and therefore it was there for only two possible purposes. The mysterious Ford was either there to quietly keep tabs on him, or it was there to eliminate him — and maybe Pecos — at the earliest feasible opportunity. With its tinted windows, there was no way to tell if the Ford was merely a scout or if it was filled with hard-faced men with Tommy guns. Jasper did not particularly care for either option.

The light switched to green, and Jasper pushed down on the accelerator. He twisted the wheel as the Peerless shot forward, cutting off the car in the lane beside him. Horns bellowed like asphyxiating cattle, and Jasper pushed his way forward into the narrow space between his lane and oncoming traffic. The Peerless's engine howled gleefully as he sent it careening back into the proper lane, cutting off another driver and creating a tangle of traffic. He worked the car's gears, and it cranked up to sixty miles per hour in a matter of seconds. His tires ate up the asphalt.

He came up to the next intersection fast and hard. Another street light had cars in his lanes stopped while a trickle of cross-traffic puttered through the light. There was no traffic coming through the signal, so Jasper crossed all the way over the double yellow line and roared past the frozen vehicles.

At the last second, Jasper punched the brakes and twisted the Peerless's wheel hard to the right. The tires squealed in protest, leaving a set of sideways skid marks as Jasper slingshotted into the stream of cross-traffic. More horns blared as the Peerless erupted amongst the commuters like a cheetah springing out of the tall grass at a herd of zebras. Panicked cars swerved in every direction to avoid the new arrival. For its part, the Peerless shimmied sidelong into the intersection and peeled off as Jasper worked the gas again.

The next light was green and mostly free of traffic, so Jasper throttled through it and turned left. He was now paralleling his original route, just one block over. Jasper let off the gas, and the

Peerless's engine noise slowed to a continuous, satisfied sigh. Anyone following him would now have to navigate the tangle of vehicles he'd left in his wake. Driving at high speeds would only draw attention to himself. Now was the time to blend back into the normal flow of cars. Checking his mirror, he did not see any Fords with tinted windows. He allowed himself to feel the smallest hint of satisfaction as he patted the Peerless's wheel and started to relax.

Suddenly, the little Ford exploded out of an alley and spun onto the street amid a screech of tires. It punched forward, right on top of his bumper. Obviously, Jasper had underestimated the Ford and its driver. The car itself had the chassis of an older Model T, complete with chipped black paint and a collection of dents, but it was a wolf in sheep's clothing. The car's guts must have been scooped out and replaced with new hardware.

Even as Jasper revved the Peerless back up to speed, the Ford remained on top of his exhaust pipe as if magnetically tethered there. Now that the other driver knew he had been spotted, he only cared about keeping Jasper in sight, not stealth. As close as the other car was, Jasper still couldn't see the Ford's driver, except for the white driving gloves. Whoever he was, he was good. He must know the city like the back of his fancy gloves to boldly plunge into Detroit's alleys and pop back out exactly where he needed to be.

Jasper twisted the car into a hard right, hoping to lose the Ford. No such luck. The black car continued its relentless pursuit. They were moving through downtown, headed for the riverfront. Traffic grew steadily denser, and Jasper had to keep his gaze focused on the road.

A mere generation ago, these roads had been used as much by horses and coaches as the first automobiles farting down the world's thoroughfares. Not all of the city's streets had been widened appropriately to accommodate the automotive revolution.

An accident had occurred ahead, and a few police officers had gathered around a car that had knocked a pole into the street. The officers were taking statements and waving traffic onto an alternate route. Amid the snarl of cars, there was nowhere for Jasper to go. Well, there was one place he could go.

He bounced the Peerless up onto the sidewalk. Pedestrians scampered in every direction as Jasper honked at them. The Ford followed Jasper up onto the sidewalk.

The cops stared in wide-eyed amazement at the scene unfolding before them. Jasper's pale, sleek Peerless cleared the startled crowd and jumped off the curb onto the street behind the accident and took off with a six-pistoned roar. Immediately behind the Peerless, the black Ford did the same.

Jasper was beginning to figure out his pursuer. If the other driver's purpose was to kill him, he could have accomplished that several times already. From such close range, a passenger could have easily riddled the Peerless with an entire drum clip from a submachine gun, but it hadn't. So that meant the Ford was here to observe him and report back. That was some small comfort, but that didn't mean the driver wouldn't be ordered back to kill him later. Better to lose the Ford now than to risk greater trouble later.

Behind him, Jasper heard two police sirens wail to life, exactly as he'd hoped. The police would give the Ford another problem to contend with — assuming the cops could catch up to the two roaring street machines. In the meantime, Jasper wasn't about to make life easy on the other driver.

Pushing the engine to nearly eighty miles per hour, Jasper jerked the wheel to the right. His pursuer fell for it, shifting to the right to remain hot on the Peerless's rear tires. Jasper then flicked the wheel back to the left and applied the brakes. The other car didn't have time to react before Jasper was next to the driver's window, leaving the cars racing side by side. Behind them, the police cars crashed into view like a pair of drunk mastiffs chasing two rabbits. Their sirens whooped, and their lights flashed, but the extra attention only caused the traffic ahead to move out of Jasper and the other driver's way.

Glancing over, Jasper tried to catch a glimpse of his opponent, but the side windows were tinted, too. Suddenly, the driver's window started to roll downward. Jasper took one hand off the wheel and reached into his jacket for his pistol. If he saw a gun barrel poke out of the opposite window, he could fill the other car with slugs in short order.

Instead, something much less expected revealed itself behind the dark windows. The other driver was a woman. She had a smooth Mediterranean complexion and dark, wavy hair that fell to her shoulders. The wind caught her curls and blew them back from her face. She wore a collared, button-down sports outfit and, of course, the little white driving gloves.

She winked at him. If she weren't driving like Satan on wheels and working for some unknown entity that might or might not want him dead, Jasper would have been forced to admit that she was exceptionally pretty.

Lifting a gloved hand off the wheel, she gave Jasper a little wave, blew him a kiss, and then proceeded to smoke the Peerless. The little black Ford pulled ahead of Jasper as if he were sitting in a parking lot.

Unless Jasper was mistaken, he'd just been challenged.

As the Ford sped ahead of him, he took the first intersection he came to. He jimmied the brake and downshifted, spinning hard to the right. As he completed the ninety-degree turn, he poured the speed back on. Just before he shot down the new street, he saw the Ford plunge into another alley like a hawk diving into a cloudbank. Both cop cars chose to follow him instead of the Ford, foregoing the tiny passageway the dark-haired woman had chosen.

He tore down the street, building as much speed as he could. The woman driver wouldn't dare drive at full speed down a dark, narrow alley. But apparently, she did dare.

The Ford burst out of an alley beside Jasper like a bullet crashing down the barrel of a gun. Its windows were up again, and all Jasper could see of the driver was a pair of white gloves as she bore down on him. Jasper swerved, and the Ford swung into place beside Jasper.

She wasn't making things easy on him.

Well, two could play this game. Jasper swung the Peerless around and shot up an alley of his own. Masonry whizzed past on either side, and the alley reverberated with the sounds of hot, angry metal.

A dumpster sat to one side at the end of the alley. Jasper eyed the heavy obstruction and quickly rolled down his own window. This was going to be a tight fit. He stuck his arm out the window and pulled his side mirror flush with the body of the car. Then he edged the Peerless closer to the wall. If he accidentally clipped the brickwork, its rough surface work would shred the vehicle's side like a high-speed cheese grater.

The white-rimmed wheels spun mere inches away from the wall. Jasper held the car perfectly straight, refusing to slow down. Looming larger and larger in his windshield, the dumpster blocked most of the alley. Residents of the two buildings on either side stuck their heads out their windows to see what the unholy racket emanating from their alley was about.

Jasper blinked as his passenger side mirror snapped off against the unforgiving metal of the dumpster, but then he was back in the sunlit streets. The Agency's mechanic wasn't going to be happy, but the Peerless didn't seem to mind.

He'd come out at a T-intersection. There was no road ahead of him, just a small green park. Behind him, the Ford and its femme fatale driver ripped out of the alley like a bat out of hell. The narrower car cleared the dumpster with several inches to spare. To his sides, the two police vehicles must have split up because the road to either side was blocked off by flashing lights and sirens. Left or right, Jasper was trapped.

So Jasper didn't go left or right. He continued straight ahead, blasting across the road. The Peerless's suspension got a good workout as Jasper slammed over the low curb and started to cut across the park. Green contrails fanned out behind him as the Peerless's tires chewed into the grass and left muddy ruts through the middle of the park.

The Ford followed him, churning up its own green spray. Jasper knew what he needed to do now. He couldn't outrun the Ford; the woman driving it was too good. If he stopped and surrendered to the police now, he'd end up in jail, and they wouldn't catch the woman anyway. His only option was to allow the Ford to follow him. He would deal with the consequences later.

Now all he had to do was lose the police. If his first interaction with the Detroit Police Department were to get arrested for a bevy of driving offenses, the Attican Detective Agency would bail him out, but it would not be conducive to a future working relationship. The cops didn't know who he was yet. At best, they had the model of his car and maybe a few digits of his license plate.

Jasper tore past a fountain at the center of the park and was soon back on the road. His little detour had cost him some speed and gave the cops enough time to wheel their cars around, going around the park. Sirens blared behind him. Jasper made a quick left. The Hotel Montclair was in that direction. All he needed to do was lose a couple of police cars before he got there.

Make that three police cars.

Another cruiser pounced out of a side street and tried to ram Jasper from the side. The officer's timing was slightly off, though, and a quick twitch to the right sent the Peerless out of danger.

Something lumbered into the intersection ahead of Jasper. The huge, ungainly shape clawed its way into the intersection, moving like a brontosaurus. Jasper was forced to tap his brakes as the beast waddled into the intersection.

It was a standard Ford stakebed truck, a distant relative of the Model T chasing him, in fact. The little truck hacked and wheezed under the strain of its load, frantically trying to get out of the way of the approaching siren. "KELLY'S HOG FARM" was painted on the driver's door, the letters so encrusted with filth as to be almost unreadable. The bed of the truck was piled six high with wire cages. Inside each cage was a big, pink pig. Straps had been wrapped over the top of the cages and cinched to the body of the truck to prevent any of the cages from falling off. The pigs were probably being driven off to be butchered, maybe even in one of Edwin Fitzhugh's slaughterhouses.

Straining under the weight of so much hog flesh, the truck couldn't get out of Jasper's way. Jasper didn't believe in cutting corners in his work, but there were always exceptions. He spun his way onto the curb again, slicing through the gap between a corner boutique and the truck. Behind him, the Ford tried a different tactic. The woman twisted the wheel and threw her vehicle into a sideways slide, bleeding the Ford's speed. She squealed into the intersection, and Jasper expected her to use the gas to jackrabbit her way out of the skid.

Instead, she just kept sliding. The truck's horn gave a panicked bleat. With a crash, the Ford slid sideways into the truck. It was a hard blow, but the Ford only collected a few more dents and lost some paint. The Model T's frame must be reinforced.

The truck didn't fare as well. Already top heavy from the stacked hog cages, it didn't take much to overbalance the vehicle. The entire stack of cages started to fall. Pigs squealed as the whole tower of hogs swayed, and the truck tipped off the ground onto two wheels. For a single, precarious second, the truck hung in a limbo between rocking back on its wheels and falling onto its side, the Leaning Tower of Pigsa.

Gravity decided the matter. The truck tipped over with a resounding crash, and wire cages spilled all over the road. The cages splintered open, releasing a platoon of terrified pigs into central Detroit. Thirty hogs dispersed in thirty directions behind Jasper and the Model T.

That left an overturned truck and a sea of pigs in front of the pursuing cop cars. The truck driver scrambled out of the overturned vehicle and tried to collect the pigs, but he only succeeded in scattering the animals further into the intersection. The police cars screeched to a halt in front of the hog stampede.

Jasper looked in his rearview mirror again. The woman in the Model T had just helped him. With the cops out of sight, Jasper slowed down to normal traffic speed, and the Ford did likewise. He still didn't know the woman's ultimate mission, and he certainly wouldn't trust her until he knew who she was working for, but he was willing to tolerate her continued presence.

Not that he had a choice.

Jasper continued back toward the Hotel Montclair. In a few minutes, he was back on his original route, approaching his destination.

The Hotel Montclair was an older, dignified-looking building. Light-colored stone paneling covered its ground floor, and four other floors rose above the street. Red awnings hung over the lower windows, and big gilded letters above the door announced the hotel's presence to the world.

Detroit was a growing city, and the lot next to the Hotel Montclair was nothing more than a dirt tract where something else had been demolished. A massive steam shovel worked the lot, scooping soil out of the earth. In a few more weeks, a new structure would start to rise from the pit and take shape next to the hotel.

Jasper wheeled into the parking lot behind the hotel just as the sound of distant sirens reached his ears. He pulled to a stop out of sight from the street. The Peerless's engine hummed happily as he came to a halt. The Ford circled into the lot and parked nose-out a few spaces further down. Its tinted windows rolled down, but its engine didn't shut off. From the driver's seat, the woman continued to watch him. She flashed him a big, toothy smile.

Sirens wailed past the hotel, presumably searching for them. Jasper had to admire the woman's driving skills, but he was equally impressed by her "disguise." A dispatcher had no doubt supplied the cops patrolling the street with a description of their cars, a big, pale Peerless and a Ford with tinted windows.

If the police chose this moment to check the parking lot, Jasper would stand out from across the lot. They'd also notice the Ford with tinted windows, but they'd lose interest the second they saw a pretty woman sitting at the wheel. Well, professional interest, anyway. Just by rolling down the windows, she could avoid all suspicion. Clever.

On the other hand, Jasper needed to do a little more to disguise his car. He got out and opened the trunk. A variety of useful tools and supplies presented themselves, but Jasper reached for a small package wrapped in plain brown paper. Its contents clanked together. He picked it up and rifled through a stack of license plates. He finally settled on one from Michigan and quickly replaced the Peerless's Illinois plate. Even if the police had seen a few numbers on his car while he was twisting and scampering down their streets, it wouldn't do much good now.

Plus, the Peerless Motor Company had its own factory in Detroit. His car was unusual, but hardly one of a kind. Now able to wander the city in relative freedom, Jasper closed the trunk and began walking toward the woman's car. He wanted to know how she knew to find him and why she was following him.

She raised a single eyebrow and then gunned the still-running engine. *Back off.* Jasper got the message and switched course for the doors of the Hotel Montclair. He had no doubt she'd run him over if she thought it necessary. Maybe back up and run over him again for good measure.

Suddenly, he stopped and turned around again, making sure he had a clear shot to the door if he needed to make a break for it. "You got a name?"

"Amelia. Don't bother trying to track me down, though. I'll hear about it."

"Maybe next time we can just get coffee, Amelia." Jasper tipped his hat and turned around. The lady had spunk. Possibly murderous intent, too, but definitely spunk.

Keenly aware of the dark brown eyes watching him from behind, Jasper O'Malley walked into the lobby of the Hotel Montclair and began the worst case of his life.

Chapter 5
With a Grain of Salt

The Hotel Montclair's lobby was a rococo design monstrosity. At some point, one of the managers had obviously taken it upon himself to attract a higher class of clientele, and he had attempted to do so by turning the lobby into a miniature Versailles.

Gold leaf clung to the molding like metallic fungus. The carpeting was a deep, swirling purple that looked like a gigantic grape juice stain. Jasper glanced at the wallpaper. It featured intertwining vines with tropical birds frolicking amongst the foliage. A chandelier hung from the ceiling, its arms dripping with glass crystals. Paintings done in various shades of tastelessness hung from the walls while businessmen and upper-class ladies filed past. Jasper was a gray smear amid the forced opulence.

The centerpiece of the lobby was a larger-than-life bronze statue of a very, *very* nude Spartan soldier. Jasper skirted around the soldier and went to search for his contact, Victor Pecos. He scouted out the front desk, which was a massive slab of cherry wood, but he saw no sign of anyone waiting for him.

Looking elsewhere, Jasper spotted a bar, or — more accurately — something that used to be a bar. There was a long, simple counter that pointed to a much humbler time in the hotel's history. The shelves behind the bar were filled with old pictures of the hotel, famous personages that had stayed there, and a smattering of awards, creating a small museum of sorts. On the counter itself, a little model of the Hotel Montclair sat inside a glass cube.

Jasper suspected that the counter and shelves had been preserved for reasons other than pride in the hotel's history. The manager was hedging his bets that Prohibition would end in the not-too-distant future. If he tore out the old bar and replaced it with something that matched the rest of the hotel's alarming style, he'd be missing out on a potential source of revenue. A repeal of Prohibition would probably see the bar fully stocked and open for business again within a week.

A man was leaning against the defunct counter, looking at the hotel model. Even though he had only a smattering of gray around his temples and mixed into his mustache, his face was prematurely creased. His skin had a tough, leathery texture that looked out of place in the posh lobby. Jasper approached him, and the man looked up. He had sad, blue eyes.

"Victor Pecos?"

"Yeah, that's me. You must be that detective we sent for." Pecos's voice was deep and gravelly, like it had been sanded down by the smoky debris of thousands of cigarettes. He wore his hair longer than was fashionable, and his suit looked like it was purchased at least fifteen years ago. The man reminded Jasper of a down-at-the-heels western rancher not happy about the fact that he needed to call for help, but stuck with the situation.

"Yes, I'm Jasper O'Malley." His Attican Detective Agency badge appeared and disappeared in the blink of an eye. Pecos seemed satisfied, and they exchanged a firm handshake.

"I'd prefer to talk about this somewhere more private, like my apartment, but my wife doesn't want us there. Her brother was one of the first men to go missing, and it would upset her."

Jasper nodded somberly. "I understand. Perhaps our time is best spent if you give me everything from the top." A notebook was suddenly in Jasper's hands. He didn't actually need the notebook — he'd remember everything that was said — but it seemed to reassure clients to see him writing things down.

"Well, the big picture is something like this." Pecos ran a hand through his hair. "As of right now, one hundred eighty-four people have disappeared from the Detroit Salt Combine mine. Poof. Gone. Nada. We don't know what's happening to them, and the police don't seem to know either."

"That's a significant number," Jasper said. "Why aren't the press climbing all over this?"

Pecos made a disapproving sound in his throat and reached into his back pocket. "There's press coverage alright, but the reporters are all chewing Detroit Salt's cud." He pulled out a clipping and handed it over.

Jasper scanned the scrap of newsprint, but the headline told him everything he needed to know. "Labor Unrest Continues in Salt Mine," it read. The rest of the details were sensationalistic claptrap suggesting that the tunnels were filled with Reds and anarchists trying to bring the company down. The article mentioned the disappearances in passing and dismissed them as a stunt being pulled by the miners.

"I take it you have a different theory."

"Damn straight I do." Pecos brought a fist down onto the counter, causing the miniature hotel to rattle slightly. "I guess it's not a theory, exactly," he said. "But I'm not going to let some fool with a press badge tell me my friends are causing themselves to disappear. Detroit Salt is trying to keep this under their hats so they can keep the mine running. A lot of us have walked out, but whenever we try to warn the new fish not to go down there, the Combine's hired attack dogs start busting heads. There was always somebody trying to organize unions or whatnot before all this, but tensions didn't get bad until after people started vanishing."

"Is there a particular reason Detroit Salt insists on keeping the mine open? If they're losing people, it seems reasonable to shut it down."

"Yeah it does," Pecos scoffed. "I suppose it's because closing the mine is their only real asset. You shut down the mine, you shut down the company. They aren't exactly diversified. All they do is sell salt, so closing the mine for any length of time would cause them to default on all their contracts and probably lose their customers to competitors." Jasper jotted something down.

"What sort of customers do they deal with? Anyone who would benefit from closing the mine?"

"They've got contracts with all sorts of groups. Salt has all sorts of uses. Aside from plain old table salt, cities buy it in bulk to de-ice their roads. Some chemical companies need it as a raw ingredient, and salt is still used to preserve food." Pecos had clearly read some of the company literature in his years there.

"The human body requires a certain amount of salt just to function. It's a sight more practical to mine this stuff than it is gold for shiny trinkets. Ever hear the phrase 'worth his salt?' It comes from the fact that Roman soldiers used to be paid in salt cakes. It's even where the word 'salary' comes from."

In actuality, Roman soldiers were paid a special stipend so they could buy salt. They weren't actually paid in the substance, but Jasper let the comment slide. "But would any of those customers want the mine closed?"

"I doubt any of them would benefit much from having their shipments disrupted, and I doubt even more that they're crazy enough to stage nearly two hundred disappearances to do it." Jasper agreed with that assessment, but it was always important to know who would benefit the most from someone else's misfortune.

"How about the police? What are they doing about the situation?"

Pecos sighed. "The police aren't much help at all. Publically, they're toeing the same line as Detroit Salt. This is officially being investigated as a labor disturbance, and if anyone in the press asks, that's the answer they're getting. Mostly, they're trying to avoid sparking a panic and public outrage because they can't find whoever's doing this."

"Have they been more cooperative in private?"

"They used to be, but something changed in the last few days. Before, they would at least try to tell us what was going on. They played their cards close to their chest, but we didn't mind that. We didn't expect them to share evidence or anything. We just wanted to know things were being done."

"And they were taking action?"

"They did what they could. Patrols were sent down at regular intervals, and they posted some permanent guards, but they never had the manpower to investigate everything. There are miles of tunnels down there, and it's expensive to take cops off the street and send them on a subterranean goose chase. As much as we want them to catch whoever is doing this, nobody expected results overnight. I can appreciate that. We all did. All we wanted was to know what, if any, progress they were making."

"Who was your contact in the police force?"

"I always talked with Captain Renfield. He's good people. Rough around the edges maybe, but he tried, and it obviously ate him up that he wasn't allowed to blow the lid off the whole thing. He wanted the mine closed until the National Guard could crawl through every crevice and shaft down there."

That sounded like a remarkably sensible plan to Jasper. He jotted Renfield's name down. "Something must have happened?"

"A few days ago everybody clammed up. We don't know why."

Wheels spun in Jasper's mind. "Do you have any suspicions about who's responsible? Is there any talk? Rumors perhaps?"

Pecos huffed through his bushy mustache and rubbed a leathery hand over his chin. "Let me put this straight right now. Nobody, and I mean *nobody*, from the tunnels has any real idea what's happening, but aspersions have been cast. A lot of the miners think Detroit Salt is orchestrating the whole thing."

Jasper lifted his pen off the notebook, encouraging Pecos to go on. From the information Jasper had, it didn't make sense for Detroit Salt to try to put itself out of business. However, Pecos seemed like a reasonable man, more than reasonable, really, so Jasper wanted to hear what he had to say.

Leaning forward, Pecos's voice dropped to a rough whisper. "Some of the boys think this whole thing is a ploy to drive us out of the mines and replace us with cheaper labor. Once we're gone, Detroit Salt will bring in blacks or the Irish." He glanced at Jasper. "No offense."

"None taken." What his client's thought in their heart of hearts wasn't his problem. It was his problem when the case had no obvious leads. Without any solid evidence about what was happening to the miners, it would be all too easy for his mind to start sliding down that smooth, frictionless highway of speculation.

Some avenues of inquiry appeared more promising than others. He would still investigate Detroit Salt, but they were a low priority.

"How many people are still working the mines?"

"A few hundred, including me."

Jasper raised an eyebrow. "If it's so dangerous, why are you still going down there?"

"Hard to say. It's the only thing I've ever known, and now I'm trying to help out my wife's brother's family, too. It's … it's just hard for me to leave behind. Plus, I'm one of the old hands. A lot of the original lads are sticking it out."

"You said the company hired some, ah, gentlemen who don't want you talking to the replacement miners?"

"Pinkertons." Pecos spat the word, and Jasper didn't entirely blame him. The Pinkerton Detective Agency was founded in the 1800s, and at one point they had more men than the United States Army. Unscrupulous businessmen hired them as strike breakers, shipping in a platoon of Pinkertons to put down worker strikes. Sometimes quite violently.

A lot of them were basically domestic mercenaries, and some of them were crooked to boot. Jasper knew of one crooked one in particular.

Jasper rubbed at the knotted flesh where his left ear used to be as he thought about the last time he had worked alongside Pinkerton agents.

"Tell me about the Pinkertons."

"When folks first started disappearing, Detroit Salt hired them to make the tunnels safer and to supplement the police investigation. A lot of guys wanted to leave, so the Pinkertons were brought in to convince us the mine could be secured."

"But they couldn't stop the disappearances."

"Nope. People continued to vanish every day. Sometimes more than once a day."

"What do the Pinkertons do, primarily?"

"There's plenty of them down in the mine itself, for all the good it does. They try to keep us separated from the new recruits. A lot of the new guys have been hired from out of town. They're basically scabs, but they think they're just keeping the mine running. Nobody deserves to walk into that mess blind. When they start disappearing and subsequently leaving, Detroit Salt just hires more from somewhere else."

"Have any Pinkertons disappeared? Or is it just the miners?"

"A couple of Pinkertons have wandered into the darkness and never come back, but that's it. I think they'd be up in arms, too, if somebody went after them in earnest."

Jasper rarely sugarcoated his words, and he saw no reason to start now. "Do you have any idea if the missing men are alive?"

"None at all. Captain Renfield said they'd found blood near the sites where some of the guys disappeared, but most of the time, the place is completely clean. The police have never found a single body. Not one. We're hoping everyone will be found alive and well."

Pecos looked as unhappy as Jasper felt about this fact set. He riffled through possibilities in his mind. It was unlikely that the person responsible was a garden-variety madman. The disappearances were far too prolific for one person to be responsible.

An ambushed group of miners could just scatter into the darkness, and the crazed attacker could never catch them all. Yet that hadn't happened. Even when the attacker struck groups of people, no one ever escaped. Furthermore, the Pinkerton agents were almost certainly armed to the teeth. If a few of them had disappeared, their attacker was one tough hombre.

Criminal gangs would have even less to gain than Detroit Salt by attacking the miners. They'd simply bring notoriety down on themselves for no apparent gain, and it still didn't solve the problem of how they captured or killed every single miner they targeted.

And where did one keep one hundred eighty-four bodies, alive or dead? With police patrolling the mine, it was only a matter of time before a secret prison or graveyard would be discovered. The mine would only have a few entrances, all of them guarded and in constant use. There was no easy way to secret bodies out of the mine.

That didn't leave too many options.

"Are there any animals in the mine?" Jasper touched his pen to his notepad again. A pack of feral dogs or even an escaped circus tiger might be able to adapt to the mine's environment.

"There's a few donkeys," Pecos said.

Jasper strongly suspected that nearly two hundred men had not been mauled to death by donkeys, but he made a note anyway to look diligent.

"We usually have to disassemble the big equipment to fit it in the shaft's elevators," Pecos continued. "It's time consuming and expensive to put everything back together and replace it when it wears out, so we use donkeys for a lot of the day-to-day hauling and lifting. Other than that, there's nothing."

"Could a large animal, or maybe a group of them, live down there unnoticed?"

"A small animal couldn't live down there, unnoticed or not. There's no water. There's no food except for a few scraps that fall out of our lunch pails. There aren't even any fossils down there. Just salt.

Life was not meant to live down in those tunnels. It's a totally clean environment."

Jasper frowned. The number of likely scenarios was dwindling rapidly, though he didn't want to say so to Pecos. Maybe there really was a rogue faction amongst the miners. They had the most to gain by imperiling the mine's operations. If fewer and fewer workers were willing to go into the tunnels, they could leverage that into higher pay and other benefits that they might not be able to chew off in regular negotiations. If some of the miners were in on the whole operation, they could organize their own disappearances at their leisure, exiting the mine under the watch of their confederates after they had "vanished." A trip out of state on an assumed name would more or less perfect the illusion and allow them to be hired back later under much more favorable terms.

The ploy would actually work better if most of the miners weren't aware of what was going on and genuinely believed them-selves to be in danger. It would sow panic amongst the ranks and accelerate the exodus.

Depending on how ruthless the group was, they might even put an end to anyone, Pinkertons included, who stumbled upon their operation or tried to defect. If the miners were disappearing voluntarily, that could very well explain why no harried survivors had been found after an unsuccessful attack.

"Out of curiosity," Jasper asked, "why did you contact the Attican Detective Agency? I trust you realize I can't guarantee that I'll contribute anything substantial to the investigation. If the police have already failed to produce results after launching a full-scale inquiry, what makes you think it's worth hiring me?"

Pecos lifted his sad blue eyes to look at Jasper. "I think it's mostly so we feel like we're doing something. Right now, we're just sitting on our asses, hoping the problem will go away. We don't have the authority or the resources to launch any sort of investigation of our own, but we can contribute something. You keep us in the loop, and you'll be our poker in the fire. It ain't much, but we don't know what else to do." Pecos was a proud man forced to admit failure, never an easy thing to do.

Jasper put his notebook away. "I'll be in touch," he said, and walked out the door of the Hotel Montclair into the smoggy Detroit sunlight. There was work to be done.

Chapter 6
Blood Diamonds

Detroit's police headquarters on Beaubien Street was a massive stone structure worthy of the expanding metropolis. The eight-story block of concrete featured high, arched windows all around its lower floors, as if a crenelated medieval fortress had made architectural love to an art nouveau apartment building.

Jasper tugged open one of the large, imposing doors and was greeted by a lobby far more understated, and far more tasteful, than that of the Hotel Montclair. Uniformed police and civilians bustled through the entryway, each engaged in their own tasks.

A sergeant waited at the front desk, filling out a stack of forms. Jasper walked up to the desk, gliding silently over the smooth floor.

"Can I help you?"

"I'd like to speak with Captain Renfield, please." Jasper flashed his Agency badge. Technically, the police were under no obligation to help him, but they generally preferred not to turn down a qualified helping hand.

The desk sergeant called over a rookie, fresh faced and not yet a cynical bastard like most of his colleagues. "Hinkmeyer, we've got a guest. Take him up to Captain Renfield's office."

"Got it. If you'll just follow me," Hinkmeyer said, leading Jasper up a set of stairs. The young man seemed eager to talk, and Jasper had no qualms about exploiting that.

"You look like a capable fellow," Jasper lied. Fresh out of the academy, the lad was still too inexperienced to be of much use around the station. "Been assigned to any interesting projects yet?"

"Not yet. People mostly just hand me the leftovers."

"Hmph. So you're just stuck here at the station, then?"

"Naw. There's always something interesting going on, even if I don't get to handle it. Everyone had their butts in an uproar earlier after a couple of lunatics started drag racing across the city. Half the squad cars in Detroit went to track them down, but they got away."

"Really?"

"Yeah. We know one of the cars pretty well. It's a Model T with tinted windows that Schackel's boys use as a getaway car. The other one's a mystery. Some big, pale, luxury car. We figure Schackel and somebody else got into a little tussle, and the other guy got chased off."

"Who's Schackel?" That explained who Amelia, the other driver, was working for. Now maybe he could learn why.

"Gerhard Schackel is the worst of the worst. He's our local crime kingpin. Everybody knows it, but we can never get enough evidence to nail him. His gang muscled into Detroit after the war. They're mostly German expatriates, the Kaiser's finest, who decided to head for greener pastures after the Central Powers lost. Did you fight in the war?" Hinkmeyer tried to pretend like he wasn't looking at Jasper's missing ear.

"Yes. I was a pilot," Jasper didn't elaborate.

"You could have done Detroit a favor and plugged Schackel when you had the chance. Most of his gang's German, former storm troopers. Call themselves *Die Ratten*, The Rats. They're nasty customers. He'll pick up anybody with skills that he wants, though. His gang's a bit of a freak show."

Jasper thought about the female driver he'd dueled with on Detroit's streets. Not many gangs would want a woman as a getaway driver, regardless of how good she was. Schackel was obviously a man who appreciated talent, regardless of where it came from.

"In a lot of ways they've done quite a bit to clean up the city, wiping out a lot of the smaller gangs on the lower end of the food chain. He just carved a swath through the city and claimed it. Mostly, he just sticks to bootlegging and a few illegal casinos, but if you cross him, you and probably all your friends are going for a facedown swim in the river. Hope your business here doesn't see you tangoing with him."

"He's that bad?" Jasper didn't like what he was hearing. Why had the most ruthless criminal in Detroit taken an interest in him?

"Schackel's as cold as a lizard and as ambitious as Lucifer. A whole paper's worth of bad news."

Hinkmeyer switched subjects, but Jasper only listened with half an ear. He pondered Schackel's involvement in this. If the German crime lord were involved, Jasper would have expected him to hinder his investigation. Instead, Amelia had actually helped him. What did Schackel have to gain out of any of this?

Jasper followed Hinkmeyer down a maze of corridors until they finally reached Renfield's office. A plaque with the man's name was stuck on the door. Hinkmeyer knocked.

Tap. Tap. Tap.

"Come in," a gruff voice called. Muffled noises came from inside the office, and Hinkmeyer opened the door.

Captain Renfield was a big, corpulent man maybe fifteen years older than Jasper. His jowly face was rimmed by a day's worth of stubble, and his hair looked like it had been combed with his fingers, or maybe gardening implements. His outrageously crumpled red tie and even more outrageously crumpled brown suit were in stark contrast to Jasper's new, perfectly creased outfit. Big, dark bags hung under Renfield's eyes. His left hand was wrapped entirely in bandages.

A seemingly random array of papers sat scattered across his desk. His ashtray was filled with a small hillock of cigarette butts, and the mashed stubs were in danger of avalanching onto his desk. The police captain had another cigarette jammed his mouth, which he puffed furiously. Part of a sandwich and some crumbs lay on a plate nearby.

"You must be Captain Renfield."

"Right on the first try. Now who the hell are you?"

"I'm Jasper O'Malley, with the Attican Detective Agency." Jasper brought out his badge again.

"Right. Your bosses were kind enough to send your file over to us. I thought you might be showing up, so I glanced over it." Renfield reached down and picked up something on the floor behind his desk. There were papers scattered all over the office in no order that Jasper could discern, but Renfield seemed to know where everything was. He lifted up a big accordion folder, stuffed nearly three inches thick with various papers written on Attican Detective Agency letterhead.

Renfield thumbed one out at random and looked at it. "Did you know that two Chicago mob bosses, the Munich *Freikorps*, and a former governor of Nevada have all placed a bounty on your head, Mister O'Malley?"

"I'm not in this business to make friends," Jasper said.

"No, you're clearly not," Renfield agreed. "You've pissed off some very important and powerful people. Therefore, I like you. Give yourself a gold star; that's a very exclusive club you've just joined. Don't screw it up." The police captain took a sip from his coffee, made a face that suggested it tasted like lukewarm wolf spittle, and took another sip.

"I spoke with Victor Pecos."

Making a different, equally unpleasant face, Renfield put his coffee down. "I can't talk about that."

"Mister Pecos said that the police had stopped communicating with him and his colleagues. As you might expect, they're getting antsy. Pecos spoke highly of you."

"The case has become more complicated, and the matter was kicked upstairs. We're not allowed to brief anyone about the situation at the Detroit Salt Combine mining facility, and I, in particular, am not allowed to talk about how if we'd shut down the mine like I suggested, five officers would still be alive right now."

"Somebody took out some of your men? Is this what prompted the communications shut down?"

"I'm not at liberty to say. If I were, I could tell you all about how one of our patrols vanished into the earth somewhere inside tunnel G, near intersection forty-four, and I could ask for your independent aid in investigating the matter. Alas, I can tell you no such thing."

"Do you know for sure that they're dead?"

"If I were to become so outraged by the imbecilic steps this police administration is taking to cover its ass that I lost all my sense of discretion, I might blurt out the fact that we found quite a bit of blood in one of the nearby tunnels, and it's now presumed at least one of the officers is dead. However, I am a man with an enormous tolerance for asinine decisions. My patience and civility are, I dare say, legendary, amid my colleagues, and I would do no such thing."

"You're really stonewalling me here, Captain. I might have to file a complaint about your lack of helpfulness. What sort of evidence were you able to collect during the course of your investigation?"

"Having been muzzled by my superiors," Renfield pulled open a drawer to his desk and pulled something out from inside, "I'm not at liberty to say."

He dropped a small velvet baggie on the desk. It clacked loudly, as if it were full of marbles. Very carefully, Renfield undid the bag's straps and upended the package.

Seventeen oddly shaped objects spilled onto the desk. Each one was slightly different from the others, but they were all about the size of Jasper's thumbnail and dark crimson, almost the color of blood. It took Jasper a second to process exactly what it was he was looking at.

"Rubies?" The rough, uncut stones glittered up at him.

"I can tell you we called in some experts from the USGS, the United States Geological Survey. I can even tell you that they're still staying at the university. Really, though, I'd be loath to tell you that they determined the stones were actually extremely rare red diamonds, not rubies. That was our first guess, too."

"May I examine them?"

"No. In fact, *hell* no," Renfield said, shoving the stones across the desk toward Jasper. Jasper picked them up. There were seventeen in all. Even uncut, they were absolutely beautiful. "I wouldn't be caught dead telling you that we've found those near the sites of several disappearances, either."

"You're thwarting me at every turn here." Jasper kept the rocks cupped in his hands and examined them. He held one of the diamonds up to the light before setting the rocks back down on the desk.

Renfield either didn't notice or didn't care that there was one less diamond on his desk. The police captain scooped the diamonds back into the bag and stuck it back in its drawer.

"Have these turned up near the site of every disappearance, like a calling card?"

"No, just some. Those are actually the only ones we've found out of the dozens of disappearances that have occurred. Usually, we're more likely to find them after a larger group vanishes. I'll tell you right now that there haven't been any thefts of red diamonds in Detroit. Or anywhere else for that matter. Until recently, only about three had ever been discovered, and they're all accounted for. These're worth a fortune. Hundreds of thousands of dollars. Maybe millions for the whole trove."

Jasper would need to visit those geologists. Any insights they might have would be valuable. If the diamonds weren't stolen, someone either had access to a previously undisclosed cache or they were naturally occurring. USGS might be able to point him in the right direction.

"What else has the investigation turned up?"

"We've got two other pieces of physical evidence. First, jack. Second, shit. There's no prints. There's no witnesses. There's no bodies, for Christ's sake. These people are just *gone,* and we don't seem to be able to do anything about it. Worse yet, we don't appear to be willing to even try for fear that it'll raise a stink." Renfield banged his bandaged hand against the surface of his desk and grimaced.

"What happened to your hand?"

"I sliced it up on some mining equipment the last time I went out to patrol the tunnels. It's fine. There are bigger problems to worry about."

"Do you have any particular suspects in mind?"

Renfield shifted in his chair, "I've never seen a case like this. We have virtually no evidence, and the evidence we do have doesn't make a lot of sense. My best guess is that we'll find Gerhard Schackel at the bottom of this turd pile."

Jasper thought about it. If the diamonds really were as valuable as Renfield said, he could probably retire on the one he'd just pilfered for evidence. If Schackel was half the criminal he had been built up to be, it made sense that he'd stick his snout down the mine. And it sounded like there was a lot of money to be made here.

"Do you have anything that actually connects him to the crimes?"

"Not exactly," Renfield said. "But we have caught a few of his people trying to sneak into the tunnels."

"What were they doing down there?"

"We don't know, and that's why we haven't run Schackel in on a rail yet. They didn't have any diamonds on them. Detroit Salt started issuing identification cards to it workers to try to keep track of everyone. We don't even know if it's connected; Schackel likes to keep moles everywhere. He might just be sniffing around out of curiosity, but I doubt it. Schackel always does everything for a reason. Usually a nefarious one. He's even worse than the Pinkertons Detroit Salt hired."

Someone knocked, and Renfield's door swung open without waiting for a response. A man stood in the doorway. He had a handsome, if somewhat pointy, face, with prominent cheekbones and a jutting chin. A carefully groomed, pencil-thin mustache clung to the slope of his upper lip. He was slightly shorter than average, but an obvious sense of cool self-confidence made him seem larger.

Two large, stony-faced men flanked his sides. Having the primate exhibit as his personal entourage should have made him look shorter, but he only seemed all the more prominent.

"Captain Renfield," Lance Basilhart said. His voice came out in the smooth, honeyed tones of a Nashville drawl. Jasper knew that voice well enough to recognize the hint of threat hidden under the polished, urbane manner. "I believe I heard someone mention the good name of the Pinkerton Detective Agency and the fine work we're doing."

"You're in charge of the Pinkerton operations?" Jasper asked.

"How long have you been out there, Basilhart?" Renfield leveled a glare that probably would have made the likes of Hinkmeyer melt into insensible blubbering.

"Long enough," Basilhart said cheerfully, utterly unaffected by Renfield's obvious distaste.

"And bless my stars, if it isn't Mister O'Malley. How's the ear, Jasper?" The Pinkerton smiled, showing his teeth.

Jasper resisted the urge to touch the place where his left ear should have been. "Mister Basilhart. It's a surprise to see you again. I see you've joined the circus and brought some trained gorillas with you. I'm sure society thanks you for departing the field of private detective work."

"I take it you two know each other?" Captain Renfield waved a pen between the two private eyes.

"We've crossed paths before," Basilhart said.

"There were some differences of opinion," Jasper added.

"So I gathered." Renfield glanced at both detectives. "If this is going to be a problem, I will throw both of you in jail right now. I will not have some petty rivalry or whatever's going on here interfere with this case in any way, shape, or form. Consider yourselves both on notice. You two do not want to test me. Now, what do you want, Basilhart?"

"I thought I should tell you in person that we've had more

disappearances," the Pinkerton detective said.

Renfield looked pained. "How many this time?"

"Five. Three of them were part of an explosive team setting charges. The other two were my guys, guarding them. First, one of your patrols, and now more of my men. Whoever is doing this, they're getting bolder."

"Thank you, Mister Basilhart. I'll get a team sent down to investigate immediately, for all the good it'll do." The police captain rubbed his jowly stubble with his uninjured hand. "Alright. You two, I need to get this organized. Get out of my office. And remember what I said."

Basilhart and his shadows backed out of the office, giving Jasper room to exit. The Pinkerton men watched him go, but Jasper didn't pay attention to them.

There was a small, hard weight in one of Jasper's pockets, consuming his attention. He rubbed the diamond with his fingers.

He needed to pay a visit to those geologists.

Chapter 7
I Bet Your Say That to All the Girls

Jasper walked down the sidewalk toward the university. There was no sign of the little black Model T or its mysterious driver. He didn't know if that meant he was no longer being followed at all or if Schackel had switched his surveillance techniques to something more subtle. Somehow, the German seemed to be wrapped up in all this, so Jasper needed to remember to keep his vigilance.

He walked past a street vendor selling newspapers, magazines, and dime novels. Jasper eyed the selection. One pulp horror magazine's cover featured a brawny man protecting a scantily clad woman from what appeared to be a dinosaur. *IT CAME FROM BENEATH THE ICE*, the header read in brightly colored letters. "Prehistoric horror preserved into the modern era," a smaller byline read. Jasper bypassed the more sensationalistic literature and bought a newspaper instead.

Finding a nearby bench, Jasper sat down and thumbed the paper open. He wasn't particularly interested in any of the articles. Instead, he wanted an opportunity to survey his surroundings, looking for any suspicious individuals. His odd green eyes flitted from passerby to passerby, looking for anyone who might be following him.

An elderly woman threw crumbs at some pigeons, but everyone else kept on the move. Jasper didn't notice anyone lingering. Minutes ticked by, and Jasper waited to see if any faces appeared again, making a second trip around the block.

None did. He certainly didn't see Schackel's lady friend anywhere.

Checking the paper, Jasper saw a short article about the Detroit Salt Combine and labor unrest implying that the police and Pinkertons were cracking down on anarchists embedded amongst the miners. There was barely any mention of disappearances, which were attributed to rogue elements being rooted out and fleeing back to their handlers in the darker, more barbarous corners of Europe. There was absolutely no mention of any diamonds, and a Detroit Salt representative, one Mr. Gerald Ransom, was quoted as saying the crisis was nearly over and order would soon be restored.

Folding the paper neatly, Jasper left it on the bench and continued walking. He knew a little something about geology, though he wasn't an expert. If the USGS people could tell him anything useful about the diamonds, he needed to know about it. Right now they were his only lead.

The university soon came into sight. A few questions at the Geology Department soon got him to the lab where the visiting geologists had set up shop. Heading down a flight of stairs, he found the correct door and knocked.

Tap. Tap. Tap.

After a minute the door opened. An impatient-looking man with a neatly trimmed beard and a bowtie greeted Jasper. His small, squinty eyes looked unnaturally large and owlish behind a thick pair of round-rimmed glasses. Despite a copious amount of cream, his frizzy hair still managed to stick up in unruly clumps. He was about fifty, and his skin had the tanned, rough look of someone who spent a lot of time outside. In fact, he looked distinctly uncomfortable in his button up shirt and slacks, and Jasper suspected he preferred the denim and short sleeves of field gear.

"Yes? Yes?" The man spoke hurriedly.

"I'm Jasper O'Malley with the Attican Detective Agency." Jasper's badge made another appearance before being replaced with his trusty notebook.

The scientist shook hands with Jasper. "I'm Doctor Baxter. Heywood Baxter. We're a bit busy packing up the last of our equipment. What can we do for you, Detective?"

"I'm investigating a matter regarding the Detroit Salt Combine's mining operations. I believe you gentlemen were called in to consult with the police?"

Baxter looked unhappy. "Yes, that's right, but if you've spoken with them, you've heard our results."

"Actually, the case has been put under strict supervision. I was hoping to gather details directly from you." Jasper lifted his blood-colored diamond out of his pocket and held it up.

"If you heard anything at all, you heard almost everything. There really aren't any details I can tell you. What you have there is an extremely rare, extremely valuable red diamond. We don't know where it came from, we don't know why they're turning up in the salt mine, and we don't know why they're connected to the disappearances. That's why we're packing our equipment up. We're taking a train back to headquarters in Denver tonight. There's absolutely nothing more we can do."

"You mean USGS is giving up on the matter?"

"We're not giving up," Baxter said. "We've told the Detroit Police Department everything we can tell them short of actually nabbing the culprit for them.

"We're not authorized to go into the mine, regardless of how badly Doctor DuPree wants to investigate. Given that these diamonds only seem to appear near the site of a disappearance rather than being found *in situ*, heading down there seemed like a spectacularly unwise decision."

"There are more of you?"

"Yes, Doctor DuPree should be in the lab just across the hall."

"Perhaps I'll see if he has anything else to add," Jasper said. He turned around and knocked on the opposite door. After a moment, it swung open. "Oh, I'm sorry. I was looking for Doctor DuPree."

"You found her."

"Oh," Jasper said again. "My apologies."

Dr. DuPree was, in a word, hot. She wore hiking boots that looked like they'd tramped through every variety of mud known to man. The boots matched a pair of worn dungarees. She was wearing a white work shirt with the sleeves rolled up to the elbows. Her bright blond hair was tied back and thrown casually over her shoulder. She had stunningly blue eyes and long, curved eyelashes. This mistake had clearly happened before.

"I'm Jasper O'Malley with the Attican Detective Agency." He flashed his badge and nearly fumbled it. "I've been tasked with investigating the disappearances at the Detroit Salt facilities," he recovered.

"You're here about the diamonds." It wasn't a question.

"Precisely."

"Doctor Sadie DuPree." She offered her hand, and Jasper shook it. Her grip was warm and firm.

"A pleasure. Again, I must beg your pardon."

"There aren't very many female geologists wandering around. Believe me, just the fact that you actually believe I work for USGS is flattering anymore. Tell me, though. Do you know how diamonds are formed, Mister O'Malley?"

"Essentially, a large amount of organic matter gets squeezed by the earth until it's compressed into a diamond."

"That's about the gist of it. Usually, the organic material comes from a swamp. As decaying vegetable matter and dead alligators and what have you build up under the water, they're eventually swallowed by the earth. They're mashed down and transformed into other substances, like various grades of coal, and if the heat and pressure grow great enough, you get diamonds."

"So why are these diamonds red?"

"There's some kind of contaminants in them. Usually, when diamonds are formed, everything but the carbon is squeezed out, but not always. If there's something else leftover, mixed in with the carbon, you usually get brown diamonds, which aren't particularly valuable. People mostly use those for industrial purposes, creating ultra-tough drill bits, that sort of thing. Sometimes, though, you get really spectacular gems that are blue or pink. Those are hugely valuable."

"Is red a rare color?"

"It's extremely rare. I can count on one hand the number of red diamonds of any size that have been discovered. These new diamonds, like the one you have there, are absolutely unprecedented."

"Would diamonds form naturally inside salt caverns?"

"No. It's the wrong environment entirely. At one point, this whole region was a shallow inland sea, much larger than the Great Lakes. The salt built up as the sea dried out and receded. You don't get the abundant plant life you need to make coal and diamonds in that environment. In fact, nothing can live in an environment that's basically just a salt bed. It should have been a completely barren area when it was buried. Probably made the Sahara look like the Galapagos."

"Do you know specifically which impurities cause the red coloring? If there's a large deposit of that mineral nearby, it might give us a place to start our search."

"Unfortunately, I can't tell you exactly what causes the unique coloring. It seems to be a variety of organic compounds."

"Would it be possible to artificially create diamonds? Could someone take a carbon-rich source, say, a lump of coal, and mechanically compress it into a diamond?"

"Theoretically, it's possible. People have tried it before, but there simply isn't a press in existence strong enough to simulate the right conditions. The best they can do is crush a lump of coal into a slightly smaller lump of coal. Unless someone has made a breakthrough somewhere, the diamonds aren't being made artificially."

Jasper considered this information. The fact that the diamonds didn't belong in the mine raised some interesting problems. Perhaps the miners were running afoul of a gem smuggling ring using the tunnels to hide their activities. If the smugglers were ruthless enough, they might choose to eliminate anyone who discovered them.

So far, he only had one name that sounded like it might be associated with such an endeavor: Gerhard Schackel.

That theory had its problems, too, though. First of all, it didn't solve the question of why none of the witnesses had escaped. It wasn't possible to track down and kill every single individual who came across the smugglers, especially when some of those witnesses were heavily armed Pinkerton detectives. Nor did it make sense to bring so much attention to the tunnels if they were trying to keep the operation a secret.

Additionally, where were the diamonds coming from in the first place? If no one had ever discovered this many diamonds before, they weren't being stolen.

"So, if the diamonds aren't occurring naturally inside the salt mine, someone must be bringing them in from somewhere."

"They have to be. That, or everything we think we know about diamond formation is wrong. If I had an opportunity to explore the mine ..."

"Absolutely not," Dr. Baxter blustered, marching into the room. "We have no idea what's going on down there. If something were to happen to you, the Director would have my head on a pike outside Denver."

Sadie scowled. "This might be the most important geological discovery of the decade, and nobody wants to investigate it except for some private detectives."

"No. It's too dangerous. We're heading back tonight."

"This is a major discovery. We need to research it. I have every confidence that, say, a capable fellow such as Mister O'Malley here could keep us safe. He gets to investigate the disappearances. We get to research and help him at the same time."

Jasper said nothing.

"Another team can handle this. They're already sending a better-equipped group. We are leaving tonight, Doctor DuPree," Baxter said.

"Another group?" Jasper asked, but he was overridden by Sadie.

"You are leaving tonight. I'm staying."

"Sadie, don't do this. The USGS won't support this. Your uncle won't support this. You won't have any funding."

"I won't need any funding beyond living expenses and maybe some equipment the university would be happy to loan me. If Mister O'Malley were to take me on as a partner, he could bill the expenses …"

"You cannot be serious. You remember what happened with Doctor Rumson. That's part of the reason you're always assigned to part of a team."

"I can take care of myself. You remember what happened *to* Doctor Rumson."

"If I could tie you up and physically drag you back to Denver, I would," Baxter said. He glanced at Jasper, sizing him up. He seemed to deflate as he realized he was defeated. "But given that I can't, I would rather you stay with someone who can provide you with some protection."

Sadie smiled. "Mister O'Malley, what do you say? Partners?"

Jasper looked at her. "You seem like you might be useful."

"Oh, I bet you say that to all the girls," Sadie said. She leaned in close. Jasper could smell the soap she'd used. "You'll take me?"

"Yes. We need each other's help."

"Thanks," she whispered close to his ear.

"Detective? Can I speak with you for a moment?" Dr. Baxter waved Jasper toward the other lab.

"But of course," Jasper said.

"I need to unpack my things," Sadie said. "Come get me when you're done."

Stepping inside Baxter's room, Jasper looked around. The room was actually a teaching lab that had been converted into temporary quarters. A cot was stuck in one corner. Low counters covered with rocks and fossils lined the walls. None of the samples were particularly great; the university almost certainly had a better collection elsewhere, but didn't want untrained students handling the rare and fragile samples. Still, Jasper recognized some crushed trilobites, fossilized clam shells, and a dozen leaf imprints trapped in shale.

"I'm not sure you appreciate the situation you've put me in here," Baxter said.

"I believe Doctor DuPree put you in this situation. I just helped."

Baxter waved that away. "Obviously, Sadie is not your, shall we say, typical USGS scientist. She's something a little different."

"I don't need to be a detective to notice that," Jasper said.

"No, I suppose you don't. However, there are other differences that are less apparent. For instance, she happens to be the niece of our current sitting director."

"Does she know what she's doing? That's my primary interest in her."

"Don't misunderstand me, Detective. She's the best, and I mean the best, at what she does. However, she wouldn't be here if not for her connections. That's not a slight on her, but it's a fact. Her uncle knows her abilities, but he won't send her on field missions. There aren't many women at the USGS, and some of our members ... well, they resent having her here. She thinks this is her chance to prove herself because of all the excitement, but I think this situation is more dangerous than any of us really understand."

"And you're worried that if something happens to her ..."

"Precisely. Sadie has been my research partner for years now. If she were to disappear, I'd be losing a friend, and I'd be lucky to get a job as a middle school science teacher. The director won't be pleased when I return to Denver without her. If she doesn't return at all, it won't end well for anyone."

"I'm surprised you're not worried about leaving her in my care. I'm more or less a stranger, after all."

"Oh, no. You don't appreciate the situation, Mister O'Malley. It's probably more accurate to say I'm worried about leaving you in her care. Doctor DuPree is, alas, incorrigible. She's a pistol, that one. I have no doubt that she can take care of herself. She'll mop the floor with you if she has cause," Baxter said.

"I'll keep that in mind," Jasper said.

"Good luck, Detective." Baxter shook his hand and resumed packing his equipment.

Jasper stepped across the hallway and knocked on Sadie's door. Once again, it swung open. He didn't blanch this time, but Tycho Vedel's voice cackled away in his head, begging him to say something stupid. *Shut up, Tycho. This is strictly business.*

"Come in," she said. "I'm almost ready." Jasper watched her lift some heavy-looking books out of a box and set them on a nearby counter.

"Need a hand?"

"Nope. Already got two." She waggled her fingers at him. "Thanks, though. Did Baxter tell you about my uncle?"

"He mentioned he's the director of USGS."

She tossed her hands up in the air. "Lovely. And now you probably think I'm some sort of debutante out on a field trip with my uncle's permission. Mister O'Malley, I assure you that my work with the USGS has been —"

Holding up a hand, Jasper stopped her. "He also told me your work was top-notch. I'm willing to take his word on the matter. If we're going to be working together, you might as well call me Jasper."

"Then I'm Sadie."

Jasper looked at the small mountain of books on the counter and pulled one out. It was Alfred Wegener's *The Origin of Continents and Oceans*. "Have you read this yet?" He flipped the book open to a random page and saw an illustration of how the fossilized remains of certain creatures could be found on multiple continents separated by thousands of miles of sea.

Wegener postulated that the continents, rather than being immobile slabs of rock, were once joined together in a gigantic *Urkontinent*. He used evidence such as fossils found on different continents, as well as the suspiciously jigsaw-perfect fit of earth's various coastlines. It had its adherents, but a significant portion of the scientific community had slammed the work. The continents were, after all, a little too big to easily imagine them skittering across the globe.

"What did you think of the Wegener heresy here?" Jasper asked.

"Is this a test?" Sadie asked, sounding amused.

"Of sorts." Jasper said nothing else.

"Alright, then. I wouldn't be much of a geologist if I weren't at least familiar with his ideas. Wegener's theory is interesting, but I'm not sure I buy it. We don't know of any geological processes strong enough move entire continents. None of the mechanisms Wegener suggested are powerful enough to rip continents apart and send them plowing across the sea floor. He thought things like the earth's rotation and tidal forces were responsible, but we know those forces simply aren't potent enough to do the sort of heavy lifting his theory requires."

Jasper considered her answer.

"So, did I pass your test?" Sadie asked, raising an eyebrow.

"It's not that kind of test. I wanted to know how you consider problems."

"Oh? And maybe I'd like to know how *you* think about problems now that we're partners. So? What do you say, Jasper? What's your take on Wegener's ideas?"

"I actually like his ideas."

"Really? I'm surprised. You're a detective. I took you for the sort who likes to have all his ducks in a row before buying into an idea. Wegener lacks a good mechanism to explain how the continents drift."

"An interesting way of looking at it, but my business isn't in the sciences. My business is people, and often damaged, deranged people at that. I don't work with scientific certainty. I look at the evidence and worry about the mechanisms later. I rarely operate with anything resembling absolute proof, so I just float where the evidence points me. Wegener's compiled a lot of evidence."

"So you don't care that Wegener has no way to explain his results?"

"I care, but I trust there's some additional process, some piece of evidence we simply don't have yet that fits the theory. The evidence Wegener collected all point to the idea that the continents were once joined together. All the other theories look good, but they can't explain the facts on the ground. I prefer to follow the facts until I have a logical conclusion. If there are some gaps working backward, I'm less inclined to worry about it so long as the evidence is in my favor."

"I still like to work with things I can actually test in a lab somewhere or see with my own eyes. I don't like relying on the idea that some nebulous something will come along later and prove my theory right. I'll tell you what, Jasper. You stick to the detective business, and I'll keep to geology. Together, we'll lick the world."

"Deal," Jasper said.

"So what's the next step?"

"I have a contact, a man named Victor Pecos. He'll get us access to the mine, and we'll investigate one of the disappearance sites."

"Sounds like a plan. I've been dying to go down there, but my chaperone keeps insisting that we handle everything about this case from a distance."

"He might be right. I'm not sure what's going on down there yet. There's no guarantee I can ensure your safety."

"I know, but I can take care of myself."

"Your colleague mentioned that as well. Who was Doctor Rumson? Something happened to him."

Sadie looked at him. "Doctor Rumson was one of the best the USGS had to offer, and he knew it. He was also an unpleasant man. He was cocky and boorish and thought everyone should be in awe of him. We were dispatched together to investigate a cavern system in Kentucky."

"Just the two of you?"

She shrugged. "It was a preliminary survey, and it was only supposed to take a few days. The cave was beautiful. Running water carved it out of limestone millions of years ago, leaving miles of tunnels and vast, open caverns filled with their own ecosystem. Apparently, he thought the low lights and exciting sights set the mood."

"I take it he was incorrect."

"You take it right. He refused to take no for an answer. We brought sleeping bags so we could stay in the cave system overnight, and he pestered me all night, wouldn't let me sleep. After hours of this, he decided it would be a good idea to try to crawl into my sleeping bag with me."

"What did you do?"

"I broke his pelvis with a rock hammer."

"Sadie?"

"Yeah?"

"I think we'll work well together. Welcome aboard."

Chapter 8
Queen of Diamonds

She lurked in the darkness, waiting. Her massive claws kept her anchored to the roof of the mine tunnel like a spider clinging to the bedroom ceiling. Jointed mouth parts clicked and snapped, cleaning her first row of teeth. Her mouth was a vertical gash, a tooth-filled fissure. The wickedly pointed teeth fit together like a giant bear trap. Their points curved inward slightly, making it impossible for anything speared on their tips to disentangle itself except by moving deeper into the cavernous maw. Bristles sprouted from her iron-hard hide like the dead trees of a blighted forest. Her skin was mostly translucent. If any light were allowed to penetrate the pitch blackness, it would have been possible to see the wires and unidentifiable mechanical shapes inside her body that ran beside her veins and organs. Four stumpy, multi-jointed legs sprouted from her body where her thorax joined her abdomen. Shortly after her second set of knees on each leg, the limbs bifurcated into two massive tarsal claws. Made from titanium and curved like giant Gurkha swords, the claw tips were embedded into the salt rock like huge pitons. Whenever she moved, her claws *tap-tap-tapped* as they sank into the rock. She looked like a Thanksgiving turkey crossed with a giant tarantula crossed with a knife factory.

Long ago, when the planet was little more than a globule of molten rock floating through space, gravity pulled many of the heavy metals downward through the plastic magma, like stones sinking to the bottom of a tar pit. The metals eventually formed Earth's dense core. However, the heat and exotic metals also formed something else. Silicon-based lifeforms, first no more complicated than metallic bacteria, appeared in the molten primordial soup. Over the countless eons since, the life forms lurking deep below had grown more complex, more bizarre, and more intelligent.

Determining whether the creature was primarily organic or primarily mechanical was impossible. Even though she existed in the curious twilight between life and automata, she still had needs and instincts and an indescribable nebula of linked perceptions that might be categorized as thoughts.

At present, her brood of minions waited patiently for a command. Most of them were humble workers, but there was a growing rank of warriors amid her entourage. They sat stock still, conserving energy while their bodies continued to change; however, a quick spray of chemical hormones could cause them to go into a frenzy or perform complex tasks for their queen.

For now, she waited. Her guts, a horrifying array of tubular organs and piston-like apparatuses, were busily digesting her last meal. The victims she hadn't eaten were tucked away in a small alcove, curled up in little balls as the change slowly began to eat its way through their bodies. Soon, they would be ready for the next stage. She would need to harvest more raw materials before then, but for now, she was content to rest near her favorite hunting ground.

Suddenly, the scent membranes that ran down either side of her mouth detected a presence in the tunnels. She didn't have any eyes because there was nothing to see. Instead, she relied on her sense of hearing and smell, and the odors she was picking up now were enticing. A wave of pheromones scattered her children into the darkness. Their twisted, inhuman limbs allowed them to scamper up walls easily and retreat into crevices, ready to pop out at their matriarch's command.

The creature waited. The scent grew stronger, and electrical and chemical bursts flashed across the tangle of wriggling neurons and mechanisms that served as its brain. The exact process she used to formulate ideas would fray a human brain apart in a couple of minutes, but the basic conclusion she reached was simple enough to understand.

Prey.

She waited. After a few minutes, the quarry had moved within one hundred yards, and she could savor the bouquet of odors. There were two of them, moving slowly through the tunnels. She could pick up a variety of chemical traces. One of the targets was wearing cologne, but was sweating heavily. That one had recently eaten a meal rich in meat. The other one was carrying something with a greasy, metallic scent. Wafting above it all was the sweet perfume of adrenaline and fear. She could also sense the electrical impulses firing away in their skulls, commanding their legs to move, telling their hearts to continue beating, wondering what lay in the shadows. She found the neural signals unpleasant.

The pair of bipedal animals were about to pass directly below her. One of them shone a flashlight from side to side while the other carried a gun, ready to fire at anything that popped out from either side. They spoke softly to each other, looking for something.

A few steps later, and they were below her hiding spot. She retracted her front claws and crimped herself backward using a pivot joint in her spine. She bent in half like someone flexing their elbow.

For a brief instant, the target holding the flashlight was aware of a rustle of movement, and then the terrible teeth clamped down over his waist. The man was confused for a very brief moment. Where had his legs gone?

Then the creature started chewing with its rows of back molars, and the man and his flashlight were reduced to red gruel. Below, the man's legs took one more spasmodic step and then fell over, blood jetting from the ragged stump where the rest of his body belonged.

The other figure screamed and started firing blindly into the spot where something had just swung down and taken his partner. "*Gott in Himmel!*" With the flashlight gone, he was cast into sudden blackness. His Thompson submachine gun thundered in the enclosed space of the mine, sending out strobes of light. Each stuttering muzzle flash revealed more and more semi-human figures crawling out from the shadows and dropping off the walls. Twisted, clawed hands grabbed him by the arms, ripping away the Tommy gun. The man screamed and tried to escape, but the inhuman hands were like bands of iron.

Above, the creature climbed down from the wall.

Tap. Tap. Tap.

Without slowing, she scooped the pair of severed legs off the ground and chewed them into a film of red juices and pulverized bone. Then, she turned to the man pinned down by her children. She paused for a moment, considering whether to devour the screaming human or convert him.

No. She had already fed, and she needed more soldiers to guard her tunnels. Tensing, the creature hunched up on its legs, almost like a frightened cat. After a moment of strain, a harpoon-sized barb slowly emerged from her body on a stiff stalk.

The creature paused for a moment. She had slower means to transform the creatures. Her very presence, through a mixture of electrical signals and pheromones from her body, would corrupt the forms of her prey over time. But time was becoming a valuable commodity now. No, she would do this the fast way.

Still trapped by dozens of clutching hands, the man screamed. He struggled and thrashed against the things holding him. If he didn't escape, there was no telling what —

Blinding pain arced through his body as something large and viciously sharp punched into his stomach. The object sliced through his skin like tissue paper, ruptured his abdominal muscles, and lodged itself in his inner body cavity.

Without further ado, the sharp object started to disgorge hot, clumpy liquid inside him. He could feel chunks plopping into his body like boiling porridge. More and more of the sick fluid pumped into him, burning everywhere it touched. His stomach burst like an overfilled balloon, spreading the poison deeper into his body.

The goop swirled through his body. It poured into his veins and soured his blood. Bubbling up his throat, the sick slurry of liquid curdled in his chest and dripped into his lungs, cutting off his screams.

His screams wouldn't have lasted much longer anyway. As the hot slime filled his body, the man's thoughts dissolved into an electric buzz of berserk static. A thick streamer of drool dribbled from the corner of his mouth as the chaos of dying consciousness cleared out to a dull, meaningless hum. The hum was slowly replaced by something else. It wasn't an idea. The man's brain was already too irreparably mutilated to ever form ideas again. Instead, it was a simple animal compulsion, a pure, hammering need.

He needed to serve, to obey. He could no more ignore the command to submit than he could the urge to breathe. Already, his body was beginning to change, reconfiguring itself to better conform to his new function.

The others began to drag him away to a quiet corner where he would go through the first delicate phases of his brutal metamorphosis. They hauled him down the tunnel by his arms, his feet trailing behind him. Two of the creatures had the tattered remains of blue uniforms still clinging to their malformed bodies. Hugh Corbett's old comrades.

They dragged the limp figure past the overturned remains of a mining truck. The truck had been all but turned inside out by Detroit police officers, led by Captain Renfield, searching for any clues as to the whereabouts of their friends. Despite a frantic investigation, the police hadn't found any fingerprints, any shell casings, any evidence at all, actually. All they knew was that the truck had been stripped of certain parts. Of course, they'd been looking for perpetrators that were still human.

Satiated, the creature used her claws to clamor back to her roost on the ceiling. Full and spent, she hung lazily from the tunnel's roof. Her power was growing, but she was still weak from eons of dark slumber. Right now, she was content to rest, but soon she would be back to full strength.

A spray of pheromones dispersed most of her children to gather the raw materials she would need to continue expanding her brood, materials both mechanical and organic. For now, she kept just a couple of specialized workers as a private retinue. The bloated, tick-like figures scampered up the wall and clung to their master like baby opossums, grooming her bristly hairs with their mouths.

Temporarily content, the creature hung from the ceiling and rested. Every day, her strength grew. Soon, weakness would be a thing of the past. Very soon.

Chapter 9
Come into My Parlor

"My good sir," Jasper said, "we're part of a parallel investigation to Lance Basilhart's. I'm with the Attican Detective Agency. I've also brought a scientist from the United States Geological Survey and a guide who knows the tunnels. Our work would aid your own investigation." He was standing in front of the mine elevator with Victor Pecos and Sadie.

"I don't give a tin shit if you're Moses here to lead your people to the Promised Land, Mack. If you ain't got the right papers, you ain't getting in that elevator." The Pinkerton agent stood with his arms firmly crossed in front of his chest.

The Pinkerton man was trying to look formidable and tough, like the proverbial immovable object before an unstoppable force. Really, though, the pose was a tactically poor choice. Jasper could level a savage chop to the man's throat before he could uncross his arms. That was certainly one way to gain access to the areas he needed to visit, but that was hardly an option.

A name tag on his lapel identified the Pinkerton man as "Hank." Jasper was hoping that invoking Basilhart's name would be enough to let them into the tunnels. No such luck, though, so he needed to play nice. Since Lance Basilhart and his Pinkertons worked for the Detroit Salt Combine and Jasper worked for the company's employees, they were nominally on the same side. Making enemies unnecessarily would only make things more difficult in the future, and Jasper had no doubt that Captain Renfield would bust anyone's chops who started a clash.

There was also the matter of a dozen more Pinkertons patrolling the grounds, all of them heavily armed. Jasper was as likely to get shot as not if he started a ruckus.

Faced with an impasse, Jasper tried a different strategy, one as old as the invention of money: bribery. "I can appreciate your position," Jasper said. "Obviously, it makes sense to require identification papers for mine employees and visitors, but Detroit Salt said it will take over a week to vet my clearance. I'm sure that an intelligent man such as yourself can recognize that sometimes exceptions need to be made to the rules, though. Perhaps we could expedite this process?" A hint of green flashed at the Pinkerton.

"Nobody gets into the mine without papers."

"My, my, my," someone said from behind them. The voice had a buttery, cultured Nashville accent. *Basilhart*. Speak of the Devil. "Fancy meeting you fine folks here. Picked yourself up some strays, Mister O'Malley?" Basilhart was still flanked by his two massive Pinkerton praetorians, and he was working a toothpick with his teeth.

"Your friend here seems intent on keeping us out of the mine."

Basilhart ignored Jasper to take a good long gander at Sadie. He stopped chewing his toothpick. "You're a tall glass of water, Miss. I'm surprised a thing like you wants to be seen in the company of this roustabout. Did this scoundrel hire you as his secretary?"

Sadie reached into one of the many pockets of her vest and pulled out a card. "I'm a geologist with the United States Geological Survey. The USGS also has an interest in some of the materials discovered in this mine."

Basilhart's expression soured. "More's the pity. Let them through, Hank. It's none of our business if they end up dead. Might even help us crack the case if we find their bodies with some evidence later."

Pecos took a few steps toward Basilhart, fire in his eyes, but Jasper laid a hand on his shoulder. They got what they wanted. There was no point in starting a fight now.

Everyone walked toward the elevator cage as Hank stepped obediently aside. Basilhart followed them, working his toothpick again. He stepped directly in front of the wire mesh doors of the elevator.

Jasper and Basilhart stared at each other through the metal lattice. "It's my professional advice that you don't cock this up like the last time we worked together, Jasper. This time, you'll end up missing more than an ear."

Before Jasper could respond, the elevator's motor sputtered to life, and the entire contraption began to clank downward. In a few seconds, the sun was swallowed by the large vertical shaft. As the darkness closed in around them, it was like descending in a primitive bathysphere into the depths of an unexplored sea. The shaft was wide enough to accommodate two elevators for miners and a much larger elevator for freight and loads of rock salt.

Focusing on keeping his breathing slow and steady, Jasper closed his eyes as the blackness consumed him. His previous experience with mines had also involved Lance Basilhart, and it had not gone well. Sitting in the rattling elevator, feeling the walls close in around him, brought back memories Jasper would have preferred to keep buried. He opened his eyes, letting them adapt to the darkness.

"You two have worked together before?" Victor pointed upward.

"Unfortunately," Jasper said. He didn't elaborate, but he had to stop his hand from rising to rub at the place his ear should have been.

The elevator continued down and down and down, scraping and grinding its gears for over 1,200 feet. If the cable snapped now, it would be like plunging off the top of a small mountain. As they dropped lower, an eerie light began to rise from below. Powerful arc lights illuminated the base of the shaft, creating the effect.

Finally, the elevator reached the bottom, and Jasper, Victor, and Sadie stepped out of the cage. As soon as they were out, miners poured into the elevator, packing it full. Once no more could fit, one pulled a lever, and the cage ascended. More miners waited for the next elevator.

Jasper looked around. "Is it time for a shift change?"

Pecos shook his head, sadness in his eyes. "No. Something else must have happened. These men are leaving for good. Detroit Salt will just hire more, though. With good pay and no warnings, there's an infinite supply of fools for them to pick from."

Stepping away from the elevator platform, they moved down a metal staircase crowded with men anxious to move toward the elevators. Eventually, they found themselves in the mine proper.

The walls and floor glittered like some bizarre fairytale castle, but the ceiling was cloaked in shadow. Every visible surface was made out of salt. Some of it was blotched with the debris from boots and machines, but on the whole, everywhere they looked was a disorienting maze of sparkling white.

Tunnels branched off in every direction from the central cavern. The cavern itself was absolutely gigantic, though. With all the white surfaces, Jasper felt like an ant sitting in a toilet bowl. A convoy of mine vehicles waited along one wall. The opposite wall sheltered a corral filled with donkeys.

Only one of the tunnels was lit. The others were all closed because it was impossible to guard all of them at once. Apparently, it was impossible to guard even one tunnel. All the tunnels were connected to one another at semi-regular junctions, so it was hardly as if the open tunnel was isolated from whoever was haunting the other parts of the mine.

Sadie looked around. Pinkerton guards were watching the exodus of miners. "I don't see any police. Word of this must have just gotten out."

"Good. This will give us a chance to investigate before too many people can interfere with the scene." Jasper walked up to the first Pinkerton he saw. "Basilhart wanted us to check things out before the cops arrived. Where'd the incident happen?"

"The boss sent you?"

"Yup. Now c'mon. We don't have all day."

"Uh, yeah. Sure. There was a lot of gunfire out of Tunnel G. We didn't have any guys in that sector, so we think Schackel infiltrated more of his crew after the disappearances earlier today. We're trying to figure out exactly who's missing now. There's a lot of blood, and it's right by where those cops disappeared. Renfield's gonna blow a stitch when he gets down here, so you better hurry."

Jasper nodded and made off for the row of vehicles. "None of those work," the Pinkerton said.

"None of them?" Pecos sounded incredulous.

"Somebody got into the engines last night after the mine closed and carried off a bunch of equipment. Just tore out random pieces and walked off with them." Jasper tried to fit this new piece of information with the evidence he already had. Now someone was pilfering the mechanical equipment, too? Why would they start doing that? He'd have time to think about it later. Right now, he wanted to get to a scene that was still fresh.

"We'll take some of the donkeys then." Turning around, he

quickly saddled up three of the animals. He grabbed some flashlights from a nearby stand and passed them out. He also patted a place on his side and felt the reassuring weight of his pistol. "Do you know how to ride?" He looked at Sadie and Pecos.

"The only way you can get to some geological sites is by mule ride. It's not my favorite mode of transportation, but I can manage," Sadie said.

"I grew up on the frontier in Wyoming," Pecos responded. "It's been a while, but there's some things you never forget how to do."

All three of them hopped onto the donkeys and began moving down Tunnel G. The donkeys clopped reluctantly down the hard, salty path. Jasper and everyone else switched on their flashlights.

It was interesting that Schackel's men chose to enter one of the closed tunnels. What had they been doing in here? So far, Jasper's main lead seemed to point toward Gerhard Schackel being responsible for the disappearances. If Schackel's men were being hunted just like the miners, though, Jasper was back to square one in trying to find some answers.

They rode for over two miles, feeling every bump and thump in the donkeys' gait along the way. The animals were getting more and more stubborn, balking every few hundred yards as they picked up something they didn't like. Jasper couldn't see anything beyond the beam of the flashlight, and the ceiling was cloaked in shadow. He was painfully aware that his flashlight was only a pinprick against the darkness, its light soon to be devoured by the hungry gloom. Some of the side chambers to either side had been filled with empty supply crates stacked five high, filling the alcoves.

A fine layer of salt dust had settled over the wooden crates, most of them apparently left there long ago. Jasper couldn't see beyond the crates to tell how deep the alcoves were. Odds were, the crates had been left where they were because it wasn't economical to haul them to the surface just to dispose of. Valuable elevator space could be filled with salt instead.

Tap.

All three of them looked up to try to find the source of the noise. The donkeys suddenly stood stock still, refusing to budge another inch. Jasper shone his flashlight straight ahead, searching for the source of the sound.

From his previous experiences in tunneling with Basilhart, Jasper knew the normal sounds of a mine settling. Normally, noises were the result of rock somewhere deeper in the earth shifting slightly. This sounded more like someone smacking the walls of the tunnel with a hammer. He lowered his voice to a whisper so only Sadie and Pecos could hear. "Stay behind me."

Pecos nodded. Sadie sad nothing.

The donkeys refused to move, so everyone dismounted and tied the beasts to a nearby support beam. Their eyes were white with panic.

Without any obvious movement, Jasper's pistol, an FN Model 1922, found its way into his hand. It was an updated version of the same weapon used to assassinate Archduke Franz Ferdinand, a handy little tool. He began to slide silently forward. His other hand kept the flashlight moving from side to side across the tunnel, searching for anything that was out of place.

Suddenly, the light picked up a shape huddled in the darkness. It was much bigger than a man. Jasper trained his pistol on the thing in the darkness and inched forward. Slowly, the light revealed a hideous sight. It was a truck, similar to the ones parked in the main cavern bay, but this one was in much worse shape. The vehicle sat flipped onto its side, and two of its doors were ripped off. Only a few shards of jagged glass remained where the windshield should have been. Rusty red blotches, dried blood, spattered the seats. More mysteriously, the truck's hood had been pried open, and most of the engine had been ripped out.

Obviously, Renfield's team had been all over the scene. The truck was roped off, and Jasper could see fingerprint powder still clinging to most of the truck. Jasper already knew the conventional policing methods hadn't turned anything up. Renfield had no idea what happened to his officers.

The truck was a few yards away from another crate-filled alcove.

Jasper was primarily interested in the scene near the truck. A Thompson submachine gun lay abandoned on the floor amid a welter of brass shell casings. The Tommy gun was developed as a trench broom, a mobile machine gun that infantry could carry into battle and clear out entire defensive positions with one sweeping pull of the trigger. Tommy guns were sometimes known as "Chicago typewriters" due to their association with underworld figures. Seeing one here now meant that Schackel's people were probably involved.

Near the gun was a large pool of blood. The blood was much

fresher than that in the truck, a few hours old at most. Some of it had soaked into the porous salt floor, but the rest was coagulating into a red mess.

Examining the walls, Jasper searched for splatter marks. If one man had shot another, as the weapon on the ground seemed to imply, there should have been sprays of blood on the walls as well, but Jasper saw nothing. Nor were there any blood trails leading away from the scene, as there should have been if a bleeding body was dragged away.

Moving further along the wall, Jasper noticed the wall of boxes again. There was something wrong about those crates ...

Suddenly, Jasper had it. The dust.

Or rather, the lack of dust. All the crates they'd seen while riding through the tunnels had been covered in salt dust after sitting untouched for years. These crates were old; the wood was dry and gray, but they were quite clean, as if they'd been moved recently.

"I don't like this," Pecos hissed. "I can't shake the feeling that we're being watched."

"I feel it, too," Sadie said. She was examining the walls as well, breaking off small chunks of rock and stuffing them in a sample case. "I don't know what you're looking for, Jasper, but look for it faster."

Jasper was looking at the crates, trying to figure out how to move them. Even if they were empty, they were stacked too high for him to disassemble the wall without the whole stack tumbling to the ground. He felt the odd sensation of being watched, too, almost like a current of electricity crackling through the air.

Between the boxes and the hard salt wall, there was a narrow black gap about half an inch wide. Jasper shone his flashlight into the gap. "I've found something," he said.

Pecos walked over, his feet crunching on the salt. "What is it?"

"I'm not sure yet, but ..." Jasper stuck his long surgeon's fingers into the gap between the boxes. Something tickled his fingertips, and he jerked his hand back.

A fat spider scurried across the back of his knuckles, heading for the sleeve of his shirt. Jasper flicked his wrist, catapulting the tiny arachnid into the darkness. He stuck his fingers back into the gap and felt around. Finally, he found what he was looking for and something behind the crates *snicked*.

Suddenly, the entire wall of crates began to move, swinging outward. They weren't actually crates at all. They had been once, but someone had broken them apart to leave a collection of panels. Then, the crate sections had been nailed together in such a way to look like an entire stack of crates. Set back flush in the alcove, it was impossible to see that the pile of crates had no depth.

The stack was actually a door, with hinges bored into the wall. Jasper shone his flashlight inside.

"You might have just cracked the case, Detective," Pecos said.

Jasper wasn't so sure, but this did add a significant wrinkle to his collection of evidence. A massive distilling tank greeted Jasper. The thing was almost the size of a small tanker truck, and it could probably keep the five thirstiest speakeasies in Detroit satisfied for a month.

There was more, though. One wall had been almost entirely converted to a weapons rack. Dozens of Tommy guns just like the one outside hung side by side. Several large chests, each of them filled with drum magazines, sat under the weapons. There were also rifles, pistols, and, *good grief*, German potato masher-style hand grenades. A man could start a small war with an arsenal like that.

As if the armory weren't complete enough, there were several crates labeled *ACHTUNG! SPRENGSTOFF.* Jasper recognized the German words. *Attention! Explosives.*

Stepping further inside the alcove, Jasper peered into the crates. They were stacked with what appeared to be sticks of dynamite. Sadie followed him inside and began examining something else. Pecos stood by the false door, clearly uneasy.

Jasper finally turned his attention to the thing Sadie was examining. He'd deliberately chosen to examine that particular item last because it was the least pleasant. It was a body, and it was in poor shape.

The cool, dry conditions of the mine prevented it from rotting very much. In fact, it looked partially mummified. It wasn't the state of decay that made the body grotesque, though. Instead, it was something much worse.

To Jasper's eye, the body looked like something that might be put on display at a second-rate traveling freak show, the kind that wasn't reputable enough to get a permit to set up within town, so it sprang up in a field just outside the city limits. The body was horribly deformed. Whoever the man was, he barely looked human anymore. Jasper wasn't even sure where to start. The dead man's jaw was oddly distended. His mouth didn't even close properly anymore, and his teeth were a jagged mess. Both of the man's hands were ravaged. It looked as if the bones in his fingers had started growing longer and longer until the skin covering his digits simply burst. Ragged bone poked out of his fingertips like claws. His feet had done something similar, except twisted lumps of bone and flesh had exploded out the tips of his shoes. The man's legs were gnarled and dramatically different lengths. He was dressed like a miner, but that didn't do much to establish his identity. Under his clothes, it looked like the rest of his body was just as horribly twisted. The clothes bulged grotesquely where they hid lumps of mutated flesh.

The whole situation was kind of gross, really.

Jasper noticed something out of the corner of his eye. He looked up from the corpse and shined his flashlight toward the door just in time to watch something rip Pecos's head off his shoulders. Pecos never even had time to realize he was in danger. The thing snuck up behind him and wrenched his head off like it was pulling a weed out of the ground. His vertebrae separated as easily as a delicate pearl necklace ripped from a woman's neck.

Victor's head, gripped in the thing's claws, blinked a few times in apparent surprise. His arms fluttered briefly toward the ragged nub of his neck, which squirted blood in foot-high geysers.

And then the body simply toppled over. The creature was already advancing toward Jasper and Sadie before Pecos's headless corpse hit the salty ground.

Jasper leaped backward. His flashlight jerked, illuminating the scene is spastic bursts. He never even heard the creature coming.

Good God, it was ugly. The thing looked a bit like the dried cadaver on the ground. However, this being was far less human. Most of its head was now a mouth. Literally most of its head. Even if it had once been human, its entire skull now opened and closed like the maw of a Venus Flytrap. The two sides of its head didn't even fit together properly anymore. Odd yellow teeth had grown between the two halves of its bifurcated skull. Whenever the creature's head snapped closed, the teeth clacked together. The thing's skull looked like Dr. Frankenstein had tried to put Humpty Dumpty back together. Where a brain would go in a normal human skull, there now seemed to be a dozen prehensile, waggling tongues anchored to the bone. With the rest of its skull hollowed out, it was now a straight drop from the crown of the creature's head down to its esophagus. It made squelching noises like a sick moose trying to free itself from a tar pit. From the neck down, the creature was just as twisted. Its body was bloated like an engorged tick, its skin stretched almost to bursting. Bulging, watermelon-sized blisters covered most of its body. Jasper could see tadpole-sized creatures swimming in the pus when his light shone on the monster's translucent skin. On each hand, the index and middle fingers had fused together into a single, brutal-looking talon. Now the hands were simply didactylous murder shovels. Like oversized owl claws.

Jasper and Sadie were trapped. There was simply nowhere to go in the shallow alcove. The only exit was blocked.

Outside, in the tunnels, Jasper could hear the donkeys braying in terror. A second later the sound was choked off and replaced with wet gagging noises. Whatever this thing was, there were more outside.

Jasper raised his pistol and started to squeeze the trigger.

BLAM! BLAM! BLAM! BLAM! BLAM! BLAM!

Gouts of yellow ichor sprayed from the monster's body. It stumbled forward, leaking great geysers of stinking liquid. Jasper looked at the unfired gun in his hand and then glanced at Sadie. A revolver smoked in her hands, its chamber empty. Six shots. Six hits.

Even littered with bullet holes, the creature continued to lumber toward them. Stinking fluid dribbled from its wounds. It raised its clawed hands to lunge.

Lowering his aim, Jasper planted a shot squarely in one of the monster's shins. The bone splintered, collapsing the leg. Hissing furiously out of its mouth hole, the creature tried to crawl toward them. Two more bullets burst out of Jasper's pistol and entered the top of the creature's head, traveled downward through its throat. Its malformed head exploded in a spray of bone and wet tissue, and the monster finally stopped moving.

Tap. Tap. Tap.

The same sound Jasper had heard before echoed down the tunnels, moving away from them at high speed. Then, there was silence.

Sadie reloaded. Jasper kept his gun pointed at the door.

"You didn't tell me you were armed," he said.

She surprised him by leaning over and kissing him on the cheek. "What can I say? A girl has to have her secrets."

"Captain Renfield and his men will be down here soon. I say we hole up here until the cavalry arrives." Sadie nodded, filling her revolver with bullets again and spinning it closed.

They sat together like that, weapons pointed toward the door and the blackness beyond, until voices and lights began to bounce down the tunnel toward them. Jasper was going to have some explaining to do when the police got here, and the Attican Detective Agency was going to owe him one hell of a bonus.

Chapter 10
Making Enemies

The creature scurried across the ceiling toward her sanctum. She was furious.

If she hadn't dismissed all but two of her children, she could have subdued the prey in the tunnels and saved them for later. Right now, though, she was spent from her previous encounter. Had the intruders arrived only a few hours later, she would have rejuvenated her energy and been ready.

Instead, she had lost one of her personal attendants and been forced to withdraw before she could even harvest the fleshy raw materials her children had gathered. She had left the four-legged beasts and the dead prey behind, where the material would soon deteriorate and lose its usefulness. And because she had gorged herself earlier, she couldn't even eat the bodies and use them for her own benefit.

Finally, she reached her refuge, her remaining attendant clinging to her great body like a remora. Sensing its master's agitation, the smaller monstrosity tried to groom its queen's mouthparts, but she was having none of it. Chomping her maw closed, she bit off one of the attendant's arms. It scampered away as best it could to clean another, marginally less dangerous part of her body.

Even if she couldn't have eaten the puny intruders, she could have at least slaughtered them both if she hadn't sensed another pack of them rapidly approaching. She probably could have taken care of the additional trespassers just as easily, but it would waste precious strength and risk injury at a critical juncture. Retreat was the wiser option, but she was still furious.

If nothing else, she now had the scent of the two creatures that had eluded her, and she would not soon forget it. For now, she would have to content herself with the slavish affections of her brood, but if she ever sensed their presence in her tunnels again, she would take care of the matter.

She waited in the darkness of the tunnels, biding her time. Soon, it would no longer matter one way or the other.

Chapter 11
Trouble Brewing

Somewhere in Detroit, a phone was ringing. It rang once, twice, three times, and then a carefully manicured hand lifted the receiver.

"Sheridan Metals," a sultry female voice said. "How may I direct your call?"

"I'd like to make a custom order," Edwin Fitzhugh III responded.

"What sort of metal would you like to order, sir?"

"Lead."

There was a pause at the other end of the line. "I'll connect you with our special delivery manager." The phone line redirected with a series of clicks and pops. Fitzhugh waited, the phone precariously clutched in the fingers of his less-broken hand. He wanted to drum his fingers on the hospital desk, but the bones were nowhere near mended.

A heavily accented voice came over the receiver. "So, I understand you have a problem, the kind that's best solved with lead," Igor Lavrov said. His voice was thick with the accent of Mother Russia. As one of Rasputin's closest disciples, he had fled before the onslaught of the Bolsheviks, resettling in a new land with new followers. Of course, he needed a way to keep up the life he'd become accustomed to under the czars.

As it turned out, that was no problem in the land of opportunity. He was but a simple man of God, and he and his followers had helped many meet Him in the course of his services.

"How much lead will you require for this job?" Lavrov asked.

"All you have," Fitzhugh said.

"Such services will not come cheap."

"I have the money. And there's one more thing." Fitzhugh paused. "I want to be there while you work. It's a personal matter."

"That will cost you extra."

"Money is no object."

"What do you need done?" Fitzhugh could hear the smile in Lavrov's voice.

"I want you to kill a man named Jasper O'Malley."

Chapter 12
Double Trouble

Elsewhere in Detroit, another phone rang. It rang once before someone snatched up the receiver.

There was no greeting from the other end. "Give me a status report, Basilhart."

"Of course, Mister Ransom." Lance Basilhart was in no mood to give anything to anyone, but Gerald Ransom signed the Detroit Salt Combine's checks to the Pinkertons. He also signed the substantially larger checks to keep Basilhart and his most loyal lieutenants on retainer for any special services Detroit Salt might want performed.

"Two of my agents were lost in an incident today. We thought we'd cleared the tunnel, but the activity has become more unpredictable as of late."

"Yes. I know, and close to a thousand of my employees quit on the spot when word got back to them. Replace the fools you lost with someone competent and see to it that this activity is slowed down. It's getting harder and harder to recruit new workers while the project goes forward."

"I've already called up fresh men from headquarters. They'll be here tomorrow."

"That is acceptable. Anything else?"

Basilhart drew in a breath. "An operative working for some of Detroit Salt's more ... rancorous employees made his way into the mines earlier today."

"How did he get into the tunnels?"

"I granted him access."

There was silence on the other end of the line.

"I thought the situation would take care of itself if I allowed him to poke his nose into the right dark corners."

"And did it?"

"Unfortunately, no. He managed to kill one of the kobold's thralls, and the police now have its body. The creature did decapitate the man who was rallying the miners against Detroit Salt, though," Basilhart hastened to add.

"Who is this operative?" Ransom's voice was like arctic ice dipped in liquid nitrogen.

"His name is Jasper O'Malley, and he has a companion from the United States Geological Survey. We're still trying to dig up some information on her. It's surprisingly hard."

Ransom spoke two words into the phone and hung up. "Kill them."

"With pleasure, Mister Ransom," Basilhart said into the empty phone line.

Chapter 13
Three of a Kind

A third phone rang elsewhere in Detroit. It rang a long time before anyone picked it up. Finally, someone lifted the receiver. "Hello?"

"We're picking up some interesting chatter. Is the mission compromised?"

"The police have two bodies. One's a full kobold thrall. The other's only partially transformed. They're examining them now."

"How did they acquire the bodies?"

"A private detective found one and killed the other."

"He's seen them alive?"

"The thralls, yes. Not the kobold itself."

"I've already dispatched a squad of our best people. You know what to do."

"Absolutely."

"This detective, what's his name?"

"Jasper O'Malley."

"He's seen too much. Kill him."

"Acknowledged." Both phone lines clicked dead at the same time.

Chapter 14
Bad Medicine

Jasper O'Malley stood in the Detroit police station's morgue with Sadie, Captain Renfield, and the medical examiner. The police mortician was a large, slightly paunchy man with a shaved head, little round-rimmed glasses, and a Charlie Chaplin mustache. He seemed surprisingly jolly for a man wearing a rubber apron meant to keep human viscera from staining his clothing.

Several hours had passed since the incident in the mine, and their weapons had been temporarily confiscated. Renfield had grilled Jasper and Sadie, both together and one at a time while the medical examiner did his gruesome work in the basement. Eventually, they'd gotten word that the sawbones had come up with some preliminary results.

There were three examination tables currently in use. The first had a plastic sheet drawn over the shape laying on the table. A bucket sat nearby.

Victor Pecos was under the blanket. His head was in the bucket. A couple of assistants were preparing to transfer the body into a refrigerated storeroom. Their surnames were stitched onto small nametags on their aprons. Jasper noted that one was Eagan and the other was Parkinson. Apparently, nobody wanted to accidentally grab someone else's potentially blood-encrusted dissection bibs. The medical examiner's name was Grainger.

Renfield started to light up a cigarette and Grainger plucked it out from between his lips. He stubbed it out and threw it into a nearby trashcan.

"So what have you found, Grainger?" Renfield asked, frowning.

"Well, I've found a lot, but most of it doesn't make a whole lot of sense."

"Start with the parts that do."

Grainger pointed to the cloth-covered table. "It should be pretty obvious what happened to Mister Pecos over there. If not for the sheer strength required to rip a human head off like that, he's fairly unremarkable. Death was basically instantaneous. Things get more, shall we say, interesting with these two specimens over here," Grainger pointed to the other two tables.

"That's one word for it," Renfield commented. Jasper watched in silence.

"Let's start with this fellow." Grainger moved around to the less deformed of the two bodies — the mummy. "Now, this is not for the squeamish. If the lady doesn't mind?" Grainger looked expectantly at Sadie.

"I'll be fine, Doctor." She didn't bother to add that she'd already seen the corpse and helped kill the other creature.

"We know a bit more about this gentleman. We found a wallet in his clothes that identified him as Klaus Gottschalk. His hands were in better shape than his companion's, so our lads were able to get a single fingerprint off of him." Grainger lifted a sheet of paper off a nearby table and handed it to Renfield.

Quickly scanning it, Renfield gave them the gist. "The fingerprint came back and confirmed that this fellow is, or rather was, Klaus Gottschalk. He's got a rap sheet that could choke a hippo. One of Schackel's boys."

Renfield held up a mug shot of the German gangster. Before, he'd been a weedy-looking man with bushy eyebrows and a shock of dark, curly hair. There was still a hint of resemblance between the picture and the body on the table, but it required a hard squint and a lot of imagination. Most of that wasn't due to the medical examiner's none-too-gentle examination techniques either.

"Was he one of Schackel's ex-storm troopers?" Jasper asked.

"Yup," Renfield said. "One of his heavies. Not a pleasant man. He knew his way around a weapon. He'd be difficult to capture against his will, so I'm surprised anyone was able to snatch him and do these experiments to him."

"Experiments? You think a person did that to his body and dumped him there?" Jasper asked. He had no idea how medical science could do anything like that to a man.

"It's definitely not natural. Wait until we get to the other body. As to how a bruiser like Gottschalk was captured, I can't say. Maybe he was caught by surprise. Or maybe it wasn't against his will at all. He might have been a volunteer," Grainger said.

"You think anyone would volunteer for this?" Sadie looked appalled.

"I'm not counting anything out," Renfield said. "Schackel might have gotten his hands on some sort of chemical weapon. He still has a lot of connections with Germany, and they're a clever lot. We've already traced most of the weapons and alcohol in that room back to Schackel's associates, so we know he's involved with all this somehow. I already put out an APB for him, so we should find out soon enough."

Jasper was less convinced. Schackel was involved somehow, yes, but nothing added up. Why the disappearances? The monsters? The diamonds?

"What else have you got for us, Doc?" Renfield asked impatiently.

"I can't speak to Mister Gottschalk's motivations, but he apparently was none too pleased with what was happening to him. He committed suicide."

"What? How?" Renfield looked incredulous.

"He poisoned himself with salt."

"Salt?"

"The man was mighty determined to kill himself. We found about four pounds of salt in his stomach. Must have chewed it right off the walls. He basically jerked himself to death, which is one of the reasons he hasn't rotted much. Salt is an excellent preservative."

"Would it normally take so much salt to kill a man?" Jasper asked.

Sadie responded before Grainger. "No. Sodium chloride, your common table salt, is necessary for human life, but it's basically a poison in too great a quantity. It affects the electrolyte balance in the human body, regulating the circulation of fluids between the body's cells. If the concentration of salt is too high in the human body, it drains all the water out of your system, and you dehydrate. Basically, you die of thirst at a cellular level. Normally, it would take a lot less than four pounds to kill a person."

"Couldn't have said it better." Grainger looked admiringly at Sadie.

"Christ," Renfield said. "Why not just shoot himself? He had an armory to choose from."

"His fingers were too deformed to fit inside any of the trigger guards properly. Probably couldn't pull a grenade pin, either."

"That's shit luck." Renfield shuffled his feet and scratched at the bandage on his hand.

"Indeed," Grainger agreed.

"How long was he down there?" Jasper asked.

"Difficult to say exactly. The fact that he basically mummified himself throws off a lot of our metrics, but he's probably been dead about a month."

"We lost track of Gottschalk five weeks ago," Renfield said. "We've been suspicious of Schackel for a while, so we started tailing some of his big hitters. Looks like we were right."

Jasper wasn't so sure.

"So he was changing into one of those?" Sadie pointed to the more-deformed creature on the other table.

"Not exactly," Grainger said. "My other patient here has some radically different physiological adaptations. Mister Gottschalk was turning into something *similar*, but not really the same. Even if he were mutating into the same creature, he would ultimately need some outside help."

"What sort of help?" Jasper asked.

"Schackel," Renfield said confidently.

"Let me show you something with this other specimen," Grainger moved to the other table. "Whoever did this is either a genius or completely out of their tree. Probably both, actually."

Grainger lifted one of the creature's malformed arms. The skin had been peeled away, revealing the muscle below. Gesturing them closer, the medical examiner pointed to the muscle.

A network of tiny wires was mixed in with the sinew like a nearly microscopic electrical grid. The scale was amazing, unlike anything Jasper had ever seen. He leaned in closer to examine some of the smaller circuits.

"That's remarkable," Sadie said.

"You can't even see the best of it," Grainger pointed to the arm.

"We put some tissue under a microscope. The wiring connects directly to the nerve endings. This body was systematically upgraded on a scale I can't even comprehend. Some of the organs and other body parts had been taken out and replaced with mechanisms we don't understand. We are fully into mad scientist territory here, folks."

"Eat your heart out, Mary Shelley," Sadie murmured.

"Do you have any idea what purpose all this serves?" Jasper asked.

"Not even the foggiest. I can tell you that Mister Gottschalk didn't have anything similar, suggesting he killed himself before he could be similarly, ah, enhanced. He was only being altered at a biological level, not a mechanical level."

Bulbous tumors covered the inside of the deceased creature's body. In some places, the cysts were so tightly packed that they looked like bunches of fleshy, malformed grapes.

Many of the polyps were sprouting teratomas, smaller, more-complex growths. Some of the tumors had clumps of teeth, matted hair, and eyeballs all mingled together. Things like fingers and tongues sprouted from other tumors. One of the growths appeared to be forming into a secondary head. It was covered in a dozen tiny mouths.

The bubbling organic chaos before him sent a little shiver down Jasper's spine. Now that all the excess liquid had been drained away from the creature's body, it looked like some sad accretion of slaughterhouse castoffs fused together with junkyard scraps.

Hinkmeyer, the rookie cop who had led Jasper to Renfield's office a lifetime ago, opened the door to the morgue and entered the room with a sheaf of papers in hand. "Captain, here's that report on — WHAT THE HELL IS THAT?" The rookie stopped dead and stared at the thing on the table, his report instantly forgotten.

Grainger's morgue assistants wheeled a cloth-draped cart into the room. The medical examiner peeked under the cloth and nodded. Hinkmeyer hadn't yet peeled his eyes off the thing on the table.

"What've you got there, Hinkmeyer?"

The younger officer swallowed hard and finally tore his gaze away. "I've got that report on that military convoy that got hit last night."

Jasper's ear perked up. Renfield noticed his apparent interest and held up the report. "Some of the local factories here are under contract with the military. The Army came to pick up one of its deliveries last night, and somebody hit the convoy on the way out. We've got a pile of missing National Guardsmen and a bunch of looted equipment. When it rains, it pours."

"Do you know who's responsible?" Sadie asked.

"Not yet," Renfield said. "But they fingered a couple of tanks and a prototype patrol plane."

"They stole *tanks*?" Sadie asked.

"Any connection with the mine disappearances?" Renfield had Jasper's full attention.

"We considered connections with the Detroit Salt Combine. The heist happened within a few blocks of the mine entrance, and the disappearance factor caught our attention, but we ultimately ruled out any connection."

"But mechanical parts have been disappearing from the mine, and it looks like they're being repurposed to go into these monsters."

"The mine elevators are on lockdown at night, so we know nobody entered or left the mine. Plus, you couldn't fit a tank in any of those elevators anyway. You can't even fit a truck in those elevators without taking it apart first. There's no way these things can take two tanks apart. Our military liaison thinks the soldiers probably went AWOL to sell the weapons."

"Were there any witnesses?"

"Just the National Guardsmen, and they're obviously not much help if they're missing."

"Well, that's just peachy," Sadie said.

"With all due respect, Captain. I don't think we know these things' capabilities yet, and I don't think they're the only thing down there." Jasper thought about that odd tapping noise he'd heard in the mine. That sounded like something big.

Renfield's face reddened, but then he sighed. He reached for his pack of cigarettes again, but stopped when he looked at Grainger. "I agree that it's too early for us to assess these things, but you've cracked the case. You've found out what's attacking the miners. Hell, you even bagged one. I wouldn't have believed it if it wasn't before my eyes, but I find it highly unlikely that anything is creating these monsters other than Gerhard Schackel. Even if we don't know exactly what he's doing, his scent is all over this case. His guys are clearly involved with these creatures, and he's using the tunnels for his distillery. Now we just need to nail whoever he's working with that knows how to rig up a monster."

Jasper didn't say anything. He didn't have any proof, nothing that would convince Renfield, at least. All he had was the memory of that tapping noise, like someone knocking on the side of the tunnel. Whatever it was, it was far too big to be just another mutated miner.

Sadie spoke up. "Jasper's right, Captain. There's something else down there. We heard it."

Renfield threw up his hands. "Fine. There's more than one type of creature down there, but I'm guessing they both came out of Schackel's freak lab. We'll have some answers soon enough."

"How about some answers right now?" Grainger asked. He whisked the sheet off his cart with a dramatic flourish, revealing a wicked-looking circular saw. "Had to call in a favor from upstairs. Normally, they use these to cut car crash victims out of their vehicles."

"Why do you need that?" Renfield asked.

"This fellow's ribcage has been reinforced with steel rods. My surgical equipment isn't built to handle anything like that, so ..." Grainger gleefully hefted the circular saw. Hinkmeyer turned a little green as the medical examiner revved the saw.

Donning a pair of goggles, Grainger explained. "The chest cavity is the only portion of the body I haven't been able to explore. I can see something wedged in there, but I can't get to it. Once I've cracked these ribs open, I can file my final report. That should tell you if Schackel is capable of anything like this."

He touched the whirring saw to the exposed ribs. Sparks flew, and an intolerable, high-pitched grating sound filled the morgue like a giant dental drill. Hinkmeyer exited the morgue to make a call on the large porcelain telephone as the first rib snapped apart.

Slowly, the saw sliced through the entire ribcage on both sides. With great care, the medical examiner shut the saw off. Grainger lifted the ribs off like an expert chef lifting the lid off a boiling pot. "Now we can finally see what —"

A tentacle whipped out of the gaping chest cavity and wrapped around Grainger's throat. Something hideous pulled itself out of the corpse and attacked the doctor. The saw clattered to the floor as the thing bit into Grainger's neck. Blood shot across the room as the cantaloupe-sized tumor creature tore out the medical examiner's throat.

The massive tumor had a beak-like jaw, now covered in blood.

Boneless tentacles erupted out of its body at random angles. Each tentacle was tipped with a bony hook. Jagged, broken fingernails erupted haphazardly from all over its body. Clusters of eyes, some of them dangling off its body on stalks, goggled at every corner of the room.

Jasper automatically reached for his pistol only to find that it wasn't there. He saw Sadie do the same thing, but their weapons had been confiscated for their interrogations. Renfield hadn't brought his service revolver; there was no need when simply traveling down to the police station's basement.

Grainger stumbled backward, clutching at the ruins of his neck. He fell over the cart and went down. He didn't get back up.

The tumor creature had already lost interest in the dying medical examiner. Its eyes all twitched in different directions.

Without warning, the tumonster lunged forward with surprising speed, heading straight for Sadie. Bits of viscera trailed behind it like grotesque umbilical cords as it sailed through the air. Sadie tried to spin out of the way, but it was too late. The creature was too quick.

But there was an even quicker predator in the room. Jasper's fist pistoned into the globular monster's flank before it could land on Sadie's horrified face. It smacked wetly onto the floor, tentacles flailing. For something that resembled a disembodied butt, it was shockingly spry. The creature skittered out of the way before Jasper could stomp on it.

Grainger's assistants fled the room out a back door. The creature squelched across the floor toward the open door. Jasper didn't even want to imagine what would happen if the tumor beast escaped into the city.

"No you don't," Renfield shouted. He shot a foot out and managed to step on one of the creature's tentacles, pinning it to the floor. It hissed at Renfield. Jasper had never heard a tumor hiss at anyone before, but it was turning out to be one of those days. Then it swung around and chomped on Renfield's foot.

Its steely beak sliced through Renfield's leather shoe like a lawn mower blade, clamping down hard. Renfield drew his foot back with a meaty ripping noise. Jasper saw one of the police captain's toes wedged in the creature's beak before it continued hell-bent for leather toward the door.

Jasper grabbed something off the floor and was dismayed to see that there was no way for him to reach the door before the squishy little hell spawn escaped. Fortunately, he didn't need to.

Sadie's heavy, military-style boot crashed into the thing's side, sending it sailing through the air like a kickball. The creature arced magnificently across the room like the god Apollo driving his flaming chariot across the sky. Except made of tumors.

It smacked against the far wall, leaving a crimson stain against the pristine green tile. Plopping onto the floor, it charged relentlessly back toward Sadie. Hefting the object he'd stopped to pick up, Jasper pulled the starter cord.

BBBBBRRRRRRRRRRRRRRRRWWWWWWWWWWWWW!

Grainger's power saw roared to life, its blade whining to a silver blur. Jasper darted forward after the sentient cyst. It leaped onto an island counter, scattering lab equipment in its wake. Jars and beakers crashed to the floor, shattering in sprays of glass and stinking chemicals. Crunching over the debris, Jasper swung his ungainly weapon at the creature.

He missed, taking out a considerable chunk of the counter in the process. The tumor creature darted around the corner of the island. Jasper rounded the corner, raised the saw to deliver the killing blow … and stood there.

The creature was gone.

Then Jasper saw that one of the cabinet doors built into the island was slightly open. Sadie, armed with a scalpel, approached the opposite side of the counter. "Where is it?" she mouthed. Jasper pointed a finger down to indicate the creature was skulking through the cabinets under the counter.

Renfield was out of commission, clutching his bleeding foot, and no help had arrived from upstairs. They probably didn't even realize there was a problem yet. The creature could pop out of any of the cabinets on either side of the island.

It chose to pop out of the cabinet directly in front of Sadie. Springing up on its clawed tentacles, it snapped at her throat. She tried to backpedal, but the beaked polypus caught her by surprise.

A tentacle flopped onto her shoulder, its claws sinking into her back. Sadie screamed as it used its fishhook claws for leverage, drawing its snapping beak closer to her face. She pushed the creature's pulsating, veiny body away with both hands, but it latched more of its tentacles into her skin, locking her in a lover's embrace.

The beak drew methodically closer and closer to her face as the creature tightened its grip around her body. It was aiming for her succulent, squishy eyes. She threw her head as far back as she could, but it only bought her a few inches.

Her arms folded inward, her muscles unable to resist the anaconda squeeze of the tumor creature. It was like fighting a hungry octopus. She tried to crush it in her hands, but her fingers simply couldn't find a grip on its spongy flesh. The awful beak drew closer, and she had to turn her head just to prevent it from tearing her nose off.

Despite her best struggle, the beak pressed closer yet. It crunched shut again, and Sadie felt a flare of pain as the razor-sharp tip raked across her skin, opening a gash down her cheek just below her eye. An inch higher, and she'd have lost the eye completely.

She was about to anyway. Sadie screamed again as the last of her strength was crushed from her trembling arms.

BBBBRRRRRRRWWWWWZZZZZZZZRRRRRRRRTTTTT!

The circular saw chewed into the top of the creature's body and buzzed straight down. Red juices spattered in every direction, like a blender full of gerbils. All the creature's tentacles performed a spastic death dance, flailing in every direction. Sadie grimaced as the ones hooked into her flesh ripped out.

Jasper continued to bring the saw down until the creature was sliced all the way in half. Both its halves plopped to the floor like a pair of overripe tomatoes.

Taking no chances, Jasper turned the saw to the twitching red ooze on the floor, cutting the creature into fourths and then eighths. He was not in the mood to take chances with it springing back to life. By the time he was done, the creature was little more than individual tentacles and red bisque. Among the tiny abomination's gooey remains were more wires and pieces of flanged metal that Jasper couldn't identify. He flicked the saw off and dropped it on the ground.

Sadie threw her arms around him. "I'd kiss you again, but you're kind of covered in blood."

"Sorry."

Just then, the morgue door flew open and what appeared to be half the Detroit police department stormed inside, guns drawn. Upon surveying the scene, two of them heroically puked their guts out. Some of them split off to help Renfield.

Others checked Grainger. The next medical examiner's first job would be to take care of the old medical examiner. Grainger was stone dead.

"It's been a long day," Jasper said to Sadie. "Can I invite you to dinner?"

Chapter 15
Going Clubbing

After cleaning themselves up, Jasper and Sadie left the police station. Renfield was recovering in the station infirmary. His amputated toe would slow him down for a while, but wouldn't seriously impair him in the future.

Jasper was in yet another of his perfect gray suits. He was going through a lot of them lately. Sadie had managed to send out to the university to have some of her clothes delivered. Fortunately, the police station was equipped with showers, so they had at least managed to get most of the blood and shredded meat out of their hair.

Sadie looked shockingly good for someone who had just been attacked by a carnivorous tumor. One of the police medics had stitched the gash under her eye, and now it was covered with a small bandage.

The sun was setting over Detroit. The evening's dying sunlight sent brilliant orange reflections off office building windows and bathed the street in warm gold hues.

They walked down the stairs of the police station's front entryway. "I don't know about you," Sadie said, "but I'm glad this day is over."

"That was rather hectic," Jasper agreed. Since this morning, he'd been involved in a high-speed chase through the streets of Detroit, seen two men brutally murdered, narrowly survived being ripped to shreds himself, and killed two abominations that had no business existing on God's green earth. A remarkably busy day, all things considered.

Walking together, they looked for a restaurant. "I say we call it an evening, grab some food, get some rest, and hit it again in the morning," Sadie said.

"That sounds like a good plan," Jasper replied as a car screeched to a halt directly beside them. The vehicle's back passenger door blew open just as a powerful hand latched onto Jasper's arm. In one fluid motion, he was thrown into the back of the car.

Jasper had been reunited with his pistol before he left the police station, and he reached into his jacket to draw the weapon. Sadie shouted, but she was cut off and rudely heaved on top of Jasper, blocking his shot. The vehicle's door slammed shut, and the car accelerated back into traffic. It had only been stopped for maybe five seconds.

Tangled up in Sadie's thrashing limbs, Jasper finally managed to wriggle free. He struggled to pull his pistol around, but something hard and heavy crashed down onto the back of his head. Bright shapes flashed across his vision, and his limbs went suddenly limp and uncooperative. The world had gone fuzzy around the edges. Still, he struggled to wrap his fingers around the pistol's grip. His fingers didn't want to obey, but pure muscle memory latched them almost magnetically into place around the gun.

Another blow crashed down onto his head. This time, the world didn't just go mushy, it shrank into a little speck of light surrounded by darkness. The last thing Jasper saw before the world was extinguished completely was the driver's white-gloved hands on the car's steering wheel.

Chapter 16
The Dark at the End of the Tunnel

Jasper was back in the mine. Not the salt mine under Detroit. The other mine. The one he saw in his dreams every night while he slept. It was a coal mine in rural Pennsylvania, not far from the border of West Virginia.

He was with his younger brother, Percy O'Malley. Like Jasper, Percy was tall and thin, with the same red hair and curious green eyes, but he always had more spring in his step, more enthusiasm for everything. He was charming and sly and forward where Jasper was reserved and guarded. Even though they looked quite similar, they possessed vastly different personalities. And that made them excellent partners. They knew each other's capabilities and how to use them. Whatever weaknesses one possessed, the other counterbalanced. Percy could schmooze his way out of hell, and Jasper could shoot the fleas of a dog's back. Each trusted the other implicitly and maybe even envied the other a bit as well.

Percy was newer to the business. Jasper had already let him cut his teeth on a few simpler cases, and he was pleased to realize his brother had a natural affinity for causing trouble, the O'Malley family talent.

The case they were working on, though, was something different. People didn't usually come to the Attican Detective Agency because they wanted to know if their spouse had been unfaithful or they thought their employees were stealing from the till. Any cheap gumshoe could do that. They asked for Attican detectives when they had a problem no one else could help with, and investigating another detective — and certainly one as established as Lance Basilhart — was just such a problem.

Jasper knew of the Pinkerton agent by reputation. People had the nasty habit of turning up dead when Basilhart was on a case.

Currently, Basilhart and his Pinkertons were in Pennsylvania to investigate a coal mine. The old mine stretched and twisted in an unmapped maze through the countryside's rolling hills, and the nearby town had long since expanded to sit atop many of the old tunnels. A group of miners had obviously seen potential there.

During two separate nights, the floors had blown out from under a jewelry shop and a bank, dropping their contents into the mine tunnels below. The debris had been picked clean. It was a clever scheme, but Percy and Jasper's interest came from the fact that the town had hired Basilhart and his squad to supplement the tiny police force. Everett Bergman, a wealthy, old industrial baron, wanted the Attican Detective Agency to dig up as much dirt as they could on Basilhart, and dig they had.

He and Percy were pretending to be there working for the bank's insurer, investigating the miners in a parallel investigation. People who crossed Basilhart had the bad habit of dying. Bergman's own brother died under less-than-clear circumstances during a case involving Basilhart. If Percy and Jasper found out anything about the miners, that was great. They could scoop the Pinkertons. Basilhart was the real target, though.

It had been a hard and fruitless investigation up to that point. The Pinkerton agents refused to talk to them about their boss. After the well seemed to run dry, Jasper thought they should break into the Pinkerton compound and make off with any relevant-looking files, but Percy had a better idea. He arranged a meeting with one of Basilhart's lieutenants, a big man named Al Dempsey. The younger O'Malley intimated that they knew of Basilhart's reputation, and they were interested in being hired out. They had a sometimes-messy case record, and they recognized a kindred spirit in Lance Basilhart. It was a stupidly simple ploy, one that Jasper probably never would have thought of, yet Percy had pulled it off perfectly.

Dempsey bought it hook, line, and sinker. He simply *handed* the file to Percy. It was delightfully damning — filled with names, dates, and payment information — and tailored to bring down Basilhart. For the right price, Basilhart was happy to rent his men out as a hatchet squad. They couldn't have asked for juicier evidence. To this day, Jasper didn't know if the entire thing had been a setup, or if Basilhart found out about his henchman's indiscretion later and chose to make the O'Malley brothers a target of opportunity.

Until they cleared out of town, however, they were still obligated to pretend they were investigating on behalf of the bank's insurers. They stuck the file in a safe inside the room they had rented and went out to shadow a group of miners they suspected of being behind the subterranean heists. In total, there were about thirty miners. Most of them were ex-convicts, though a few of them were just local hard cases. They tended to travel in a big pack, like feral dogs. When they weren't working in the mine, they were usually drinking and whoring at a ramshackle bordello located just outside of town. The ringleader was a hoary-bearded geezer with brown teeth by the name of Theophilus Crane.

Crane had spent most of his adult life in prison for slashing a man's throat in a bar fight. He was one of the most genuinely unpleasant individuals Jasper had ever met. His scruffy white beard was stained yellow with dribbles of tobacco juice. He made a point of hating just about every ethnic group on the planet and kept a stable of the choicest slurs on the tip of his tongue. Naturally, the red-haired O'Malley brothers caught sixty-seven flavors of verbal invective whenever they were on the mine grounds to investigate. From their observations, Crane's favorite hobby seemed to be shooting cats off fences in his neighborhood.

The O'Malleys staked out on a hill overlooking the mine that night, the moon shining bright overhead. With their binoculars, they had a perfect view of the mine entrance. This would be the last time they staked out the mine before leaving. They'd even debated skipping the duty, but Basilhart's Pinkertons would be patrolling near the mine property, and their absence might draw suspicion. Neither one of them expected to see anything of interest, but it was a special night.

Shortly after midnight, they spied a furtive figure scampering alongside the mine's chain link fence. It was Theophilus Crane himself, shockingly sober. More often than not at this time of night, Crane would have been passed out in puddles of various things at the bordello. The man produced a set of bolt cutters and chopped his way through the fence. A few minutes later, the rest of his gang skulked into view. They passed through the fence carrying various tools, not the least of which was a plunger for detonating explosives. The crew of miners snuck through the mine complex, easily evading the trio of Pinkertons wandering the property by sticking to the shadows. Soon, they all passed into the mine unnoticed.

It was Percy who decided they should follow the miners. With the information they had, Basilhart was about to get dropkicked from the case. If they caught Crane and his gang red-handed, the Attican Detective Agency would effectively win Basilhart's uncompleted contract, and they could probably expect some modest bonuses. Jasper was more reluctant. At this point, there was no reason to endanger themselves in case Crane caught them, but he allowed himself to be persuaded.

They crept away from their vantage point, the dew-soaked grass swallowing their footsteps. The shadows were equal opportunity, hiding them just as effectively as they hid Crane and his team of cutthroats. They followed the faint light of the lanterns ahead of them. Just as their lack of lanterns effectively sheathed their movements in darkness, the lanterns ahead revealed every turn Crane was making.

Blowing their way into the town's businesses from below was a clever technique, but Crane wasn't necessarily the shiniest apple in the crate. Probably the only reason he'd chosen tonight to strike was because he'd spent all his ill-gotten booty from the previous heists on a different kind of ill-gotten booty at the brothel.

Percy and Jasper could hear voices ahead. Crane cackled a series of orders, and a slurred voice responded. Apparently they had hit a dead end and he was arguing with one of the other tunnel pirates about where they were on the mine map. If they were wrong about that, they'd simply blow a random hole in the topography above without any reward. The argument continued for quite a while until the world ended around them. That's what it sounded like, at least. The blast ripped through the mine as a gigantic concussive blast. The sudden, violent change in air pressure nearly sent Jasper's lungs crawling out of his nose.

During the war, Jasper once saw a German artillery shell land on the lip of a trench. The men directly below were spared the deadly wave of shrapnel, but a change in pressure from the huge blast basically turned their lungs inside out.

For a brief moment, the entire mine was illuminated in a sun-like flash. Every shred of shadow was stripped away from the tunnels, and an enormous roar like the sound of the Earth tearing itself in two consumed Jasper's mind. Parts of the tunnel started to collapse around them. The cave in began closer to the mine's entrance and moved inward, taking support beams with it. Tons of stone and coal plunged downward. Jasper and Percy ran deeper into the mine, toward Crane's position as chunks of earth rained down all around them.

Behind them they could hear the growing roar of collapsing rock. The tunnel's roof and floor were coming together like a giant press, moving toward them at the speed of a freight train. The sound built and built behind them, growing in volume until it was even louder than the explosion that had triggered it. The ground bucked and heaved beneath them. The ceiling spat rubble above them. All hell was breaking loose behind them, and in a few seconds, they expected to be smashed into a quivering jelly, buried forever in this pitch-black tomb. The sound of the collapsing tunnel was almost directly on top of them. Smaller rocks plunged from the roof and battered them bloody. Suddenly, Jasper felt a pair of hands at his back, and he was shoved forward. He stumbled, fell to his knees, and waited for his swift and inevitable end.

It didn't come.

He'd landed just on the far side of a tunnel cross section, where one part of the mine connected with another. The ground continued to rumble and tremble for a moment and then grew still. The structural feature had saved them.

Jasper felt around for his brother in the darkness. He didn't find him. A sense of hard-edged panic started to grow in his chest. He felt around again, and, again, he couldn't locate Percy. Slowly, blindly, he backtracked to the wall of rubble now blocking the exit. Frantically grasping in the darkness, Jasper cut his hands pawing at the jagged rubble. He felt around the base of the heap, and his hands landed in something warm and wet.

Percy hadn't made it.

Jasper didn't remember a whole lot of what happened next. He was trapped in the mine with a gang of backcountry psychopaths. If they found him, they'd very likely blame him for setting off the explosives that triggered the mine collapse, and it was unlikely he'd survive much past that. Of course, that was probably just delaying the inevitable. There seemed to be a few small crevices supplying fresh air, but they were trapped underground with no food and only a few greasy, stagnant puddles for water. Rescuers would begin drilling toward them soon, but there was no guarantee that they would reach the chamber in time. He did have one advantage, though. Crane's men didn't know he was in the tunnel with them. Their lanterns shattered by the massive blast, the only way they could find him would be by touch and sound.

Crane, who had survived the blast, also seemed to realize the severity of the situation. A partial collapse at his end of the mine had caused its own problems for the miners. Crane sorted out wounded and crippled miners and had the healthy men kill them with pickaxes. That solved the food situation, at least for a while. Now there were only ten miners left.

Keeping to the far edges of the tunnels, Jasper managed to remain hidden for nearly two weeks. He tended to stick close to the edge of the collapsed tunnel, though, near his brother. During that time, Jasper had found a couple of rats and some beetles, but other than that he had abstained from the available food supply. The miners were beginning to dig up their comrades who had been crushed, even though they had started to spoil. Pandemonium reigned in the darkness.

Perhaps most maddeningly of all, they could hear the rescuers drilling ever closer, but they couldn't communicate with them or even tell how close they were. They might be hours away from rescue. Or weeks. There was no way to tell.

Eventually, the healthy miners began eliminating their weakest comrades, keeping themselves strong on the flesh of their friends. By rights, Theophilus Crane should have been first, but he had a hold over his followers like a mad-eyed prophet. Besides, there was so little meat on Crane's scrawny bones that it almost wouldn't be worth the effort of killing him. His creaky, heckling voice was constantly echoing down the tunnels like a mad goblin king.

After close to a month, Jasper was dying. His naturally reed-thin physique had been reduced to wholly skeletal thinness. Everything hurt as his body slowly cannibalized itself, sucking up first his small reserves of body fat and then his muscle mass.

He had cholera, or at least something very much like it. There were dangerously few fluids in him, but his body was doing its best to expel them anyway. His vital functions were slow and erratic. Sores had developed on his arms and legs, and the cuts on his hands were badly infected. His gums bled, and his teeth felt loose in his jaw.

Crane and his people were faring a bit better, but at an extraordinary cost. There were only five of them left. Two of them had died after eating tainted meat. Their scavenger's diet had left them sick and impacted.

Even though they were only marginally more alive than Jasper, he still did his best to avoid them. At this point, they would simply view him as prey. They were aware of his presence, though. As the number of living bodies in the mine dwindled, it became harder to dismiss a distant scrabble of rocks or the scuff of a shoe. Even moving as silently as he could, Jasper couldn't navigate the pitch-black environment of the mine without occasionally stumbling or stepping on some gravel. Of course, the same applied to the miners, and they were much clumsier than Jasper. He always had plenty of warning when they bumbled into his part of the tunnel. At least one of the miners apparently thought he was a ghost. To the extent that Jasper was still capable of feeling amused, he got a kick out of that.

He'd been laying near the tunnel cross junction for hours. Maybe days. He didn't know anymore. The sound of the rescue drill grew constantly closer, but he'd accepted that he wasn't going to live long enough to see it. Still, he had needs. Right now, he was thirsty. He was always thirsty, but the thirst had slowly grown into a crackling dryness that he couldn't ignore any longer. He could feel every inhalation of breath rattling down the dusty corridors of his throat and down into his struggling lungs.

Slowly, painfully, he crawled to one of the few remaining puddles left in the mine. Walking on two legs required too much effort anymore. Aside from some thick, black mud at the bottom, the puddle was nearly exhausted. He swilled some of the muck in his mouth, drawing what moisture he could out of the silt. It wasn't enough to sustain him. It wasn't even enough to slake the ugly throb in his throat. In fact, it only seemed to focus his attention even more on how dehydrated he was.

Finally, he spat out a mouthful of mud. His teeth were gritty with the stuff. More crawling took him back in the direction of his brother's grave. Perhaps it would be best to simply give up when he got back, just peacefully expire next to Percy. He was already in hell. What's the worst that could happen?

As he slumped back to the tunnel junction, he became aware of a sound. Crane and his cronies had moved into his part of the tunnel. Crane was talking, jabbering away as he always did, but that wasn't what got Jasper's attention. There was another sound.

Crunching.

Lip smacking.

Chewing.

Whether they were hunting by scent or they had stumbled upon him by pure, blind luck, Crane's men had found Percy.

Jasper's hand brushed against something, and it shifted under his touch. His fingers wrapped reflexively around what he now knew to be a wooden handle. He hefted it, ran his fingers along the length until he reached the end. A pickaxe.

Now armed, he moved forward primarily by sound. A rustle of cloth. A stifled belch. A leathery ripping sound he didn't want to think about. Soon, he had the positions of all five men fixed in his mind. Even though he couldn't actually see them, they burned brightly in his mind.

The first they became aware of his presence was when Jasper's outstretched hand rocketed into the first man's throat. The delicate muscles collapsed under Jasper's bony fingers with a sound like someone dropping a load of wet laundry on the floor. Gagging, the man collapsed, his windpipe crushed.

Next to the downed man, another miner started to react when Jasper swung the handle of the pickaxe like a baseball bat. A wet crunch echoed down the tunnel, loud as a rifle shot.

That left three men, including Crane. They rose and turned to defend themselves against the unknown force attacking them. One of them barreled into Jasper, nearly knocking him down. The miner tried to use his arms to pin Jasper against the mine's rough wall.

Jasper lashed out with the butt of the pickaxe, catching his attacker across the chin. The vibration traveling up the tool's rough wooden shaft and the hearty snap of bone told Jasper he'd broken the man's jaw. Swinging the pick end of his weapon down like a broadsword, Jasper placed the metal blade firmly in the miner's neck.

There was a hideous puncturing noise followed by a wet sucking sound. Jasper wrenched the blade up and away, ripping several of the man's vertebrae out with it.

Two left.

Jasper knew he was using his last reserves of strength. Whatever he had left in him might have been enough to keep him alive for a couple more days, but he didn't care. He was using it all right now. Those chewing sounds had snapped something inside of him.

A skinny, feverishly hot body leaped onto Jasper like an angry monkey. Theophilus Crane screeched something incoherent, pelting Jasper's face with warm, fetid spittle. Crane's grubby, blood-encrusted beard whisked across his face like steel wool.

Jasper threw his weight to the side, smashing Crane against the wall, but the man clung tenaciously to Jasper's body. He pitched his weight to the side again, and he body slammed Crane into the rocks for a second time.

Crane darted his head forward and bit Jasper's left ear off with his sharp, brown teeth. Jasper shouted as blood ran down the side of his head, feeling the pain like it was being beamed in from a weak signal very far away. He spun and used his shoulder to leverage the spindly miner into the wall a third time, finally peeling him off.

Jasper didn't have time to deal with his ear right now. He could hear the last miner, who was significantly larger than Crane, lumbering toward him. Hefting the pickaxe, Jasper brought it up over his shoulder and brought it straight down like a mallet.

The spike plunged neatly through the top of the man's head and sank up to the tool's shaft. It passed all the way through the man's cranium and emerged out of the base of his lower jaw. Jasper's arms were trembling so hard he almost couldn't draw the pickaxe back up and out of the man's skull. He was operating on pure will power. His body no longer had the ability to provide the sort of energy he was using.

"Crane," he called.

Jasper's knees wobbled, and he nearly fell. He'd torn something in his back, and his hands were growing numb around the wooden shaft of the pickaxe. The weapon drooped in his hands, the metal head clanging against the floor of the mine.

He could hear something, but the noise was distorted by the blood oozing into his ear canal. All of a sudden, Jasper realized that the noise was the sound of Crane chewing on his ear, chewing and swallowing.

"CRANE," he called again.

A sound came from directly behind him, the faintest shift of rock underneath a boot. Jasper spun, bringing the pickaxe around in a savage, upward swing. The blade sliced through the air and punched into Crane's gut. It kept going, burrowing into his sternum and up under his ribcage. There was a sharp intake of breath, and then Jasper was truly alone in the tunnels.

Jasper dropped the handle, letting it fall as Crane pitched forward onto his face. Jasper tried to take a step forward, but his legs crumpled beneath him. He collapsed, limp and boneless, beyond exhausted. He fell a few feet away from Crane. His breath came in weak, shallow gasps. He wasn't sweating. There wasn't enough liquid left in his body to spare for sweat. Blood oozed down the side of his face from his severed ear, and his heartbeat pounded in his head. The pounding was horribly loud, and he realized it was being supplemented by the pounding of the rescue equipment, but he was too tired to care.

Jasper's eyelids felt as if they were weighted down with bricks. He couldn't keep them open any longer. All he wanted to do was fade quietly into sleep. After a moment of brief resistance, his eyes finally drooped closed.

He didn't know how long they stayed closed, but he opened them again sometime later. It could have been minutes, hours, or days. His eyeballs were gummy and crusted with sand, virtually blind.

There was a shape standing in front of him, reaching down for him. The shape was backlit by a bright light. For a brief second, he thought it was Percy, but then consciousness started to fade from him again.

The shape was saying something, but it was faint and distant, as if coming from very far away. "Mister O'Malley? Mister O'Malley?"

Chapter 17
In the Flesh

"Mister O'Malley? Mister O'Malley?"

Jasper jolted awake as the smelling salts were waved in front of his face. He tried to stand, but rough hands pushed him back into a plush chair. Jasper looked around, disoriented. A lump throbbed on the back of his head.

For a moment he was still trapped in the past. Waking up in the hospital. Traveling back to the room he and Percy had rented only to find that someone had drilled through the lock of their safe and stolen the file on Basilhart. A day later, his boss had told him that Everett Bergman, their client who wanted information on the Pinkerton detective, had been found garroted two days after the mine collapsed around the O'Malley brothers.

To Jasper, it was pretty obvious who was behind the incident, but he had no *proof*.

"Mister O'Malley?" The soft, lightly accented voice finally snapped him back to the present. Jasper looked up and stared at the small, compact man sitting across from him. He tried to stand again, and the same pair of hands shoved him back into the same posh chair.

"Gerhard Schackel, I presume?" Jasper forced his mouth to form the words. His brain was still sputtering from being knocked unconscious.

"In the flesh."

Detroit's most ruthless gangster was a short man with close-cropped gray hair and flat features. He was maybe twenty pounds overweight, and his off-the-rack suit did nothing to hide his small paunch. A pair of prissy librarian glasses were perched on his blunt nose. Schackel looked more like a certified public accountant than a man half the city's police force seemed to live in fear of.

He sat on the other side of a large desk in a plain study. Jasper looked around the sparsely decorated room. Aside from the desk and chairs, the room was basic and unpretentious. Sadie sat in a chair beside him, saying nothing. Jasper could sense a large, looming presence directly behind him, ready to push him back into the chair, if necessary.

The white-gloved Model T driver stood to Schackel's right. Her dark, mysterious eyes watched him intently. Under other circumstances, he might have mistaken it for interest. Maybe it was, but that seemed like a long shot given the way her hand kept teasing along the grip of the pistol holstered in her sash.

"My apologies for your, ah, less-than-gentle treatment, Mister O'Malley." Schackel sipped at a cup of steaming tea. "Do you mind if I call you Jasper?"

"Yes."

"Very well. Can I get you anything?" He raised his cup of tea.

"No," Jasper said, shaking his head. "What do you want?"

"Your hostility is understandable given the manner in which you arrived here. I'm sure you've heard some stories about me since your arrival here, too. Don't worry, though, I've brought you here for entirely friendly reasons. Let's get down to brass tacks, shall we? I'd like to speak to you about employment."

"I'm already on a job."

Schackel gave him a weighted look, like a father humoring a mouthy teenage son. "I'm already aware that you're on a case, Mister O'Malley. You're investigating the disappearances in the Detroit Salt Combine mines. You seem to be a man who gets results, as I've heard you've already made some headway in the case."

"I've also discovered one of your private stockpiles down there. The police seem convinced that you're involved with these disappearances."

"But that's not what you think, is it, Mister O'Malley?"

There was a pause. "No."

"And why is that?"

"First of all, the evidence doesn't point to you. Even assuming you had access to the sort of technology needed to make those creatures, you have no reason to. You're obviously using the salt mines as a depot. You keep your distilleries and arms down there because the police and Prohibition Bureau normally never have any reason to go down there. Even if they put a token group of investigators down there, it would take them years to explore every inch of those tunnels. You could move your assets around inside the tunnels, and they'd never find even a quarter of it."

Schackel was smiling.

"With all the activity inside the mine, your activities are virtually invisible. With a little digging, I'm sure it would come out that you pay some miners a little extra to look the other way when your supplies are shipped in or out. To any outside observer, it looks like business as usual. Attracting the attention of the police by staging those disappearances is arguably the single dumbest thing you could do. You've created a literal criminal underworld underneath Detroit, and invisibility is one of its greatest assets."

"I like that. A literal underworld. I hadn't thought about it in those terms before. Yes, I run my operations out of the mine, and yes, these disappearances have played royal hell with everything. What about the diamonds, Mister O'Malley? Any theories on how those fit into things? The police have probably told you I'm smuggling them down there."

"They're not yours. Altogether, just the ones that have been found are worth millions. Probably tens of millions. Henry Ford standing on William Randolph Hearst's shoulders probably couldn't afford that many red diamonds, and you wouldn't be leaving them behind. Even if they were comparatively cheap uncolored diamonds, it seems unlikely that your men would be careless as to drop them near the scene of the crime." Jasper could tell he was being tested.

"That seems logical. But there's more, isn't there? You can tell these facts don't add together, and it's eating you up isn't it?"

"The creatures."

"Yes. The creatures."

"The police seem to think that you have contacts back in Germany who have been working on this for you. Funding for some mad scientist-type."

"Again with what the police think. What do you think?"

"I don't care what contacts you have. They aren't capable of this. Those things in the tunnel were so outrageously twisted that it's impossible to even call them human anymore. Even if you knew how to alter a human body like that, it's impossible for you to install the sort of mechanisms that we found in the corpses. No one even knows what half those devices do; they just know that they're incredibly complex. If you were the one responsible for this, you'd make a fortune off of perfectly legitimate patents rather than turning your men into monsters and setting them loose in the Detroit Salt Combine tunnels."

Schackel sat back and threaded his fingers behind his head. "I'm well aware that I'm the police department's favorite whipping boy, but if I'm not responsible, that raises the question of who is."

"Are you trying to suggest I should help you?"

Without saying anything, Schackel pushed his chair back and carefully removed a small key from his pocket. He bent over and unlocked one of the drawers of his desk. He reached in and pulled out a large envelope, which he tossed to Jasper.

Jasper grabbed it out of the air and slit it open with his thumb in one smooth gesture. A single photo fell out of the envelope onto his lap. He looked at the picture. It was grainy and out of focus, and the black-and-white square showed only a corner of its subject, but it was enough.

Most of the picture consisted of a white blur, and it took Jasper a second to realize that the perspective had turned a massive claw reaching for the photographer into a distorted smear. The creature's gray skin was saggy and loose on its frame, but it was covered with dozens of lopsided bumps, almost like a plucked turkey set out for Thanksgiving dinner. Unhealthy-looking bristles, each about the width and length of one of Jasper's fingers, stuck out of its body at irregular intervals, like tombstones in an old, ill-cared-for cemetery.

The creature didn't have a head precisely. Its body tapered into a short neck of sorts, which simply ended in a vertical column of jagged fangs. It looked like someone crossed a dragon and a tarantula and then ran it over with a pickup truck a couple of times. At the moment the photo was taken, the mouth was flared open like a deadly flower, and Jasper could see straight down the beast's gullet. What looked like an endless succession of additional teeth retreated down the monster's throat. Far in the back, Jasper thought he could see another set of jaws. The creature's mouthparts were stretched out toward the photographer.

"What is that?" Sadie asked, speaking for the first time.

"I don't have a good answer to that," Schackel said. "But it's killed too many of my men. When the disappearances began, I decided to move my operations out of the mine for a while. I sent down some of my men to pack everything up. Most of them came back, but a few didn't."

"So you sent more down to take care of things."

"Precisely. The men I brought over from Germany were all former *Sturmtroopen*, the finest fighting men Europe had to offer. I was able to carve a niche into the criminal ecosystem here because my men are experienced, disciplined, and organized. For most people, this is a difficult, deadly business to break into. Needless to say, I am still here and my former competitors are not. My point is, when I want a matter cleared up, it is cleared up."

"But this time was different."

"*Ja*. One of the teams disappeared. That alone should have told me that this wasn't the work of some petty rival trying to even a score. The camera that took that picture is all we found of the team. Once we developed the film, it became apparent just how unpleasant this problem was going to be."

"So why did you keep sending people into the mines? Like Gottschalk?"

"I heard you found dear old Gottschalk. He was a good man. Had a young son who showed a lot of promise." Schackel sounded genuinely aggrieved. "I only kept a few men in the tunnels under the guise of miners to keep an eye on the situation. I was surprised Detroit Salt didn't shut down their operations as the crisis grew."

"They seem to think they can fix the security situation."

"And what a fine job they've done," Schackel noted, the words dripping with acid. "That is no way to treat those under you. Gottschalk was one of the men I kept in the tunnels. For the most part, his job kept him near the mine's entrance, which seemed to be safe enough and gave me access to a pair of ears underground."

"So what happened to him?" Sadie asked. "It doesn't look like you're taking particularly good care with your men either."

Schackel scowled. "I don't throw them away like Detroit Salt does. One day, Gottschalk came out of the mine acting strangely. Irritable. I didn't take much notice of it when he reported back, but he began acting increasingly erratic over the next few days, spending longer and longer in the mine."

"He wanted to spend more time down there?"

"He was miserable away from the mine. One day, he simply didn't come back at all. That's when I finally withdrew all my men from the tunnels. The darkness down there is like a poison."

"But didn't you send more men down today? We found a Tommy gun and some fresh blood near the entrance to one of your caches."

"No. They were two of Gottschalk's friends. They went of their own accord to continue looking for him against my express orders. If I'd known what they were doing, I would have taken it out of their hides."

"So where do we fit into this?" Jasper asked. "Why did you bring us here?"

"I want you to work for me. I want you to kill that thing."

"I don't work for your type."

Schakel reached down into his desk again and pulled out two objects. The first was a thick file. Jasper's file. The one that no one except the police force was supposed to have access to.

The other object was a Luger. Schackel set the pistol casually on the table. He rifled through the file and pulled out the single sheet of paper he had been looking for. "Mister O'Malley, you served in the war, did you not?"

"Yes. You have my record right there. I'm rather curious as to how you acquired that."

"I served in the war as well," Schackel said. "I was a colonel in Germany's military intelligence branch. Believe me when I tell you that I can get any piece of information I want. There's something I'd like to ask about, though."

"Ask, then."

"You were a reconnaissance pilot. Why? You strike me more as a man who would appreciate logistical work or military police duty. Perhaps even intelligence, like myself."

"When you're a reconnaissance pilot, they tell you to get pictures of a particular section of the trenches and not to get killed while you're doing it. Then they send you up, maybe with some fighter escorts, maybe not. I appreciate the ability to do things my way, a rare commodity in the military."

Schackel pursed his lips and nodded in apparent approval. "I suppose that is ultimately the reason I've brought you here."

"Yeah, about that," Sadie said.

The German turned his gaze to Sadie. "I wasn't speaking to you," he said flatly. "You're here by a fluke. If Mister O'Malley requires your presence to finish this case, then so be it."

"I need her," Jasper said. That was no longer technically true. He didn't know everything about the diamonds yet, and he probably didn't need to. There was something much bigger afoot, but they'd gone through a lot together in just a few hours. It was the first time he'd worked closely with anyone since Percy's death. He hadn't really thought about it, but aside from taking messages from Tycho Vedel, he hadn't shared his work with anyone these past few years, and it felt good sharing it with someone.

"Very well," Schackel waved that away. "It says here that you shot down four enemy planes during the war, one short of making ace. You piloted a one-person reconnaissance plane. How in the world did you manage that? Did you retrofit the aircraft with guns? I knew some pilots from my side, and reconnaissance planes were sheep for the wolves."

"They always sent me up with a pistol. Technically, it was so I had something to fight with in case I was forced to land behind enemy lines. Your skies were usually thick with Fokkers, but your pilots were cocky. All they saw was a slow, defenseless recon plane, so they liked to swoop in close and take their time adjusting their sights. I'd wiggle around a bit to make it harder on them, force them to draw in closer to get the perfect shot they wanted. Then I would empty my pistol's magazine into their engine block. Anything that didn't crunch into the engine whisked right through to the pilot's seat."

Schackel considered this for a moment, considering the odds of hitting another moving aircraft with a handgun. "That ... is an impressive trick."

"You do what you have to."

"Mister O'Malley, you said that you had no interest in working for 'the likes of me.' Those were your exact words. But we're actually very similar, you and I."

"Forgive me if I disagree."

Schackel hefted Jasper's file and let it drop onto his desk with a bang. "Consider. Do you know why my associates are called *Die Ratten*? It's a label they wear with pride."

Jasper sat in silence.

"When Germany lost the war, the Entente Powers ordered our military all but disbanded. I had been in the Kaiser's armed forces for almost all of my adult life, and suddenly I was thrown out into the streets with a pat on the head as thanks for my service. I wasn't merely jobless; I no longer had a purpose in the cold, new world I'd entered. All the skills I'd spent a lifetime honing, all the experience, was suddenly useless. It had no application after the war, and I was a worn-out piece of wartime detritus. Useless.

"It was a condition felt all across the country. Men who had spent years fighting and dying came home to faces that didn't understand or appreciate what they'd been through. They were already ghosts. Their past selves died in those trenches. Everyone expected us to transfer quietly into the civilian world and let life go back to what it was before the war, but that was impossible. Training and experience had whittled them down to some of the finest killing machines the world had ever known, the best of their generation, and all of that was rendered inapplicable overnight. Not everyone could successfully navigate that transition. It's a strange melancholy knowing that you're the best at something horrible, Mister O'Malley, and I hope you never have to experience it because nothing can ever quite fill that void.

"Some ex-soldiers joined paramilitary groups or became revolutionaries. Others, painters or writers. I hope some of them found peace in that, but from my experience, most of them are bitter assholes. As I said, it's a sad feeling knowing you've reached the apex of your powers and then having no use for those skills.

"I took the only skills I had, and I moved them here. I knew foot soldiers, and I knew German brewers. I also knew how to run a large organization capable of enormous violence. Put those people and those skills together in a land that has prohibited alcohol, and you have the formula for a very interesting new life. Organized crime? Bah! There was only crime here before. *We* brought the organization.

"We call ourselves *Die Ratten* because you can trap us, gas us, do everything you can to eliminate us, and yet we will always come back. We are everywhere, scurrying through the shadows. We feed off of the debris of the very society that reviles us."

"That's very nice, but I still won't work for you," Jasper said.

"Oh, Mister O'Malley. Don't you see? Where would you be if your actions became unsanctioned? If you were cast out from the detective business? You've been a man whose entire purpose has been wrapped up in his work ever since you lost your brother. If you didn't have the justification of your employment, people would think you a dangerous misanthrope. Is it really so hard to see yourself following my example if you had nowhere else to turn?"

"Yes," Jasper said stiffly.

"Very well." Schackel let the issue drop, sensing he'd scored a point. "Ultimately, though, I'm not asking you to work *for* me. I'm asking you to work *with* me. I know your type. You don't like unfinished business regardless of what form it takes. You want this thing, whatever it is, dead just as badly as I do. What I'm offering is conditional help. You want guns? I can provide them. You want information on anyone in this city? I can provide it. You want an armored battalion? Well, that will take some doing, but I'm pretty good at pulling strings."

"You said conditional help. What sort of conditions are we talking about?"

"I want Amelia to go with you." He gestured to the dark-haired woman standing against the wall.

"Absolutely not." Sadie nearly shouted the words. Jasper and Schackel both looked at her in surprise.

"Jealous?" Schackel asked.

"No," Sadie said, sounding decidedly unhappy.

Schackel smirked and reached into his seemingly bottomless desk drawer again. His Luger sat on top of the desk, waiting. He pulled out another file, much thinner than Jasper's. With a flourish, he removed two single sheets.

"Miss DuPree, your record is much less distinguished than your colleague's. In fact, it's almost entirely empty. You've published a few papers, under a pseudonym, I might add, but no one has paid any serious attention to them."

"How did you find out about any of that?"

"I assure you, I can gain access to nearly anything. And, unless the USGS has taken to encrypting and hiding their files at a greater level than the highest echelons of your American military, that is the entire depth of your résumé, Miss DuPree. You seem competent ... but ultimately unnecessary."

"You son of a —"

"Now, Miss Rio here," Schackel gestured to his driver, "is supremely capable. Aside from her driving skills, which I believe you can attest to, Mister O'Malley, she is proficient with a weapon, as well as hand-to-hand techniques. She's fluent in three languages, and she is entirely qualified to aid you in any of your endeavors. She will be completely unobtrusive, extremely helpful, and wholly loyal to me. Do you object, Mister O'Malley?"

"I don't believe I require any more help."

"Look, don't be dense. You're looking a gift horse in the mouth, as you Americans say. I will make this easy. I want a source of information that I control on your little team. You can still act independently, and you'll have the great benefit of one of my most competent people by your side, and believe me, I have many people of great competence to choose from."

He picked up the pistol to make the point perfectly clear. "If you do not voluntarily allow Amelia to help, I will have her replace your current assistant. It would probably be an improvement, actually."

Schackel leveled the Luger casually at Sadie. A pair of heavy hands preemptively wedged Jasper into his seat in case he tried anything stupid.

"Keep in mind, Mister O'Malley, I have over seventy guards on my grounds right now. If you were to adversely react to this decision, you might be able to make it out of this room alive. You're very talented. That's why I'm interested in you. However, you would never make it out of the building with your life."

Jasper took a breath. He had the good sense to know when he was beaten. Even if he didn't like it, it looked like the second woman was here to stay. "Amelia, was it? A pleasure to make your acquaintance."

"Charmed," she responded, finally moving her hand away from the pistol in her sash. "Amelia Rio. Happy to help."

Sadie made a little disgusted noise in the back of her throat. Everyone ignored it.

"Seeing as you're being ever so helpful," Jasper turned to Schackel, "I don't suppose you have any more information about the mine disappearances?"

"As a matter of fact, I do have something you may wish to look into," Schackel said. "Obviously, this thing, this creature, is a complete unknown. It might be a good idea to learn more about it."

"Brilliant. Why didn't we think of that?" Sadie was clearly unhappy with this turn of events.

"There is a man who frequents one of my establishments. He is what you call a regular. He is also a high-ranking mine engineer with the Detroit Salt Combine." Schackel produced a strip of paper and jotted down a name and address and handed it to Amelia. "If you were to travel here and ask for this man, you might be able to learn something useful."

"Is that a suggestion or an order?" Jasper asked.

"It is a piece of information. How you choose to act on it is entirely up to you."

Chapter 18
Tanks a Lot

The creature sat in the darkness admiring the toys her children had brought. Soon she would have time to tinker with them and salvage materials. They had carried the tanks down the side of the mine shaft like ants carrying a dead beetle down the trunk of a tree. When they all worked together, they could lift inordinately heavy objects and carry them great distances. Their new limbs, with their grasping claws, were perfect for latching onto sheer surfaces and climbing straight up or down. That was one of the reasons she transformed them from their prior useless shapes.

She admired the metal trinkets. Yes, there was much she could do with these. The thick metal plating was useful in and of itself, but there were also heavy-duty motorized elements that could be scavenged and reassembled. This was a rich bounty indeed.

Perhaps even more valuable were the additional thralls her children had brought her. These were fine specimens, and their flesh was already bubbling away into something new and better. Sometimes one of them made sick mewling noises from the ground, where they were curled up into little balls. More common was the loud, hearty crunch of a bone snapping or separating from the rest of the meat as their bodies changed and altered in different ways.

Each of her children was different, unique snowflakes of diseased flesh and teeth. They each served specialized tasks. Some, the majority, were workers. They found materials and disassembled them, whether they were natural or organic. Her bloated, tick-like groomers were much less common. There were only a few of them at any given time. She constantly needed to make more, as she had the habit of eating them when they annoyed her or she became bored. Still, they were as completely devoted to her like all the rest. Her favorites, though, were her growing ranks of soldiers. They usually performed similar tasks as the workers, but they were much hardier and could do more heavy lifting. So far, they hadn't seen much use, but the creatures working the mine were becoming bolder.

The fact that one of her attendants had been killed today was a reminder of that. The primitive, fleshy creature that killed her servant … She had not sensed that one's presence in the mine before, but she was ready if she ever sensed it again. She was ready and hungry.

Chapter 19
Bottoms Up

Jasper stood in front of the speakeasy. The door was a graceless metal affair that looked like it could stop a bomb blast. A little sliding slat stood at eye level. It was currently closed. Jasper knocked.

Tap. Tap. Tap.

The slat slid open, revealing a pair of bloodshot, angry-looking eyes. "What you want?"

"I'd like to speak with someone in there." This looked more like the sort of speakeasy Jasper was familiar with. The door was in a filthy back alley behind a garage. Trash and stains that Jasper didn't care to think about covered the concrete. This was a far cry from Madame Mai's establishment.

"Piss off, hotshot." The slat slammed shut.

"Well, this has been productive." Sadie still wasn't very happy.

"Let me try," Amelia said.

"This'll be good." Yes, Sadie was not pleased.

Amelia tapped on the door. There was a pause, and then the door's slat ripped open again. "Look, you stupid bastAAAHHH! Miss Rio, please! I'm sorry. I didn't see you there. What can I do for you? Please, let me offer you a drink."

"Can we come in?"

"Yes. Yes. Of course. Please." The door creaked opened with an unoiled squeal to reveal an enormous, burly man in a wife beater. His arms were plastered with tattoos of varying designs and quality. He had a bald head and a nose that had been broken multiple times, and he had an old knife scar running down the side of his cheek. He was all but whimpering as Amelia walked inside.

"Can I get you anything, Miss Rio? Anything at all?"

"I'm fine, Max. Thank you."

"Please don't tell Mister Schackel. I just didn't recognize your, ah, friends."

"It's alright, Max. Is Roger Ackley here tonight?" Amelia was looking around, trying to spot the Detroit Salt Combine engineer who supposedly frequented this bar.

"Yeah. He's just over there." Max waved a thumb to the far side of the room. There was a hunched figure, his back to them, drinking alone at one of the tables. "You need him thrown out? Our records say he's paid up, but if you want him out, I'll get him out of here."

"No, Max. We just need to talk to him. Mister Schackel thinks he might have some useful information. You're doing a good job, Max. Just go back to handling the door."

They started to wander over in Ackley's direction. Max gave Jasper and Sadie skeptical looks, but didn't say anything.

"Well, that was impressive," Jasper said.

"There are advantages to having friends in high places. Especially when those friends aren't averse to killing everyone who displeases them."

"Point taken," Jasper said.

"More like friends in low places. I hope Schackel doesn't suddenly decide that we displease him as soon as we finish this job," Sadie said.

"Don't worry, he won't," Amelia said.

"How reassuring," Sadie commented.

Jasper ignored the commentary happening around him. He was focused on Ackley. The man was clearly half past drunk, but it looked like he'd been putting some serious effort into this particular bender. He had a thick crop of stubble growing over his cheeks and weak chin. His hair looked like it had been combed with his fingers several days ago, and it had obviously been a while since he had a haircut. His eyes were bloodshot and glassy, and they barely moved. They just stared straight ahead at the mug of beer in his hand. A fly buzzed down from the ceiling and landed on the lip of the glass. It sat there for several seconds, rubbing its front legs together. It finally flew away when Ackley raised the glass to his lips and took a long drink. His Adam's apple bobbed as he took several heroic swallows of the questionable-looking brew.

Finally, he put the glass down. A ring of beer foam clung to his upper lip. After a few seconds, Ackley wiped it away with the back of his sleeve. Most of the glass of beer was gone, leaving only a sad, little puddle sitting in the bottom.

"Roger Ackley?" Jasper asked.

The man looked at him and blinked. "Yeah?"

"I'm Jasper O'Malley with the Attican Detective Agency." Jasper's badge made its obligatory appearance. "Could my friends and I borrow a moment of your time to speak with you?"

"Uh-huh. Sure. Whatcha need?" Ackley's words slurred together.

Jasper sat down at the table. Sadie and Amelia took the other two chairs. Amelia stepped in front of Sadie to take the seat next to the gray-clad detective. A venomous look passed from Sadie to the other woman.

"You work for the Detroit Salt Combine, correct?"

"Yup. I'm one of the senior engineers."

"I'm sure you're familiar with the current problems that are going on at the mine."

"Yeah. That's a real pisser."

"Could you tell me about them?"

"Well, sure," Ackley slurred. "It started about two months ago. Everything was normal as ... well, as pie. Apple pie. Yeah. We sent a crew down to the end of Tunnel F to do some blasting, and they just never came back."

"That was the first disappearance?"

"Yeah, it was. We just figured it was an accident. We always blast the tunnels to break the salt rock into manageable sizes. You know, break it off the wall into smaller rocks so we can cart it back to the elevators and send it up to be processed. Running at peak capacity, we could do eight thousand tons of salt any day of the week. Let me tell you, partner, that is a metric buttload of salt."

"I'm no expert, but I'll take your word for it. Tell me more about the first two disappearances."

"Say, you're awfully pretty," Ackley said in Sadie's general direction.

"Mister Ackley," Amelia said, trying to snap his attention back to the task at hand.

"Oh, hello there. Say, you're awfully pretty, too."

Judging from Ackley's pale, stretched skin and glazed eyes, he'd been in this state for quite a while. Jasper suspected there was something more potent than alcohol running through the man's system. He glanced at Ackley's veiny arms and saw a network of tiny scabs tracking across his flesh. Needle marks.

"The disappearances, Mister Ackley."

"Terrible business, that. We should have closed the tunnels when it started, but Mister Ransom wouldn't let us. Said the mine needed to stay open. Had us start building the cage."

"The cage? What's the cage?" Ackley was growing less lucid.

"When the first group disappeared, we thought it was an accidental explosion. Poor fools buried themselves in a tunnel collapse. We found the salt rocks, but we didn't find the miners. They'd blasted into some sort of chamber or something. We just assumed they'd been crushed when the rocks came down. Not the first time it's happened. But we always found bodies before. What was left of them, at least."

Jasper had to push the memory of his brother out of his mind. It was hard. He sat perfectly still for a moment. Sadie looked at him questioningly.

"You said something about a cage?"

"I can't talk about that," Ackley said. He drained the last of his beer. It looked like the glass hadn't been cleaned in a long time. The man sat sullenly, obviously wanting to tell his story to someone, but aware that he'd be in trouble if he said anything more.

Raising a hand, Jasper gestured to Max. The bouncer wandered over, glancing worriedly at Amelia.

"What sort of beer do you serve?"

Ackley perked up.

"The cheap kind."

"Bring us a pitcher of your finest swill." Max scurried away, and Jasper looked at Amelia. "Are all of Schackel's establishments like this?"

"No. This is the bottom rung. He's got a couple of places that make The Ritz-Carlton look like a sewer. Strictly black tie affairs. The boss likes to have something for everyone, though."

Max came trotting back with a foaming pitcher and some cleanish glasses. He set them on the table, and Jasper removed two neatly folded dollar bills from somewhere inside his jacket. The beer probably wasn't even worth half that, but Jasper didn't care. He'd be billing Schackel for it.

"No, it's on the house." Max waved the money away.

"Consider it a tip."

The bouncer glanced at Amelia. She nodded slightly, and Max took the proffered bills from Jasper's hand. He took up his post by the door again, the money wedged in his pocket. The money wasn't for the pitcher of beer. It was for the spilled beer someone would have to clean up in a minute.

Reaching over, Jasper selected the cleanest of the glasses and slowly, carefully poured beer into it. Ackley watched the golden liquid fill the glass an inch at a time, longing in his eyes. The sudsy brew came to the top of the glass, and Jasper stopped pouring. A thin head of bubbles barely rose over the rim of the glass.

Jasper slid the cool glass in Ackley's direction, but he kept his hand wrapped around its base. Ackley grabbed the glass and tried to lift it, but Jasper didn't let go. "I'd like to know more about this cage you mentioned. And who is Mister Ransom?"

"I can't tell you about that."

"Very well." Jasper pulled the beer out of Ackley's grasp and held it out, away from the table. With the same deliberate slowness with which he'd poured it, Jasper tilted the glass and let the foaming alcohol spill onto the floor.

Max watched from his post by the door, apparently more curious than concerned. The floor was already sticky with unknown substances and littered with cigarette butts and peanut shells. Given the aggregate mess, the additional puddle of beer wasn't much of a custodial hardship. Maybe someone would clean it up eventually. Maybe not.

Ackley watched the beer dribble out onto the floor with desperate eyes. Jasper shook the glass, and the last few drops of foam inside the glass escaped onto the floor. He repeated the process, filling a fresh glass. The mining engineer watched the entire process with a piteous expression. That was the gaze of a man who wanted to forget something but couldn't.

Jasper slid the next glass toward Ackley. The pitcher was now about half empty. Ackley's hands trembled as he stared. Jasper had seen men with the same expression trembling in field hospitals, men hit with shell shock. If Ackley wasn't careful, those urges would eventually destroy him.

"I'd very much like to know about that cage you mentioned. Why would the Detroit Salt Combine need a cage?"

"This is cruel," Ackley said. He was right, of course. He needed help. He was clearly a wasted, shriveled husk of whoever he had been before. Jasper wouldn't be surprised if Ackley ended up dead from the poisons flowing through his veins within the next six months. Right now, though, Jasper needed whatever information Ackley had about the mine and the creature living in it.

Ackley didn't volunteer any more information.

Saying nothing, Jasper poured the second glass of beer out over the floor. The tremble in Ackley's hands became more pronounced. Jasper poured a third drink. Most of the beer in the pitcher was gone.

"I ... I don't have to put up with this. I can buy my own drinks. I don't even have to stay in this pit; I can take my business elsewhere."

"No, you can't," Amelia said.

"Of course I can," Ackley blustered.

"Wrong. I can have you tossed out of every joint in town. If I say so, every place connected with Gerhard Schackel, which is most of them by the way, will have your name and know to ban you. If I say you have unpaid debt, the other places won't give you the time of day. We share our blacklists, Mister Ackley. There is a bit of honor among thieves, you know? All we want is a bit of information. If you don't want to spend the rest of your days straining rubbing alcohol through pieces of burnt toast in a back alley somewhere, I suggest you cooperate."

"I ... I ... You ..."

Jasper sloshed the third beer onto the floor and started to fill the fourth, using up the last of the pitcher. He slid the final glass toward Ackley.

"But Mister Ransom will kill me if I tell you," the engineer pleaded.

"There's no way he'll know it was you," Jasper said. He lifted the final glass of beer off the table and started to tilt it. "Last chance."

"Wait," Ackley said, his voice hitched, and Jasper realized the man was trying to hold back drunken sobs. "Here. I can give you this. That's all I can give you. That's it. Mister Ransom will kill me."

Pulling a pen out of his pocket, Ackley snatched up a napkin and began scribbling on it. Wrote down an address in wobbly letters. It was barely legible, but Jasper could still make it out: *1332 Van Buren Avenue.*

He passed the note to Amelia. "You know Detroit's streets. Is this place nearby?"

"Van Buren's on the edge of the industrial district. Warehouses, mostly. It's about a mile from here."

"Thank you, Mister Ackley." Jasper set the beer back on the table, and Ackley snatched it and lifted the cool glass to his quivering lips. He took a big gulp, probably not even tasting the watery booze.

"Amelia, please see to it that Mister Ackley is cut off after this. He's had enough."

Ackley's eyes popped open. "You son of a bitch!"

"He's been a good customer," Amelia said.

"Write him off. It's for his own good." Jasper got up and started to move away from the table. His companions followed him. Ackley was blubbering behind them, shouting. Maybe he'd be able to get his life on track again, maybe not. Gerhard Schackel's establishments were not the place to begin that process, though.

As they made for the door, Ackley gave up and stared sadly into his glass. It was decidedly half empty. He raised it up and prepared to finish it off.

They were interrupted before they could leave the speakeasy, though. As it turned out, Jasper's previous assessment that the front door could withstand a bomb blast was actually incorrect.

A controlled explosion ripped the door off its hinges, flinging it inside the bar and knocking Max, the doorman, off his feet. Brickwork and masonry cascaded inside.

Stunned, Jasper had just enough time to duck behind a table as a wave of bullets buzzed through the cratered wall. Sadie and Amelia dropped down beside him. He flipped the table over, creating an improvised shield against the lead tsunami.

Behind them, his reflexes fogged by alcohol, Ackley turned around to see what the commotion was. A bullet smacked him in the face just below the right eye, rattled all the way through his head, and punched out the back of his skull in an exit wound the size of a toddler's fist. He plunged out of his chair and fell to the floor in a tangle of limp limbs. The bar's other patrons screamed and tried to escape out the back door in a drunken stampede.

A figure carrying a compact submachine gun stepped through

the gaping hole in the wall. The man was casually dressed except for a vest lined with dozens of overlapping pockets. Without slowing his pace, he leveled his gun at Max's stunned form and pulled the trigger. A dozen bullets spurted out of the gun's muzzle and all but obliterated the doorman's torso.

Jasper didn't recognize the type of gun, but he didn't have time to examine it. The weapon swiveled in his direction.

Jasper's drew his pistol and snapped two rounds into the man's chest. The intruder stumbled, pushed backward into the wall. Then he wheeled around and raised his weapon in Jasper's direction again.

That wasn't right. With two slugs in his chest, the man should have gone down like a sack of cat turds. Instead, he was alive and well and about to blow Jasper's head off. Underneath the man's odd vest, which now had two neat holes in it, Jasper could see the dull gleam of steel. Dozens of small steel plates rattled as the man moved, creating a nigh-impenetrable shield. The man must have been in remarkable shape to carry so much metal around. Jasper had seen attempts to make bulletproof shields for infantry during the war, but they were all so heavy that they could only be used by immobile troops like machine gunners.

They also had another major downside.

Jasper shot the man in the face, aptly demonstrating the armor's primary shortcoming. The armor couldn't protect everywhere.

Their attacker slumped to the ground, but two more men stormed into the speakeasy in his place. They, too, were dressed in civilian clothing, but equipped with the armored vests and strange guns.

"Amelia, who are these guys?"

"Probably Schackel's thugs, here to double-cross us," Sadie said. She stuck her head above the table and fired off a couple of rounds from her big revolver. The rounds went high, and the two men flipped over a table of their own across the room.

"These aren't Schackel's people. I don't know who they are. They look like jumped up G-men," Amelia shouted over the chatter of submachine gun fire. Jasper didn't know who they were either, but right now he agreed with Amelia's assessment. They were too well and oddly equipped to be part of a local crime syndicate.

Bullets thumped into the thick wood in front of them. None penetrated, but that wouldn't last long. The rounds were already starting to chew the table apart.

A third man entered the bar. Amelia shot him in the groin with her own pistol. He howled and collapsed in the doorway. There were more men outside the door, waiting for an opportunity to force their way inside.

This was not good.

Jasper tried to peek over the edge of the table, but about a thousand pencil's worth of lead forced him to duck back down. Two more of the men outside took the opportunity to dash into the embattled speakeasy. They went right, trying to flank Jasper's position. The first two men provided cover while the second pair leapfrogged forward.

Dammit. These guys were trained, they had better equipment, they had more people, and their primary purpose seemed to be murdering the hell out of Jasper and his colleagues. Not good at all.

Amelia lay flat against the floor and poked out from the side of the table. She shot one of the mystery men in the throat. His legs ran for a few more steps before he pitched over. It was a damn good shot. Another bullet thumped high of the second man's vest, near the protective gear's edge, spinning him around. A third shot took out a hefty chunk of their attacker's shoulder, but he managed to duck behind a ratty pool table. They weren't flanked, but it meant that Jasper's group had to split their attention between the threat in front of them and the threat to their side.

Nope. Not good at all.

Jasper needed a plan. He looked around. To their right, more men waited behind the smoldering remains of the front door, and the injured gunman was still a threat. Straight ahead of them, the overturned table hid two more goons. On their left were the bar and the back door. Those were the elements he had to work with.

Jasper had his plan. More bullets flogged the surface of the table, chewing it to toothpicks. "Amelia, you keep the one on the right occupied. Sadie, make sure the two in front keep their heads down for a second. Ready? Go."

Both women sprang up and unloaded their weapons at their assigned targets. Sadie's rounds pounded one after the other into the opposite table. Amelia peppered the area to the right with bullets, hitting the man hunkered down there. He screamed and hit the floor.

Jasper lunged to the left and rolled behind the bar, which offered a modicum of safety. Amelia and Sadie dropped down behind the table again to reload.

Everything Jasper needed was directly in front of him. He grabbed a bottle of cheap booze. For a drink to burn, it needed to be at least forty percent alcohol, 80 proof. The bottle of rum in his hand was labeled as 120 proof, more than half pure alcohol. Jasper prayed the bottle wasn't watered down too badly. Uncorking it, the smell that reached up and smacked him in the face told him it would work nicely. It smelled like industrial solvent. Next, he produced a lighter and grabbed a cleaning rag.

Sadie and Amelia had just finished reloading as two more of the armored attackers dashed into the speakeasy. As they stepped inside, a flaming missile arced out from behind the bar, sailing toward the door. It smashed on the ground directly at the intruders' feet. Alcohol splashed out of the shattered bottle and instantly ignited, burning a hot blue. The flaming rum sprayed all over the two men trying to muscle their way inside. All around them, the floor erupted in a lake of blue flames.

One of them ran back out the door, little more than a streak of screaming fire. He looked like a low-orbiting comet. The second man collapsed into the flames, shrieking. The small alcohol fire wasn't anywhere near hot enough to melt the steel plates inside their bullet-proof vests, but they did conduct heat, like a pan on an oven.

Jasper couldn't completely ignore the smell of burning flesh and hair that was already beginning to fill the bar as he readied another incendiary. The growing fire blocked the front door, making it impossible for more of the mysterious gunmen to enter the speakeasy. It also left the two men who were already inside cutoff. They seemed to realize this at the same instant Jasper lit the wick of another bottle bomb.

Before Jasper could throw the improvised explosive at them, they popped up and fired their submachine guns at Jasper, as well as Sadie and Amelia, forcing everyone down.

The gunmen made for the back door, where Jasper had been planning to escape through. He sprang up to fire at them with his pistol. If they escaped and took up positions back there, Jasper, Sadie, and Amelia would be trapped from both sides in a building that was now on fire.

Almost seen as he stuck his head above the counter, Jasper ducked down again as the bottle beside his face shattered under a hail of bullets. Glass shards and cheap hooch sprayed his suit.

The first gunman threw the back door open. His head exploded into a mist of hot blood. The sound of a high-powered rifle boomed through the speakeasy. At the same time, the now headless corpse of the first man slumped to the ground and a hail of smaller caliber bullets ripped through the back door and tore the second man apart. His armor plating spared his chest, but the gunfire shattered his legs, tore one of his arms off at the elbow, and left his face a cratered ruin. If Jasper had thrown the door open himself ...

What in the hell was happening? Why was there a second group of gunmen out in the back alley? Whoever had set up shop in the alley was very well armed, but what were they doing here? Were they here to attack the other group or had the first group of gunmen simply gotten in the way?

Jasper took advantage of the temporary reprieve to hop over the counter. He had a dozen tiny cuts on his face from where the bottle had burst next to him, but he ignored the droplets of blood starting to seep down his cheek.

Were these newcomers on his side? Carefully, he poked an eye around the edge of the back door.

He had to jump back as a hellacious typhoon of hot brass blew through the doorway. A split second after he moved his head, a chunk of the doorframe was blown to smithereens by another overpowered rifle shot.

Well, that answered that question. The enemies of his enemies were not always his friends. In fact, they might be worse.

His quick glance told Jasper that the alley was filled with dumpsters, fire escapes, and about thirty armed men. Unlike the goons at the front of the bar, these fellows looked local. They were dressed in street clothes and carrying mismatched weapons. Many of them were bearded. Some of them had Tommy guns while others packed sawed-off shotguns and hunting rifles. And at least one of them had a Mauser 1918 T-Gewehr. Jasper didn't need to be an expert on weapons to recognize the sound of its blast. The T-Gewehr was a heavy caliber, high-velocity, bolt-action rifle designed for one very specific purpose: killing tanks. Its half-inch cartridge could peel right through the armor of a British Mark IV tank from one hundred yards out, but it was accurate for up to five times that distance. Aimed at a person, it didn't even have to hit a vital part of their anatomy to kill. Assuming it didn't simply rip the person in half, it would still leave a big enough hole that the trauma would probably kill them regardless of what kind of medical attention they received. Handled improperly or by someone too weak to take the recoil, it would break its wielder's collar bone or dislocate their shoulder. It was the kind of weapon that could catapult a man right the hell off this mortal coil, past heaven, and somewhere into orbit around hell. And somebody out there was very good at using it.

The speakeasy was filling up with smoke as the fire spread. Sadie and Amelia scampered over to join him behind the bar. Their eyes were watering from the burning fumes.

"Any ideas, hotshot?" Amelia asked.

"We've got some options," Jasper said.

"Out with them."

"First, we can stay here and burn to death."

"Pass," Sadie said.

"Second, we could try to force our way out the front windows, get shot in front of the bar."

"Keep talking, O'Malley," Amelia said.

"Finally, we can go out the other door, face ten-to-one odds and get shot behind the bar."

"Great," Sadie said.

Amelia looked around. "There is a fourth option."

"Illuminate me," Jasper said. The fire was rapidly consuming the front entry of the speakeasy, sending out plumes of black, choking smoke. It was becoming difficult to breathe.

"We could take the stairs to the roof and only *maybe* get shot up there."

"I like this plan," Jasper said.

"I do, too," Sadie added. "But I don't see a staircase."

Slipping past Jasper, Amelia moved to the end of the bar and looked up. There was a bare light bulb directly overhead, dark and dusty and seemingly long dead. She stood up on her toes, grabbed the bulb near its base, and yanked downward. The plaster ceiling cracked and gave way in a narrow rectangle. Dust rained down around Amelia as a rickety folding ladder slid down from the ceiling, extending to the floor in front of Jasper and Sadie.

"These places are built with trouble in mind," Amelia explained. "Now get up there before some of our guests get any bright ideas."

Jasper didn't object. He all but shoved Sadie up the ladder. Amelia went next, leaving Jasper alone in the bar as the front windows burst inward and a flurry of grenades thumped inside.

"That's not good." Jasper scurried up the ladder like a spider on a hot skillet. He made it into the speakeasy's attic just as the grenades went off, obliterating half the furniture in the bar. Jagged pieces of shrapnel sawed through the air like hungry little teeth, burrowing into the walls and pincushioning the surviving tables and chairs. Anyone left downstairs would have been shredded into dog food.

Up above, Jasper followed Amelia and Sadie through a small crawl space. Even crouched, Jasper barely fit. Cobwebs brushed his face. The space was hot from the fire below. Smoke was starting to sift up from below.

"Over there," Amelia pointed. There was a small hatch on the far side of the attic, next to some crates, a ruptured keg, and a decapitated mannequin. "C'mon." She pushed past Sadie and thrust the tiny door open. She started to creep outside onto the building's flat roof.

"Wait," Jasper said, halting her. He squeezed past and stuck his head into the cool night air. He peeked around and saw the back alley. It was still packed to overflowing with thugs. Some of them were shifting around uneasily, speaking in what sounded like Russian.

Up on one of the fire escapes was another man, a huge rifle grasped in his hands. The rifle's bipod was balanced on the iron railing, and the man's bearded face was pressed to the gun's sights, all his attention focused on the door leading out to the back alley.

The sniper had long dark hair and a thick, unruly beard that looked like it might have small animals living in it. A gray streak ran through the man's hair like a lightning bolt across the midnight sky. His eyes were sunk deep into their sockets, and his fishy lips were pursed with grim determination. The man was striking, certainly not in a handsome way, but he had an odd magnetic intensity. Even so, he was overshadowed by the massive figure standing next to him on the fire escape. *Edwin Fitzhugh*. He was somewhat worse for wear, which shouldn't have been a surprise, but it was definitely him. One of his legs was locked in an elaborate brace, probably the only thing allowing him to stand, and his broken hand was wrapped with a massive cast. His smashed thumb and black eye rounded out the appearance of someone who had received a sound thrashing.

Amelia stuck her head out next to Jasper's and her eyes narrowed to tiny, predatory slits. Jasper would not have cared to have that gaze focused on him. "Lavrov," she breathed.

"Who?" Jasper whispered.

She nodded. "The one with the rifle. Russian cultist. Freelance assassin. Keeps a crew of disciples with him. Nasty character. Looks like he's got a customer with him."

"Yeah. The customer and I are acquainted."

"What'd you do to twist his panties in a bunch?"

"Long story. If we can make it to that fire escape over there, we can go through that window and make it to street level."

Jasper glanced over at the other side of the building. The strange secret agent types were still out there, but some of them had breached through the shattered windows and entered the bar. It was only a matter of seconds until they noticed the hole in the ceiling and figured out what happened.

Obviously, neither group had expected the other here. Lavrov and his thugs were here for him on Fitzhugh's dime. Jasper still didn't know for sure what the other gunmen wanted or why they wanted it, but killing Jasper and his friends seemed to be part of their designs.

Suddenly, two long, black cars rumbled into the alley behind Lavrov's men. Muzzles poked out of the windows and fired. Several of the Russians went down, their legs kicking. They'd arranged themselves to ambush anyone coming out of the speakeasy, not to defend against an attack from the rear. Caught out in the open, several of them dashed through the bar's back door for cover, and gunfire erupted from inside.

On the railing, Lavrov swiveled around and fired at one of the cars. The shot went cleanly through the passenger door. A gaping hole appeared in the door as the metal crumpled inward; it was as if it had been struck by a massive fist. Jasper knew that the blast from the rifle shot would send spall and bits of the car's metal exterior scissoring into the vehicle in a tiny shrapnel storm. He didn't envy the car's occupants.

The cars looked like they had been fitted to protect their passengers against small arms fire. That might have been adequate against most weapons, but the T-Gewehr was not most weapons. You could hunt a tyrannosaurus with the damn thing; the vehicles were no match for its anti-tank rounds.

Jasper recognized an opportunity when he saw one. With

everyone distracted, Jasper, Sadie, and Amelia could run for it. It was only a short leap from their roof to the fire escape of the apartment building next door. "Let's move," he said. The two women dashed across the roof with Jasper just behind them. He glanced over as the men inside the black cars swarmed out of their vehicles. There were a lot fewer of them than Lavrov's people, but they were organized, and they had the element of surprise.

Of course, organization and surprise weren't everything. Lavrov pulled the trigger on his oversized rifle again, and one of the men from the cars ceased to exist from about neck to navel.

A big figure, almost as big as Fitzhugh, stepped out of the rear car, and Jasper nearly stopped moving. It was Al Dempsey, Basilhart's top lieutenant. The one who handed Percy a certain collection of files. That explained who this third group was. They were part of Basilhart's crew. Were they here to take him out, too?

Dempsey spotted Jasper running across the rooftop, and even from that distance, Jasper saw the glint of recognition in the Pinkerton's eyes. Basilhart's man greeted Jasper by raising his revolver to fire at him. Jasper felt something whiz past his face at the same instant he saw the muzzle flash.

Okay. The Pinkertons were also here to kill him. Jasper was glad that was cleared up. At least the night had some consistency. Had every murdering psychopath in Detroit converged on their position just to kill him? How flattering.

Perhaps Lavrov caught a glimpse of the running figures out of the corner of his eye, or maybe he turned to see what Dempsey had fired at. His severe, penetrating eyes locked onto Jasper, and he racked another thumb-sized bullet into his rifle with unbelievable quickness.

On his own fire escape, Lavrov was roughly level with Jasper. For someone of Lavrov's skill, it would not be a difficult shot. Fitzhugh hobbled around to get the best view. He licked his lips. Lavrov raised his huge rifle. Its bore looked like a howitzer to Jasper. For all the T-Gewehr's enormous power, it was an unwieldy thing, much like the tanks it was built to hunt. The Russian was fast, very fast, but he simply couldn't compensate for the fact that the rifle wasn't meant to be used in a quick draw contest.

Jasper snapped off a shot with his pistol just as Lavrov fixed his sights on the private eye. The pistol round roared through the short distance between Jasper and Lavrov and hit the assassin off center in the chest. Lavrov was pounded backward. His back hit the low fire escape railing, and he went up and over, plunging from sight like a partridge blasted out of the air by a hunter. There was a clatter as the rifle hit the asphalt and a crunch as Lavrov did the same.

Fitzhugh bellowed something, but Jasper was already off and away. The air rippled with bullets from every grade of small arms known to man. Time to move.

Jasper sprinted across the roof and leaped across to the fire escape, leaving him opposite to the sputtering Fitzhugh. Sadie and Amelia were already waiting for him. He tried the window.

Locked.

Using the butt of his pistol, Jasper bashed in the window. Clubbing the rest of the glass away from the edges, he slid through the opening. They all stole through the window, landing in somebody's apartment. The apartment was cramped and disordered, but it was, fortunately, empty.

They went through to the door and quickly exited down to the front lobby. Jasper poked his head outside. He didn't see anyone. The eruption of gunfire had cleared out the streets near the speakeasy.

Amelia's Model T was parked just across the way. She waved them forward, and they scuttled across the road as fast as they could. Jasper and Sadie piled into the passenger seats, and Amelia took the wheel. The Model T's deceptively powerful engine roared to life just as another long, black Pinkerton car slid into view from around the corner. Dempsey's backup.

The Model T's lights flashed on, and the car bolted like a jackrabbit out of a cannon. Basilhart's men poked their heads out the windows and fired a few desultory rounds at the fleeing Ford, but the vehicle sped off and left them in the dust. Jasper and Sadie bounced and slid across the seats as Amelia swerved over most of the road.

"You still want to head to 1332 Van Buren Avenue?" she asked.

"Yes," Jasper responded.

"It's not as if things can be worse there than they are here," Sadie said.

Chapter 20
Things Get Worse

"So tell me," Sadie said to Amelia. "How exactly did you end up as part of Schackel's organization? You don't exactly look typical stormtrooper material."

Amelia laughed. "No, I suppose I don't, and you don't exactly look like your typical geologist. But Schackel's only picky about talent. He doesn't care about established crime families or paying respects to the old country. The man's meritocratic in a very utilitarian way. Most of his gang is German because he had connections to a lot of the Kaiser's finest.

"Even so, he likes to pick up additional people that wouldn't fit in anywhere else. Maybe he feels a certain connection with people who can't find applications for their unusual skills. Maybe he just likes to collect us. I don't really know.

"His accountant, Theodore Geertz, can make a financial statement say whatever he wants. He's a numbers wizard. Even if some crusader at the IRS gets it into his head to go after Schackel, every single sheet of paper he submits will come out clean."

"If he's so good, why'd he join up with Schackel? Why not work for a big firm? He'd probably make just as much."

"He's black. His grandparents were all slaves. Teddy's completely self-taught. There isn't a company in town that'd touch him. Nobody needs to tell him that. It doesn't matter that he can turn a balance sheet inside-out; he'd be mopping a factory floor or cutting hair or down in the mine if not for Schackel. The man gets to be a numbers nerd all day long, and Schackel pays him. He's the happiest man in the world for it."

"How about Lavrov?" Jasper asked. "He seemed awfully good with a rifle. A little too good, in fact. Why doesn't Schackel have a leash on him, too?"

"Yeah, Lavrov's one of the best, but he's crazy."

"Was one of the best. I shot him."

"Trust me. I wouldn't start talking about him in the past tense yet. Lavrov's been shot thirty-seven times before, and he came back and killed everyone responsible each time. It's part of his mystique. Schackel actually scouted him out one time, but never had any interest in retaining his services. The man's damn good at what he does, but he's a liability."

"Define 'liability.' You had half of Detroit's patrol cars worked up to beat the band not twelve hours ago."

"Fair point. Let's see. Where to begin? Lavrov's crazy will toast anybody else's crazy and slap some jam on top for good measure. He was one of Rasputin's disciples, but he went into hiding after his mentor kicked the bucket and the Reds took over Russia. Supposedly, he fought for some of the loyalist groups, but was kicked out for some sort of debauchery.

"Eventually, he made his way here and stuck out his shingle as an assassin for hire. His groupies are really just a freaky little cult rather than an organized gang. Instead of keeping it bottled up, they think the only way to expunge sin from their souls is to let it out for a romp. The greater the sin, the purer they are afterward. I doubt the Roman Senate in its glory days could top the shenanigans Lavrov likes to put on. If you're into orgies and murder, it's a knockout set up.

"Combine Lavrov's persona, his reputation, and his personal brand of hedonism, and he's managed to attract every psychopathic loser in the state. He's like the opposite of Schackel. So long as he can manipulate them and exercise complete control over their lives, Lavrov doesn't care who he recruits.

"They're untrained, but zealous, which makes them dangerous in their own way. Schackel's never had occasion to face off against Lavrov. The Russian would lose, but it would cost us a lot to wipe out his gang of fanatics."

"How about you?" Sadie asked. She seemed to be thawing out a little bit now that Amelia had saved their lives. "How'd you get tied up with Schackel?"

"Believe it or not, my dad was a cop," Amelia said.

"That's an interesting family trajectory," Jasper commented.

"Yeah, but Dad's actually the one who taught me how to drive. My mother died when I was very young, so Dad pretty much raised me. Taught me self-defense and how to handle a gun, too. When I turned thirteen, he started letting me steer his cruiser around an empty lot. It was one of the first cars on the force, and he taught me all the moves the police used to chase people down. It was electrifying. I loved every second of it. Eventually, he saved up enough money to buy an old Ford, and I used to beg him to let me race around in it." Amelia's eyes were wistful.

"Of course, that all changed. Dear old Dad had been drinking himself to death for years, and it finally caught up with him about the time Prohibition took effect. The problem with living fast isn't that you die young, it's that you get old early. Things started to give out. His liver was shot. He needed a lot of medical help, and there was no way to pay for everything.

"That's when I robbed my first store. It wasn't hard. I took Dad's police pistol as a persuader, actually — something the department probably wouldn't have appreciated. One weekend I simply left with the car and came back a few hours later with some money.

"There was no way Dad's pals on the force could have caught me. I'd been tinkering with the car's engine for months, slowly getting more speed and power out of it by adjusting this and that, trading a few parts out, that sort of thing. Plus, I knew every trick in the police playbook. They couldn't have stopped me if they had a month to prepare. I blew through three more stores that month.

"I'm pretty sure Dad figured out what was going on when he started to see reports of a lady bandit in the paper and I somehow kept coming up with money to pay the doctor's bills. At first, I think he thought I was working the streets, so the fact that I was just robbing shops came as a sort of relief to him.

"I'd become quite the little nuisance, so his buddies stepped up patrols in my favorite neighborhoods. The press thought the whole thing was a hoot, and the Commissioner was losing face. And if there's one thing the Commissioner could not stand, it was losing face. That's probably half the reason he's keeping the Detroit Salt details under his hat. It would make the department look bad if anyone knew just what was going on under there.

"I had to outrun a couple of patrols on my next two runs. Easy business, but it told me that things weren't going to get any easier, and I was right. I hit up a few other neighborhoods, but they had protecttion rackets. Schackel has wiped out the gangs that were running them since then, but it made things a lot more dangerous. I walked into one place at the wrong time and had to leap back into my car when some greasy, little troll who was already shaking the place down pulled out a shotgun. That convinced me to go back to my usual haunts. I was practically a celebrity there, if not particularly well-loved.

"One day, I came back home, a pillowcase full of small bills on the seat beside me. I'd managed to leave two prowl cars in the dust by cutting through a construction site, and I was feeling pretty slick.

"But when I got home, there were cops everywhere. I figured the jig was up. Somebody must have recognized me and called me in. There wasn't anything I could do about it. I decided I'd go quietly, turn myself over with some dignity, and maybe a pinch of drama for the papers.

"But when I parked and got out of the car, nobody paid any attention. They weren't even looking in my direction. They were all focused on the apartment. That's when the front doors opened, and a couple of big, beefy cops led Dad out between them.

"Later I found out that they'd managed to trace some of the money back to him. I guess one of the doctors was suspicious where all the funds were coming from when we were obviously flat broke otherwise.

"I rushed up. I think I was crying, but I don't really remember. Dad just looked like a crumpled-up paper sack between those two huge internal affairs officers. They were telling him how it was going to be a scandal and they were going to throw the book at him and how he'd shamed the entire force.

"One of them saw me approaching and tried to push me away. Like I said, Dad taught me self-defense in addition to driving. I broke three of his fingers and dislocated his ribs before six more policemen tackled me.

"When they searched the car, they found the money and put two and two together pretty quickly. I ended up doing a short stint in the ladies' klink. The trial judge took an odd sort of pity on me I guess, so I spent less than a year there even though it could have been a lot longer.

"Dad died a few days after they brought him in. Just dropped dead of a massive heart attack about the same time I was being arraigned.

"Once I was out, I didn't have too many prospects. I tried to get a job as a seamstress, but nobody would hire me with my record. Normally, I might've gotten married and lived quietly at home, but all the men I had any interest in were far too squeamish to try courting a former jailbird, and I wasn't interested in any of the men who were.

"That's when I got a letter from Schackel. It was embossed with gold leaf, like the kind you might send to a queen, and it read like a fan letter. He wanted to meet me and possibly give me a job. I'll tell you, I wasn't about to turn down an offer like that. Not at that point.

"Schackel wanted to bring me on as his personal driver. Some of his rivals had tried to shoot his vehicles up in the past, and he needed someone who could maneuver under pressure. I happened to be the best, so he asked me on."

"Nobody gives you any trouble?" Sadie asked.

Jasper thought back to her tale of the unfortunate Dr. Rumson.

"Don't get me wrong. I have to put up with plenty of less-than-sterling behavior, but Schackel's people are used to tight discipline, and I'm high enough up the food chain that they know not to cause too much nuisance. They know Schackel would gut them for stirring up trouble, and that works as a pretty strong detriment."

"Maybe the USGS could learn a thing or two from your boss," Sadie said.

"We're getting close to the address," Amelia said.

"Park out of sight," Jasper ordered.

Amelia killed the Model T's headlights and slipped the black vehicle into the pool of darkness between a couple of broken streetlamps.

The address Ackley had given them was not located in the best part of Detroit. The lot was a large warehouse, nearly identical to the other structures lining the street. A few weeds poked out of the dirt surrounding the lot and through cracks in the asphalt. A pair of large trucks sat next to the building along with a collection of cars.

"Looks like people are still working," Sadie said.

"At this time of night?" Amelia looked skeptical and checked her watch. It was approaching midnight.

"Let's take a look around," Jasper said, sliding out of the vehicle. He shut the door and stepped back into the shadows. Sadie and Amelia followed.

A perimeter fence lined the entire lot. Jasper circled the lot once, remaining behind cover when he could.

The building itself was a fairly standard, if cheaply constructed, warehouse. Its walls were made of corrugated tin, blotchy and discolored in places. There were no windows to speak of, and the steepled roof sagged in places. A large sign, almost unreadable with rot and rust, claimed the building in the name of the Detroit Salt Combine. Even if the building had seen better days, the chain link fence surrounding it was new and in very good condition. It was topped with several reams of barbed wire. There were only two gates, a large sliding one to allow vehicle access and a smaller one for people. Both of them were fitted with some of the finest locking mechanisms money could buy. There was a small guard booth next to the big gate, but it was empty.

Jasper looked around with suspicion. The place was locked down tight, and there were apparently people inside, but he didn't see any guards. He was surprised that there weren't at least a couple of rented watchmen to man the gates. Really, though, he would have expected a troupe of Basilhart's Pinkertons prowling the grounds like barnyard tomcats.

Instead, the place was abandoned.

"I've seen banks with cheaper locks than this," Amelia whispered, examining the gates.

Jasper lifted one of the locks delicately.

"I don't suppose you brought any wire cutters?"

"Something better, actually." He pulled a lock pick out of his pocket. The lock popped open in Jasper's hand. The smaller gate swung open on well-oiled hinges.

"You know, if you're ever looking for a job, I bet Schackel would triple your salary."

"I'm happy on my side of the law, thank you very much."

"We're breaking into a secure, private facility. Are you sure you operate on the right side of the law, Jasper?" Sadie asked.

"I didn't say I work on the right side of the law. I work on my side of the law."

"I think I like you, Mister O'Malley," Amelia said as they stepped through the gate. Their feet crunched on the gravel as they stepped onto the premises.

"Why would Ackley send us here?" Sadie looked around. "It looks like a pretty normal storage depot."

Jasper peeked into the guard house. There was a folding table with a half-finished game of solitaire and a newspaper set up next to a chair. A modest pile of cigarette butts sat in an ashtray nearby. It all looked very normal except for the small pool of blood drying on the floor.

"We might have company," Jasper said. He pointed to the puddle of blood. "Probably the same mystery crew that barged into the speakeasy. Lavrov and Fitzhugh wouldn't have any interest in the place, and Basilhart wouldn't turn on his employers."

Jasper thought back to the men in strange body armor wielding unfamiliar guns. They were clearly trained. However, he had no idea what they wanted beyond killing him.

"Who *are* these people?" Amelia asked.

"I don't know, but they must have started here before moving on to Schackel's place. They act more like a military unit than a gang or a rogue detective agency. Are there any mercenary groups based in Detroit? Bounty hunters, perhaps?"

"None that I can think of."

"Alright, let's be careful," Jasper said.

They crept forward, watching the building for any signs of activity. There was nothing. That might have been a good sign, or it might not have been.

Jasper noticed something interesting. There were tire tracks in the dirt near the building. Several large vehicles had been here and had only recently left. The tracks were still very well-defined, not at all eroded by the wind or natural subsidence. Only a few hours old.

They reached the warehouse's large sliding door. It was closed tight. A much simpler padlock and chain kept the door shut. Jasper made short work of it and slid the door incrementally open. There was a surprising amount of resistance. He pressed an eye to the gap.

"What's in there?" Amelia asked.

Rather than answering directly, Jasper simply pulled the door open all the way. Sadie and Amelia both jumped back as a pile of fresh corpses tumbled out of the door in a tangle of limbs.

"Are ... are these the missing miners?" Amelia looked a bit green and for good reason. There were about thirty bodies, and it was obvious that they had been lined up facing the door and mowed down by automatic gunfire. Jasper had sometimes seen similar things from the air during the war, just a solid line of dead infantrymen sprawled in a line in the middle of No Man's Land after they charged into a zone of machinegun crossfire.

This was different, though. This was a mass execution, a regular massacre.

Chapter 21
Countdown to Midnight

"No, these aren't the miners," Jasper said. There were several distinct groups amid the corpses. One group was younger and dressed in cheap suits. Jasper pointed. "Unless I miss my guess, those fellows were the Pinkertons guarding the place."

A couple of the dead men were older. Maybe not too old to work in a mine, but they were dressed in much nicer clothing than the Pinkertons. Furthermore, they were soft and pudgy, slowly melting into fat with age. Salt miners, almost by definition, were tough, brawny creatures covered in callouses.

"Most likely Detroit Salt's people. Executives. Probably here to oversee whatever was going on at this place."

The remainder of the bodies appeared to be scientists. Many of them were wearing lab coats, now stained uniformly crimson. Jasper spotted some tweed among the charnel house ruins at his feet.

"Oh my God," Sadie said. "It's Doctor Winston."

"Who?" Jasper and Amelia asked at the same time.

"He used to work for USGS. Worked with my uncle back when they were both just grad students out running wild with the survey teams. I'd heard he quit, but he must have been doing work for Detroit Salt." She trailed off.

Jasper put an arm over her shoulder. His touch was slightly cold.

"I'm sorry, Sadie." She brushed his arm off.

He leaned over and patted down the better-dressed bodies. Feeling something, he pulled out the dead man's wallet. His license identified him as Gerald Ransom. Jasper recognized the name as one of the higher ups in Detroit Salt. If he was in charge of this facility, he was probably also responsible for hiring Basilhart and his crew. It appeared he and Detroit Salt had been outmaneuvered in this little game, though.

"Let's go," Sadie said. "Maybe we can at least figure out why he was here."

The exterior of the warehouse was deceptive. The corrugated door was so heavy and difficult to move because a steel plate was screwed onto its backside. The rest of the warehouse was similarly retrofitted, effectively turning the place into a fortress. Whoever had cleaned the place out was either very stealthy or had inside help.

Jasper was more interested in what he saw scattered around the warehouse. Several filing cabinets had been overturned, sending a blizzard of notes and papers across the floor. Some of them were sodden with blood.

Among many things in the warehouse that caught Jasper's attention, the most immediately impressive was Ackley's cage. It was made from six-inch-thick steel bars slotted firmly into an equally impressive base and top. Altogether, it was somewhat bigger than a freight train car. Jasper spotted several latches where the thing could be collapsed for transport, but otherwise the cage looked like something a dinosaur zoo might use.

In another corner of the warehouse stood a long stainless steel table. A corpse lay on the table, a corpse that was similar to that of Gottschalk. If anything, it was even more thoroughly mutated than Schackel's man had become. Someone had poked and prodded at this one in their own clandestine autopsy. Chunks and snippets sat in sample jars filled with formaldehyde. A few of the pieces were moving, tapping at the glass like particularly stupid goldfish as they attempted to escape.

Upon closer examination, Jasper noted that someone had pumped the creature so full of lead that entire sections of its body were little more than gummy meat and torn tissue. Jasper assumed that this was the handy work of one of the armed Pinkertons patrolling the tunnels with the miners. Maybe the man had survived this encounter or maybe not. There were shreds of blood-stained fabric, like the kind that might be used to make a suit of middling quality, stuck to the creature's gnarled teeth. Mostly likely, the Pinkerton was no longer among the living.

"There's something you don't see every day," Amelia said.

"Spend more time with us and you might," Sadie replied.

For now, Jasper ignored the corpse. He preferred not to tamper with it and risk another incident like the one in the police morgue. There were airtight workstations lined up against one wall, like the type people used when mixing dangerous chemicals that could give off toxic gases. Each box had an object inside. Jasper moved to get a closer look.

All the objects were mechanical in nature, their purpose Delphic and inscrutable. They'd clearly been removed from the corpse and placed in the isolation chambers for safe keeping. Bits of flesh still clung to many of them. The objects seemed to be constructed piecemeal, just lumps of scrap from disparate sources that had been recombined in enormously complex ways. For some reason, they reminded Jasper of a shipwreck survivor on a desert island using bits of scrap from the wreckage to create makeshift tools and comforts. Some of them appeared to be supplemental mechanical organs. Others served no purpose that Jasper could discern. They were all frightfully alien-looking.

Amelia picked up a sheet of paper off the ground and read a few lines. "Anybody know what a 'kobold' is?"

"What have you got?" Jasper asked.

"It's a Detroit Salt report tracking something's movement through the tunnels. They're calling it a 'kobold.' I assume that's our creature."

"I've heard a bit about kobolds," Sadie chimed in. "Supposedly, they would lead medieval miners through the tunnels by tapping on the walls of the shafts. Some people thought they were good spirits warning miners about imminent cave ins. Most people considered them malevolent hobgoblins, sort of like evil, tunneling gnomes, leading miners to poisonous ores. We actually derived the word 'cobalt' from kobold because it's usually mixed in with deadly arsenic.

"Lots of cultures had their own version of the creatures. Kobolds themselves are from Germany, but Tommyknockers, tsuchigumos, pookas, and other creatures were common explanations for the mysterious sounds and calamities that constantly surrounded pre-modern mines. Sometimes miners would leave food in the tunnels to try to appease the tunnel monsters. People used to always blame kobolds for whenever there was a tunnel collapse or gas explosions."

"According to this paper, those things over there," Amelia gestured at the body on the table, "are the kobold's doing. Apparently, it can either inject you directly with some sort of mutagen or spray pheromones and you turn into one of those. They're like ants serving their queen."

"I think I'd prefer to just get eaten," Sadie shuddered.

"As would I," Jasper said.

"Yeah, well, hold onto your socks, boys and girls. It gets worse. The thing has some sort of, and I quote 'corrupting influence' that comes from just spending too much time in the mine. That's why those little trinkets there are under glass. They were starting to affect people's heads. Apparently, you'll slowly turn into one of those things even if you just spend too much time down there."

"Gottschalk," Jasper said.

"You think that's what happened to him?"

"Schackel said he started to act erratically, wanted to spend more and more time in the mine after he was stationed down there. He didn't have any mechanical upgrades, so the kobold itself didn't get ahold of him. He must have killed himself when he realized what was happening to him."

"It might explain why some of the miners stuck on even after the disappearances started, too. They're not operating entirely of their own free will anymore," Sadie said.

"However the kobold works, Detroit Salt was obviously studying it. I guess they were going to use Ackley's cage to catch it."

"But why?" Amelia asked.

"I think I know," Jasper said. He walked over to one of the tables. Three small objects were sitting on the table, none of them much bigger than Jasper's thumbnail, but all worth more than his entire life's pay. More of the richly colored red diamonds.

"I assumed Detroit Salt wasn't involved with this because, as Pecos said, the salt mine was their only real asset. Without it, they'd quickly go out of business. That wasn't entirely correct, though. They had another asset once the kobold showed up."

"The diamonds," Sadie said.

"Precisely." Jasper took the diamond he'd borrowed from Renfield and set it next to the others. "By keeping the mines open, Detroit Salt could harvest these diamonds. If they could collect enough of these, they'd rival De Beers almost overnight. Just one of these rocks is probably more valuable than a decade's worth of salt."

"So is the kobold digging up the diamonds? Making them with those contraptions? They're obviously connected with this monster, but where exactly are they coming from?" Amelia asked.

"That I don't know yet, but Detroit Salt is putting peoples' lives on the line to get them. Any thoughts, Sadie?"

"None yet. Maybe we should all search for some answers. There's a lot of paperwork scattered around here. It might provide us some clues."

"Good thinking," Jasper said. "Search the warehouse and gather anything that looks like it might be useful. At some point, another shift of Basilhart's Pinkertons are going to come by, and you can bet they won't be happy to find us here."

The three of them split up and started rooting through papers. The place had apparently been sacked by whoever killed the people working here, but Jasper couldn't tell if anything had been taken. And they had left the bodies where they fell rather than disposing of them? Who on earth were these people?

Jasper dove into the papers, looking for answers. There weren't many to be had. He found reports on the chemical compounds found inside the diamonds, as well as assessments of their value. It was all very standard fare. What surprised Jasper was that the diamonds themselves hadn't been taken. They were enormously valuable, all the Detroit Salt papers agreed on that point. So far, he didn't have any definitive motive for the group that had done this. One possible answer was that they wanted the diamonds for themselves or their bosses. Certainly, a good many people would be willing to kill for such a valuable commodity. But the evidence didn't add up. They hadn't taken the three diamonds that were here unless there was a much larger cache that they'd made off with and simply forgotten the remainder. That seemed unlikely, though. This group was very well organized and equipped. If they were here for the diamonds, they weren't likely to forget any.

Besides, why would they then go after Jasper and his friends at the speakeasy? They couldn't have known he'd be there unless somebody told them. Given how they cleaned this place out, it was much more likely that they'd shown up at the speakeasy for Ackley, and Jasper, Sadie, and Amelia had merely been targets of opportunity.

He picked up another sheet of paper and read a few lines. It was thick with scientific jargon, but he understood the gist of it well enough. The paper suggested that the creature had been embedded in the salt field for untold millennia, some atavistic throwback from before the dawn of history. Or maybe an alien. Or maybe just a straight-up demon. The paper used very precise and scientific terms to explain that no one had a damned clue beyond the fact that the thing was very old. That paper was written on Detroit Salt letterhead, and it was dated to about the time the disappearances started.

Someone had added a handwritten addendum directing the reader to look at Dr. Winston's report. After a couple of minutes of scrounging, Jasper found the former USGS man's notes. Apparently, he was the one who termed the creature a kobold, and he thought the monster was some kind of bio-mechanical organism, something that normally lived much deeper in the earth.

While pulp stories frequently used the trope of prehistoric monsters locked in the ice thawing out and wreaking havoc, salt also had preservative qualities. That's why it was used to keep food from spoiling, after all.

Jasper turned around to show the paper to Sadie. She was gone. He looked around. Amelia was sifting through what appeared to be a pile of internal financial statements. "Sadie?"

There was no response. Amelia looked up from her pile of papers, too. They were suddenly aware that they were the only two in the main part of the warehouse. He checked his watch. It was about a minute to midnight.

The warehouse had a few storage closets built into the back wall, but other than that, there was nowhere to go except out one of the back doors. Jasper had been so engrossed in Dr. Winston's paper that he'd lost track of his surroundings. Did she go outside to check something out?

He walked over to the door, Amelia following him, and stuck his head out. Nothing. "You check those closets, I'll check these," Jasper said, gesturing. Amelia walked over and opened a closet door at the same time Jasper opened one of his.

"Uh, Jasper?"

"Yeah. This one, too." His closet was filled with a large canister-shaped object rigged up with wires and a cheap clock. Unless he was mistaken, that was a fire bomb. A very large one.

Balls.

That explained why the crew that cleared this place out didn't bother to clean up or hide the bodies. This mess was rigged to dispose of itself, and judging from the display attached to the bomb, it was set to go off at midnight, meaning they had maybe forty-five seconds to escape to a safe distance, which was probably at least one city block away.

"Let's get out of here," Jasper said, already halfway out the door. Amelia didn't need to be told twice. They had other problems, though.

The sound of tires crunching across gravel reached them. A car door slammed, and the entrance to the warehouse rolled open. Al Dempsey stared at Jasper in stupefied surprise for a full second before drawing his gun. The Pinkertons were back, fresh from their clash at Schackel's speakeasy.

Jasper and Amelia dove out of the way as gunfire threw sparks off the walls and floors. The sound was deafening in the steel-plated confines of the secret Detroit Salt laboratory. They were outnumbered and out of time.

Thirty seconds until midnight.

Snaking his pistol around the edge of the desk, Jasper fired off the entire eight-round magazine in rapid succession. He didn't have a good shot at any of the Pinkertons pouring into the warehouse, so he just fired blind.

Basilhart's men ducked out of the way for a second, which was all the time Jasper and Amelia needed. They sprang up and darted out the back door as more gunfire smote the air. Jasper slammed the door shut and scampered around the side of the building, his heels kicking up gravel. They needed to get away. And fast. But the Pinkertons, who hadn't discovered the bombs yet, had other plans.

Two Pinkertons dashed around to cut them off. Jasper was out of bullets, and there was no time to reload. Amelia shot the first Pinkerton, but the second took cover behind one of the nearby parked cars. The surviving man took potshots at them, forcing Jasper and Amelia to duck behind one of the big cargo trucks.

Footsteps thudded inside the building, chasing after them. In a few seconds, they'd be cut off and annihilated before the bombs could even go off.

Amelia smashed in one of the trucks windows and unlocked it. "Get in," she shouted, all but picking Jasper up and shoving him inside the cab. Jasper didn't object. He leaned over and unlocked the driver's door as she scurried around to the other side of the truck. She piled in and leaned over to pry open the truck's wiring.

Fifteen seconds until midnight.

Almost immediately, the truck roared to life. Jasper was impressed. She kicked the hotwired truck into gear, and it roared forward like a diesel-powered dragon.

A very slow dragon. Maybe an old, arthritic dragon with two bum knees and a cane.

Twisting the wheel, Amelia sent the truck snorting through the parking lot. She didn't bother to maneuver; she simply barreled along in a straight line, plowing the smaller cars aside. The Pinkerton who had taken cover was forced to leap out of the way to avoid being crushed.

Gunfire chased after the truck from the side and behind. One of the back tires exploded in a spray of rubber, sending the truck slewing. Momentum kept them grinding forward, but it made it harder for the lumbering vehicle to gather more speed. Jasper slammed a new magazine into his pistol and emptied it almost as quickly, trying to keep the Pinkertons at bay.

The truck smashed into the perimeter fence, plowing through it with a screech of metal. Barbed wire wrapped itself around the truck's grill and trailed behind the vehicle as it dragged a length of the fence behind it.

Five seconds remaining.

Amelia poured as much power as she could into the truck as it bumped onto the road, but they clearly weren't going to make it a safe distance away from the rigged warehouse. A bullet starred the windshield with a spider web of cracks. Steam billowed out from under the truck's hood where the radiator had been pierced, but the vehicle continued to limp away from the blast zone.

Jasper saw the light a split second before he felt the heat or heard the blast. It was like they had been in a bubble of darkness that suddenly popped. The entire street lit up, bright as high noon. All the shadows suddenly evaporated out of existence. Then the blast hit. The truck lifted off its rear wheels and came down hard like a bucking bronco. Jasper slammed against the door in a blizzard of glass as the truck tipped over onto its side. Amelia landed on top of him.

Fiery debris started to rain down all around them. It looked like a disastrous Fourth of July celebration meets Gomorrah. The truck's cab protected them from the worst of the blast and some of the smaller pieces of debris, but a lot of the rubble wasn't small, though. A fiery mass landed directly next to the truck. Jasper realized it was one of the long, black Pinkerton cars, blown into a nearly unrecognizable husk of flaming metal. It bore no more resemblance to a car than a swatted lump of goop bore to a healthy fly.

More debris arced into the street and nearby buildings. The warehouse's steel door, on fire and twisted roughly into a bowtie shape, crashed through the wall of one of the depots across the street. Flames began to pour out of the second building as its contents ignited.

Jasper felt the heat from the blast. It was hot. Horribly hot. Turbo-crazy-flaming-taco-truck hot. Hotter than Satan's cheer squad. Hotter than high noon on the surface of the sun.

Most of the truck's windshield had been blown out by the initial blast, so Jasper was able to easily kick out the last few jagged edges. He squirmed out from under Amelia and crawled out through the gap.

The asphalt was blistering and covered with shattered glass. Jasper's palms tried to stick to the surface like burning meat on a hot griddle. Closer to the obliterated Detroit Salt warehouse, the street was just a river of melted, bubbling tar.

Leaning down, Jasper helped Amelia out of the truck. The entire neighborhood was starting to go up. Something exploded in the distance. Acrid fumes made their eyes water and their lungs ache. They made their way down the street, the soles of their shoes sticking to the hot street as they moved. Amelia held a sleeve over her face, coughing as the contents of the warehouses all around them went up, adding to the fiery maelstrom.

The blast had wiped out the Pinkerton guards and just about everything else nearby. All the evidence, all of Detroit Salt's experiments, everything was gone. Someone was not playing around.

After a few minutes, they made it through the worst of the firestorm. The entire neighborhood was quickly becoming a hell furnace. Sirens clanged in the distance, drawing nearer. That would be the fire department, not that they'd be able to do much about this catastrophe.

Jasper turned around to look at the flaming, cratered remains of the Detroit Salt warehouse. A great deal of potential evidence had gone up in the inferno, but Jasper wasn't thinking about that.

Sadie ...

Amelia put an arm around his narrow form. She looked at his grim, glass-sliced, soot-blackened face. What she saw there didn't look like sadness. Burning red in the reflection of the fires, it looked a lot more like anger.

Chapter 22
Look on My Works, Ye Mighty, and Despair

Even as explosions rocked the surface of Detroit, the kobold paid no attention. Her ultra-acute senses could detect the minute vibrations of the explosions, even a quarter of a mile under the earth.

If she wanted to, she could zero in on the rumble of individual freight trains as they brought materials into Detroit and products out. It was how she had known to send her minions out to snatch the tanks and other equipment from the surface.

She still hadn't pulled those toys apart yet. They were the biggest and most interesting objects her little changelings had acquired, so she was saving them until she needed their unique parts and mechanisms. For now, they were stashed away for safe keeping.

Right now, she had bigger concerns than either the tanks or the distant explosions. She huddled over something attached to the mine wall. It was a slimy, twitching sack. This is what she had been waiting for.

The sack was made out of a pulsating, veiny membrane. A thin cord of organic material kept the sack anchored to the wall. There were several dozen beach ball-sized objects inside the sack, dangling off the central cord like bunches of grapes.

More sacks were stuck all over the walls of the tunnel. Some of them hung from the ceiling, dripping juices onto the ground. The sacks throbbed and pulsed unnaturally.

All her workers were currently busy tending to the sacks. Even her personal retinue of groomers was busy with the task.

Suddenly, the sack in front of the kobold split open, sliced apart from the inside. The round objects inside were starting to burst apart. Several tiny versions of the kobold spilled out. They were perfect miniatures of their mother, fully formed and already crawling away on their oversized tarsal claws. She bent down to examine one as it tried to scamper away into the darkness.

It looked vaguely like a spider that had grown to approximately the size of a Boston terrier, an arachnophobe's worst nightmare. Its skin glistened with unspeakable fluids, matting its stiff bristles to its body.

Sensing an enormous presence looming above it, the tiny kobold nymph looked up and made a soft mewling sound. The noise cut off as the mother kobold crunched down on the infant with her bear-trap teeth. The tiny creature popped like a pressed olive in her cavernous jaws.

More of the miniature kobolds scurried across the floor in a mass exodus away from their brood chamber. Many of them hatched out of their eggs and immediately pounced on one another, slashing and tearing with both teeth and claws. Hundreds of them were torn apart within their first few seconds of life. Any that were victorious over their siblings but injured in the process were quickly devoured by their compatriots in a flash of evolution at its most brutal. Any of the kobolds that did not represent the very pinnacle of their species died almost instantly.

Some of the workers couldn't get out of the way quickly enough as more of the oothecae exploded open with horrible, writhing life. The kobold nymphs instinctively attacked the first thing they came into contact with. In large groups, they ripped into the much larger workers like piranhas tearing apart cattle.

Each of the kobold nymphs faced a two-pronged threat. They had to fend off their ravenous siblings as soon as they were born, but they also had to contend with their matriarch. She bent down and shoveled dozens of them into her mouth at a time. Wet popping and smacking noises emanated from her mouth as she chewed the spider-like babies to mush. Juices dribbled out of her lipless maw. She needed to regain her strength after caring for the nest for so long, and she couldn't even dent their numbers. There were thousands more for every nymph she ate. Teeth and claws flashed in the bedlam. They would spread outward, fighting each other until there were only a few left. Whittling their numbers down from hundreds of thousands to only a handful. Eventually, they would seek out new crevices in the earth for their own long hibernation. For now, though, they were all simply so much prey.

This is what she had been waiting for. Once she no longer had to attend to her brooding chamber, the great kobold queen could focus on making these tunnels her own. Before, she only took what she needed to sustain herself. Now, she could exercise total dominion over the mine.

Of course, there were still threats, though. The creatures that had killed one of her workers earlier proved that. They had come from above, from the surface, and her realm could never be truly secure with that looming danger. Even though they had sustained her thus far, she would need to eliminate most of the surface creatures in the region, keeping only a stock for her personal feeding.

Well, that's what her warriors were for. She spurted a cloud of pheromones, and shapes more twisted than any of the workers materialized out of the shadows. They unfolded themselves out of crevices, slid down ropes of silk from their spinnerets, or crawled across the ceiling to assemble in front of her. They waited adoringly, ready for any command she gave.

She did not disappoint them. Another spray of pheromones, and they dispersed to carry out their tasks.

The kobold waited, pleased. She had put a great deal of effort into her warriors. Machinery and twisted flesh came together to create the ultimate minion. They would not fail her now that the time was ripe.

Chapter 23
Smorgasmorgue

"Is Captain Renfield back yet?" Jasper asked Officer Hinkmeyer.

Hinkmeyer handed Jasper a mug of steaming coffee. It was nearly 7:00 a.m. Jasper took the coffee and stared at it. He didn't bother to sip. The smell alone told him that the brew was strong enough to knock the humps off a camel.

"Nope. He wanted to check something out at the mine. Didn't say when he'd be back." They were back in the morgue under the police headquarters. The room was significantly fuller than the last time Jasper had visited. With no one to attend to the new arrivals, the corpses had simply piled up.

There were guests of nearly every stripe. Aside from Grainger, the former medical examiner, Pecos was still here, as was Gottschalk, and the creature. Someone had hosed down the green tiles that covered the floor and walls, but there was still some viscera stuck to the ceiling from Jasper's last visit. They were going to need somebody with a ladder and a mop for that. Jasper saw a group of Lavrov's men stacked on a tarp on the floor. There was simply not enough space for everyone, so the medical examiner's assistants had started sorting bodies apples to apples until something could be arranged. Lavrov's men were riddled with bullets.

On the opposite side of the room were some equally bullet-riddled Pinkertons. There were fewer of them. Jasper didn't know if that meant they'd gotten the better of things in the fight at the speakeasy or if there simply weren't as many of them to kill. Judging from the relative size of the corpse piles, though, it was evident that a lot of Lavrov's men had gotten away.

The bodies that were getting the most attention were those of the mysterious men who had first assaulted the speakeasy and killed Ackley. There weren't many of them, so apparently they had done their best to collect their dead. Jasper doubted it was for reasons of honor. Odds were, the bodies they had stolen away had probably been dumped in a lye-filled ditch somewhere, rapidly being rendered unidentifiable. The corpses they couldn't collect were already burned beyond easy identification.

"You willing to share who you think these guys are yet?" Hinkmeyer took a sip of his own coffee and made a face.

"I've got ideas but no proof, and nothing that wouldn't sound stark raving mad." Things were starting to take shape in Jasper's mind, and he didn't like it. Not one bit. It would make for some ungodly paperwork afterward as well.

"Have your men finished analyzing these bodies yet?" He pointed to the group of deceased gunmen.

"Yeah, and they didn't get a whole lot back. None of them had any sort of identification on them whatsoever. We're still going through our fingerprint records, but nobody is holding their breath on that front."

"I'm not surprised," Jasper commented.

"No dental records on this fellow, obviously." Hinkmeyer pointed to the man whose head had been taken off with Lavrov's anti-tank rifle.

"Any unusual scars? Things that might help identify them?"

"Our first fellow here does have something interesting. It'll help, but probably not tonight. Seems he had the name of his alma mater tattooed around his bicep. We've tried calling them up, but they were closed for the night, so it'll be a while before we gain access to their records. Plus, even if they have photos of him, they'll probably be from the shoulders up, which is a lot less useful than it normally would be."

"Which school did he go to?"

"None less than the hallowed halls of Stanford. Bit unusual, dontcha think? Somebody comes out of a place like that and joins some sort of — I don't know — paramilitary group? Gang?"

It was unusual, and it only seemed to confirm Jasper's suspicions about what was going on. Hardly definitive proof, but it fit in with the current breadcrumb trail of evidence he'd been following.

"Have your men finished sorting out the bodies from the warehouse explosion?"

"Not even close," Hinkmeyer said. "It's ... it's kind of a mess."

Jasper was aware of what the cops at the warehouse were probably dealing with.

With their enamel, the teeth were the toughest, most resilient part of the human body. Some of those people at the epicenter of the inferno, the cops might only find their teeth. Everything else, including the bones, would have disappeared in the impromptu cremation.

"I'm sorry about your geologist friend." Hinkmeyer patted Jasper on the shoulder.

The detective's face grew longer. He shook his head, clearing out unhealthy thoughts like bats rattled out of an attic. "What about my driver? Can you release her?"

Amelia was being held at the city jail due to her connections with Detroit's most-wanted gangster. She hadn't told any of the cops that Jasper was also technically working for Schackel at the moment, and he wasn't about to volunteer that information to Hinkmeyer.

"Sorry. You're not getting her back. Renfield put in orders to arrest anyone connected with Gerhard Schackel on sight. It's been a long time coming."

"I need her," Jasper said. "She's the only other person I can trust who knows what's going on."

"I'm not sure I would trust anyone affiliated with Schackel. She has quite a record. Did she tell you about the robberies she was involved with when she was younger?"

"As a matter of fact, yes. I don't care. I trust her, and I need help with what's going on. Look, I know what you and Renfield are up to. With all this chaos, you're just trying to keep me here so I don't gum up your investigation."

"Hey now. I don't think that's entirely —"

The sound of gunshots erupted directly outside the front door of the police station, interrupting Hinkmeyer. Jasper hadn't allowed himself to be disarmed this time. His pistol appeared in his hand.

A few more shots sounded. There were evenly spaced and deliberate, not the frantic *pop-pop-pop* of a gun battle. Someone was trying to get attention, not start a fight.

A second later, the sound of screeching tires reached Jasper's ears. Whoever it was, they weren't sticking around.

"I'll check it out. You stay here," Hinkmeyer said, starting for the door.

"I think not," Jasper responded, following the officer. There wasn't much Hinkmeyer could do to stop him short of chaining Jasper to one of the tables, and that wasn't about to happen.

They piled up the stairs. Some of the other cops joined them to see what the commotion was about. They burst out the front door as a group.

There was a body at the base of the stairs.

Some of the cops shooed curious pedestrians away from the scene as they roped it off. Jasper scanned the small crowd for threats, but he saw nothing more than a few harmless insomniac rubberneckers.

The corpse was a man laying face down on the sidewalk, his face mashed into the concrete. From where Jasper was standing, it didn't look as if he'd been shot. He'd apparently been beaten to death with a blunt object. His skull was dented in, and it looked like both his arms were broken at the elbow. His leg also looked like it had been crudely snapped. Only the one, though. The man's other leg was missing below the knee. Jasper's heart sank.

Hinkmeyer also took in the scene. "Poor bastard," he said. "Looks like somebody did a number on him and then dumped him here to make a statement."

The cops already working the scene flipped the body over to check for a pulse, and Jasper's fears were confirmed. The dead man was Tycho Vedel.

Someone must have driven to Chicago, grabbed him, killed him, and dumped him here. There were probably quite a few people the Attican Detective Agency had collared who probably wouldn't mind seeing Vedel dead, but so far as Jasper knew, only one of them was in Detroit, and only one would be interested in leaving Tycho's body specifically in a place where Jasper would be sure to find it.

Fitzhugh.

There was a note attached to the body. It had been nailed to the man's chest like a psychotic version of Martin Luther posting one of his theses. The note was splattered with blood, but it was legible enough.

We have your friend. Hotel Montclair. Room 217. Come alone.

Just then, a police cruiser came barreling down the road and screeched to a stop in front of the headquarters. A cop jumped out and flailed his arms at his fellow officers. "Somebody's hit the jail! They cut the phone lines and blew up most of the east wall. I dunno who they are or who they were trying to spring, but half the damn prisoners have escaped! We need everyone who can hold a gun over there now!"

The note didn't mean anything to the cops yet. Until they figured out Vedel's identity, this would probably just look like another senseless gangland killing, but the message was clear to Jasper.

The city jail was where Amelia was being kept. *We have your friend.* It wasn't a jailbreak. It was a kidnapping.

Hotel Montclair. Where this crazy journey started when Jasper talked to Victor Pecos for the first time.

Most of the cops in the crowd moved toward the garage, readying the paddy wagons so they could pick up as many escaped prisoners as possible. The morning's paperwork could wait.

Hinkmeyer started to move with them, but then remembered he was supposed to guard Jasper. "C'mon, we better stay here in case anything else comes up." He turned around, but Jasper was gone.

Looking around, Hinkmeyer saw that the bloodstained note had been snatched off the body. Frantic, he scanned the area.

There was going to be hell to pay for this if he let the detective escape.

Chapter 24
Hell to Pay

Lavrov grimaced as one of his followers tended to the wound in his chest. A few inches lower and the bullet would have pierced his heart. The injury would have killed a lot of men outright; however, Lavrov wasn't a lot of men, and he wasn't dead. Mostly, he was just pissed. His big, bushy beard only seemed to amplify the scowl on his face. He'd survived worse, but the wound still throbbed and dribbled blood. Lavrov wanted to get up and pace the hotel room angrily, but his medic was still busy scrubbing the hole with disinfectant. Instead, he sat and frowned at the beautiful woman tied to a chair in the center of the room.

She still wore her civilian clothes rather than prison garb. The jail hadn't had time to process her before Lavrov's team struck. A gag was cinched firmly over her mouth to prevent her from speaking, and her limbs were strapped to the heavy wooden chair. A pair of Lavrov's men stood with their guns trained on her.

"O'Malley should have been here by now," Fitzhugh said. They'd been waiting all day. They'd dumped the body that morning, and now darkness was setting in again. Fitzhugh perched on one of the room's posh chairs. The unfortunate furniture creaked and strained every time Fitzhugh shifted his weight. He sat awkwardly in his casts.

Lavrov's scowl blossomed into an even more intense glower, as if he was trying to make Fitzhugh's head explode with his mind. The big man seemed impervious to such treatment.

"I know his type. The detective will try something clever. He is making us wait, hoping our defenses will waiver," Lavrov said. He got to his feet. He was slightly wobbly from blood loss, but that would soon pass. Shrugging on a long black cassock made from finely woven silk, Lavrov walked over and ran a finger down Amelia's cheek.

"Are your men prepared for something clever? I wasn't exactly impressed at the speakeasy." Fitzhugh fidgeted in his casts, trying to get comfortable.

The Russian turned slowly toward Fitzhugh. "What happened at the speakeasy was a fluke. Here, we have every advantage. My men have the lobby covered. They have the stairs covered. They have the hall covered. They have the roof covered. Clever is good, but it does not work miracles. Clever does not outrun a bullet. He cannot save his woman without coming through some entrance in this hotel, and every avenue is guarded. If he should decide to bring a swarm of your police, we shall simply kill her and escape." Lavrov made a slashing gesture with his hand.

Fitzhugh nodded, approval in his eyes. Lavrov looked at Amelia, bound and gagged. A very different expression flamed in her eyes than Fitzhugh's.

Lavrov moved to the window and glanced at the construction zone next to the hotel. He liked the Hotel Montclair. Its zeal for ornamentation and pomp reminded him of the old Russian imperial palaces where he had once rubbed shoulders with the Romanovs and their inner circle. What fine days those had been! So much of Detroit was like the crass factory cities the Bolsheviks dreamed of, full of dull people performing even duller tasks, but here was an island of luxury amid the concrete sea.

"I am rather hoping your friend takes the bait." Lavrov returned to Amelia's side. "It has been a difficult day for my people. Their trials have been harsh. They should be rewarded for their continued faith. Perhaps a sacrifice would cleanse their souls of the day's burdens." He appraised Amelia.

Amelia managed to move one of her feet just far enough to stomp on Lavrov's toes. He ignored this and backhanded her, rocking the chair backward onto its rear legs. A thin trickle of blood rolled from Amelia's nose.

"What say you, Mister Fitzhugh? Do you care what we do with

this wayward lamb?"

"Hey, I don't mind either way. I just want O'Malley. If killing her makes your souls feel all squeaky clean, fine by me. But I'm paying you to ice the detective. He comes first."

Lavrov nodded. He pulled a wickedly curved blade out from the folds of his cassock. He dangled the deadly looking knife in front of Amelia's face. "Your friend thought he could kill me. He was not the first. I've been shot thirty-eight times now. Thirty-seven of the men who did this are now dead. What do you think will become of your private detective?"

Amelia looked away.

"I will tell you. I will gut him with this. And you will watch. I imagine it will be a very unpleasant experience for the both of you. All we need to do is wait." Lavrov walked back to the window and stared out at the construction site again. His blood ached for vengeance, the same as Fitzhugh. Waiting for O'Malley was proving tiresome.

As it turned out, he didn't need to wait very long. A pair of floodlights suddenly blazed to life in the construction yard, not on the ground, but level with Lavrov's window.

Down below, Jasper sat at the controls of the steam shovel he'd seen that lifetime ago when he walked into the Hotel Montclair to meet Victor Pecos. He'd scouted out the hotel and come to the same conclusion as Lavrov: every entrance was too well guarded to assault. Therefore, he decided to make his own entrance.

The steam shovel lifted its mighty steel arm. Lavrov was silhouetted in the window as Jasper sent the huge machine rumbling forward.

A bullet pinged off the metal beside his seat. Jasper looked up and saw a dark shape leaning over the hotel's roof line with a rifle.

Jasper drew and fired in a single motion. The figure pitched forward off the roof and fell four stories to the hard-packed ground in front of the machine's treads. Jasper didn't bother to change course. He raised the shovel's arm and sent it punching straight through Lavrov's window. The Russian managed to dodge out of the way, but one of his men started to raise his gun toward Amelia. Pulling a lever, Jasper opened the shovel's claw. The shovel snatched the man in its grip before he could pull the trigger. Its steel jaws were built to chew through rock and impacted clay. Gnashing its blades together, the machine tore its prey apart like a dinosaur snatching up a rat.

Suddenly, the room to the right of Lavrov's lit up with gunfire. More of his disciples had been waiting there as backup, and now they were firing out the window at Jasper. There were five or six of them, more than Jasper could guarantee hitting with the seven remaining bullets in his pistol clip.

Instead, he swung the machine's arm sideways. It plowed through the wall like a rhinoceros, sweeping the plaster from its path. Jasper continued to pivot the arm sideways like the blade of a giant blender. The shovel's arm smashed the men against the wall and then burst through the exterior wall itself. Brickwork and crushed body parts rained to the ground below, like manna from hell.

Jasper swung the claw back around to Lavrov's room. The Russian was scrambling to retrieve his anti-tank rifle. It had a worthy opponent.

Lavrov's second guard tried to escape out the door after seeing what happened to his colleague. Even after Lavrov snarled something at the man, he didn't stop. Lavrov shot the man in the back with the anti-tank rifle from close range. The man exploded, and the bullet probably traveled through the length of the entire hotel, passing through walls and maybe guests alike, until it flew out into the early morning darkness.

Racking a fresh round into the rifle, Lavrov turned around to face the steam shovel. Then he froze for a brief instant. The shovel's claw was poised directly over his head like the sword of Damocles. It hovered for a split second, and then Jasper yanked another lever and sent it straight down.

Lavrov and the shovel blade disappeared as part of the floor gave way. Jasper sent the flat, mashing surface of the shovel all the way down until it crunched into the floor of the lobby below. Just for good measure, Jasper brought the claw up and smashed it down a couple more times, pulverizing anything unfortunate enough to be small and fleshy down there.

That only left two people up in Lavrov's room. One of them was tied to a chair. The other had his leg in a brace and was frantically trying to hobble toward the door. Fitzhugh gave his escape the old college try, but he was too slow. Just before the claw came down on him, the man turned and threw his arms up in supplication, but Jasper was having none of that today, and neither was his roaring mechanical steed. Nope.

The shovel latched onto Fitzhugh and ripped him out of the room and into the night. The machine began swiveling sideways, gathering speed. As it spun faster, the claw rose higher, and then, like a discus thrower, it released Fitzhugh. There was a wailing sound as Fitzhugh flew over the moon and into the starry night. A few seconds later, there was a distant little *splat*.

Working carefully, Jasper raised the claw back up to Lavrov's room. He locked the controls and used the steam shovel's arm like a bridge. Lavrov's men would still be scattered throughout the building, and this was the safest route up. There was just enough room for him to put one foot in front of the other as he danced up the narrow length of cantilevered metal.

Finally, he made it up and jumped into the ravaged hotel room. The walls were demolished. A cavernous gap ate up the floor. Most of the furniture was little more than splinters. Jasper had probably done tens, if not hundreds, of thousands of dollars of damage in the span of less than a minute. All in a day's work.

And in the middle of it all sat Amelia, still tied to the chair.

Glancing around, Jasper spotted a nasty-looking knife abandoned on the floor. He grabbed it and cut Amelia's hands free. She ripped her gag out as he sliced through her leg bindings.

"Took you long enough," she said, and smiled.

"Glad to see you, too. Here." He handed her a Tommy gun that had belonged to one of Lavrov's thugs a minute ago.

"Oh, how did you guess? It's exactly what I wanted. Gimme." She took the drum-barreled submachine gun and cocked it.

"Lavrov's men are going to be coming up the stairs any second. You ready to shoot your way out of here?"

"Why Mister O'Malley, first you make a big fuss in picking me up, then you give me presents, and now you've practically read my mind. If I'm not careful, I might just fall for your charms." Despite everything that had happened, Jasper smiled.

The door swung open, and one of Lavrov's men leaped inside. Jasper and Amelia fired at the same time, blowing the man back into the hallway.

"Now come on. I've got some scores to settle," Amelia said.

"Me, too," Jasper said.

They sprang into the hallway, covering each other just as Lavrov's men appeared in the stairwell doorway. A few of the hotel's guests had opened their doors to see what on earth was going on, but they quickly ducked back inside as lead flew down the hall.

The stairwell doorway made a perfect shooting gallery, and Amelia laid down a heavy burst of fire from her Tommy gun. Bullets mowed down the assassins, forcing them to retreat down the stairs. Lavrov's men had been expecting to defend the building from outside intruders, not from people who were already inside. Now their positions were compromised. At the speakeasy, Lavrov lost a lot of men because they were caught by surprise in a poor position, and now it was happening all over again.

Jasper and Amelia rushed the stairwell, not giving Lavrov's corps of psychopaths a chance to regroup. Leaning over the bannister, Jasper saw a group of attackers taking up positions below them. A couple of bullets whizzed past him, forcing him to duck back. He frowned. It would be difficult to clear them out, and every second they wasted waiting gave Lavrov's men time to reorganize and develop a strategy.

"Here," Amelia said, placing something in Jasper's hand. It was a grenade taken from one of the nearby bodies, probably stripped off one of the speakeasy's other dead attackers as booty.

"Thanks." He ripped out the pin, lobbed it over the railing, and ducked back. There were shouts and the sound of mad scrambling from below, and then a rattling explosion. Jagged petals of shrapnel tore through the air, embedding themselves in the walls and anyone unfortunate enough to be hunkered nearby.

Jasper and Amelia leaped down the stairs three at a time. The Russian assassin's organization had been all but annihilated tonight.

There were only three men left in the lobby. Two of them raised their weapons to fire. Jasper shot the one on the left, and Amelia took out the one on the right.

The third man dropped his gun and started to run away. Jasper was cleaning up this town, and he was loathe to leave a job unfinished. He drew a bead on the final assassin as the man scrambled for the door, but before he could pull the trigger, a line of bullets stitched across the man's back. Jasper lowered his sidearm. Smoke wafted from the barrel of Amelia's Tommy gun. She lifted the weapon to her lips and blew the smoke away.

Glancing around, the Hotel Montclair's lobby lay in shambles. The ceiling was partially collapsed. Shrapnel was embedded in virtually every surface. The steam shovel had lopped the head off the statue of the naked Spartan warrior. The Attican Detective Agency was going to get a very large bill for all this.

The bodies of Lavrov's men were sprawled across the floor. Lavrov himself wasn't so much sprawled as splattered nearby. It really didn't matter what sort of luck or healing grace he'd had before; he wasn't getting up from this. He was nothing more than a very robust stain on the carpet.

Now that the gunfire and explosions had ceased, the night manager and a few guests began to poke their heads out from their various hiding holes. "Let's get out of here before the police show up. I'd rather not get carted back to jail twice in twenty-four hours," Amelia said.

"Good idea," Jasper responded. The only reason the police weren't already here was because they were probably stretched too thin already.

Taking the red diamond he'd been carrying around in his pocket, Jasper tossed the gem onto the hotel's shrapnel-crusted front desk. That would pay for most of the damage. They stepped through the hotel's front doors into the evening twilight.

"My Peerless is close by. Want to see if there's any place open where we can get coffee?"

Amelia stretched her arms, still feeling the ache of being bound up. "Oh, that sounds heavenly," she said.

Something exploded in the distance. Jasper looked up and saw a column of fire rise into the night. The fireball cast a pale glow over the street, and, even from here, Jasper could feel a faint heat on his face.

The explosion had come from the direction of the salt mine. Jasper watched the plume of fire fade into a dull shadow of smoke against the night sky.

"I'm afraid you're going to have to take a rain check on that coffee."

"No rest for the wicked," Amelia sighed as they set off for Jasper's Peerless.

Chapter 25
Salting the Land

Jasper pulled the Peerless to a halt a block away from the Detroit Salt Combine mine. Another massive explosion rocked the night, rattling the ground beneath the car's wheels. Some of the surrounding buildings were on fire, and Jasper spotted several cars engulfed in flames further up.

From inside the Detroit Salt facility itself, there was screaming and the crackle of gunfire. Stepping out of the car, Jasper looked around.

"What on earth...?" Amelia breathed. The place had turned into a warzone.

A figure leaped out of the shadows, and Jasper nearly gunned it down. The figure wasn't trying to attack them, though. Jasper recognized the man. He was the Pinkerton who had resolutely blocked his and Sadie's access to the mine until Basilhart intervened. *Hank*. He was still wearing his nametag. Now he was wild-eyed and terrified.

"We can't stop them," the man shouted. "It's not safe. We need to get out of here."

"Who can't you stop? What's going on here?" Jasper asked.

"The creatures. USGS. Everyone. Come on!"

"USGS? The United States Geological Survey?" Amelia looked around.

Jasper took this information in stride. He'd been expecting this shoe to drop for a while now. "Calm down and start from the beginning. What's going on?"

"The Survey people showed up late in the afternoon. They wanted to bring equipment into the mine. Their permits checked out, so we let them. They've been taking huge crates down there all night. Then everything just fell apart. Get in the car. We need to get out of here," Hank said.

Suddenly, a bolt of intense blue light shot out of the darkness like a wad of ball lightning. It struck the man in the back. He didn't even have time to scream. The ball of energy sublimated most of his body, instantly converting solids into superheated gases. Essentially, the man's body exploded in a cloud of blood steam. Jasper and Amelia leaped back in surprise. Where the Pinkerton had stood, there was now nothing but a puddle of hot stroganoff and a flaming shoe.

Something emerged from the shadows behind the Pinkerton. The thing looked like an upgraded version of the monster from the medical examiner's office. It approached them, hissing softly. Technically, it was walking backward toward them. Its head had been wrenched around so it was now facing the opposite direction a standard issue human head would normally be pointed. There were other adjustments over the typical Mark I head as well. Metal plates had been attached, crudely welded directly to the skull. Everything from the nose up was simply armored sheeting. There were two holes punched out for the eyes, but the things staring at Jasper didn't look very much like eyeballs. There were just two faintly glowing lenses swiveling and twisting inside the sockets. The lenses moved independently, allowing the kobold soldier to focus on Jasper and Amelia with one eye and check its surroundings with the other, like a chameleon.

The creature had no lower jaw. At least not a proper one. The teeth of its upper jaw were grotesquely overlong, metallic-looking daggers. There were far too many of the unnatural fangs crowded together, and they pushed against each other and poked out at odd angles. Below the upper teeth, there was a long gap because the creature's pelvis had been retrofitted to serve as its new lower mandible. The rest of its upper body had been hollowed out to make way for the artificial jaws. Foot-long, stalagmite-like fangs sprouted from the bone. In some places, the teeth apparently hadn't grown in properly, so they'd been ripped out and replaced with lengths of sharpened rebar. With its maw open, the creature's gigantic "mouth" actually made up most of its body.

To accommodate this radical transformation, the kobold thrall's spine and ribcage had been removed. Now, two pantographic hydraulic lifters could spring up and down, opening or closing the mouth. Bands of cables ran up the beams and disappeared inside the creature's throat, presumably leading up to the brain and transmitting whatever impulses the corrupted organ sent. Thick wires that looked like they'd started life out as a pair of jumper cables protruded from the creature's shoulder blades and ran down its back, punching back into its body just above the navel. The creature's arms had been wrenched out of their sockets and migrated downward to create a secondary set of legs. All four of the legs ended, not in a hand or a foot, but with two huge, steely claws. Each of the claws was curved like a small scimitar. Balancing on all four limbs like a fleshy stool, the monster stared at them.

In place of the arms were two weapon barrels. Each tube had a diameter a little wider than Jasper's fist and was about three feet long. The metal was grafted crudely onto the creature's flesh, which was cratered and pitted where it had been pulled out of shape to fit the huge weapons. The skin near the base of the tubes was cooked through from the heat of firing the weapons. The parts that actually touched the metal were singed black and crunchy.

The kobold thrall's grotesque, distended stomach was now a backpack of sorts. The guns' power source was located there. More armor covered the creature's back, but an eerie blue light seeped out from between the spaces in the crudely soldered metal.

Still hissing, the creature scurried toward them. With its mouth closed, it was very squat and almost crab-like. Its claws clacked across the asphalt.

Suddenly, it opened its mouth all the way, extending back up to the height of an average person. A blue glow shone through the skin at the back of its mouth, where the mysterious power mechanism was embedded in its flesh. A faint, ghostly radiance began to glow deep inside the weapon barrels as they gathered power. The air filled with a crackling charge.

Jasper slammed into Amelia, pushing her out of the way just as a bolt of energy shot out of the creature's biomechanical cannons. There was some sort of power source inside the creature itself, like an organic generator. However it worked, it allowed the kobold soldier to launch energy projectiles. The apple-sized ball of concentrated death looked like a sprite of St. Elmo's fire as it crackled past. All the hair on Jasper's arms and neck tried to stand on end as if he'd just passed through a field of static electricity.

Sailing onward, the plasma orb hit the wall of the building across the street. It instantly released all its energy on contact, vaporizing a large section of the wall in a blinding flash of light. As the flashbulb flare faded, Jasper saw a burning hole about eight feet in diameter in the wall.

He looked back at the kobold warrior and rolled out of the way just in time to avoid being blown into a pile of scorched atoms as another deadly bolt slashed into the asphalt where he had been a second before. The blast excavated a hole deep enough to bury a body in and spewed burning rock and tar into the air.

Jasper leaped to his feet as the monster scuttled forward. It came at him with its claws. Taking aim at the thing's skittering legs, Jasper pulled the trigger of his pistol. The bullets tore out chunks of flesh, but didn't slow the kobold warrior in the slightest. Where the bullets had hit, Jasper could see the gleam of metal. Apparently, most of the creature's skeleton had been ripped out and replaced with hardier materials, and the parts that couldn't be replaced were now covered with sheets of plate armor.

If he'd known this was what he'd be facing, he would have grabbed Lavrov's anti-tank rifle. He might as well have been hunting grizzly bears with a BB gun. How was he supposed to fight something like this?

Pressing its advantage, the kobold thrall slashed at Jasper's belly with its claws. Jasper jumped backward to avoid being disemboweled, but the thing remained right on top of him, keeping up a constant assault with its lethal appendages. A set of claws raked toward Jasper, and it was all he could do to avoid being slashed apart like a cow in a slaughterhouse. The claws caught his sleeve, tearing the cloth as easily as tissue paper. If he couldn't open up some distance, he wouldn't last more than a few seconds.

Raising its front claws high, the kobold readied a vicious killing blow. Jasper tried to squirm away, but the creature was simply too fast. He was about to be cleaved apart.

Suddenly, a storm of bullets rained down on the kobold's back. Its armor absorbed the rapid hammer blows from Amelia's Tommy gun, but they distracted the kobold.

Hissing as its prey slipped out of reach, the kobold opened its massive mouth. The artificially enlarged maw gaped from mouth to groin. The blue, alien luminescence glowed again, shining through its skin.

Seeing it gave Jasper an idea. It wasn't a very good idea, but if he didn't do something soon, both he and Amelia were going to die right here.

As if the demonstrate that point, the blue glow began to emanate from the creature's weapons again, and the air filled with expectant energy. Jasper dove out of the way as the first sphere of fatal light shot out at him. The ball of energy went high and slammed into a parked car. The front half of the car disappeared in a flash of released energy. A sick, metallic smell filled the air as what remained of the car's engine block melted like warm chocolate.

Jasper was prone on the ground as the monster aligned its second shot. It carefully lined up the barrel of its remaining gun with Jasper's still form. But even as the creature was taking aim, Jasper was mirroring its movements with his pistol. The kobold thrall's mouth was still open, revealing that startling blue glow through the back of its throat, virtually the only part of its body that wasn't armored. In the few seconds it spent charging and aiming its shots, the creature's power source was vulnerable.

At least, Jasper hoped it was. If he was wrong, he was about to see what it felt like to have all the molecules in his body fly apart and scatter in a million different directions. He squeezed the trigger of his pistol again and again in a tight cluster near the center of the unearthly glow. The bullets pierced the soft tissue, penetrating into the creature's body.

Suddenly, the glow in the kobold's remaining barrel went out as if someone had pulled a switch. Amelia ran over and helped Jasper to his feet. The creature stood where it was, apparently stunned. Then Jasper became aware of a high-pitched whining noise. It grew in intensity, like a circuit frying out. There was a rough, rattling undertone as something started to come undone inside the creature. The kobold soldier jittered madly, like a death-row inmate in the throes of the electric chair, and still the whining sound grew louder. The creature had lost all interest in them, even as Jasper clambered to his feet.

"We should get behind cover," Jasper said. Amelia nodded.

As they scampered away, the creature tipped completely over, its legs curling up toward its body like a dead spider on the windowsill. The whining noise grew to an earsplitting roar, and the grating sound grew rougher and harsher. It sounded like an airplane engine overheating and starting to tear itself apart.

Jasper and Amelia ran and slid behind a car about one hundred feet away from the creature. Unearthly blue light sprayed out of the creature in a miniature supernova, growing more and more intense. Soon, the twisted figure was barely even visible at the center of the ungodly light. They ducked down just as the monster went critical. A massive jet of blue flame spewed toward the sky, forming a small mushroom cloud. A shockwave swept the ground, knocking both Jasper and Amelia off their feet and bounced them across the ground. Glass tinkled around them as the windows of nearby cars and windows blew out.

Heat buffeted Jasper as the shockwave blasted him. The blue flame gave off an intense, lingering warmth that felt somehow unhealthy, feverish. They both cringed against it.

The sound was absolutely deafening, nearly bursting Jasper's eardrums. Even as the roar of the blast faded, his ears rang as if they were trying to pick up a distant radio station.

He and Amelia had to roll underneath the car as lumps of molten asphalt and metal plummeted to earth all around them. The largest chunks, about the size of grapefruits, plunged down from the sky like flaming meteorites.

After almost a full minute, Jasper and Amelia rolled back out from under the car. There was a massive crater further down the street. All that remained of the creature was a caldera of fused, black glass. A nearby fire hydrant had burst and was filling the hole with water. Cracks radiated out from the basin in crazy zigzag patterns. Even looking down on battlefields from above during the war, Jasper had never seen so much pure destructive power. It was like a tiny pocket apocalypse had just been unleashed in front of the Detroit Salt Combine facilities.

The sound of continued gunfire reached him again. He needed to see what was going on. He skirted the edge of the crater, and he could feel the lingering heat through his shoes as he approached the entrance to the facility.

Pushing open the gate to the mine complex, Jasper ducked as a burst of submachine gun fire chewed past him. The scene was utter pandemonium. One of the elevator's had already descended into the mine.

The armored mooks who had attacked Schackel's speakeasy were loading equipment into the remaining two elevators and firing at anything that moved, but they weren't having an easy time of it. Lance Basilhart and his Pinkertons were holed up in one corner of the compound. They were under fire from both the unidentified human attackers and the kobold soldiers alike. All three sides were trying to exterminate each other.

Basilhart had the best position: one whole end of the compound where it would be difficult to flank him. He also had the most men, which counted for something, but he was also going through them at a rapid clip. They weren't trained for this. Even as they peeked out from behind crates and equipment to fire at the mysterious gunmen and the kobold's minions, their cover was being systematically blown apart by energy weapons. There were bodies and parts of bodies scattered all over the compound.

There were only a few of the kobold thralls loose in the compound, but they were doing a disproportionate amount of damage. One of the monsters clamored up out of the elevator shaft and immediately blew an armored gunman into crackling red vapor. Jasper realized that the monsters were scaling the inside of the shaft's walls.

Even though there were only a smattering of the kobold warriors and they were caught between the two groups of gunmen, they were more than holding their own. Each of the creatures was slightly different from the others, but they were all armored like living tanks and carried a lot more firepower. The constant hail of gunfire meant they couldn't rampage freely without risking serious damage, but they still managed to fire their weapons and slash at anyone foolish enough to draw too close.

The mystery gunmen were obviously well trained and disciplined. They were rapidly, but efficiently, loading a gigantic box into each of the remaining two elevators while their friends provided covering fire. Jasper wasn't sure what was in the boxes, but he guessed it was bad.

They successfully loaded the first elevator, and several of the men jumped in with it. As Jasper looked again, though, he noticed they had someone with them, someone who wasn't like the others.

One of the men pulled a lever, and the elevator started to descend into the darkness beneath Detroit, carrying its cargo, the gunmen, and Sadie DuPree.

Chapter 26
Razing Hell

"Was that who I think it was?" Amelia asked.

"Yes. Come on. We need to hitch a ride down."

The second crate was almost loaded into the remaining elevator.

"We're screwed if they lower that last lift. It's the only way down," Amelia said.

"Follow my lead," he said. The enigmatic gunmen finally managed to fit the last crate inside the elevator. Five of the gunmen piled in behind it. Their giant crate practically filled up the entire space, leaving only a narrow strip for the men to squeeze into. One of them yanked on the elevator's controls and the device began to descend into the earth.

"Now," Jasper shouted, dashing forward. Amelia followed just behind him. In all the confusion, they were barely noticeable. The remaining armored gunmen were retreating, their task finished. They were leaving the Pinkertons to deal with the monsters.

Sprinting, Jasper came to the edge of the shaft. Without slowing down, he vaulted the waist-high safety railing that circled the pit. There was no time to look before he leaped. If he hesitated, he'd either be gunned down up here, or the elevator would descend out of range. He plunged feet first into the darkness. If he was too slow or had miscalculated ...

But no, he landed on top of the elevator's roof not ten feet down.

He dropped into a crouch to absorb most of the impact as Amelia landed beside him.

Directly below his feet, Jasper heard shouts of surprise. His entry hadn't exactly been stealthy. He lowered his pistol and fired it through the roof of the elevator, and Amelia did the same with her Tommy gun. Below, the men in the elevator were packed in too tight to raise their weapons without bumping into each or to move out of the way of the barrage. It was like shooting heavily armed fish in a barrel.

Jasper listened for any sound of movement below after the boom of gunfire ceased, but there was nothing but the clank and whirr of the elevator steadily lowering itself into the shadows.

A new and greater threat immediately presented itself. As the elevator descended, it passed something crawling up the shaft's sheer rock wall.

"Look out," Amelia shouted.

On the wall, the kobold warrior swiveled around, bringing its oversized cannons to bear on the two figures riding on top of the elevator. Amelia emptied the last of her drum magazine at the monstrosity, the rattle of gunfire echoing up and down the shaft in a roar. Bullets peppered the creature's armored hide, causing it to stagger slightly before it lost its grip on the wall. Shrieking like a broken steam engine, it plummeted one thousand feet straight down into the black abyss. Amelia began to reload her Tommy gun just as the elevator passed another of the creatures.

Apparently learning from watching the demise of its comrade, it didn't stand still to use its guns. Instead, it pushed away from the wall like a giant jumping spider and landed atop the elevator. Swatting Amelia out of the way, it went straight for Jasper.

Amelia rolled across the top of the elevator, tumbling toward the edge. Jasper lunged for her, but the kobold warrior moved to cut him off. Ropy saliva dripped from it upper jaw onto the metal roof of the elevator. There was nothing Jasper could do as Amelia plunged over the edge with a scream.

At the very last second, she managed to throw out a hand and grab onto the lift's mesh siding. Her Tommy gun slipped into the gloom below, quickly disappearing from sight. "Jasper!"

"Just a second," he called down. The creature's claws clacked across the roof of the elevator as it moved toward him. There was no need for the creature to use its cannons here. Jasper was trapped with no room to maneuver; it had every advantage with just its claws, and it was plainly aware of that fact.

Both its strange lensed eyes stopped bobbing around and focused directly on Jasper. The eyes glowed malevolently, two blue embers in the suffocating darkness. Moving like a crazed crab, the monster charged forward.

Jasper let it come. His pistol had a bullet in the chamber, but then the magazine was empty. He was going to need to make it count. As the creature lunged forward, Jasper braced his feet.

The creature approached at a dead charge. Its gigantic front claws came up like the Grim Reaper's scythe, ready to slice Jasper in half. Just as they started to arc down for the finishing blow, Jasper pivoted to the side. It was essentially the same move he had pulled on Fitzhugh, letting his opponent think victory was imminent, encouraging carelessness. The attacker became so focused on delivering the killer blow that they stopped thinking about anything else.

Jasper let the claws swing through the empty air where he'd been a split second before. The brute's forward momentum meant it couldn't immediately recover, even as it turned its head to look at Jasper with an expression that might have been surprise.

The kobold warrior stood inches away when Jasper raised his pistol. He pulled the trigger just as it started to wheel around. Recoil kicked Jasper's arm back as the bullet traveled down the barrel of the pistol, surfing a wave of rapidly expanding explosive gases. A series of tiny grooves along the inside of the barrel caused the bullet to spin as it traveled toward its target. It coughed out the end of the pistol in a burst of flame, a miracle of carefully engineered mechanical parts and chemical reactions all working in perfect harmony.

In a span of time so incrementally small that the human mind couldn't actually measure it, the little brass projectile accelerated to a speed that could be measured in the thousands of miles per hour. With only a short jaunt to its target, the result was effectively instantaneous.

The bullet sailed directly through the glowing lens that served as the kobold warrior's right eye. Bright blue light poured out of the hole as the lens shattered like a child's belief in Santa Claus. Sparks shot out of the beast's skull as it lurched backward, but it didn't slump over and die. Even though the bullet had probably scrambled whatever was left of its brains, the thing was as much machine as beast.

Jasper pressed his brief window of advantage and darted forward.

He lifted a leg up and used all of his strength to shove the creature toward the edge of the elevator. It was already off balance, thrashing and squalling like an angry tea kettle. The push sent it teetering to the precipice.

But even as it screeched and tottered over the void, it reached out and grabbed the only thing within reach: Jasper. A set of razor-tipped claws reached out and snatched the lapels of Jasper's jacket and started to yank him toward the abyss.

There was nothing within reach for Jasper to grab onto. His feet began to slide across the smooth metal roof of the elevator. The creature screamed at him, blowing hot, stinking breath that smelled like dead beavers and burning insulation. He tried to wriggle out of the gray jacket, but it was no use. Slowly, his toes slid toward the edge.

Then, with a loud rip, the cloth gave way under the kobold's weight. The creature hovered for a second, and then, in almost comical slow motion, it tipped over backward and dropped into the seemingly bottomless cavern below. Jasper could hear it shrieking all the way down.

"Uh, Jasper?" Amelia was still dangling by her fingers from the side of the elevator.

"Oh, right," he said. They still had a long way to go, and things were only going to get worse the lower they went.

Chapter 27
U-235 Complete Me

The elevator finally ground to a halt at the bottom of the shaft just in time for Jasper and Amelia to watch one of the mine's flatbed trucks disappear into a tunnel. Strapped to its back was the gigantic crate they'd seen earlier. Jasper didn't see anyone else in the main cavern, so it stood to reason that they'd taken Sadie with them as well.

He and Amelia needed to follow that truck. Jasper looked around and spied something useful. It was another mining truck, but it had been retrofitted. Somebody, presumably the same gunmen who had just disappeared down the tunnel, had attached a machine gun to the back of the vehicle. Mostly likely, it had been left as an escort vehicle for the men in the second elevator.

Well, they certainly weren't going to be using it. No doubt they wouldn't mind if Jasper and Amelia borrowed it. Jasper hopped onto the platform. He pointed to the truck. "Can you drive that?"

"Hell yes, I can drive that. You're going to take the gun?"

Jasper nodded.

Jumping off the platform, they moved to the truck. The door was unlocked, and the keys were even dangling from the ignition. Perfect.

Amelia jumped in the cab, pulled the choke, turned the key ... and nothing happened. She restarted the process, carefully checking each step.

Still nothing.

She ran around to the front of the truck and lifted the hood. "Well, here's the problem," she said. "The spark plug's missing. Without that, we're not taking this thing anywhere."

"They must have taken it," Jasper gestured toward the now-empty tunnel. "That, or one of the creature's scavenged it for some repairs."

They were so *close*. Everything was coming to a climax, and they were stuck here. If they hit the tunnels on foot, even if they survived, they'd never catch up.

"O'Malley," a voice breathed.

Jasper and Amelia both looked up. The voice had come from somewhere behind a large conveyor belt.

The voice came again. "O'Malley."

Jasper recognized that voice. "Renfield?"

"Get your ass over here." Renfield's voice sounded weak and strained. It was also wet and slightly bubbly, as if he were fighting to talk through a bad cold. Jasper crept toward the stack of crates. He kept his hand on his pistol, just in case. Once he reached them, he peeked around the corner, not sure what to expect. He vaguely recalled Hinkmeyer saying that Renfield had gone to check something out at the mine, but Jasper hadn't expected to find the police captain alive.

Renfield was sitting on the ground with his legs splayed out in front of him, his back to the crate. His hands were clasped in his lap, only they weren't really hands anymore. They were just misshapen claws.

Jasper thought back to the report at the Detroit Salt warehouse explaining how prolonged exposure to the kobold's corrupting influence could start to warp people, physically and mentally. He thought of Gottschalk, Schackel's henchman who spent more and more time in the tunnels until he disappeared entirely. He remembered Renfield keeping a bandage on his hand when they first met, explaining it away as an accident from the time he'd spent searching the mine. But a mere bandage couldn't hide Renfield's transformation anymore. His skin looked like it was rotting on its bones, and one side of his face was starting to sag, as if he'd suffered a massive stroke. Pimple-like abscesses covered his face. As Jasper watched, one of them burst and spilled pasty white goo down the police captain's cheek.

"O'Malley," Renfield gurgled.

"Captain Renfield," Jasper said.

"You want ... truck?" Renfield croaked. He seemed to be having a hard time putting his thoughts in order.

"We better get you out of here, Captain." There was no way for them to pursue that vehicle on foot, so Jasper shifted his focus to what he could actually accomplish. Once the mess above cleared, they could bring Renfield to the surface. It seemed unlikely, but maybe time outside the mine would have some sort of restorative effect on the man. Or at least prevent him from changing even further.

"Inside my front pocket," Renfield said. He poked his chin at the breast pocket of his jacket.

Jasper leaned down and stuck his fingers inside Renfield's pocket. They emerged holding a spark plug.

"You stole this to prevent them from taking the truck?"

"No," Renfield answered. "Just took it. Don't know why. Visions in my head. Told me to."

Jasper thought about how the creatures had stolen pieces from the mining equipment, apparently for use in their transformation. They didn't seem to be intelligent enough to know what to do with the materials, so they just instinctively grabbed whatever struck their fancy, like crows snatching up shiny objects.

"Amelia!" Jasper tossed her the spark plug. She caught it out of the air in a single deft motion. "Does that fit?" She disappeared for a second, and then the truck roared to life. He took that as a "yes."

He turned back to Renfield. "Captain, we need to track down that other truck. When we get back, we'll get you evacuated to the surface. It's not safe up there right now. You're lucky. I'm surprised those creatures didn't kill you."

"Recognized their own. Favor?" Renfield asked.

"Of course."

Renfield mumbled something, and Jasper had to crouch down beside him to hear.

"You're sure?" Jasper asked.

The police captain's lips peeled back to the gums in what might have been a smile or a rictus of agony. His gums were covered in a ghostly white fuzz in places, like some kind of mold. Renfield nodded and closed his eyes, his expression sliding back into something that almost resembled peace.

Jasper reached down and unholstered the policeman's gun. The metal was cool and remarkably heavy in his palm.

There was a pause, and then the chamber erupted with the sound of a single gunshot.

Jasper ran back to the truck, alive and thrumming now. Just as he jumped onto the truck's bed, the elevators behind them began to rise. Someone up top had summoned transport. Presumably, the creatures could crawl back down the side of the shaft if they were forced to retreat, so that left three possibilities. First and least catastrophic, the Detroit police had arrived on the scene and cleaned up the remaining fighters up top, and now they were on their way down into the tunnels. Odds were, they would arrest Jasper and Amelia on sight and launch their own expedition into the tunnels, maybe catching up to the other truck and maybe not.

Second, it could be Basilhart and his remaining Pinkertons. Given that Ransom was dead and Detroit Salt probably ruined, Jasper wasn't sure that Basilhart would have any professional need to kill them. Maybe.

However, if the two detectives had anything in common, it was the fact that they didn't like to see a job left unfinished. The Pinkerton would want to eliminate any witnesses to his misdoings and would probably think it was a gas to wipe out the remaining O'Malley brother in another mine, effectively closing the book on both cases. But even if Basilhart was in a cooperative mood, Jasper might shoot the Pinkerton down himself. Lance Basilhart had cost a great many people, himself included, very dearly over the years.

Finally, the elevators could be coming with the last of the armored gunmen. They seemed more inclined to shoot first and ask questions later. Jasper had an idea of who they really were, but he didn't fancy the prospect of sticking around to ask them.

Jasper pounded on the roof of the truck with the flat of his hand. Inside the cab, Amelia had found one of the advanced-looking submachine guns. The truck rumbled forward, chugging and rattling but gaining speed.

On the back of the truck, Jasper was painfully aware of how exposed he was. Anything ahead of them could see the headlights coming from a mile away, giving it plenty of time to set up an ambush just outside the pathetic cone of light the truck could carve out of the darkness. Fortunately, though, Jasper had an equalizer with him. The Lewis Gun mounted on the truck's bed was a military surplus weapon from the Great War, an all-purpose machine gun used to slice down entire infantry battalions or to harass low-flying enemy aircraft. A massive, ninety-seven-round pan magazine rested on top of the gun, near the sights, rather than under the gun. The pan magazine, basically a drum magazine that had been flipped onto its side, made the weapon look like a Tommy gun's bigger, uglier brother. It was not a weapon to be trifled with.

Something leaped out of the darkness and attempted to trifle with Jasper. It was one of the kobold's lesser thralls, one of the workers.

Jasper pulled the trigger of his anti-trifling device, and the creature simply blew apart. The Lewis gun's .30-06 bullets chewed into the monster's soft tissues like a hot chainsaw through a butter sculpture.

In the distance, Jasper could just make out a pair of taillights. Amelia must have seen them, too, because she pressed harder on the gas, forcing a tiny gasp of speed out of the truck.

Their vehicle closed the gap. The other truck was weighted down by the enormous bulk of the crate strapped to its bed, and it couldn't muster the speed needed to escape. With their headlights closing behind them, there was no way they weren't aware they were being followed. Maybe they thought the second truck was filled with more of their people, and he and Amelia could draw closer in relative safety.

Nope.

Something exploded about one hundred yards in front of Amelia's windshield, too far away to do them any harm. Now that they were getting closer, Jasper could see two of the gunmen standing on the truck bed.

One of them lobbed something behind the vehicle, and another explosion followed, closer this time. They were tossing grenades at their pursuers, trying to find the right range. Amelia began weaving the vehicle from side to side, making them a harder target.

Jasper could easily hit the two gunmen from here simply by emptying the Lewis Gun's magazine in the general direction of the truck. With that much lead in the air, he would barely even need to aim. But Sadie was in the truck's cab. If he just started firing blindly, the odds that she'd be hit were too great.

Amelia managed to coax a bit more speed out of the truck as Jasper pounded on the roof again. He let the Lewis Gun drop back to its stand and pulled out his pistol. Once upon a time, he'd been able to hit enemy pilots as they swooped down on his reconnaissance plane. Those were difficult shots, but at least he had the advantage of surprise. The fighter pilots never expected to face anything with teeth, so they weren't afraid to come in close for the kill.

These two knew Jasper was coming for them, and they weren't about to make things easy for him. Jasper had eight bullets in his magazine. If he tried to shoot the men riding the back of the truck, he would have four chances per target. Even if he hit one of the men, their body armor would likely stop the round, and if he missed, he still might hit Sadie. Meanwhile, his own truck bumped over the floor of the mine.

Another explosion went off in front of the truck, only thirty yards away this time. Jasper felt something whiz past his head. Several pieces of shrapnel *thwacked* into the front of the cab, embedding themselves in the metal.

Leveling his weapon against the roof of the truck, Jasper took aim the best he could. The wind buffeted his face, forcing him to squint, and the truck rattled over the ground like a crazed grasshopper flitting across the landscape. He fired, and the bullet sailed harmlessly into the darkness straight ahead. The men in the back of the truck saw what was going on and decided to switch tactics.

Another bullet ripped out of Jasper's pistol, this one burying itself in the salty floor. Obviously, the men in the truck hadn't been expecting trouble. Aside from the grenades pinned to the front of their vests, they weren't armed.

The one on the right tapped on the truck's rear window. The window slid open, and someone shoved a submachine gun into the man's eager hands. Unlike Jasper, they had no reason to be discreet with their aim. They could simply spray the front of the truck with lead.

On the left, the other man readied another grenade. Jasper narrowed his focus down to his gun and his target. His breath slowed. His finger started to depress the trigger.

Then something lunged out of the darkness at the first truck. It was one of the kobold warriors. Latching onto the side of the vehicle with its large talons, it swung itself up and grabbed the man on the left in its scrap shearer jaws, grenade and all. The man didn't even have time to react. The creature made vulgar chewing motions, mutilating the gunman like a child's doll run over by a lawn mower. Turning to confront this new threat, the man's partner pointed his gun at the fiendish aberration, but before he could fire a shot, the grenade went off inside the creature. The explosion ripped the horror in half, turning its soft insides to mush. While the upper half flew off into the darkness, the lower half dropped off the side of the truck like a dead barnacle, trailing a mixture of its own and its victim's intestines behind it. Even as their truck blew past the broken remains, Jasper could see that the creature's belly was glowing a brighter blue as its power unit began to overload.

The remaining man hefted his gun again. He brought the weapon to his shoulder, preparing to rake the front of their vehicle with a long, deadly sweep.

A dazzling blue blast lit up the tunnel as the kobold soldier exploded in a wave of energy. With the distance the trucks' had built up, the explosion was little more than a tremor, no worse than any of the other rough patches in the mine tunnel. However, the blast was incredibly bright. It lit the tunnels up like a flashbulb. Jasper had his back to the explosion. The gunman was facing it. He recoiled, shielding his eyes from the flash. Jasper wasn't affected to nearly the same degree. He leveled his pistol again, and this time, the shot was true. The right rear tire of the truck exploded in a burst of rubber. Already blinded, the gunman lost his balance as the truck dropped onto its rim.

The driver, unable to correct in time, smashed into the side of the tunnel. The truck scraped against the wall in a welter of sparks, and the driver overcorrected, whipsawing the truck to the left. Thrown off balance, the gunman tipped over the side of the truck with a scream.

Amelia didn't bother to change course. Jasper held on as the vehicle went over a particularly large bump.

Ahead of them, sparks flew as the truck's wheel rim ground against stone, desperately spinning. The vehicle began to slow until it eventually crunched to a halt.

There was a short pause. Jasper kept his pistol ready and aimed at the driver's door. He couldn't see what was going on inside the cab because the massive crate in the truck's bed blocked his view. Amelia stepped out of the truck with her newfound submachine gun. Whatever was about to transpire, it probably wasn't going to be friendly.

The driver's side door flew open. A man with a shaved head stepped out of the truck and immediately ripped his passenger out in front of him as a human shield. Sadie looked at Jasper, her eyes wide. The man jammed the barrel of his submachine gun up under her chin. The weapon pressed cruelly against the soft skin of her throat.

"Help," she mouthed.

Jasper kept his attention, and his pistol, trained on the man holding her captive. The man hid most of his body behind Sadie, leaving only his arm exposed where he gripped her. His face was mostly eclipsed by her blond head, leaving only an eye visible. Sweat poured down his face, but he didn't wipe it away.

"Drop your guns!" the man shouted. His bald head shone in the truck's headlights as more sweat glistened on his brow. Jasper didn't lower his weapon. "Drop them! I'm going to count to three. If you haven't put your guns on the ground by the time I'm done, I'm going to blow this broad's brains all over the fu —"

Jasper shot the man. The bullet punched into his skull just above the left eyeball, missing Sadie by a couple of inches. The man's expression slackened into something resembling mild bewilderment. His eyelids fluttered once, and then he tipped over backward.

Sadie blinked once in surprise, and then she started to run toward the truck. "Jasper!"

"Stop right there, Sadie," he ordered. He switched the pistol in her direction. She froze where she was.

"Jasper, what are you doing? It's me!" Still, she didn't try to come any closer.

Amelia cast an inquiring glance up at Jasper and then shifted her own weapon to point at the geologist.

"What's this all about, Sadie? What's in the crates?"

"I don't know! These men just snuck in and grabbed me at the Detroit Salt warehouse. They grabbed me before I could even ..." She trailed off as Jasper raised a hand for her to stop.

"What's in the crates?"

Her manner stiffened, grew colder. She gathered herself up like an angry blond lioness, ready to pounce. "I don't know. Those men just dragged me down here as a hostage."

"Those men? You mean your USGS colleagues?" Jasper laid his cards on the table. Amelia's eyebrows shot up, but she didn't say anything. Sadie did her best to look flabbergasted by this accusation, but she didn't do a very good job.

"That's ... that's quite a leap in judgment, Mister O'Malley."

"Not really. At Schackel's speakeasy, only four people knew we would be there. Me. Amelia. Schackel. And you. I know I didn't want myself killed, so that narrows down who blabbed the information to Lavrov, the Pinkertons, and those gunmen.

"Schackel just had us in his clutches. If he wanted us dead, he would have done it before we went to that speakeasy. Since then, Amelia has enjoyed numerous opportunities to kill me, but she has actually been a great aid in keeping me alive.

"That leaves you. Now I might have shrugged the attack off as mere coincidence. The USGS men did wipe out the Detroit Salt facility before coming to the speakeasy. Maybe they just came for Ackley and we got in the way; however, that doesn't explain how Lavrov and Basilhart also arrived there at almost the exact same time. They had no interest in Ackley.

"Someone must have tipped them off that we were there, giving specific instructions not to kill one member of the party. Come to think of it, you were also the only one who didn't shoot any of the attackers at the bar. You fired over their heads to keep them in cover, but that was it."

"This is preposterous," Sadie fumed. "There's no way I would have —"

Jasper cut her off. "Then, at the warehouse, you disappeared because you knew about the explosives hidden there. You found Doctor Winston there, dead, a former USGS man who'd gone into private practice. He was your mole, wasn't he? He tipped your people off about what was going on here, but he knew too much, and he'd been exposed to the influence of the tunnels through his work with the Detroit Salt Combine. To completely cover your tracks, he needed to go just like everyone else.

"USGS knew about this thing and put together a task force to eliminate it and contain the situation. You attached yourself to me because I was a convenient way to gather more information, and when it became obvious that the situation had truly spiraled out of control, you were ordered to kill me and everyone else with too much knowledge. When Schackel demanded that Amelia travel with us, you were angry because it spoiled your easy opportunity to knock me out of the game."

Sadie threw her head back and laughed. It wasn't the reaction Jasper was expecting. "Very good, Jasper. Very good. Do you remember when Schackel had my file and said that it was either unremarkable or protected with even greater secrecy than top military files? Well, I think I've proven that I'm involved with some fairly remarkable business ventures, don't you?"

"Tell me what this is all about."

"Consider what I told you about kobolds, Jasper. They were unpleasant imps who lived in medieval mines and caves. But medieval mines were rarely much more than a ditch with a ceiling. But with the Industrial Revolution, it became possible for much deeper shafts to be excavated. Not only was it possible, but it was practically necessary. The new era required coal to fuel its innovations, and that, in turn, required deeper and more complex mines that delved further underground.

"The only problem was, humanity had no idea what was down there. Kobolds, proper kobolds at least, are basically just offshoots of humanity. Blind, little gnomes that dig and tunnel underground. They're unpleasant, but nothing that can't be slaughtered with a pickaxe. The worst they can do is undermine the tunnels until they collapse.

"As you go deeper, things become much worse, and humanity was completely unprepared for that. Some creatures survived the great extinction at the end of the Cretaceous by traveling deep into the crevices and fissures of the earth. Their descendants are still alive today, huge, sightless pseudo-reptiles wandering the natural pockets and caverns lining the earth's crust. There's a massive underground lake we discovered under California with Precambrian carnivores the size of whales. After a while, 'kobold' just became the generic term for any new underground monster USGS found.

"Then there's the things even deeper underground. Things we can't even begin to classify. Someone who simply stumbled across these things would probably label them as demons. They ... might not be entirely incorrect.

"This thing in the tunnels, it's from deeper underground than we've ever seen before. Every other creature we've encountered is something that evolved on the surface and then adapted to living underground. However, that's not true with this thing.

"The monster down here is from an entirely different branch of life. Its body isn't even carbon based. As far as we can tell, it's more like a naturally occurring robot, made mostly from a mixture of conductive and heavy metals. It's much older than us. I don't just mean humanity. It's older than all life on earth. These things already existed down at the earth's deepest depths when life on the surface was just heaving itself out of the primordial soup. We're just upstarts compared to this thing.

"It has a gift for technology we don't understand. Hell, it's basically living technology. We need to stop this thing, and the USGS is the only group that can do it.

"USGS was established in 1879, and it has always quietly maintained a branch to deal with these things. A lot of countries have something similar to us, though they fold it under different organizations. Our budget is par with the Army, and we've developed a lot of our own tools. However, with mining interests plunging their drills to ever newer depths, the situation has started to get out of hand. We've kept our secrets from the public for years, but we've reached a critical juncture here."

"Why not disclose this to the public or turn it over to the military? Why keep it secret?"

"It's one thing to contemplate hell. It's another to know its mouth might be directly below your feet. If we made our files public, very few people would ever show up for work at a mine again, I assure you. As for the military, they don't have our expertise, and they'd just waste our specialized equipment." Sadie pulled something out from one of her vest pockets.

Jasper needed a moment to figure out what the device was. If he'd recognized it in time, he would have shot Sadie down then and there, but it was too late. Her finger was already poised over the detonator's trigger.

"You wanted to know what was in the crate? It's a uranium bomb. USGS has been contemplating what we should do if there was ever something we simply couldn't handle, and this was our solution. These are by far the most powerful weapons on the planet, and we've placed over a dozen down here."

"I've never heard of such a thing," Jasper said, looking into the distance just beyond the truck's headlights. He needed to keep Sadie talking.

"*You* wouldn't have," she scoffed. "Trust me, we developed these for our own use a while ago, and we got permission from the Russians to test a few at Tunguska back in 1907. We haven't exactly been keen to share them. The military would have simply pissed them away against the Germans during the war. No, we were saving these for a rainy day."

"So you're going to collapse the tunnels?" Jasper asked.

"More than that, I'm afraid. You underestimate just how powerful these bombs are. They won't just destroy the mine. They'll hollow out a huge empty space under Detroit, and the city will fall into the caldera."

"That's insane," Amelia said. "You can't wipe out the entire city!"

"Originally, we didn't plan to. We were just going to detonate a few bombs in the parts of the tunnel that extend under Lake Erie, flooding the tunnels. But as I followed you, it became increasingly obvious just how bad things had become. The kobold had moved its sights to the surface, using its thralls to take down that military convoy.

"We have no way of knowing just how deep its corrupting influence has taken root. Even if we flooded the tunnels and killed the creature, we couldn't guarantee that its poison hadn't already spread to the surface. There's a good chance the entire city is already slightly affected. This kobold isn't like anything we've ever faced before. If we don't eliminate every trace of it, we might lose a lot more than just Detroit."

"You know we won't let you leave," Jasper said.

"I know," Sadie sighed. "That's why I have this." She hefted the detonator. "We just can't risk this creature's influence spreading to the surface."

"Wait," Jasper shouted. He just needed a little more time.

Sadie paused, her hand still on the detonator.

"There's one thing I still haven't figured out."

"And what's that?"

"The diamonds. How do they fit into all this?"

"Jasper, remember when I told you that diamonds are just organic matter that's been squeezed down mostly to pure carbon? The diamonds are carbon with some contaminants. Human beings are basically just carbon with some contaminants. The kobold isn't transforming all its victims into thralls. It's eating some of them, and its guts operate under incredibly high pressure. The diamonds are just monster shit."

He thought back to the diamond he'd taken from Renfield. It was disheartening to think that he'd been carrying all that remained of one of the missing men around in his pocket the whole time without realizing it. Detroit Salt hadn't just been harvesting the diamonds from the mine, it had been keeping the mine open so it could feed the workers to the kobold and gather its highly valuable dung.

Cripes.

"Is that everything, Jasper?"

"Yeah, I suppose it is."

"I'm sorry, Jasper. I really am."

"So am I."

Tap.

Sadie looked up just in time to see the kobold directly above her. She screamed, but the giant monstrosity swung down and clamped its mouth down over her. It sprang back up, leaving behind only Sadie's boots, her feet still in them. A horrible chewing noise sounded from the ceiling.

"Go," Jasper yelled.

Amelia hopped back into the truck's cab and gunned the engine while Jasper leaped up to man the Lewis gun. The kobold skittered across the ceiling toward them.

Shooting forward, the truck passed directly beneath the bus-sized monster. Jasper ducked as one of the massive claws whipped down to snatch at him. The kobold seemed to remember who he was, and it was out for blood. The claw ripped through the truck's roof as easily as if it were opening a sardine tin, taking the Lewis Gun with it. Skittering around on its steely claws, the kobold queen shrieked its outrage after the fleeing truck, but the vehicle was already surging away. Jasper soon lost sight of the creature in the darkness.

He leaned over the newly convertible truck cab and grabbed the map of the mine he'd seen earlier. They passed a tunnel intersection marked by one of the hundreds of position indicators located there like a surface street sign.

"Take the next right, follow it for three intersections, and then hang a left," Jasper shouted above the wind. "That'll take us to the tunnel that leads under Lake Erie."

"Why do you want to go there?"

"Let's set off one of those uranium bombs."

Chapter 28
Salt in the Wound

"Those are some big bombs," Amelia said.

There were eight of them packed into the tunnel, and each bomb was almost the size of a rhinoceros. Filled with conventional explosives, anyone of them could have probably razed one of Detroit's skyscrapers. If Sadie was to be believed, though, they were even more powerful than they looked.

Hundreds of feet above their heads was the floor of Lake Erie, one of the Great Lakes. Containing 116 cubic miles of water, it was the tenth largest lake in the world. There were approximately 127,729,589,400,000 gallons of water in the lake, more than enough to fill Detroit Salt's mining facility and drown the evil that had hatched here. The shoreline probably wouldn't even change perceptibly if they blew a hole in the bottom.

Now there was simply the matter of detonating the bombs and escaping alive. Easy-peasy.

This part of the tunnel appeared to be some sort of brooding chamber. There were dozens of odd sacks hanging from the walls, all split open like flesh balloons. Pieces of equipment that Jasper couldn't identify were scattered all over the tunnel. Some of the machinery hummed and glowed while other pieces seemed to be under construction.

Jasper didn't know how the kobold designed its devices, but

many of them had semi-regular designs. They reminded him of wasp nests, beautifully and intricately designed in mathematically complex patterns by creatures that were actually quite dim. He suspected the kobold, which was apparently part mechanical itself, operated as much off of some crude machine instinct as any sort of coherent thought process.

The burst egg sacks were a more disturbing sight. More kobolds could only spell trouble at any size. There was no way of knowing how long ago the clutch hatched or where the creatures were now.

This was also where the kobold had stocked most of her building materials. There were great heaps of junk piled around, waiting to be turned into more infernal machines. Jasper recognized some of the equipment as being taken from mine vehicles and excavators, but there were also things that had obviously been ferreted away from the surface, including an entire cigarette vending machine, a phonograph player, and an electric stove. Apparently, the kobold's minions had been more active on the surface than anyone had realized.

There were also non-mechanical, organic parts lying around. There were limbs and other pieces of human beings scattered throughout the alcove. Some of the parts had been heavily modified with motorized doohickeys and alien tchotchkes whose purpose Jasper couldn't even begin to guess at. Maybe the kobold assembled its warriors piece-by-piece like a Ford assembly line.

As fascinating as it all was, Jasper was less interested in the junk collection and the array of mechanized limbs than he was in the military equipment. Two small tanks sat in the corner, fresh off the factory floor. Their cold steel skin gleamed in the dim glow of the truck's headlights. They were so new that they hadn't even been painted. With all the activity, the kobold must not have had time to disassemble the vehicles into their constituent components.

What really caught Jasper's attention, though, was the airplane. The biplane was quite a bit more advanced than the little "pusher" plane he'd piloted during the war, but the controls were basically similar. Even though it was apparently some sort of prototype scout plane, it had guns mounted under its wings. There was a second seat behind the pilot's, allowing a passenger to either work the rear machine gun or the photographic equipment installed in the plane's belly.

Jasper turned his attention away from the aircraft to focus on the uranium bomb stashed in this section of the tunnels. There would be more elsewhere, but Jasper only needed this one for the plan in his head to work. A three-person USGS team lay dead nearby, torn to shreds by the kobold. He walked over to the unpacked bomb, which resembled an egg laid by a giant mechanical chicken.

"Do you have any idea how to arm that?" Amelia asked.

"Not really," Jasper said, keenly aware that he was tampering in matters he didn't understand.

The bomb had a manual override, in case the remote detonator didn't work or was otherwise destroyed. Currently, Sadie's detonator was floating around inside the kobold's guts, and Jasper had no interest in trying to retrieve it. Fortunately, there were steps for how to activate the bomb painted directly next to a large lever, an analog timer, and a plug on the side of the bomb. Jasper read the instructions. They were somewhat vaguer than he would have liked, clearly intended for trained engineers who were already intimately familiar with the weapon's workings and capabilities.

The final instruction was especially unhelpful. "Retreat to a safe distance." He intended to be all the way out of the mine by the time this thing went off. When these bombs blew, they were going to unleash a flood that would make Noah soil his drawers. Anyone left in the tunnels would be in serious trouble, so he needed to build in quite a bit of time.

An hour ought to do it. Yes, an hour would give them plenty of time, even if they were forced to detour through the tunnels to avoid an emergency. He pumped the lever, priming the bomb. Then he removed the plug and connected the appropriate clamps.

Immediately, the analog timer flipped from straight zeros to its maximum time limit: fifteen minutes.

Well, crap.

He was sorely tempted to write an angry letter to USGS about the quality of the instructions that came with their doomsday weapons.

"Amelia, do you think you can drive that truck back to the mine entrance inside of fifteen minutes?"

"Maybe. It's a few miles away, and this vehicle wouldn't exactly tear up the streets. Wait. Why?"

"Get in the truck."

"You set it to fifteen minutes? Why the hell did you set it to only fifteen minutes?"

"I set it for the maximum," Jasper said testily. "Now get in the truck. We need to get out of here right now."

The seconds ticked down on the bomb's timer.

Before Amelia could toss open the truck's door, a loud rumble filled the tunnel in front of them. Jasper drew his pistol, not that it was likely to do much good against whatever was approaching.

Suddenly, Jasper caught a glimpse of shapes moving amid the blackness, and he swallowed. About a dozen motorcycles howled into the tunnel, their headlights flashing. The riders were also armed with Thompson submachine guns. Jasper would have expected nothing less from Gerhard Schackel.

Fourteen minutes remaining.

Schackel himself stepped off one of the motorcycles. "Ah, Amelia," he said. "I'm so glad I found you. And my dear Mister O'Malley. A pleasure to see you again."

"We need to get out of here, Gerhard" Amelia said. "This place is rigged to blow. We'll hitch onto the back of your motorcycles; they're a lot faster than the truck we were going to use."

Schackel threw up a hand, halting her. "I know all about the bombs. We captured one of the USGS men above while they were trying to escape. He proved most talkative after he was properly motivated."

"Amelia's right, Schackel," Jasper said. "I've already activated the bombs. This place is about to blow sky high and flood out the tunnels."

"Deactivate the bomb." Schackel's men shifted their Tommy guns slightly, bringing them to bear in Jasper and Amelia's general direction.

"What?" Amelia shouted.

"You asked me to kill this thing," Jasper said. "I'm about to do just that."

"*Natürlich.* I provided you with the one motivation that would allow you to overcome your own misgivings and work with me. Mostly, I just needed the other interested parties, Detroit Salt and USGS, eliminated so I could have the creature for myself. Having you around as a wildcard helped play them off each other. Your work was admirable, by the way. Now, deactivate the bomb, please."

"This is a bad idea, Gerhard," Amelia said. "You don't know what this thing is capable of."

"No. I'm actually quite aware. I recovered some ... artifacts related to the creature, small devices it's created. This beast is worth an incalculable fortune. The diamonds alone are worth considerably more than their weight in gold, but if someone were to license and patent the technology it's been producing, well, let's just say that Mister Ford would no longer be the king of Detroit."

Thirteen minutes remaining.

Either Schackel honestly thought he could use the kobold for his own purposes or the "artifacts" he'd found had corrupted his thinking the way the kobold seemed to poison everything it touched. Neither option was good.

"Gerhard, you really don't want to do this. Those artifacts are affecting your mind," Amelia started. She was speaking in the calm, reasonable voice one used to speak to a child who had found a gun and was pointing it at you.

Schackel drew his Luger and shot her. She sat down with a soft *oof*, clutching the hole that had suddenly sprouted from her lower abdomen. Blood gushed out of the wound, quickly staining her shirt and pants crimson.

"Do not question my judgment," Schackel said, a wild expression in his eyes. For a second, the look softened, and he looked down at the gun in his hands as if surprised to find it there.

Jasper's pistol was instantly in his hand, but an abundance of Tommy guns focused on him before Amelia even hit the ground. She was staring at the wound in shock. If she didn't get medical treatment very, very quickly, she would almost certainly die.

Then Jasper remembered that they'd probably all be obliterated in a massive fireball before she could bleed out. Schackel's Luger twisted around to point at Jasper.

"Disarm the bomb, if you would be so kind." The strange look was back on Schackel's face.

Twelve minutes remaining.

Amelia lay on the ground whimpering. She looked up at Jasper.

Behind Jasper, there was nothing but a hard wall of salt and the bomb, rapidly ticking down to their deaths. Jasper wasn't even sure he *could* disarm the thing. Even if he did disarm the bomb, it wasn't as if Schackel would allow him to live.

"Mister Schackel, you are my de facto employer at the moment, a situation that I find most unfortunate. When you contacted me, or rather abducted me, to hire out my services, I'm afraid we didn't have time to discuss some of the specifics in the standard Attican Detective Agency contract. Namely, I can unilaterally cancel any contract in which the client becomes uncooperative or otherwise unduly interferes with an investigation. Unfortunately, and to my enormous regret, I must cordially entreat you to go fuck yourself."

Schackel's mouth quirked upward in a smile. "If you just requested to be terminated, I assure you, I am more than happy to oblige you." He pointed the Luger at Jasper. His finger started to tighten against the trigger.

Suddenly there was a noise from deeper inside the tunnel. Schackel and his men whipped around. It wasn't the tapping sound of the kobold clamoring across the roof of the tunnels, but it was similar. The sound was more like a clatter, and it grew louder, rapidly approaching. Schackel's men cradled their weapons and looked at each other.

Jasper used the opportunity to go to Amelia. He quickly examined her wound. It was bad, and it no doubt hurt like hell. But the right medical care might save her. Maybe.

"*Was ist das?*" Schackel's men bunched together. Jasper gazed up, waiting for some towering beast to appear. The noise grew louder.

Suddenly, something burst into the truck's headlamps and stood before the assembled men like some proud jungle beast that had deigned to show itself to the pathetic humans entering its realm.

It was also the size of a chicken. The creature was a miniature kobold, exactly like its larger counterpart in every way except for its diminutive size. This must be one of the creatures that had inhabited the egg pouches scattered all over the chamber.

Schackel looked at the tiny creature. *"Fuerer frei,"* he ordered, and his men immediately opened fire. A dozen bullets hit the little monster at once, shredding it into something that looked like a hearty soup whose secret ingredient came from the nightmares of children.

"Hmph," Schackel scoffed.

There was a moment of preternatural silence, and then more creatures began to boil out of the tunnel in a massive swarm, moving straight for Schackel and his men. Even as they came, they were all fighting, ripping at each other, tearing legs off and eating them, puncturing each other's bodies with their massive tarsal claws. The sound they made as they moved was like a freight car having a seizure.

Thirty of them were killed and devoured by their own comrades just in the time it took the first wave to move fully into the light, but it made no difference in their overall numbers. They were legion. Schackel shouted for his men to fire, and they emptied their Tommy guns into the approaching horde. Bullets sliced into tiny, hissing bodies and pinged off the floor, ricocheting into the darkness. Some of the creatures stopped to devour the remains of their slaughtered siblings only to be consumed in turn by the carnivorous parade behind them. Hundreds of the creatures died in the span of a few seconds, but Schackel might as well have been trying to order the tide back by shooting it.

The tidal wave of tiny writhing bodies collided with the first row of Schackel's men and swept over them. They attacked the men's legs, chomping their feet, slicing Achilles tendons, tearing off knee caps. Shrieking in German, Schackel's elite guards went down and were immediately covered in a carpet of writhing, hungry bodies. The wave of tiny monstrosities bounced and struggled for a moment, like someone caught under their sheets thrashing their way out of a bad dream, and then the shapes buried underneath the forms went still.

Nor were the creatures particularly discriminate. They bit the leather seats off the motorcycles, tried to eat the tires, dug apart the engines with their claws.

Eleven minutes remaining.

Jasper jumped up, leaving Amelia, and ran back to the far end of the tunnel. They couldn't use the truck anymore. Even if Amelia was in any shape to drive, they simply couldn't outrun the blasts at this point, so that left only one option. Jasper was going to have to fly the scout plane through the tunnels and out to the mine's entrance. Granted, that plan was probably insane, but his other options involved being incinerated, being drowned, being eaten alive, or any combination of those three things. If ever there was a time to rely on insane plans, this was probably it.

Operating almost from muscle memory, Jasper started the plane's engine. Jasper went over a quick preflight checklist in his mind.

Fuel?

Check.

Wings?

Attached to plane.

Perfect. He was good to go. He ran back to grab Amelia.

Schackel's men were trying to retreat, but the kobold tsunami outpaced them. The Germans hosed the endless stream of miniature monsters with streams of bullets, but they might as well have been trying to put out a five-alarm fire with squirt guns. If anything, the scent of blood and splattered viscera only urged the baby kobolds in the back to push forward harder.

More of Schackel's men went down in a scramble of kicking legs and slashing claws. Hungry little mouths tore flesh from bone. The surge of kobolds was as unstoppable as a magma flow, consuming everything before it.

One of Schackel's remaining men turned and ran, not that there was anywhere to run to. Schackel gunned the man down with his Luger, executing him on the spot, but it was too late. Seeing one of their comrades scamper away from the dwindling position automatically triggered some primal panic instinct, and the line dissolved. The couple of men who stood firm were almost instantly overrun as the surging swell of kobolds washed over them.

It didn't really matter that the tunnel was a dead end. Faced with the sight of their friends being eaten alive, even seasoned storm troopers might break down into raw, unthinking fright.

Ten minutes remaining.

Jasper grabbed Amelia. She gasped in pain, but there was simply no way to be gentle about it. One of the tiny creatures scampered forward, and Jasper shot it. It burst like a lanced boil, and two more instantly took its place. He dragged Amelia backward as quickly as he could, grabbing her under her arms. Amelia was breathing hard through clenched teeth, her heels dragging against the salt rock floor.

They were almost to the plane now. One of Schackel's men was trying to climb into the pilot's seat. Jasper shot him, and the man tumbled off the side of the aircraft. Several of the others piled into the waiting tanks, closing the hatches overhead.

Jasper ignored them. If the tanks didn't melt down to hot metal tallow when the bombs went off, they'd be crushed when the roof of the mine collapsed. If they weren't killed when the roof of the mine collapsed, they'd all drown when Lake Erie flooded the tunnels. No matter what, they weren't Jasper's problem, and that's all he really cared about right now.

"You're heavier than you look, Amelia," he grunted.

"Oh, eat it, Jasper," she managed to say. He was trying to keep her from going into shock.

Another kobold charged Amelia's trailing legs. Jasper fired his pistol at the creature, but he couldn't keep a good grip on Amelia and aim at the same time. The bullet missed, kicking up a spray of salt from the floor.

He tried to stomp on the creature before it could get to Amelia. That was a mistake.

Quick as a snake, the little kobold twisted around and barred its vertical mouth. Lunging forward, the creature clamped onto Jasper's foot. Its razor-like teeth snipped through the leather and tore into his foot. Leather, skin, muscle, it all dissolved to red rags. Jasper shouted and shook his leg, but the beastie clung on.

He unwrapped one arm from Amelia and leveled his pistol squarely at the tiny kobold. He pulled the trigger, blowing the creature off his foot like sticking a lit cigarette into a leech.

What was left of the end of his foot dangled uselessly from his leg as if it had been partially sawn off. The pain was unbelievable. It roared up his leg like red lightning, pounding in time with his heartbeat. Nevertheless, he grabbed Amelia again and continued to walk backward, balancing on his heel. It was awkward and painful, but he couldn't stop now.

They reached the plane, and Jasper hefted Amelia roughly into the passenger seat. She screamed as he manhandled her into the bucket seat, but there was nothing he could do about it. Even with two good feet, it would have been impossible to lift her in gently. With one foot partially chewed off, it was an effort of pure will to maneuver her into the seat.

He hobbled around to the pilot's seat, stepping gingerly up the rungs built into the side of the fuselage. The wave of kobolds was nearly upon them.

Suddenly, a calloused hand smacked down on Jasper's shoulder and peeled him off the side of the plane, tossing him backward. Jasper landed on his bad foot, and the world went black and white with pain for a second as he tumbled onto his back. His pistol fell to the ground beside him, just out of reach.

Nine minutes remaining.

Schackel stood on the rungs of the plane looking down. "Sorry, Mister O'Malley, but there's only room enough for one on this flight." Jasper pawed for his pistol, but his hands were slick with Amelia's blood and his senses dumb with pain.

Slowly, almost lazily, Schackel drew his Luger with one hand and aimed it at Jasper's chest. The crest of the kobold swarm was only a few feet away, scuttling toward Jasper at an alarming rate. His bloody fingers strained for the grip of his pistol. A young kobold darted forward and attacked the pistol, testing to see if it was food. Jasper snatched his arm back as the creature spat out mangled metal.

"Goodbye, Jasper," Schackel said, cocking his Luger. He seemed to be enjoying the show.

Without warning, a hole suddenly appeared in Schackel's chest. Two more appeared in quick succession. He looked down in surprise as blood frothed out of his body.

"Oh," Schackel said. The Luger fell from his fingertips and clattered to the ground. He wobbled for a second, and then pitched forward at the base of the plane. The German lay face down, not moving.

"You can't fire me. I quit," Amelia said, clutching her own pistol in the passenger seat. Her face was pale and drenched in sweat, and it looked like it took her enormous effort to hold the smoking weapon. She waved. "Hurry, Jasper."

Jasper clawed his way forward, keeping inches ahead of the kobold horde. He bounced up onto his one good leg, leaving a slimy trail of blood. Hobbling forward, he scooped up Schackel's Luger to replace his own lost pistol and scrambled into the plane as quickly as he could. Putting any weight at all of his ravaged foot was pure agony.

Still, the alternative of being ripped apart and eaten alive was a powerful motivator, and Jasper lurched up the rungs away from the brood of kobolds. The kobolds descended on Schackel's body like an army of crabs feasting on a beached whale. He plunked himself into the pilot's seat and worked the controls. The plane began to roll forward.

It was significantly more complicated than riding a bike, but Jasper still remembered how to operate an airplane. The propeller howled in the confined space, kicking up salt dust in a whirlwind.

Eight minutes remaining.

The plane gathered speed, crushing dozens of little kobolds beneath its wheels. Jasper hit the guns, blowing a path forward through the mass of scrabbling abominations covering the floor of the mine.

All the tunnels were essentially straight lines radiating out from the mine entrance like the spokes of a wheel. Jasper simply needed to barnstorm the entire length of the tunnel until he reached the central entrance. He opened the throttle, and the plane pushed forward across the carpet of writhing creatures, creating kobold roadkill. The plane accelerated, pushing down the tunnel like a bullet down the barrel of a gun. With another push of the throttle, Jasper was suddenly airborne, buzzing into the darkness.

Chapter 29
Pillar of Salt

Seven minutes remaining.

The plane had a set of powerful lights for landing at night. Without them, Jasper and Amelia probably would have died within a couple of seconds after leaving the ground.

There was almost no room to maneuver. The wheels were only a few feet off the ground, and the wood-framed upper wings were only a few feet away from the ceiling. Flying dead center in the middle of the tunnel, the wing tips were never more than a yard from the rough-hewn walls. One wrong twitch on the controls and they'd become a pile of flaming wreckage spread out across a quarter mile of tunnel.

Jasper flew as slowly as he could without stalling out, keenly aware that he was also racing the clock. But the tunnels weren't actually completely straight. They'd been carved out with explosives, and then chiseled down by the miners. In some places, the tunnels were marginally wide or dreadfully narrow. In other places, they meandered ever so slightly where a point of unexpected resistance had crimped the mining efforts. Any miscalculations would lead to a flaming hot, Cajun-style, fiery death.

Unfortunately, that wasn't the worst of Jasper and Amelia's problems. While the plane's landing gear had crushed a lot of the toy-sized kobolds, the struts served as a convenient grasping point for others. A kobold used its hooked claws to climb up the side of the plane toward the passenger compartment.

"There's something on the wing," Amelia said. Her voice was weak and strained. She wouldn't last much longer.

Twisting around with Schackel's Luger, Jasper shot the beast; it slid off the wing and fell into the darkness. Another one immediately tried to take its place, and Jasper fired another round, severing the creature's front leg. The creature fell away, but its oversized claws and leg remained attached to the side of the plane like an organic piton.

Something started to burrow through the floor of the pilot compartment. Jasper aimed the Luger directly between his feet as a hole crumbled away there and was replaced by a ferocious little mouth. The mouth disappeared with a shriek as a bullet punched into it. He just hoped the creature hadn't chewed through anything vital, like a fuel line.

The plane was like a dog beset by giant fleas, and Jasper had no idea how many bullets were in the Luger. He hadn't grabbed any ammunition off Schackel. Once this clip was empty, he was dry.

He risked a glance back at Amelia. She had both her hands clamped over her wound. Blood was still seeping out from between her fingers. She was in no shape to be shooting. "Give me your pistol," he ordered. The weapon was placed in his hand, supplementing his firepower.

Six minutes remaining.

They were maybe halfway to the mine's entrance, making good time. Jasper might have allowed himself a modicum of hope if he didn't have to spin around and shoot another kobold off the plane's fuselage.

Another of the devilish creatures appeared at the front of the plane, near the propeller. Jasper pointed the Luger at it and pulled the trigger.

Click. Empty.

He stashed the weapon away and switched to Amelia's pistol. It barked once, and the kobold exploded like a Thanksgiving turkey stuffed full of firecrackers. Ichor splashed over the plane's skin.

More of the creatures were making their way to the top of the plane or chewing through into the passenger areas. Jasper made short work of them.

"Reload," he handed the pistol back to Amelia. He didn't want to risk taking both hands off the controls. The weapon was taken from his hand, leaving them temporarily vulnerable.

Another creature appeared on the rim of the pilot's compartment directly next to him. It hunched itself up, preparing to leap at him. Jasper reached for the nearest available weapon he had on hand, the severed kobold leg still stuck to the side of the airplane. He yanked it out of the plane's skin like a gigantic sliver and jabbed at the creature with the makeshift dagger.

The viciously curved claws skewered the small kobold, pinning it to the edge of the compartment like an alien entomology display. Jasper reached back, and the gun was planted in his hand again. He quickly dispatched several more little kobolds, but he was starting to lose ground.

Suddenly, a faint blue glow appeared just beyond the plane's landing lights. Jasper thumbed the machine gun trigger. The plane's weapons sent a thunderclap of metal roaring into the tunnel, but he was too slow. A crackling ball of energy blasted straight toward the plane. Jasper didn't even have time to warn Amelia to hold onto something as the aircraft violently dipped, its landing gear bouncing hard against the ground.

The energy projectile sizzled past, blasting a hole in the mine's ceiling. Molten salt rained down behind the plane like a cloudburst in hell.

Jasper kept his finger pressed to the trigger. He couldn't really see what he was aiming at, but he didn't need to when he could turn the mine shaft into a bullet cauldron.

All of a sudden, a gout of pulsating blue energy erupted outside the reach of the landing lights. *Bullseye.* In a flash, Jasper passed over the kobold soldier. It was rapidly overloading, jittering madly like an out-of-control paint shaker. In the blink of an eye, the sight was behind them.

This time, Jasper was able to warn Amelia to hold onto something. He only got a groan in response. Ignoring the little kobolds that were swarming the plane for a moment, he braced both hands on the controls. A few seconds later, the entire tunnel flashed brilliant blue, nearly singeing Jasper's corneas out of his skull. Before he could even blink, the compression wave from the explosion hit them from the rear.

In the confines of the tunnel, the explosion couldn't disperse properly, so it spread out laterally. The wave of hot air battered the aircraft, but the plane was traveling fast enough that they were already at the very edge of the compression envelope. Any closer and they'd have been tossed straight into a wall or simply vaporized.

Some of the baby kobolds fell off the wings as the blast rattled the plane. They lost their grip on the side of the aircraft and plummeted to the ground. Jasper used his pistol to pick off the last few stragglers.

Five minutes remaining.

It was still dark, but the gloom was growing less pervasive, less oppressive. They must be approaching the mine entrance. Jasper could hardly believe it. He could see the proverbial light at the end of the tunnel. They were nearly home free! So close!

Yet so far. Something swung down from a crevice in the ceiling and clipped the plane. The airplane shuddered for a second, and Jasper looked over.

The entire left wing was gone.

The kobold queen had set up a trap.

If Jasper had been flying higher, the sudden loss of control surfaces would have sent the plane spiraling out of the air and auguring into the ground in a plume of smoke. As it was, he didn't have far to fall.

Pure momentum dragged the plane forward at a relatively stable pitch for a few seconds, and that was enough time for Jasper to put the plane into a controlled drop. He forced them down hard on the landing gear just as they burst into the mine's entrance chamber.

One of the gears snapped, and the plane collapsed onto its belly. The salty ground acted like a giant sheet of sandpaper, grinding away the bottom layers of the aircraft. In front of Jasper, the propeller clipped the ground and tore itself apart, pelting the surrounding cavern with sharp-edged debris. Flames spurted from the engine as the plane ground to a stop.

Jasper looked around. Lance Basilhart looked back at him.

The surviving Pinkertons had evidently gone into the mine to track down him and Schackel's crew. Now they were gathered around a mining truck, an array of parts from other vehicles spread out around it. Evidently, all of the remaining vehicles had been picked apart by the kobold workers, and Basilhart was trying to build a single working vehicle from the parts left over from the dozen or so other mining trucks.

Four minutes remaining.

"You always did know how to make an entrance, Mister O'Malley." Basilhart reached into his jacket and pulled out a revolver. The weapon's handle had been refinished with ivory inlays, and the initials "L.B." were done in a fancy script printed in gold leaf. It was a dandy's weapon, but that didn't mean it couldn't blow a man's head off, and the Pinkerton had him dead to rights.

"Your employers are dead, Basilhart. USGS wiped out the warehouse where they were performing their studies. You don't have a horse in this race anymore. You don't stand to gain anything by killing me."

"*Au contraire*, I stand to gain a great deal of satisfaction. Ever since I found out you survived that incident in Pennsylvania, you have been one of my few pieces of unfinished business. Besides, there are more of the sort where Gerald Ransom came from. I'll be reporting to someone new for the exact same purposes within a week. They won't be particularly eager to see you walk away from this alive, either."

There was a sound from the tunnel like the end of the world, a dreadful screech that made everyone cringe. Suddenly, the kobold emerged from the passageway. It was colossal, bigger than three circus elephants. The kobold queen bellowed again, and everyone reacted as if heated railroad spikes had just been driven into their ears. The sound echoed and re-echoed off the walls.

Basilhart took one look at the monster and put his pistol away. He smiled at Jasper. It was not a pleasant expression. "Actually, I have a better idea. There would be a certain sort of poetry in leaving you to die yet again in yet another mine, don't you think? And besides, if this thing eats you, I might just ask for a bonus when Detroit Salt sells the resulting diamond. Goodbye, Jasper." Basilhart gestured to his men, who kept their own guns pointed at Jasper while they scurried toward the elevator.

Only one of the elevators appeared to be working. One was a pile of crumpled metal at the base of the shaft, and the ropes for the other were weirdly slack. They must have been destroyed during the battle at the surface. Jasper knew from experience that it took the elevators a little over three minutes to make a round trip from the top, down to the base, and back up to the top. He checked his watch.

Three minutes remaining.

Even if the other elevators worked, the blast would catch up to them. It would displace the air out of the tunnels and send it hurtling all the way through to the mine entrance in a superheated mass. Even if the blast didn't knock the elevator off its cables, it would very likely cook them alive.

Then there was the kobold to worry about, and she was not a happy camper. She shrieked again and lumbered forward like a living calamity.

Basilhart stepped into the remaining elevator with his men. He waved goodbye as he closed the cage door and pulled the lever. The elevator ascended toward the surface, leaving Jasper and Amelia behind. Now this was a dilemma.

"Are all of you private dicks such smug bastards, or did you two have to take a special class?" Amelia asked. Her voice was distant and frail.

"It's a gift." With Basilhart and his thugs out of sight, Jasper shimmied his way out of the plane. There was a growing pool of blood on the floor. Some of it was from his foot, and some of it had seeped forward from the passenger seat. He gritted his teeth as he landed on the ground. The world flared out of focus and went wobbly for a second. It felt like his foot was on fire.

Then the kobold bellowed again and snapped him back to reality. He'd heard artillery bombardments that were gentler on the ears. The creature began to approach them. It moved with a lazy confidence, like a lion coming over to investigate a toddler that had fallen into its enclosure at the zoo. It seemed to remember Jasper, and not fondly. Showing its teeth, its mouth parts clacked menacingly.

He started to lift Amelia out of the plane. "*Mmfph*," she grunted, trying to wave him away. Her eyes were drooping, as if she were on the verge of going to sleep. This was not good.

Jasper had a plan. It was a terrible plan, but terrible plans had kept them alive this far, and he didn't have anything else at this point. He wasn't leaving Amelia behind, though.

Grabbing her with rough hands, he hoisted her out of her seat. She screamed again, but at least she seemed to wake up a little bit. He dragged her away from the plane.

Some of the kobold's posse were beginning to emerge from the tunnel behind their master. Jasper spied warriors with their otherworldly cannons and workers and more of those poor, bloated things that seemed to tend to the kobold itself. They slowly fanned out, cutting off access to the other tunnels. Behind Jasper, creatures emerged from their hidey-holes and blocked the path to the tunnels on that side of the mine as well.

They were completely cut off.

Two minutes remaining.

The elevator continued to whir and grind as Basilhart's car rushed toward the surface. All around them, the kobold's minions were creeping closer, tightening their circle around them. Jasper undid his belt and used it to lash Amelia to him, freeing up his hands. She was fading again.

"Stay with me, Amelia," he said. She mumbled something in response. He lifted her pistol, the only loaded weapon they had between them, and panned it across the sea of nightmare faces all around them. It was a panorama of corrupted flesh and dead souls. Jasper felt much worse for these ruined creatures than he did for victims who at least were provided the dignity of death. These poor bastards were being forced to serve the very thing that had robbed them of their humanity, like unwilling participants in some Haitian voodoo curse.

At least to Jasper, there was some comfort in the fact that he'd never become one of those things. The blast from the uranium bombs would blast the flesh off his bones. If it didn't, Jasper still had the pistol, and he could give Amelia and himself a merciful end.

He retreated toward the bank of elevators at the center of the shaft, but there was nowhere to go. Right now he was simply delaying the inevitable.

The kobold towered above its thralls. Jasper could have shot at it, but at best, he'd succeed in annoying it. She seemed to be enjoying this, playing with him.

Gnarled, clawed hands reached for him, and he backed up to the very base of the elevators. There was nowhere else to go. Basilhart's elevator continued to clank from somewhere overhead.

Suddenly, he felt something. It wasn't a physical sensation. There was something inside his thoughts, slithering through his mind. The kobold was trying to get into his brain, the same way it broke Gottschalk and Renfield.

He tried to shut it out, but it scratched at the edge of his thoughts like hungry wolves pawing at a cabin's flimsy door. The mental blockade only succeeded for a few seconds before the kobold thrust its way back into his head, penetrating his every secret, his every memory, profaning everything it touched. It felt like the creature was rifling through his thoughts like a filing cabinet.

Without warning, the kobold withdrew from his mind with a sort of psychic sucking sensation. His entire brain tingled.

What had it wanted from him? Was this just part of its game?

Jasper quickly found out. Amelia, who had been slumped against him, suddenly juddered bolt upright, nearly jerking Jasper off his feet. Before he could even react, she twisted around and tried to clamp her teeth down on his neck. He managed to block her by throwing a shoulder up.

She bit down hard, but the gray cloth of his suit kept her from tearing down to his skin. It would still leave a semi-circular bruise, though. He yanked his shoulder away, a clump of the suit ripping away in Amelia's mouth in the process.

The kobold was in her head. In her weakened state, it could pull her strings like a puppet, and it was commanding her to attack him. After probing his mind for easy access, it moved on to Amelia and found her too spent to resist.

Jasper thrust an arm up under her chin, pushing her head back and preventing her from biting anymore. Instead, her arms came up and tried to scratch his eyes out. He stretched as far as he could from her grasp, but they were tied together with his belt.

As he leaned back, he bumped into something behind him. It was one of the kobold workers. The creature didn't really have a face anymore, just a crazed blight of crooked rodent teeth. He raised Amelia's pistol as its claws reached for him. The pistol barked once, and the creature's head popped like an overripe melon left out in the sun. Another horror had taken its place before the first had even slumped to the ground. More arms reached out for him.

Amelia went limp. A string of drool dribbled from the corner of her mouth. Then, the kobold was back in Jasper's head, punishing him for killing the worker. He screamed and went to his knees. It felt like a hook-studded whip was flagellating his cerebral cortex.

He couldn't even move. The pain was sizzling, corrosive, like his brain had been dipped in boiling lard and stuck back in his skull to simmer.

One minute remaining.

Suddenly, something swooped down from above and landed directly behind Jasper with a heavy *thud*. This was what he had been waiting for.

In principle, cable elevators were very simple machines. The rope was looped around a grooved pulley which was then attached to an electric motor. At the pull of a lever, the motor would activate and either lower or raise the car. However, to work most efficiently, the car needed a counterweight at the other end of the cable. The counterweight weighed about as much as a typical carload. Thus, when the elevator was full of miners and cargo, the sheave really only had to overcome the force of friction, because the car and counterweight were already more or less in balance. The car would then ride on a set of guide rails as it traveled up and down. As the car was moving, the counterweight was moving in the opposite direction. When the car was at the bottom of the shaft, the weight dangled from the top, a great load of potential energy. When the car was at the top, they switched roles, and the counterweight slid to the bottom of the shaft.

Jasper flopped backward and hurled himself on top of the large metal block that served as the counterweight. At the last second, the kobold seemed to pick out his plan from his mind, and it screeched in his head. It wasn't so much a sound as it was a blast of mental pressure, like a wave of cosmic halitosis. He felt a sensation like cold rat feet scampering across the inside of his skull. The kobold's thralls all surged forward at once on some silent order, suddenly desperate to stop him.

Somewhere 1,200 feet above his head, Lance Basilhart would be throwing open the door to the elevator, most likely grinning from ear to ear. Well, Jasper had something to say about that.

The wire cable supporting the counterweight was too thick to saw through with anything short of a blowtorch, but the pin that connected the cable looked considerably more fragile. Jasper wrapped his hand around the cable and lowered Amelia's pistol. He pulled the trigger and blew the pin tethering the cable and counterweight into oblivion. There was a split second of slack, and then gravity grabbed the elevator high above.

One of the kobold thralls snatched at Jasper, but he ripped away from its grasp like an Old Testament prophet booking it directly to Heaven. Jasper's arm nearly pulled out of its socket as he hurtled violently upward. The kobold's grip on his mind rapidly faded to a dull buzz and then shriveled into nothingness.

Amelia clung weakly to him. The belt keeping them together held as they rocketed up faster than a rookie cop's gorge at his first murder scene. He gripped the cable tight. To slip would mean death.

Exactly halfway up the shaft, Jasper met Basilhart again. He and his men were still in the elevator as it plunged uncontrollably toward the bottom. The other Pinkertons were screaming their lungs out in terror, but, for the briefest of seconds, Basilhart and Jasper locked eyes. Then, in a flash, they passed each other in opposite directions.

Jasper's eyes began to burn as they ascended. It was dawn on the surface. After so long in the dark underground, even the weak light of a new day was almost too much for him. He squinted, his eyes watering against the wind. The weight of the elevator at the other end of his cable meant he was essentially falling straight up.

He needed to keep his grip painfully tight around the cable. It was smooth and slightly greasy, in constant danger of slipping out of his hands. His fingers were starting to cramp up, but the light was growing brighter and brighter.

Looking up, Jasper could see the elevator control gears silhouetted against the pale Detroit sky. Thousands of people would be walking to work, lunch pails in hand. Birds would be chirping. Life would be going about its normal business. That sounded mighty swell right now to Jasper.

Now he simply needed to escape the elevator shaft before the bombs went off.

Zero minutes remaining.

Chapter 30
Fire in the Hole

They zoomed upward toward the gears, the cable rapidly spooling upward. Suddenly, the world flashed white from below, as if a small sun had just ignited inside one of the tunnels. Even from miles away and even looking in the opposite direction, Jasper was almost blinded. He closed his eyes. Everything turned tan and was overlaid with a network of blood vessels as the infernal light assaulted his eyelids.

Jasper came level with the surface, and the cable suddenly bunched up. Down below, the elevator had smashed into the base of the shaft. Momentum briefly continued to carry Jasper and Amelia upward before gravity reasserted itself.

Before they could plunge back down the shaft, Jasper swung the cable out over the edge of the pit like a crazed urban Tarzan. He sailed past several very surprised looking cops.

"Get back!" Jasper yelled, dropping to the ground. His foot went apoplectic on the landing, and he nearly passed out again, but the sheer simple pleasure of being on the surface again kept him conscious. He scrambled away from the shaft, shouting for the cops to follow him. Some of them helped him carry Amelia along.

They obeyed in confusion, probably as much so they could subdue him as because they understood what he was saying. A split second later, a jet of burning air spewed into the sky like a giant middle finger from the earth's core. The blast knocked the cops off their feet and onto the ground. They scrambled across the suddenly burning ground on hands and knees, their palms sizzling. Jasper's hat spontaneously ignited and he threw it off his head.

Sadie had been right. The bombs were more powerful than he'd ever imagined. This was the result of just one bomb. A roar filled the air like the end of the world, drowning out all other noises. Every window within four blocks of the Detroit Salt facility suddenly shattered inward. Jasper's wounds practically cauterized themselves as he crawled away, Amelia still tied to his side. He could slap a weenie on a stick and hold it over his head, and it would all but roast itself.

The blast furnace effect did its best to melt the skin off his face and boil his eyeballs in their sockets. Around the edge of the pit, the earth started to crumble away. The gantry and gears that supported the elevators tumbled down into the widening hole. All they needed was a little brimstone to turn the mining yard into a cozy approximation of hell.

Almost every citizen of Detroit turned at once to look at the column of flame rising above their city. Pedestrians stopped dead and cars smashed into each other as their drivers gawped.

Out on Lake Erie, a geyser suddenly erupted as the lake bed was thrust upward in a violent jolt. Fissures opened up deep under the surface, and old tires, beer cans, and a few unfortunate fish were sucked into the boiling depths and instantly translated into atomic steam.

Water gushed downward into the tunnels beneath the lake, gurgling downward like a giant bathtub. USGS seismographs scattered throughout the region scratched madly as millions of gallons of water flooded the salt mine.

Kobold workers and warriors that hadn't been instantly incinerated thrashed and convulsed underwater as the tunnels were inundated by the great deluge. Bright blue secondary explosions rippled through the tunnels as the kobold soldiers overloaded.

The raging crush of water smashed everything in its path as it swept forward into the darkness. Mining trucks were tossed aside like toys and sent crashing down the tunnels, breaking them to pieces.

Nearly all the newly hatched kobolds were fried black and blasted to dust, but a few managed to survive by burrowing underneath their peers. They were busily snarfing down the cooked flesh of their siblings when the wall of water crashed down on them. In an instant, both the living and dead kobolds were swept away.

Slowly, the pillar of flame faded. The ground immediately around the hole glowed a merry red. Jasper knew that as deep as the blast had been, this wasn't really the main explosion. This was basically the last gasp, the shockwave that followed the explosion proper. A gigantic chili belch from deep within the earth. After a moment, the earth next to the hole cooled to black glass, brittle and hot.

Jasper turned to Amelia. Her hair and eyebrows were singed, but she was still alive. A variety of emergency vehicles were scattered over the property, not just cop cars. Several fire trucks had been dispatched to quench the flames that had been surging out of buildings earlier that night. There was also a large, unmarked cargo truck that looked like it belonged to the military but didn't. A man in a black suit with smoked glasses stood next to the big vehicle. Jasper spotted the bulge of a weapon under his jacket. The man eyed Jasper with apparent distaste.

He had two similarly dressed counterparts who were hurriedly gathering kobold corpses and lifting them into the back of the truck, where they were quickly covered with a canvas sheet, away from prying eyes. Judging from the lumps under the sheet, there were about five of the creatures under there. The remaining USGS troops were nowhere to be seen. This was just the cleanup crew.

There were also ambulances parked nearby, which was what Jasper really wanted. He waved a pair of medics over and unlatched himself from Amelia. Rolling over onto his back, he stared up at the vibrant morning sky. It was a glorious sight.

Letting his head roll to the side, he looked at Amelia. Her eyes were dull and far away, but they swiveled around to focus on him. They lay like that for a few seconds, utterly exhausted, half-delirious from pain, gazing into each other's eyes.

"Thanks," she managed to breathe.

Jasper nodded, too tired to move as the adrenaline drained out of his system. The medics rolled a gurney over and carefully lifted Amelia onto it. Another set of medics came over to examine Jasper. Aside from his foot, most of his injuries were superficial. They started to remove the remains of his shoe, cutting it off with a knife.

"Will she be okay?" Jasper asked, nodding in the direction Amelia was being carted.

"Hard to say right now," the medic said. "She lost a lot of blood, but it looks like the bullet missed anything vital. That definitely puts the odds in her favor."

"Good," Jasper said, too tired for further comment. He'd been awake for roughly forty-eight hours, and on the move nearly the entire time. Even the pain in his foot couldn't completely cut through his exhaustion.

Several police officers came over to look at him, including Hinkmeyer, who didn't look particularly happy. Some of them said things to him, but he was mostly deaf from the explosion, and his brain was mushy and sluggish. His thoughts buzzed in his head. God, he was hungry, and the medics looked delicious.

But still, some shred of unease continued to gnaw at him like a lump in his gut. There was something wrong, something not quite right. He watched the subtle pulse of the medic's jugular vein in the man's throat, imagined ripping it out with his teeth and bathing in the hot warmth that spilled out.

Suddenly, it dawned on him what the problem was, and he sat bolt upright, startling the medics tending to him. "Sir, please. Just lay back and try to relax. This will only take a minute."

Jasper most decidedly had no intention of relaxing at that particular moment. He grabbed the man by the shoulders.

"We need to get out of here," he shouted. The second orderly tried to restrain him, but he brushed the man's hands aside.

He now recognized the buzzing in his head for what it was. It wasn't just a side effect of fatigue and injury. There was a foreign presence in his head, crawling stealthily across his synapses, trying to hijack his thoughts. The sensation exploded tenfold across his mind as it became aware that he'd discovered its presence.

It felt like a large clot moving through the capillaries in his brain, creating a dam and backflow inside his head. The sensation wasn't a physical presence, but it was an invasive lump of psychic energy, and he could feel it probing around in the back of his mind, growing stronger.

"Everybody needs to leave right now!" Jasper shouted. No one moved. They simply stared at him as if he'd gone insane. The medics' hands tried to restrain him again, but instead he clamored to his feet.

Hinkmeyer approached, making conciliatory hand gestures. "Mister O'Malley, you've been through a lot. Maybe it would be best —"

"It's not dead!" The buzzing was growing louder in his head, trying to overpower his thoughts, but Jasper was still strong enough to resist.

There was a frustrated shriek from inside the pit. Everyone turned in surprise at the sound. Even if it couldn't match the sheer volume of the explosion, it was far more dreadful. People began to slowly back away from the hole as a sound began to emanate from inside its walls.

Tap. Tap. Tap.

Howling its rage again, the kobold queen suddenly appeared over the lip of the mine shaft. The monster was in poor shape, but obviously still very much alive. A lot of its skin had been burned off, leaving a twisted armature of charred organic matter and smoking electronics. That obscene blue glow that Jasper knew all too well shone from many of the exposed mechanical elements.

Tatters of smoking meat hung from its steel-frame skeleton. Jasper had no idea what was keeping the creature alive, but then he realized that he didn't know if the monster had ever been truly alive in the first place.

Behind Jasper, the two medics ran away. The ambulance carrying Amelia screeched down the street the second its driver saw what was emerging from the hole.

Hinkmeyer and the rest of the police officers automatically drew their service weapons and began firing at the creature. Their bullets bounced off its frame, leaving no visible damage but clearly annoying the kobold. The black-suited men with the truck pulled out complicated-looking submachine guns and emptied their clips at the monster.

A panel slid back on the creature's side, and a weapon swiveled smoothly out of the opening. It was significantly more advanced than the guns grafted onto the kobold warriors, but it clearly worked on the same basic principles. The cannon jerked around, seemingly with a mind of its own.

After a brief pause, it fired a ball of energy at one of its attackers. Hinkmeyer disappeared in a horrific exclamation point of burning guts. The energy cluster almost completely consumed his body.

Jasper was already moving as fast as he could while the monster was distracted. He had a goal in mind. More bolts of searing energy lanced out and hit anyone foolish enough to stand out in the open.

The kobold's weapon was unnaturally powerful, but it had no penetrating power. The first thing the crackling balls of death touched absorbed all the energy and flew apart. Of course, anyone hiding behind those objects tended to face a spray of burning shrapnel, but that was at least marginally better than being blown apart at a molecular level.

Staying low, Jasper slid from cover to cover, heading toward the truck he'd seen. The man in the black suit was reloading when a jabber of hot blue energy hit him, and he proceeded to scatter himself over the landscape.

Nearby was the corpse of one of the USGS troopers, still sprawled out where he'd fallen. The police hadn't had time to remove all the bodies from the scene yet. He had a string of grenades strapped to his vest, ready for action.

Snatching the grenades, Jasper moved up next to the truck. Several dead kobold warriors were in the back of the vehicle. Most of them looked like they were fairly untouched by bullet marks. They probably had their brains scrambled when the uranium bomb exploded and cut off their contact with the queen.

Screams and gun shots filled the open-air compound. The kobold was making quick work of the men arrayed before it. Blasts of infernal light rippled across the loading area in rapid fire, cutting down a group of police trying to flank the creature's side.

Even preoccupied with raining death on all those around it, the kobold kept a toehold in Jasper's mind. He couldn't completely block it out of his thoughts.

Jasper didn't think it was reading his mind, precisely. At least, not in the way occultists and mediums claimed telepathy worked.

Maybe it would start out trying to influence and twist his thoughts, the way it had Schackel, or it might push to completely override his physical movements the way it had temporarily controlled Amelia. If it was in there long enough, it could probably trigger the release of various hormones and chemicals, slowly transforming the victim into a kobold thrall without the benefits of technological upgrades, like it had done to Renfield and Gottschalk.

In case he was wrong, Jasper did his best to shield his thoughts, letting his plan unfold moment by moment. He didn't want to accidentally trigger any warning for the monstrosity.

He poked his head around the edge of a crate to see what the kobold was doing. Its cannon was currently focused on a group of police holed up behind a group of concrete barriers. The creature hadn't moved from its position at the rim of the hole. It could lay siege to the entire compound from there.

Jasper shuffled out from behind the crate and lunged into the truck's open cab. The vehicle was already running, set to go. Opening the clutch, Jasper punched the gas, and the truck lurched forward. Amelia would have managed a more artful start, but Jasper was out of the gates and away. He grabbed one of the grenades and laid the remaining bunch on the seat beside him.

The kobold's cannon flicked in Jasper's direction. It had been waiting for him to emerge out into the open, biding its time against the other attackers until it had a clear shot at him. Intense blue energy coalesced around the cannon's barrel before launching out at the truck. There were maybe three hundred feet between the truck and the kobold.

Exactly as Jasper had anticipated. The creature was keeping a presence in his mind so it could tell the exact instant he was out in the open. Rather than rushing straight at the creature, he had already swerved the truck out of the way.

A snarl of blue energy impacted the ground where the kobold had anticipated Jasper would be. Earth kicked up into the air, crackling and fusing into molten glass, but Jasper was already in the clear. The creature wasn't aiming directly at him, precisely. It was aiming where it thought he should have been. Jasper focused on a particular area ahead of him but let his hands steer the wheel almost at random.

Another shot of brilliant plasma smashed into the ground where Jasper had been focusing, closer than the last one. The truck's left rear tires caught fire. Right now, Jasper was simply delaying the inevitable. He couldn't dance around the creature's projectiles indefinitely, and eventually it would catch onto his game.

Case in point. As Jasper directed the vehicle behind a row of supply crates, they disintegrated under a violent cascade of energy. Any closer and the truck would have been reduced to a molten puddle of slag.

He was close to the kobold now, less than fifty feet away. Its cannon was depressed almost as low as it could go, trying to track him. Jasper gunned the engine, trying to coax every bit of speed he could out of it. The truck obstinately gathered speed.

Above him, growing brighter and brighter in the windshield, the freakish blue light began to shimmer inside the barrel of the creature's cannon. Jasper was now too close to maneuver, too close to turn back. This was it. The blue light above grew in luminesce until it was a hostile sun directly above Jasper's head, a pulsating ball of pure malice.

Now.

Jasper took the grenade in his hand and ripped the pin out. At the same time, he opened his door and hurled himself clear of the truck, lobbing the grenade back into the cab at the same time. The explosive landed next to the satchel of USGS grenades on the passenger seat.

He landed on the still-hot ground and rolled. Something tore in his injured foot, and even his gritted teeth couldn't contain the scream of pain that bubbled up from his lungs. He tucked himself into a ball, protecting his head but subjecting his arms and ribs to a savage bruising.

Sweeping forward, the truck collided with the kobold, knocking it backward, where it teetered at the edge of the pit. Flailing its quasi-mechanical legs, it desperately sought purchase, but there was nothing to grab onto. The eerie blue light shorted out from the monster's cannon as it wobbled precariously at the edge of the hole.

Shrieking and spitting, it flooded Jasper's mind with horrible, inhuman thoughts. They were things he could never commit to words, for no words in any language on earth could convey the atrocious things squirming through his mind.

Then, like the Titanic disappearing beneath the waves, the kobold teetered backward and was sucked into the darkness along with the truck. A second later, the rattle of explosives reached Jasper's ears. The grenades had gone off. Another shriek sounded in his skull.

But Jasper wasn't counting on the grenades to kill the creature. He doubted they would do much more than scratch and dent its mechanical endoskeleton. It had already proven that it could take worse. Nor did he trust the thousand foot fall to kill the kobold. The monster was damnably hardy. No matter how deep the mine shaft was, Jasper didn't think a mere fall would end the monster.

Jasper clamored to his feet and hobbled away from the edge of the hole as fast as he could. No, he was relying on the truck's cargo to do the deed. The grenades would rip apart the truck, ravaging the dead kobold warriors loaded into the back as well.

If just one of them began to overload, Jasper was predicting it would set off a chain reaction, causing all the creatures to explode at once. Whatever energy source they were powered with, it seemed to be considerably stronger than any conventional explosives when it went off. The kobold queen also had a cannon, a much larger cannon than that of her minions, which seemed to be powered using the same properties. Jasper guessed it had a power source to match, and if that source could be ruptured ...

He tried to drag himself away from the pit faster, but it was slow progress. He wanted to be well clear when everything went off.

Suddenly, there was a blue flash behind him. The squealing in Jasper's head ascended to a crazed gobbling, like a burning turkey farm. Even though the jabbering was all in his head, it was deafening, overwhelming. Jasper staggered away from the pit, hoping his own head didn't explode like a squeezed grape in the process.

Without warning, the hurricane of crimson noises swirling through Jasper's head burst into a flurry of static, and then faded out of existence. At the same time, the entire city of Detroit was lit up in psychotic shades of blue as a massive burst of energy erupted out of the mine shaft.

Crackling fingers of blue plasma shot into the lower stratosphere, miles up. The reverse lighting burst up out of the earth and assaulted the sky. It looked as if Hades had stolen Zeus's lightning bolts and decided to attack the mortal world. For the second time in just a few minutes, the citizens of Detroit stared at the sky in frightened awe.

Jasper heaved himself forward. The lightening wasn't hot, but it made all the hair on his body stand on end. His teeth vibrated unpleasantly in his jaw. Some of the lightning whipped randomly out of the hole and grounded itself against nearby buildings, scoring their walls like burning claws. The concrete and brickwork dissolved like hot wax and dribbled downward. He had no interest in getting fried to a crisp by a stray finger of plasma.

The ground also rumbled beneath his feet. Jasper navigated the quaking landscape like a sailor moving about the decks in a rough storm. A nearby storage warehouse collapsed in a puff of dust.

Behind Jasper, the earth around the pit was black and bubbling from sustained plasma strikes. The edges started to crumble away, falling into the hole. He looked back and saw the earth kicking and bucking like a living thing. More of the ground disappeared behind him.

Moving as quickly as he could, Jasper shambled forward. He moved like a corpse that had been partially reanimated, half-dragging his crippled foot. The hole continued to expand, gaining on him. Boxes and parked emergency vehicles tumbled into the hungry earth. Though the ground was no longer melting, it was collapsing in on itself at an alarming rate.

Jasper tripped as the violent tremors knocked him off his feet. He crawled forward, unable to find the balance to get back to his feet. The ground roared as it crashed in on itself.

There was less lightning now. Only occasional bursts shot out of the ground rather than a vast tangle of branching and forking energy. Jasper didn't wait around to see if the rate of collapse would also slow. He did his best to move forward over the shifting landscape, crawling past an abandoned police car.

Struggling toward the street, Jasper could hear the roar of tumbling dirt gradually begin to slow. He risked a glance backward. The edge of the pit was less than thirty yards away from him, a mere stone's throw.

Just behind him, the police car was sucked into the devouring pit. Jasper couldn't move any faster across the ground, but the hole opened up behind him like a massive mouth. Now, the edge of the pit was a mere ten yards away from him. He crawled for his life. To be swallowed would mean certain doom.

More ground gave way, burrowing a path toward Jasper's heels. A final bolt of energy shot out of the hole, arcing into the sky. Deep in the pit, the angry blue glow faded, receding into the darkness.

Another cleft of earth separated, and Jasper's feet suddenly hung over the darkness. He could feel the ground under his hands beginning to sag and crumble as the hole continued to destabilize. The entire block was no longer shaking, but that didn't mean the destruction was over. It was winding down and becoming more localized.

A small crack in the earth appeared directly in front of Jasper as his platform of rock began to disengage itself from the surrounding deposits. Jasper lunged forward like a crippled frog just as the ground gave way beneath him.

His hands caught the ledge, and he dangled above the darkness. He grasped the edge, waiting for it to give way and plunge him into the abyss.

He waited, but the final descent into darkness never came. The earth below made grating noises, but it was temporarily satiated. For now, the hole had stabilized.

Bruised, exhausted, and aching in places he didn't know he could ache, Jasper pulled himself up over the rim of the massive caldera. He laid on his back and let the morning sunlight fall on his face. It was over.

When he reported back to Chicago, he was going to ask for a bonus. Come to think of it, he had one other request as well. For now, he was happy to simply lay back and let the glorious sunlight wash over him.

Chapter 31
Salt of the Earth

The hospital was bright and smelled faintly of antiseptic and cleaning chemicals. Aside from the occasional hushed voice or the occasional squeak of a wheelchair, it was mostly silent.

Amelia Rio lay on one of the beds in a private room. She hadn't had any visitors, at least not any that she'd cared to speak with. Aside from an aunt who had long ago disowned her, she didn't have any surviving relatives, and her surrogate family members, Schackel's community of criminal outcasts, were either dead or in hiding.

Detroit's criminal underworld had wasted no time in trying to fill the power vacuum left after Schackel's death. Several smaller gangs had stepped up, trying to extend their influence into the niches Schackel had monopolized. Some of *Die Ratten* had already found new homes with new organizations, basically renting themselves out to the highest bidder as elite criminal mercenaries. Others had tried to go straight. Amelia didn't imagine she'd see any of them again.

Her only visitors had been an endless stream of policemen who had come to question her. If she were well, they'd have thrown her right back in the jail where they'd tried to keep her before. As soon as she was strong enough for transfer, they would. Her room was guarded twenty-four hours a day by at least two hulks in blue.

Schackel's death wasn't just an opportunity for the lesser gangs of Detroit. It was also an opportunity for the police. A lot of bribe money had just dried up, and people were scrambling to cover their asses. The police commissioner had been arrested on corruption charges in a massive media brouhaha that competed for space on the front page of the paper with the tragic mining accident at the Detroit Salt Combine's facilities.

The cops were trying to jump on the little operations with both feet before they could grow into a larger problem. As the only high-ranking member of Schackel's entourage that they had been able to capture, Amelia was a prize pig to distract the papers with while the cops purged the corrupt members of the Detroit Police Department.

There was a noise outside her door, muffled voices. It sounded like they were arguing, but she couldn't make out the words. The first voice growled something, and there was a cool response. Again, the first voice said something and rose in intensity.

Suddenly, the door opened and Jasper O'Malley walked into her room. He moved with a slight limp that he was clearly trying to hide. The two cops standing outside her door looked unhappy. Jasper made a shooing gesture with his hand, and they reluctantly shut the door behind him.

"Hello, Miss Rio," he said, his odd green eyes twinkling.

"Jasper! You're the first friendly face I've seen since they brought me here. At least, I hope you're a friendly face. You haven't been hired to pile on me, too, have you?"

"Not yet," he said. "Here, I brought you something." The gray-clad detective held up several books.

"Oh, thank goodness. Do you have any idea how many flecks are on that ceiling tile right, there? One hundred and eighty-eight. I've been counting them over and over to amuse myself."

"I was hoping the newsstand out front would have had something a little more sophisticated," Jasper said, handing Amelia several pulpy-looking titles that seemed to cover the range from haunted castles to medieval love pirates. He placed a small vase of flowers on the table beside her.

"I don't care if you picked up a bunch of manuals on typewriter repair. They've kept me locked up in here to stew the whole time. Every cop in town has marched in here to give me their good cop–bad cop schtick. I could've screamed. How have you been?"

"The doctors managed to save my foot. They're a clever bunch. I would have probably amputated it, myself. Strictly speaking, I'm not supposed to be up and about yet, but I've been just down the hall, mostly filling out paperwork to send back to Chicago. The doctors tell me that you've been recovering nicely."

"Yeah, well, I'm better than I was, at least. I guess I never thanked you for dragging me out of that hole. Some people would have just left me there as dead weight."

Jasper waved that away. "You're a valuable partner, Amelia."

"A valuable partner? Way to woo the ladies, O'Malley."

She saw just the faintest hint of color on his pale cheeks. "So when are you going back to Chicago?" she asked, trying to sound casual.

"I imagine I'll return shortly after you're well enough to be moved."

So he was sticking around until she could be transferred to a prison infirmary. Truth be told, she didn't want him to leave. Her old life had been blown apart by all this. In some ways, this was worse than when she'd lost her father. She'd always been thankful that Schackel was there when she'd had nowhere else to go. It was highly unlikely that any of the other organizations in town would want her, even if she didn't spend the rest of her life in prison. This was worse than starting over from square one.

Even if Jasper was a spook, and perhaps even a bit of a dork, he was an oddly principled one. She trusted him, and he was maybe the only person in the world she could say that about right now.

"How are you doing?" Jasper asked.

"Like I said, I'm healing, bit by bit."

"I can read your medical charts. What I really want to know is how you're feeling. You've been through a lot, and I can't help but feel partially responsible. How are you holding up through all this?"

She told him. It had been a long time since she felt like she could speak openly with someone, but she told him. About how alone she suddenly was. About how she felt like she'd lost her place in the world. About how she didn't want to spend the rest of her life in prison.

Jasper stood and listened to her, letting her pour it all out without interrupting. She surprised herself. Everything had fallen apart, and she felt like he was the one person left she could turn to.

When she finally finished, Jasper nodded solemnly. He removed an Attican Detective Agency badge from his pocket and held it up with his long pianist's fingers. "I've never had much skill at comforting people, but I might have some good news for you." He continued examining the badge.

"Oh?"

"I've been in correspondence with my superiors in Chicago. Once they understood the situation, they began communicating with certain individuals here in Detroit. Given that we more or less cleaned the Detroit underworld from top to bottom, my bosses impressed upon certain city officials that a certain amount of goodwill was owed to the Attican Detective Agency. We cashed in some chips and had the charges against you dropped. Once you're well, the hospital will discharge you, and you'll be free to go. The paperwork just came through. I had to show it to your guards to gain access to this room."

Amelia was flabbergasted. She'd been expecting to rot in some forgotten prison for most of the rest of her life, growing old and bitter. What would she do? Where would she go? She would face the same problems that drove her into Schackel's arms in the first place.

"There is another thing," Jasper said. "I made a special request back to Chicago. It required considerable persuading, maybe a few threats, but in the end, I convinced them."

"What's that?"

"I'm getting a bonus."

"Lucky you," she said, still contemplating what she would do with herself.

"Oh, and I recommended that they make you a job offer." He tossed her the Attican Detective Agency badge. AMELIA RIO was engraved across the bottom in big block letters. "After reading my report, they agreed to draw you up an employment contract immediately. What do you say? Partners?"

She smiled at him.

Chapter 32
The Hungry Earth

Deep beneath Detroit, inside the cold darkness of the flooded tunnels, something moved.

The nuclear explosion that rocked the tunnels had done more than blast a hole up into Lake Erie. The atomic fire had been concentrated by the confined space, trapped, and unable to properly spread out. In addition to carving a path upward to let the water into the tunnels, the explosion had punched a massive crater downward. The blast seared through hundreds of feet of rock, slicing into an underground lake, isolated for millions of years.

The waters there were unfathomably dark, cut off from the sunlight for a seeming eternity. Now, a wide crack in the roof of the cistern connected the lake with the newly flooded salt tunnels.

Something suddenly glowed in the darkness. It was a fish, or at least what served as a fish in the bottomless depths of the lake. Eons of isolation had sent the life forms inhabiting the lake in wildly divergent directions from the things that lived in the surface seas. The creature's bioluminescence flashed again as it ascended toward the large crack.

Thrashing its sinuous, spike-studded body back and forth, it entered the gaping fissure. Horrible-looking needle teeth glistened in its maw as it swam upward. The creature was large enough and mean enough to rip the guts out of a full-grown great white shark.

It only had small, mostly vestigial eyes, but its other senses were heightened. The beast's blunt snout pointed it toward the surface like a living torpedo. It was a sleek, finely tuned killing machine. In a moment, it would become the first creature from its realm to cross into the surface world since before the dinosaurs.

Suddenly, a shape emerged behind the creature, an inkblot among the lake's liquid shadows. In the utter darkness, it was impossible to say what the other creature was, only that it was big.

Very big.

The smaller monster's bioluminescence flashed in danger as it was chased up the underwater chasm. Despite its efforts, the creature's flashes were in vain.

A set of truly gigantic jaws clamped down on the smaller creature, biting it in half. The fish creature popped like a meat balloon between the leviathan's teeth.

With a few flicks of its scaly tail, the larger monster swished its way up to the edge of the fissure. Its sensory glands scented the waters above. Numerous signals tingled it senses. They were strange, foreign scents.

But they were also full of prey. With no further thoughts save its insatiable hunger, the creature swam upward, toward the surface.

ABOUT THE AUTHOR

Jonah Buck wanted to learn everything there was to know about pale, semi-human creatures that flit across the sunless landscape to terrorize the living, so he became an Oregon attorney. His interests include professional stage magic, history, paleontology, monster movies, and exotic poultry.

Press
Presents

For more Jasper O'Malley adventures, be sure to check out *ATTACK! of the B-Movie Monsters: Alien Encounters* and *Cranial Leakage: Tales from the Grinning Skull, Volume II.*

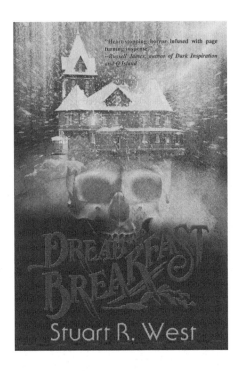

It's the worst snowstorm Missouri has ever seen, and nine strangers, each harboring their own secrets, find themselves sharing a roof at the Dandy Drop Inn, where everybody is treated like family.

Jim and Dolores Dandy wouldn't dream of turning anybody away, especially not on the worst night in Missouri's history, because that just wouldn't be neighborly.

Before the storm is over, blood will flow.

Who will survive to see the storm finally pass?

Something lurks beneath the surface of Cooper Lake. Something hungry. Something intelligent. Something that preys on those who venture too close to its domain. The native Indians had a name for it. ONIARE In 1939, its victim was a young drifter. Dave Longo fought and killed it then, but it won't stay dead. It returned in 1956 to claim the lives of two young men. For Dave, its return was a reunion in Hell. It's now 2014 and the creature has returned again, but Dave Longo is not around to face it a third time. The task becomes the responsibility of Ryan Lowell, a child the oniare had terrorized back in '56, but can he overcome his childhood fears to vanquish the oniare once and for all.

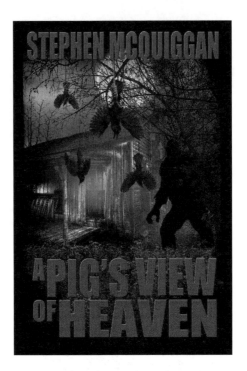

There's something in Troughton's Moss that speaks to the people of Ellsford; it whispers in their ears, burrows into their minds, like a Brainworm, and tells them what to do.

THE MADONNA
Twenty years ago it spoke to Paul Cunningham and set the wheels in motion.
He brutally murdered, then raped a young woman.
A short while later, within the narrow confines of her grave, she gave birth to ...

THE CHILD
Grown to young adulthood, it moves undetected among the people of Ellsford with only one purpose.

THE END TIMES
The time has come. The Moss is beginning to give up its dead, sacrifices made in its name throughout the ages.

THE CHOSEN ONE
Dobson Heather, a child of the Moss himself, has been marked. But is he Ellsford's salvation, or their damnation?

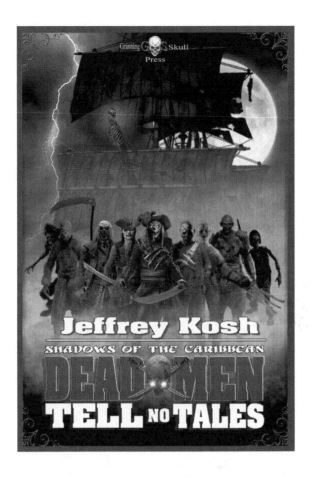

The Caribbean Sea, 1708 AD. In Port Royal many have heard the legend of the Black Brig, a ship of the damned bringing a fate worse than death to the isolated colonies of the Caribbean Sea. But few know the true story behind the tavern tales. As the war between the Northern Alliance and the League of the Antilles looms on the horizon, an old captain is ready to embark on a venture to cease the blight of the Black Brig once for all and have his revenge. Set in an alternate historical setting, where a supernatural plague caused the fall of the European powers and where what was left of humanity struggles to survive in the New World, *Dead Men Tell No Tales* narrates the ghastly voyage pirate captain Daniel Drake Davies underwent in 1676, and the events that will force him to confront those same horrors thirty years later. For the dead do not rest peacefully in the Devil's Sea. Pirates, voodoo, and seagoing undead await you in this fantastic journey in a land that never was.

Made in the USA
San Bernardino, CA
24 March 2017